THE
FRIGHTENED
MAN

THE
FRIGHTENED
MAN

Kenneth Cameron

Minotaur Books ⚏ New York

This is a work of fiction. All of the characters, organizations, and events portrayed in this novel are either products of the author's imagination or are used fictitiously.

A THOMAS DUNNE BOOK FOR MINOTAUR BOOKS.
An imprint of St. Martin's Publishing Group.

www.thomasdunnebooks.com
www.minotaurbooks.com

Library of Congress Cataloging-in-Publication Data

Cameron, Kenneth M., 1931–
  The frightened man / Kenneth Cameron. — 1st U.S. ed.
    p. cm.
  ISBN-13: 978-0-312-53896-5
  ISBN-10: 0-312-53896-0
  1. Novelists—Fiction. 2. Murder—Investigation—Fiction. 3. Prostitutes—Crimes against—Fiction. 4. Jack, the Ripper—Fiction. 5. Serial murderers—Fiction. 6. Serial murders—Fiction. 7. London (England)—Fiction. I. Title.
PS3553.A4335F75 2009
813'.54—dc22

                                                                2008051245

First published in Great Britain by Orion Books, an imprint of
The Orion Publishing Group Ltd

First U.S. Edition: May 2009

10 9 8 7 6 5 4 3 2 1

THE
FRIGHTENED
MAN

CHAPTER ONE

The door was made of thin panels, cheap stuff he could put his fist through. She was screaming on the other side. He hated the screams. He raised his fist and saw a knife in it, and he knew where he was then, always this place, this point in this inescapable hell. He shouted at her, meaning to quiet her, but the voice wasn't his own, something heavy, sinister, frightening: 'Lily! Lily!' Her name like blows on the door. He raised his fist and the knife flashed and he

woke. *The old dream.* The dream more real for a few seconds than the room. He never dreamed of her any more except in this one horror, bellowing her name with a knife in his fist.

He was slumped down in his armchair, one shoulder painful, his neck with a crick in it. Sitting up, rubbing his neck, he came completely to in the present: not the young husband of a suicide but a kind of collage, pieces of him from here and there – that town, the war, the farm – the creation a paste-up of contradictions: an American in England now, a soldier who sought peace, a farmer in a heaving city, a nobody who had become a literary lion. He shook his head the way a dog shakes off water and shouted for companionship.

'Sergeant!'

His voice disappeared into the carpets and the curtains and the padded furniture of the room, which smelled of his cigarettes, of polish, of coal, of gas, of fish that he had had for supper.

'Sergeant!'

He heaved himself up, grumbling, strode down the room through

I

the arch, past the alcove where he kept a spirit stove and dishes and bottles, down to the end of the room where a turn to the left led to the stairway and the upper shadows, and to the right was the door down. He opened it, put his head through. 'Sergeant!'

At the bottom, a door opened, a fan of green-grey gaslight widening on the floor. 'Well, what is it?' Then, before he could answer, 'We've got a bell, you know.'

The old argument. 'You know I don't like to use the bell.' He meant that he didn't like summoning a man with a bell, but he wasn't arguing, only going through the motions because he was grateful for another voice.

'This ain't a democracy, General. You pay me enough to call me with a bell, just like a dog. Plus I don't like being shouted at, do I?'

'You got some biscuits down there?'

'Biscuits!' Biscuits were, the voice said, unimaginable. In fact, Atkins was chewing something as he said it. 'I could rustle up a biscuit, I suppose.'

'Bring some up, will you?'

'Cheese, too – you want cheese, I suppose.'

'If you have it—'

'Apples? Nice apples in the shops now. Cheese and apple, very tasty.'

'Anything, anything.'

'Oh, yes, my eye!'

Denton closed the door. He was smiling now. The sergeant's performances always cheered him, as they were meant to. Sergeant Atkins, ex- of the Fusiliers, pretended he had missed a career in the music halls, now believed he had found it with his employer. And in fact he had; Denton had hired him for the cheeky persona. He walked back down the long, sparsely lighted room, which he no longer saw with any great interest. A year of living in it had dulled his taste for green velvet, gold fringe, dark wood, Karamans bought second-hand. The books, on the other hand – the books were another matter, his and other people's, in ranks on either side of the bow-topped black stone fireplace, books rising to

2

the dark cornice that loomed into the room at the top of every wall.

He sat again in the same chair – big, deep, green, comfortable – and touched his moustache and his upper lip, an old habit. The moustache now grizzled, worn rather long, the lip thin, fingers big and hard that had held a plough and harnessed horses in cold so deep it made the trees pop like rifle shots, now softer, calluses gone; the pen may not be mightier than the plough, but it is easier on the hands. His nose was too big, a beak, a proboscis, a scimitar, a nose for Mr Punch, thin down the bone with deep-flared nostrils, dominating the face, somehow not comical at all but rather threatening. Consider this nose an eagle's beak, it seemed to say – never mind the chin, that's irrelevant, watch the nose and the eyes, which have all the warmth of two dry pebbles until the mouth smiles and the wrinkles form above the cheeks; then you may relax a little and know I won't bite.

'What a mess,' the sergeant groaned, coming through the door. He hadn't seen the remains of the supper tray yet; saying it was a mess was merely habit. Now he was halfway down the room and could see the tray; 'A right mess,' he said with gloomy satisfaction. He was carrying another tray in both hands, on it two kinds of biscuits, Stilton, Cheddar, something smelly that proved to be an Italian cheese he identified as pecorino, meaningless to Denton.

'Join me?' Denton said.

'Not tonight, thanks. Port?' Atkins unfolded a two-tiered biscuit table and began to lay things out.

'Have some yourself, if you like.'

'You finished with me, then?'

'You're in a great hurry to be gone. What've you got down there, a woman?'

'I'm writing me memoirs, *Thirty Years a Soldier-Servant*. Some of the scenes of polishing boots are quite exciting. Actually, I'm having a good read through Lever again. You lonely, want my company?'

'I'm going out.'

'I *know* that! I've laid out your clothes, haven't I? What time – half-ten?'

'Eleven.'

'Opera don't let go easily, does it?' Denton was meeting a woman named Emma Gosden after the opera, but he wouldn't sit through it with her. The sergeant was nibbling a biscuit now. He said, 'See here, General.' A typical Atkins opening.

'Now what?'

'What would you say to a mechanical safety razor?' Atkins, unlike many ex-soldiers, didn't believe that buying a pub was the key to heaven: he saw his future as a captain of industry, preferably in domestic goods. He was attracted by 'getting in at the start' of some money-making business.

'I'd say it was daft.' Denton had already heard about a self-sealing chamber pot, a carpet sweeper that sprayed scent and a bicycle-powered mangle.

'Winds up with a key, like a clock. Put it to your face, turn it on, does all the work.'

'And then you send for the ambulance service.'

'Ten pounds, I can have a third of the business. The latest thing.'

'You'd do better with a tip on a horse race.'

Atkins nibbled another biscuit and said, 'Hmm,' and then, 'Faint heart never won fistfuls of money.' He picked up a third biscuit. 'Coming in later or shall I double-lock?'

'I'll be back, but I'm not sure exactly—'

The outer bell rang. The sergeant threw down the biscuit. 'What the H?' He went to a door, almost opposite the fireplace, that led down to the street entrance. 'Shall I answer it, or am I off duty?'

Denton looked at the mantel clock – ormolu, ugly as sin, came with the house – saw that it was only a few minutes before ten. 'Better see.'

The bell rang again; Atkins groaned. 'Oh, Chri – crikey.' He opened the door. 'All right, all right, I'm coming, don't put the bell through the bleeding door—' His voice dwindled down the stairs. Cold air blew in from the lower hall, a depressing space that existed only to give an entrance to Denton's rooms at the side of the house, the rest of the lower storey being rented to a draper, as it had been when he had bought the place. Denton had put a carpet and a settee down there to no avail; a marine painting on the wall hadn't helped, nor a bit of Scottish genre picked up cheap; the space remained an excuse for the stairway and the door under it to the sergeant's part of the house.

Denton heard a male voice, not Atkins's, some sort of negotiation, the slamming of the door. More voices, so whoever it was had been allowed in.

The sergeant clumped back up the stairs. Pulling the door closed behind him, he said, 'Rum sort calling himself Mulcahy. If I say a bowler hat and a cheap suit, will you get the picture? Wants to see you in a desperate fashion.'

'Why?'

'If I knew, I wouldn't have him down in the hall, would I? Just said he must see you, mentioned life and death, looked awful. I can tell him to come back tomorrow.'

Denton glanced at the clock again, thought about half an hour of solitude, said, 'Send him up.'

The man who called himself Mulcahy was small, one of a million Britons – Atkins was another – from the manufacturing cities who hadn't been fed the right things when they were children. He had a sharp face, vaguely rodent-like, narrow shoulders, a pot belly just beginning to show. Denton, standing, judged him to be about five-six, weak, forty, bad false teeth, and felt an immediate sympathy, then a kind of revulsion. When the sergeant tried to take his hat, Mulcahy held on to it as if stopping a theft; then he let go, and Atkins exchanged a look with Denton, rubbing his fingers over the greasy brim and making a face.

'Uh-*hum*,' Mulcahy said, clearing his throat. He was intensely nervous, his fingers moving constantly, one knee jerking inside his baggy trousers. Denton went through the courtesies, got the man seated, established that neither cheese nor biscuits nor port was welcome. 'You wanted to see me,' Denton said.

'Yes, ah – yes – alone.' Mulcahy's eyes slid aside towards the sergeant. 'Confidential.'

Denton raised one eyebrow. Atkins picked up the empty tray and went on down the room, pausing to open the door of the dumb waiter, installed by a former owner when the rear half of the space had been a dining room, thus allowing the sergeant to hear what was said from the floor below. He went out.

'Well, now,' Denton said. 'I have to go out soon, Mr Mulcahy.'

'Yes. Well.' Mulcahy hunched in his chair, his nervous fingers joined over his middle. The chair was too big for him, made him seem a child called in for punishment. 'Something terrible happened. To me. I'm in a right state.'

'You should go to the police.'

'No!' Red circles showed on his grey cheeks; the word heaved his body up and then let it go. 'That's why I came to you. I can't—' He looked into the shadowed corner towards the street, licked his lips, said, 'Just can't.'

'Well—'

'I know who you are, you see? I mean, everybody knows. Fact, right?'

Not everybody, but many people, indeed knew 'who he was', which was to say not who he was but what he had been for barely six months, twenty-five years ago – the American marshal who had shot four men and saved a town. It was part of his myth despite himself, despite his having come to England to get away from it. Newspapers loved it, regularly trotted it out if he wrote a new book or even so much as had tea with the Surbiton Ladies Literary Society.

'Well— I don't see what I can do, but tell me what's happened and maybe I can advise you.'

'I need *protection*, I do.'

'Tell me what happened, Mr Mulcahy.' He made a point of looking at the clock.

Mulcahy looked at his trembling fingers. 'I seen— I saw the man they call –' he clenched his hands – 'Jack the Ripper. And he seen me!'

Denton's interest sagged. The Ripper had been gone for fifteen years; people who saw him or heard him or got in touch with him in seances were loony. Denton managed a tight smile that was meant to lead to 'Goodnight'.

6

'And he recognized me! I know he did; I could see it in his eyes. He's after me!'

Ripper stories popped up like daffodils in spring. They were trotted out by the newspapers for space-fillers. Denton, aware that he was dealing with one of the (he hoped) harmlessly deranged, said gently, 'How do you know it was the Ripper, Mr Mulcahy?'

Mulcahy worked his mouth, studied his hands again. 'We was – were – boys together.' He looked up. 'In Ilkley.' Then, 'There!' he said, as if he had scored a point.

Denton had heard of a woman who said she'd been married to the Ripper. Also one who claimed to be his love child. If Mulcahy had not so clearly been terrified, he'd have eased him out right then. He looked at the clock again, then at the little man, felt again revulsion but also a somewhat clinical interest. A psychological case study, in his own parlour. He could spare seven minutes more. 'Tell me all about it,' he said.

Mulcahy needed to look at the door twice before he began; he seemed to need to know that the door, the way out, was still there. He did look shockingly bad, his face sallow in the gaslight, his cheeks grey where his beard was beginning to show. He touched his forehead, then his nose, and said in spurts and starts with many pauses, 'We was boys together up north. He was never right, but I kind of palled about with him, I did. He was older. Nobody else would, because he was— A kid like me maybe didn't notice what he was. I don't mean I was with him all the time, you know, but off and on like. Couple of years. Just – somebody, you know – we'd walk out to where there was some green, you know, and he set snares, for rabbits, he said, but he never caught nothing. Birds – prop a box on a stick. Nothing ever came into the box. Anyways.

'I was, maybe, fourteen. I *was* fourteen. He got himself a girl for walking out, he did. He made jokes about her to me but they walked out. Elinor Grimble. She was fat, not a pretty girl, glad even to have him, I suppose. He told me things about her – said he, you know, did things to her—' Mulcahy looked up to make sure that 'did things to her' was understood. 'She let him do things, if you follow.'

Denton wondered if Mulcahy's was some sort of sexual insanity. The kind of man who bothered women? Some form of compulsion, like exhibitionism? A number of the books on Denton's shelves were about such men.

'He said – he said I could watch if I wanted. There was a place they went to outside of town, down a railway cutting, a kind of little grove sort of, trees. In there. So I hid there and he brought her and they were in the trees and she let him, you know – he put his hands on her, you know, up top. And she didn't like it, I could see, but he got quite excited, and when she said that was enough, stop, and so on, he got more excited and more excited and he *hit* her.' He didn't look at Denton but seemed lost in the tale – and excited by it. 'He *hit* her.'

Too late, Denton had a sick sense that he was being used. Like being forced to watch a man masturbate.

'He got rougher and took some of her, you know, her upper clothing off, and she got nasty and he hit her again, and that went on, I mean him hitting her, and he took out his pocket-knife and he *cut* her.' Mulcahy paused. The idea of cutting a woman seemed to astonish him. He was sweating. With his eyes closed, he said, 'First, he did it to her. He violated her. And while he was still – you know, he was, um, inside of her, he cut her. *Throat.*' His voice was hoarse.

'All right, all right—' Denton stood.

'And then – it was awful, oh, God! – he went to stabbing her and cutting her and him half-naked, his thing hanging down, cutting her and cutting her—! He cut right into her female place and cut through the skin of her belly and then he reached up inside and—!' He was bug-eyed. Shaking with what seemed like real fear now, but somehow *excited*. 'It made me puke!'

Mulcahy must be eased out; even a little man could be danger-ous if he was crazed. Mulcahy was, he saw, using him to arouse himself – maybe hoping to arouse him, too. Perverse. He went to the door.

Mulcahy didn't seem to notice him. 'Then he run off. Right off. Disappeared.'

8

'So you were well rid of him.'

'Not half.' Mulcahy's voice was a whisper. 'I didn't hear nothing for six years. Then— Then comes a letter from Germany with bits of newspaper in it – that funny-looking lettering. They was about three murders. Women. I knew it was him.'

'I'm afraid I don't see how you could know that.'

'Couple more years, I got a letter from France. Nothing but clippings – more women cut up, murdered. Then Holland!' He looked up. 'He was keeping me up to date, see?'

Denton had his hand on the doorknob. 'I'm afraid this is all the time I can give you, sir.'

'My mum was dead by then, nothing to hold me. I moved on to a couple of places, and the letters they stopped. Couldn't find me, and good riddance! I was free of him, see? And then, tonight—' He put his face in his hands. 'Tonight – oh, my dear God! – I'm walking on the street and—'

'Well, sir, you know, we see people who look like people we used to know, but—'

A crash sounded from below and the house shook. Denton heard the sergeant curse. Mulcahy jumped to his feet, shouting, 'It's him— !'

Denton strode to the dumb waiter. 'Sergeant – sergeant, you all right?'

'What d'you think, bloody silver tray on my head?' Over the words was the sound of running steps on the stairs, two at a time, going down, and then the front door crashed. Denton walked back down the room. Mulcahy's chair was empty, the door open. Denton looked down, saw that the hall was empty, too. Mulcahy was gone.

'Mental case,' Denton muttered. He shouted over his shoulder, 'I'm just stepping out, Sergeant – then I really have to dress—'

Denton trotted down the stairs and opened the door. It was two strides to the gate, which was open; beyond it, Lamb's Conduit Street was dark. Denton looked to his right; not until he saw one of the whores who gave the street its reputation did he see another human being. She hadn't seen anybody, she said, worse luck. He strolled back the other way. Somebody coming out of the Lamb had seen a man running up towards Holborn.

'Damned little loony.'

The sergeant was waiting at the top of the stairs. 'Left his hat,' he said. He waved it. 'Valuable object.'

'How much did you hear?'

'A lot, until the dumb-waiter clutch gave way and dropped the dishware on my head. Mad story, I thought.'

'Mad, yes.'

'You don't believe him!'

'I believe he was really frightened, but I think it's all inside his own head. And maybe he really did see something as a kid – although it could be the sort of fantasy a certain type might invent to entertain himself.' He looked at the clock. 'Men like that pull a lot of details out of the newspapers.'

'One more crackpot trying to climb on the tired old Ripper's back.'

'Why come to me?'

'To be able to say he'd laid his mad tale on you. Good story with the girls. "How I Met the Sheriff." You're going to be late.'

'Mmmm.' Denton doubted that Mulcahy told this story to 'the girls'. Mulcahy, he thought Krafft-Ebing would say, was one of those men who had difficulties with women. Probably impotent. He started towards the stairs at the rear. 'Still, these cases are interesting.'

'And you say you don't like opera!'

'Well, he didn't sing.'

As he dressed, he thought about the story, the obvious inventions. The newspaper clippings, for example – Mulcahy hadn't said anything about getting them translated, but surely he didn't read German, French and Dutch. And not a word about the uproar that would have followed such a murder as that of – what was her name? – Elinor Grimble. Of Ilkley.

There didn't seem to be anything that needed to be done about Mr Mulcahy, and as for his tale that the Ripper was back, that was merely stupid. Mulcahy was a sad freak, to be forgotten, at least until he returned for his valuable hat.

Denton went off to Emma Gosden's. He carried a derringer in his coat pocket out of habit. A certain caution, never lost. The rain had stopped, leaving an occasional misting drizzle that was pleasant to walk through, the streets wet and shining, lamps reflected in long, shivering tracks down puddles.

Alice, the elderly maid, recognized him and took his damp coat, hat and stick and let him into the small drawing room, which he knew well enough to know which was the most comfortable chair. When Emma came in, he was staring into the coal fire, already thinking of her, but he stood, and she smiled but stopped well short of him and so postponed his kiss.

'I thought I'd be ahead of you,' he said. 'How was the opera?'

'Awful people with me. I don't know why I go out so much.' She had moved to the small fireplace, a dark red love seat behind her, clashing with her dress, also dark red but the wrong shade. She was remarkably pretty, nonetheless, the dress cut low, her arms bare.

He moved a half-step towards her, the beginning of something he never finished; he would have embraced her, kissed her, started them upstairs.

'Not yet,' she said, holding out a hand, palm towards him. She smiled. 'I wanted to have a word with you first. Down here.' She laughed. 'Where it's safe.' They looked at each other. Her smile was brilliant, slightly false.

'Well, Emma, what?'

She chuckled, surprising him. 'This is more difficult than I thought,' she said. The smile became more brilliant. 'I've found somebody else, Denton. There!'

At first, he didn't make sense of 'finding' somebody else. Then he understood: she'd found somebody she preferred to him and was giving him his walking papers. He wondered later if he had closed his eyes, because he couldn't see her for one sightless instant, a moment of horrendous rage that deafened and blinded him. When he could see again, she was smiling at him.

'Now, now,' she said. 'Take it like a man.' *Smiling*.

He governed himself. 'While you take it like a woman? A

professional woman?' He managed to force his violence down into words, words alone. She had meant that tonight would be their last time together, but that there *would* be tonight. That she had found somebody she preferred so much that this would be the last, *but this would happen* – that she would open herself to him while she had already decided on the other man, undoubtedly had already opened herself to him too.

Her face flushed; her eyes widened.

'"Take it like a man,"' he said, 'what the hell does that mean – take it from you and then jump in bed with you and then leave you for your new man to—?' He crossed the little room to her in two strides, still not able to control himself fully but getting enough control so that he wouldn't do something terrible. 'Goddamn you!' he said very low. 'How long have you been going to bed with both of us?'

'Long enough to know which I prefer.'

He wanted to say *But you're mine*, to shout *You belong to me*, but he knew she belonged to nobody, never had; it was what he liked about her. He was panting, his collar seeming to strangle him. 'You whore,' he said.

'Get out of my house,' she said in a voice so low it sounded like a growl.

'Christ, woman—' He leaned towards her and she backed away, leaning on the love seat and putting it partly between them.

'I gave you a chance to make me admire you, Denton. You failed.' She was still flushed but very much in charge of herself. She chuckled. 'I gave you the chance to act like a gentleman, and you showed yourself to be the vulgar American oaf everybody thinks you are. Get out!'

He tried to stare her down, failed, turned in a rage and tore the door open and rushed out. The elderly maid was there in the dark hall, frightened, recoiling when she saw him but muttering, 'Coat, sir, your coat—'

He rushed on, tore open the front door, thinking *To hell with the coat*, thinking *To hell with her and everything*, hating himself and her for what she had done to him and for what she had said.

The drizzle was in the air again, beading up on the black shoulders of his dinner suit. He went down the stone steps in two jumps and raged up the street, leaping a puddle to run across and turn at the first corner, to put her and her house and her words behind him. He walked, then broke into a run to the end of the street, then another, heart pounding and breath coming hard. Then he stopped. Looked around, momentarily lost, and then, breathing more slowly, he began to walk.

He headed towards Regent Street without knowing it; the people he began to pass looked at him – hatless, coatless in the rain, somebody crazed or drunk. In the end, he went into the Café Royal because he found himself there and it was bright and warm and he felt battered. He headed for the tables along one side where he wouldn't know anybody, ordered brandy and glowered at anybody who looked his way. By being rude to people he knew, he managed to drink alone, his thoughts ugly; then a cadger of drinks named Crosland came by trying to sell anybody for a shilling apiece the news that Oscar Wilde had died in Paris. Then people were weeping and shouting – the Royal had been Wilde's hang-out, his table, until his trial, a salon – and Denton was caught up in what became a wake. There were shouted arguments about who had supported Oscar and who had abandoned him; Denton, who had known Wilde only slightly but who had by then drunk too much, was doing some of the shouting. Then he was talking to a man he didn't know about the perfidy of women, and then he was standing on a table with the notorious writer and editor Frank Harris, who was proposing a toast to the dead man's memory, and when the response wasn't quick enough to suit him, Denton roared, 'On your feet, you bloody bastards! You killed him, now you'll damned well drink to him!'

Then the room was half-empty and Denton was alone, looking down at Wilde's old table, a heap of flowers that had accumulated on it. Peeping out from one side were the remains of a dried and pressed green carnation. Somebody's secret past, pressed flat. Denton turned to share this insight with the world, and he stumbled and would have fallen if Oddenino, the Royal's manager, hadn't caught him.

'Taxi, sir?' Oddenino said.

'Certainly not!' He could make his own damned way home!

The streets were dark and silent. He was standing looking up at a row of houses he didn't recognize when a boy came towards him. Denton saw him only as a shape until he passed under a gaslight, thought then it might be a woman or a small adult.

'Newspaper, sir? 'Stonishin' murder, sir. Girl cut up like the Sunday joint.' The boy pulled a newspaper from a sack he wore over one shoulder by a piece of rope. 'Oscar Wilde dead in Paris, sir. Bobs says boys will be home by summer. Paper?'

Denton read *Grisly Murder in the Minories.*

He took out a coin, fumbling and at last aware that he was drunk, and the boy ran off into the drizzle without giving him change – clearly aware that Denton was drunk, too. Denton, swaying, opened the newspaper under a street lamp. *Horrors Committed with a Knife. Unspeakable Mutilation of a Young Victim.*

How mad was Mulcahy now?

CHAPTER TWO

Sergeant Atkins came on his tiptoes into the parlour-cum-all-purpose room at five in the morning, no stranger to doors that banged at an hour when his employer was supposed to be happily between the sheets with his lovey, or to gents who drank too much to wash away some trouble. Indeed, there was Denton in his armchair, snoring; there was the mostly empty decanter; there were his boots, his sodden tailcoat, his necktie. And, in one of his pockets, a box of Café Royal vestas.

And there was the newspaper. *Grisly Murder.*

Atkins picked up the coat and the tie and took them downstairs to dry in front of the coal stove. He went up again and got the decanter and carried it to the pantry, got the newspaper, took it downstairs, put his feet up on his own fender, read it. Cutting through the journalistic fustian, Atkins concluded that not a great deal was known except that a woman 'of evil reputation' had been murdered in the Minories – disembowelled and probably, the prose a little murky here, something cut from her body that had formerly been part of it.

He read the rest of the newspaper, concentrating on the personals and skipping over the international news (*Small change to me what you do in India now I'm not there*) but glancing at the Boer War stories to see if any of his old mates were catching it. The court calendar also took up a little of his time. Oscar Wilde's death got only a grunt. At six, he went upstairs again with coffee and put the tray down beside Denton.

Denton woke. He looked like hell.

'Coffee, sir?'

Denton, still sprawled as he had slept, looked up.

'Water,' he croaked.

Atkins poured water from the carboy in the alcove. Handing it to Denton, he said, 'Big night at the Royal?'

'Oscar Wilde was dead.'

'Still is, according to the paper.'

'You hear me come in?' he said.

'Hard not to.' Atkins knelt to light the kindling in the grate. 'I don't see your coat or hat.'

'Oh, Christ. I must have left them at the Royal. No, no – I was in Jermyn Street without them in the rain – they must be at Mrs Gosden's.' He drank the water and held out the glass for more. 'Mrs Gosden gave me my walking papers. I shouldn't tell you that. Bad form, right?'

'You're the boss.'

Denton laughed – a kind of strangled cough. *Boss* was a word he'd taught Atkins to use instead of the nicer *employer* or *master*. 'I wasn't the boss last night – either of her or of myself.'

'You want me to go and get your coat and hat off her?'

'No.' He drank more water. 'I wouldn't put you through that.'

'All one to me. Servants' entrance, everybody polite but a bit chilly, here comes the coat and hat, off I go.'

'No!' Perhaps Emma would send it back. *Get this out of my sight.* Except it wouldn't be in her sight; it would be in old Alice's sight. Oh, well. Except that it was a very good coat. And it had his derringer in the pocket. 'Send the boy,' he said.

'What boy?'

'Whatever boy you send with messages.'

'I send any body happens to be loitering about.'

'Well, do that, then.'

Atkins made a face. 'Any kid I can find on this street would have your coat and hat, not to mention a gold-headed walking stick, at the Jew pawnbroker's quicker than I could say Gog and Magog. I'll go for them myself.'

'No!' Denton had shouted the word; he pulled himself back. 'Sorry. Just—' He made a patting motion, palm down, in the air between them. 'Leave it.'

Atkins shrugged.

Denton finished the water. 'I'll be going out later.'

'To make some money, I hope. The bills ain't been paid yet this month.' Atkins, always nervous about money, knew that Denton was, as he put it, 'a little close to the edge.' 'Better spend your time finishing a book, I say.'

'Don't say!'

'If I might suggest—'

'Don't suggest!' Denton lay back in the chair. 'Bring up a couple of eggs at eight and, oh, you know – bacon. Gammon, whatever the hell you call it. Bread – plenty of bread!'

Atkins said no more but went out on tiptoe, as he had come in earlier. He had run into the savage mood before. *Inside every gent, a savage. Lost his honey, is it. Bloody murder.*

Two hours later, Denton still lay collapsed in his easy chair. The back pages of the newspaper lay tented next to him on the floor. Atkins was standing, a breakfast tray and the front section of the newspaper in his hands, wearing an ancient velvet robe given him in India by some long-dead officer.

'You look like a down-at-heels maharajah,' Denton said.

'Happy to give you the name of my tailor. You want tea?'

'No, I want to know what you think of Mulcahy's story now. What he said was very like what happened to this tart.'

'I think it's bollocks, just like I did eight hours ago, no, ten hours ago, how time flies when you're up early waiting on the master. Eight o'clock, you asked for eggs.'

'Put them down and sit, you make me tired standing there. Why bollocks?'

'It doesn't hang together.' Atkins hooked a straight chair over with his left foot and sat in it, the newspaper still in his hands. 'What've we got here?' He rattled the paper. 'Some poor bint got her throat slit and other unmentionable damage inflicted, and so we're supposed to believe it was the reincarnation of the Ripper, so as to sell more papers. Mulcahy barges in here and gives you a long tale about cutting up women and being boys together with the Ripper, so you jump to the conclusion he was telling the truth. It's bollocks!'

'Coincidence, that he told the story last night, and last night the woman gets murdered?'

'Maybe he's one of them psychics. More likely getting his jollies by telling tales.'

'He was really frightened, though.'

'Probably scares himself for the fun of it. Like a kiddie. Why didn't he bring them newspaper clippings he talked about? Why didn't he give you this boyhood chum's name? Eh?'

'He did give me the name of the town and the man's first victim. I could tell somebody I know in the police.'

'"First victim," oh, yes! My hat! You going to some pal in the coppers because of Mulcahy? Name of God why?'

'Maybe it's evidence.'

Denton slouched deeper into the chair and began to peel his right boot off by pushing on the heel with the toe of the left one. Atkins said he would ruin his boots and bent down to help, and Denton swung his legs away, muttering that he could take off his own damned boots. 'Give me that,' he said, meaning the paper. He read as he went on ruining them, then flexing his toes when they were off. '"Young woman of evil reputation named Stella Minter." Evil reputation, good God.'

'In short, a tart.'

Denton grunted. '"Discovered about midnight in a horribly mutilated condition in the squalor of her bloodstained room in the Minories." I wonder when she was killed.' He was eating the eggs and the bread with one hand, holding the newspaper with the other.

'Because you're thinking that Mulcahy could of done it and then come here, right? That's far-fetched. I'll have some of that tea, myself. Was Mulcahy bloodstained? Had he just washed all his clothes, including that suit that looked like it was made out of old blankets? Was his hat red with gore? I think not.'

'But his story makes a kind of sense in one way, Sergeant – it puts a man who mutilates women in London so that he and Mulcahy see each other; then Mulcahy comes to me and the murderer goes to, what's her name? Stella Minter.'

'Who says that Mulcahy and the murderer saw each other in *London*, if they saw each other? Could of been Birmingham, for that matter, what with modern trains. Why d'you suppose the Ripper never struck in Birmingham, by the bye? Pure prejudice.'

Denton dropped the newspaper to the floor. 'We should talk to Mulcahy again.'

'Oho, "we". Well *we'd* better do something about our condition if *we* are going looking for a needle in a haystack. You've brandy sloshing about in your eyeballs like the bubbles in a mason's level. You ever looked for a little nobody like him in London, even stone-cold sober, Captain?'

Denton grunted again. He saw the size of the undertaking. 'Any help in that hat of his?' He was half asleep again. The ruined breakfast plate was on the floor next to him.

'Thought you'd never ask. Initial R – R. Mulcahy. Randolph, Robert, Reginald, Rex, Ronald, Richard, Roderick— No address, no shop name, maker's mark almost erased by his sweat but can be read as that of the cheapest, biggest hat-maker in England. No help there.'

'R. Mulcahy. We'll work on it.' Denton stood, not too steadily, and groped his way down the long room to the stairs. 'I feel like hell.'

His bedroom, which was directly above the alcove, the dumb waiter, the breakfast table and part of his parlour, served also as his workroom. The bed, narrow to the point of monasticism, took up only the wall towards the street; then came an enormous armoire, hideous but essential in a room without a closet; then his desk, a vast structure intended for two partners working face-to-face, filled by him with the mess of one man working alone – at the moment, a half-finished novel that he was having trouble with. Regrettably, it represented his best chance for filling his bank account. Here, he spent most of his mornings, writing with a stub of pencil, drinking French coffee, staring straight ahead over a brick wall, two back-to-back privies, and the rear of a house that faced the next street. Now, seeing it in the double gloom of a hangover and Emma's dismissal, it all looked grey – the desk, the windows, the rain, the blurred wall of the other house.

'Grey as a ball of lint,' he said aloud. His voice was husky. He cleared his throat. He found he didn't like 'grey as a ball of lint'. He cleared his throat again. 'Grey as the bottom of a boot.' Better. But so depressing that he felt even worse. 'Damn her!' he groaned. *Still.* He fell into the desk chair and wrote Emma an apology and then sent Atkins to find a boy to deliver it to her. Atkins, always worrying about clothes, reminded him that he was supposed to be going out to dinner that evening; Denton cursed, because Emma would be there, the reason in fact that he'd been invited in the first place. He wrote another note, this one to the hostess, pleading illness. He couldn't face Emma. Alone again, he stared at the pile of manuscript, tried to think about it, found his mind sloping off to Mulcahy, Emma, the dead tart. He stood up, leaned his hands on the desk, stared down at its scarred surface.

Odd, that he should end up at a desk. Or perhaps he wouldn't, as it wasn't yet the end. 'We all end up in a box, sooner or later,' he muttered. Like the woman who had been mutilated and killed, or the other way around, last night. For her, the box had come much sooner than later. A dangerous profession, prostitution. Much safer to be a 'nice' woman like Emma Gosden. Damn her.

He kept headache powders in a drawer; the search for them was irritating and over-long. He gulped more water, the white powder drifting in it like sand, then headed up the stairs to the top floor, thinking about nice women and women who weren't nice. *Nice, not nice.* What was 'not nice' about a sixteen-year-old who'd just come to town from a farm? Was she less 'nice' than Emma, who'd had at least four lovers before him, had visited a whorehouse in Paris so she could look on from a hiding place, and had had him and somebody else on the string at the same time? How contradictory, now he thought about it, that Emma was 'nice' at all, the quality preserved by – what? Manner? No, money. And the whores, what was not 'nice' except their doing openly what Emma did in private?

In the attic, he forced himself to pick up a forty-pound iron bar. Each curl seemed to push all his blood into his aching head.

'Bad,' he gasped aloud. He was thinking of Emma, her behaviour towards him – his towards her, for that matter – but the word would have done for all sorts of things he'd done in his life. Or so it seemed from the perspective of the hangover. Or all manner of things that men did to women. Like Stella Minter, the extreme case. He screwed his face up, wondering if that was what he had wanted for Emma in that moment of red blindness. *God, no.*

He finished twenty curls and put the bar down with a thump. The attic smelled of dry wood, a whiff of fir, dust, smoke from below, the fresh odour of rain. He had two Flobert pistols up there, 'parlour pistols' some called them because their charge was so weak you could shoot them in a parlour. Or so they said. It was Denton's view that if you hit somebody in the eye with one of the little bullets, you might find yourself a murderer. He perhaps had too much respect for firearms. But, then, a lot of experience.

Nice women, 'not nice' women, the illusions of chastity and virginity. He'd never had a virgin except his wife, and what a horror that had been. They had both been nineteen, the Civil War just over. Huddled in the cold bedroom of a boarding house.

'Cruel to her,' he said aloud. He set up a target and walked the length of the attic and aimed. He had been over his marriage ten thousand times in his mind; it always made him wince with shame. He could have waited, he knew now, been gentle with her, helped her. But he had thought that consummation had to be immediate or she would escape him, become his sister and not his wife. At nineteen, he had known no better. So, tears, bloody sheets, a terrible train journey north and west with her in pain. When she'd got pregnant, she'd fled the farm for her parents' house in St Louis, had had both the boys there, gone back to the farm each time with reluctance. But died on the farm.

Like the murdered tart, in the box sooner, not later.

He fired one pistol, then the other; reloaded, fired; reloaded. His head was spinning, his breath was foul, but he didn't miss at this distance. He fired again, both pistols, and when he walked down and looked at the target, he could have covered the six bullet holes with his thumbnail.

He went to a rowing contraption and made himself row for half an hour.

As he strained, he thought about Mulcahy, the girl, Emma.

Mulcahy had certainly been terrified by *something*. Whether he'd actually seen what he'd described or not was another matter. Was Mulcahy one of those lunatics who lived horrors that existed only in his own mind? Had Mulcahy opened a window on some inner hell and been appalled by it? But then why had he lied about it – for surely he'd lied? And why had he thought he needed protection? Or was that simply some extreme realization of his fantasy, as Atkins had suggested?

Pouring sweat, his robe discarded and the old shirt unbuttoned, Denton rested on the oars, panting, heart pounding, his head aching to the beat of it. He pulled himself up, his legs weak, and towelled himself and then lay down next to a hundred-pound dumb-bell. *The iron mistress. Like being in bed with it.* Emma weighed only fifteen pounds more. *On top of me, she felt light. Sweet. The sweetness of women, warm, soft—* He dragged the dumb-bell on top of him, arching his back and raising his abdomen so the bar rested on it, then getting his forearms under it and hoisting it above him. Twenty lifts, the later ones forcing the blood into his head again so that it felt as if the veins would explode.

Had Mulcahy murdered the girl? Was it as simple as that? But why come to Denton, then?

He had his cap-and-ball pistol from the American Civil War; he removed it from its case, checked, as he always did, that it wasn't loaded (but he knew it wasn't loaded, hadn't been loaded in ten years), and stood with the pistol held at arm's length for five minutes, holding the sights on the target. Despite brandy, hangover, strenuous exercise, the pistol never wavered.

He was at the Metropolitan Police Additional Headquarters before eleven, a ridiculous Gothic building from which passers-by expected to hear groans and sighs, perhaps muffled screams. The building had in fact been a warren of legal offices and dismal flats before the expanding police, already bursting out of New Scotland Yard, had acquired it 'temporarily'. Its blackened stones were grim at best, horrible in the rain, and now that it was an annexe for the police, it had the air of a prison. The vast and sombre exterior led visitors to expect inside huge, shadowed vistas with topless staircases and vaults and chains; as it was, Denton was merely irritated by what he found − a setting for bureaucratic tedium. Long, uncarpeted passages led to enclosed staircases with, nonetheless, dark newels and banisters, and here and there were floors that sloped, others that abruptly took a step up or down. It was said that new occupants got lost in trying to get about the building. It made the hung-over Denton dizzy.

On the third floor, past the gloomy entrance hall and the atrium that poked up through the building as if seeking light and air, up some stairs and around a balcony that looked down into the well, and up and around again and up, was the office of the Assistant Under-Secretary to the Assistant Secretary (not to be confused with the Permanent Under-Secretary to the Permanent Assistant Secretary, both career civil servants) who was in a sense responsible, although in fact not really responsible, for the apparatus that investigated the Metropolitan Police − not in a criminal sense, but a business one: its stated goal was efficiency. The Assistant Under-Secretary was a man named Hector Hench-Rose.

'Denton!' he shouted. 'Ha-ha!' Hench-Rose had ginger hair and a ginger moustache and was, at forty, already seriously into belly after years of pouring himself into the uniform of one of the higher-numbered regiments. He was affable, courageous and useless as an administrator, and so had been given the equivalent of the rank of superintendent and put one step down from the top of the division with no more experience of police work than if he had spent his life running a home for foundlings.

'Hector.' Denton liked Hector Hench-Rose in a qualified way; they were opposites without ever being enemies. Hench-Rose was energetic, cheerful and happy; Denton was listless, dour and doubtful that happiness existed. He liked to warm himself at Hector's fire now and then.

'Place stinks,' Hector said now. He was leading Denton to a chair in an office so dark it could have been used to store coal. One window gave on to an air shaft; the only other light came from a gas lamp above the desk. The rain, nonetheless, managed to reach that only window and trickle down it with sooty smears. 'Something in the chimney. Birds, I think. Place full of smoke half the time, then we get a puff of wind and this unspeakable smell.'

'I had raccoons in a chimney once,' Denton said.

'Raccoons! Those are the buggers with eye-rings, aren't they. Look like burglars in an operetta. What'd they do?'

'They stank.'

This amused Hector mightily. He offered a cigar, tea, an early drink; Denton refused them all. Hector made social small talk, mentioned the opera by way of getting to Emma, as if he knew about her and Denton. His tone was a little odd, perhaps more inquisitive than usual; Hench-Rose was an enthusiastic gossip but usually discreet. Did he know already that Emma had thrown him over?

'Emma all right?' Yes, he knew.

'Fine, of course.'

'Didn't see you with her at the opera.'

'And never will.'

Hench-Rose showed his teeth in a tight smile, seemed about to say something, thought better of it and turned to the question of weekend parties. 'You shoot?' he said.

'Nobody recently.'

'Oh – ha! Ha-ha! Meant birds, man. Grouse, partridge, like that.' He talked about shooting driven birds, which Denton found about as interesting as the opera – shooters stood at assigned posts and waited while a small army of beaters drove everything that could run or fly past them to be slaughtered. 'Make some fantastic scores,' Hector said. 'Certain royal party knocks down hundreds in an afternoon.'

'And then eats them all that night.'

'Hmm? Oh, ha-ha. No, actually, the birds go off to the markets. Very important part of the process, selling the kill.'

'The purpose of the exercise, in fact.'

Hector frowned, a rare expression on his smooth face. 'Well— Yes, in a sense.'

'The shooting party is in fact a cog in an economic machine.'

'What *have* you been reading? You sound like an anarchist, Denton. Is this for a new book?' In fact, Denton had figured out the economics of shooting for himself because he was an American, an American who had started with nothing and was always near ruin; it gave him a point of view. And earned him some insults – *parvenu, nouveau*. He wasn't sure why there was recourse to French when 'Johnny-come-lately' or 'counter-jumper' would have served so well. Something about the upper-class English and French: they decried French morals but envied French culture, adopted French words, even when they couldn't pronounce them. *Soi-disant, beauté de singe, nostalgie de la boue, elle s'affiche.*

Hench-Rose waited while an overweight young man brought in a tea tray and poured two cups, even though Denton had already refused it. 'I like something going down the gullet,' Hench-Rose muttered. He helped himself to scones.

Denton said, 'I've come on a kind of business.'

'Oh, really?' Hector seemed astonished that such a thing as business might even exist.

'The newspapers are full of a new tale about a prostitute being murdered.'

Hector groaned and said he knew it; it was terrifically boring. He held up a buff-coloured file. 'I don't have time for the interesting stuff. I'm supposed to respond to an endless minute on the cost of helmets written by that dried-up dog's leavings Mortimer Asperley, the Permanent Under-Secretary. He's written five pages to do with a three-page file.'

'How accurate are the newspaper accounts of the new murder?'
Hector looked blank. '*The Times* is always accurate.'

'Hector, I mean I want to know the details of the crime.'

'Ah, aha. Writer's curiosity, eh? Well, you've come to the wrong shop for anything having to do with police work; I might as well be in Whitehall monitoring the clothing regulations for other ranks in hot climates as here, for all I know about what the police are doing.' He rang the overweight young man back into the room, told him to ask Detective Sergeant Munro to step round, looked pleased with himself for moving so briskly. 'Munro will set us straight,' he said. 'Munro knows everything.' He smiled the brilliant and open smile that made up for many failings. 'Munro is a real policeman, not an ex-army officer dropped into a sinecure, like me.' He beamed.

'I was an ex-officer, once,' Denton said.

'Yes, but you hadn't cousins in the senior civil service, had you? You mustered out and went to work – lucky you, Denton. Look at you now.'

Denton grunted. He had mustered out as a temporary lieutenant (three months' worth, a sergeant jumped up to demobilize what was left) after the American Civil War; 'going to work,' as Hector put it, had meant going to an unploughed piece of prairie and trying to turn it into a farm. Going to work, indeed.

Detective Sergeant Munro was huge and walked with a limp. His massive face widened as it went downwards from his eyes; the jaws, seen straight on, were enormous, as if he could have chewed up iron bolts. He had a trace of a Scots accent, something else unidentifiable. His contempt for Hench-Rose was clear, even to Hector, who seemed amused by it.

'Mister Denton is a famous author,' Hench-Rose began. 'He's interested in a lady of the night who was murdered yesterday.'

Munro looked at Denton, expanded his circle of contempt to include him. 'Yes?' he said.

Hench-Rose smiled more fiercely. 'I thought the first paperwork might have made its way up to us, and we could share it with him and send him on to the right people in CID.'

Munro's great jaws widened, the effect of a smile. 'Not our crime, Mr Hench-Rose.' Dripping with contempt. Hector, not the swiftest of intellects, stared at him. 'Crime was apparently committed in the Square Mile, sir.'

Hector frowned. 'Oh, dear,' Hector said. He looked at Denton. 'Mr Denton's American.' Munro grinned at Denton, offering not a drop of pity for his being American. Hector explained. 'The Square Mile is the City of London, Denton. My fault for not having realized it; I paid no attention to the location when I read the tale in the paper. We don't get crimes from the City; the City of London Police get them.' He looked up. 'Sorry, Munro.'

'I can go, then?'

'Well— Perhaps you know somebody over there Mr Denton could go to see.'

'Not very hospitable to journalists right now,' Munro said. He apparently meant the City Police.

'Mr Denton's not a journalist.'

Munro looked him over, apparently concluded that Denton was no better than a journalist, whatever he was.

'Oh, come on, Munro!' Hench-Rose's voice was wheedling. Denton could imagine his using it on a sergeant major, one of those invaluable men who do the real work of a regiment. 'You must know somebody over there who can lend a hand.' Hench-Rose smiled, the kind of smile that would remind even a sergeant major which of them was the superior officer. 'Munro, I insist.'

Denton had been making small noises, but neither of the others paid any attention. He had muttered that it wasn't important, that he would go, that he'd been stupid. No good. He was left feeling embarrassed, as he always was by British displays, however subtle, however polite, of upper-class leverage.

'I'll just see what I can do then, sir,' Munro was saying. 'If you're ready to go, Mr, um, Denton, perhaps you could come along with me.'

'There!' Hench-Rose displayed his wonderful teeth. 'You see, Denton?'

Denton made a face – lower lip pushed up, corners of the lips pulled down, eyebrows raised – and thanked Hector for his help and went out behind Munro, turning to cock an eyebrow again at Hench-Rose, who seemed vastly amused.

They paced along a dark corridor that looked as if it ran the length of the building, perhaps of several other buildings as well, a smell of coal and drains just noticeable. The corridor was bitterly cold. Munro seemed determined to say nothing, and Denton, who had lived among all sorts of people, felt no impulse to change things. They came at last to a varnished door much like all the others they had passed, and Munro grasped the handle as if he were going to yank it out of the wall and threw the door open. Several clerks looked up with frightened faces.

'This is where we shovel the paper,' Munro said. He led Denton towards another door. 'Raw police reports find their way up here; we copy them out in a fair hand, three copies each, and send one to Files, one to Prosecution and one to your friend.' He jerked his head towards the north, the direction meant to include Hench-Rose. 'No idea what he does with them. In ten years or twenty the gods may see fit to give us a typewriter.' Munro went through the door into a dismal office piled high with faded brown folders, fell into a chair behind the only desk and began to rummage in a drawer. 'I'll give you a message to somebody I know in City CID. That's all I'll do. Coppers don't like civilians much.'

'I know. I used to be one.' Munro looked up. Denton said, 'A place called Railhead, Nebraska.'

'What was that, two whorehouses and a dog?'

'Just about. I was the entire police force.'

Munro stared at him. His huge cheeks looked unhealthy in the gloom. 'Well, you know how we feel about civilians putting their nose in, then.'

'I don't intend to put my nose in.' He told him about the visit from Mulcahy, Munro staring at him the whole time. When he was finished, Munro said, 'You mean you have evidence to offer. Why didn't you say so?'

'I'm not sure it's evidence.'

'Leave that for City CID.' He handed over a piece of paper. 'Go and see this man. Detective Sergeant Willey. Tell him what you told me. Don't tell him you're a writer.' He stood; Denton stood.

'Were you in CID?' Denton said.

'Used to be. Metropolitan, not City. Then I was crippled.' He hesitated. 'Fell off a roof.'

'Line of duty?'

'Pointing the chimney at home.'

Denton went out. Munro had never smiled, he realized. Nor, he guessed, had he.

Detective Sergeant Willey barely knew Munro, as it turned out, but was glad for a chance to get out of the bustle of Bishopsgate Police Station and sit down to listen to Denton's 'evidence'. He had a clerk there to take it down in shorthand, along with the questions and answers that followed, all the things that Denton had already been over in his own mind. Willey, long-headed, stooped, tired, was as sceptical as Atkins, but he was polite because Denton was at least nominally a gentleman. 'Many thanks,' he said when they were done. 'We appreciate citizen cooperation. Every bit of information of value.'

Denton wondered how many murders the man had investigated, as he seemed nervous and defeated already. Contrary to what Hench-Rose had thought, Denton knew London pretty well, could have told him that the Minories were in the City if he'd stopped to think about it – knew, too, that City police probably spent most of their time on business crime, not murder.

Denton said, 'I'm afraid I'd like something in return.' Willey's face froze. 'That's why I originally went to Mr Hench-Rose. Is it possible for me to see the corpse?' That idea had come to him as they had talked. Why did he want to see a mutilated female corpse? Emma had swum into his consciousness; he had refused to believe there was a connection.

'Absolutely not.' Shocked.

'Isn't there going to be a post-mortem?'

'Of course.' Stiff now, defending the procedures of the City Police.

'Post-mortems are sometimes open.'

'Mr Denton!' Willey leaned towards him, hands clasped on the scarred desktop. He had hairy backs to his hands, dark curls like wires springing out. 'This is a sensational case. Do you really think we want details of the poor woman's body known to civilians?'

'There've been a good many descriptions already, and she's dead. Plus, she was a tart. Anyway, I'm not about to write about it. I simply want to—' He wanted to say *to know what frightened Mulcahy*, but Willey would misinterpret that, he was sure. So he said, lamely, 'To follow up.'

Willey was a cynic, like most policemen. 'Oh, yes?' he said in a tone that said everything about men who wanted to see post-mortems on female bodies.

'To compare it with what the man told me.'

'That's police business, and you're to stay out of it.'

'Where's the post-mortem?'

Willey stood. He was two inches shorter than Denton but secure of his mastery on his own turf. 'We're done here.' He nodded to the clerk, who got up and went out. 'Thank you for your information, Mr Denton. I'll show you out.'

Denton went back to Hector Hench-Rose, missing his lunch – it was now after one – and so accepting Hector's offer of scones because the hangover had turned to nausea, and got from him the information that the post-mortem on Stella Minter's body would be at St Bartholomew's Hospital at two, with Sir Frank Parmentier wielding the scalpel. Hector found this out only by sending five messengers in as many directions to other offices. 'You owe me a lunch,' he said when he'd got the news.

'How do I get into the post-mortem?'

'Oh, do you really want to? Well, as it's at Bart's, it's probably in the theatre and so open to the students. You could just go in, probably, but—' He took a piece of rather grand letterhead stationery and scribbled on it, signed with a huge and illegible flourish, then sent the young man off to get it stamped and initialled by the commissioner's clerk.

'Won't it be under City Police control?'

'The worst they can say is no, Denton.' He twitched his ginger moustache. 'Why ever do you want to go to a post-mortem?'

Denton dragged a version of the truth from the clutches of the hangover. 'I want to see if they were in coitus when he slit her throat. Mulcahy said that's the way he saw it done long ago.' Yes, well – there it was. He'd been shutting out an insistent image of slitting Emma's throat while they made love.

Hench-Rose said hoarsely that you shouldn't even think such things.

'I find myself more and more interested in these mental cases.' Not quite true, unless he was himself a mental case. Still—

CHAPTER THREE

The operating theatre was circular and steep, the central well thirty feet across with only three steep ranks of seats rising around it. A lantern rose from the roof above, giving only gloomy light because of the rain, augmented by standard gas lamps in a rough circle around the wheeled table that was the centrepiece. The unheated space felt arctic; a coal stove on the far side was unlit. Fewer people than Denton had expected sat as audience, all men, most in over-coats as he was. Denton didn't register as a separate fact that the only woman in the room was the dead one until he had looked around, got bored and begun really to see. He would, on the other hand, have been surprised to find a living woman there. He would not have been able to articulate why he would have been surprised. Now, he thought about it. Why was the murder of a woman a solely male concern?

On the table lay, presumably, what was left of Stella Minter, covered with a much-washed white cloth, some old stains barely perceptible as yellowish blooms. Sir Frank Parmentier stood a few feet away next to a table of instruments, consulting with, or giving orders to, a smaller man. Parmentier was tall, thin, fully bearded, an apparently virile man in his fifties with a full head of rather long, possibly curled, hair. Denton judged him something of an egoist, as he seemed to like poses that threw his head well back. Both men were wearing day clothes – dark coats and waistcoats, Parmentier's in the rather outdated style named after the late husband of the Widow of Windsor. For the third time since Denton had come in, Parmentier consulted a pocket watch, and at the same moment three men came in from the staff entrance, one of whom Denton recognized as Detective Sergeant Willey of the City Police. If Willey recognized him – unlikely in that gloom, that crowd – he gave no sign; he was muttering with Parmentier, who was gesturing impatiently. Willey and one of the other policemen (such they had to be, Denton thought) went up into the seats; the third put a chair near the table of instruments and took out a notebook and a pencil.

'I am about to begin,' Parmentier announced. It was said the way a stage magician might have announced that he was now going to lock himself into a trunk. The audience of mostly medical students, who had been making a good deal of noise, shut up as if a curtain had been dropped. Parmentier pulled on rubber gloves that looked very white in the brightness and glanced in Willey's direction. 'Belatedly,' he said in an acid tone, but Willey didn't react.

'I am about to perform a post-mortem examination on the body in a police matter of a victim named Sarah Minter.' The accent was upper-class, the voice accustomed to inspiring awe.

The man with the notebook said something. Parmentier frowned. '*Stella* Minter,' he said. He let several seconds pass. Then, deliberately, he selected a bone-handled scalpel from the tray of instruments, turned back and in one swift gesture strode to the table and whipped the cloth aside. The rubber gloves, coming high on his arms over his coat sleeves, gave him a vaguely rakish look, the gauntlets of a pirate or a highwayman, at odds with his clothes and his voice.

Denton, like others, gave no outward reaction when the body was exposed, but, to someone standing close and looking directly at him with a good light, he could have been seen to narrow his eyes, a kind of blink; looking closer, a dilation of the pupils would have been visible. The widespread effort to show no reaction made the theatre quite silent as even breathing stopped.

Stella Minter lay on her back, nude, legs together, head sticking a few inches beyond the end of the table so that her light-brown hair fell back and down and the slash across her throat gaped.

She was painfully thin; her ribs showed clearly; but her breasts, flattened by her position, were nonetheless large, the aureoles dark. Her skin was greenish-grey, the light unkind to it; she had no hint of warmth, of the pink that is life. Using a cheap pair of opera glasses picked up on the way, Denton could see the curled, grey-brown edges of wounds on her breasts and abdomen. Two inches below the navel, the abdomen was open, and unidentifiable organs lay on her joined thighs, as grey now as pickled specimens. Denton counted eleven wounds on the upper half of the torso. Visible blood was brown but very scanty; the body, he thought, had been washed. *The bloody sheets of his wedding night. Not a lot, but it seemed so, his new wife in tears, wanting to wash the sheet before it was discovered. So much of women was about blood.*

'The subject is a woman, somewhat but not excessively under-nourished, height—' Parmentier gestured; the assistant handed him one end of a tape, and Parmentier walked to the feet. The assistant muttered to him. 'Five feet, four and one-quarter inches.' He let go of the tape. 'Age—' He walked to the middle of the body, felt over first one hip and then the other; walked to the head, felt the top of the head; returned to the middle and leaned over the pubis, apparently studying the rather sparse, sandy hair. 'Perhaps sixteen or seventeen; if we had time, we would excise one tip of the pelvis to study bone growth.' He started again for the head and paused at the breasts, again leaned forward until his eyes were directly above the right breast. With his left hand, he touched the nipple, rubbed the tips of the fingers together, sniffed them, then leaned still farther and examined the other breast. 'Evidence of lactation in both breasts, which also appear to be engorged.' He straightened. He looked halfway around the circle of men. 'What does this suggest to us, gentlemen?' He waited and waited until somebody at last said in a gruff but hesitant voice, 'Had a baby?'

'Recent parturition, exactly, albeit crudely put. We speculate tentatively that subject has given birth within perhaps six months.'

He continued up to the head and examined the face, then the top of the head, parting the hair with one hand. The assistant made measurements – circumference of the skull, eye-line to back of the head, ear-to-ear width.

'I find two contusions on the right side of the face, one on the maxillary, one two inches lower.'

Denton studied the face through the glasses. The bruise on the cheekbone was blue-grey. *He hit her and hit her.*

Parmentier straightened. 'In certain cases, we would remove the cranium.'

He took a step backwards and spread his hands a little wider than his hips; the scalpel caught a light, winked.

'The subject has been virtually exsanguinated,' he said. 'Exsanguination was undoubtedly the result of wounds visible even before examination – as you can perhaps see. However, as to which wound was the principal cause—' He raised his heavy eyebrows. 'Note the throat.' He touched the body again, this time at the tip of the small chin. Pushing with one finger, he tried to force the head back; when it would not move because of its position on the table, he signalled to his assistant, and the man took the shoulders and drew the body a few inches towards him. The wound gaped wider and the head sank back. The surgeon probed the cut with a finger, then forced the head farther back still, reaching in with his left thumb and index finger. 'The right carotid artery has been severed, as we suspected – reason enough for exsanguination, but –' he straightened and gestured with his scalpel – 'we must never speculate.'

– and he cut her—

He put his eyes close to the wound and worked in it with his fingers. 'Wound is deepest on victim's right side, slightly less so in the centre, suggesting a cut from right to left that also tended somewhat downwards, exiting through the left sternocleidomastoid muscle, where I can follow an increasingly shallow incision that ends in a faintly jagged tear hardly visible to the naked eye. I deduce that the point of a blade was inserted on the right, then pulled across – not, let me say, the cut with the long edge of a blade that is suggested by the vulgar gesture of drawing the finger across the throat.' He then made measurements with a flat ivory or bone instrument – Denton couldn't tell which – that gave imperial measurements for what he had just said. The deepest thrust, on the right, had gone in more than three inches, actually striking into a vertebra. Parmentier measured the stabs in the torso with the same showy precision, counting fourteen, the deepest five inches. 'Nine of these wounds show abrasion beyond the edges of the wound itself, in five of the cases the same pattern of ridges parallel with the blade. I take these to suggest – suggest, gentlemen, not prove, not yet – that a large clasp knife was used that, when thrust to the full depth of the blade, brought the end of the handle, and hence the bolsters, into violent contact with the skin, leaving the ridged patttern I have noted – that is, the marks of the bolsters.'

Then, for the first time, he used his scalpel. With one sweep, he cut the torso from the breastbone to the navel. Denton, with even his minimal knowledge of orchestral concerts, was reminded of a conductor. 'In the event, what I am now doing is probably redundant, but *it pays to be sure*. We want to know that the victim did not die of poison or internal damage or any of the vicissitudes that await the human body.' He handled a lung, cut a slice from it, then straightened, the tissue resting on his left palm. 'The victim was in relatively good health, in fact, with no outward sign of disease to the lungs or stomach. I shall of course do the kidneys and liver separately. If enough blood remains in the spleen, as I expect it to do, we shall take a sample and test it for the grosser poisons.' He handed over the piece of lung without looking towards the assistant. A slight smell of something like sewage spread through the theatre.

'Now—' The surgeon moved down the body. He was still immaculate, had not rolled up his sleeves or put on an apron, as his assistant had. Again, he held the scalpel up as if it were a cautioning finger. 'To the organs that most interest the police.' He looked down at the mass of tissue lying on the thighs and at the brutal gashes above it. 'A crude semi-oval of approximately six inches by four inches has been cut, or perhaps I should say *hacked* in the abdomen, penetrating the muscle wall and damaging the intestines, although they were not, I believe, the goal.' He was probing the terrible wound. 'The spleen is untouched, sheer happenstance. Small intestine is perforated in at least three places, slashed right through in at least one; this isn't our primary concern. Rather than damage to these organs, what has been so crudely attempted is an excision of the womb, cutting it – or perhaps tearing it, I cannot yet tell – loose from its connections so that it could be exvaginated through the vulva. In short, the most primitive sort of methods have been used to, as it were, surgically remove the most female parts of the body.'

He reached up inside and—

He then handled the tissue lying on the thighs, slit the exvaginated portion and opened it out. Denton was reminded of a fish or a bird spatchcocked for broiling. Around him, men were making notes or looking on without expression. He thought that they were all keeping themselves under tight control, as was Parmentier, he supposed, never mentioning the dead woman's humanity, the horror of the crime; it was as if they were all dealing with the unpacking of a suitcase. Denton looked around the faces again. Control, yes – a considerable feature of English life, the part he found least likable, least sympathetic, dropped only in special environments: the whorehouse, the battlefield. But control of what, really? Superficially, any response that would show weakness, he supposed, or anything 'undignified'. But the savagery of the woman's injuries were far beyond dignity or respect, rather in the realm of madness. Was this male control partly the suppression of a desire, or at least – he winced at the memory of his wanting to hurt Emma – the suppression of a recognition of a possibility? Had they all murdered her, in fact? Had he murdered Emma so, in his mind?

Parmentier was ordering the body rolled over, then opening the back to get at the kidneys and the liver. Organs were weighed, put into bottles; at last the corpse was covered again with the cloth and the organs were wheeled out of the theatre. Parmentier made a summary – exsanguination, multiple stab wounds, blood in the trachea and lungs suggesting possible asphyxiation after the carotid artery was severed; the inference to be drawn was that this had been the first wound, although not impossible that the others or at least some of the others were done first, but this notion not supported by the lack of bruising or other signs of response to extreme pain. No indication of restraints on wrists, ankles, or mouth. One interesting detail lay in the lifting of part of the scalp from the cranium, probably by the assailant's free hand, pulling the head back as the throat was slashed.

'An exceedingly violent act by an exceedingly powerful person, perhaps in an extreme state caused by alcohol or other substance, perhaps not, the many stab wounds allowing us to speculate as to his or her mental state.' Parmentier put down his scalpel at last. 'Questions?'

The questions were of two kinds, the incomprehensibly scientific and the banal. Parmentier dealt with the first at the same level of incomprehensibility, the second with ridicule. 'Frenzy? What do you mean, sir, by *frenzy*?' Then, ignoring the student's stammered response, 'I do not deal in *frenzy*. I leave such conclusions to the police.' Staring into the near-dark of the audience, for the light had clouded in the lantern above him. 'You, perhaps, have embarked on the wrong career, and would be better off to think of one in some more emotional field.' And then, playing to the house: 'Perhaps journalism.' Uneasy, then relieved laughter.

Denton asked no questions but made his way into the arena as soon as Parmentier announced that they were done. Detective Sergeant Willey was making his way down from the other side but coming slowly, talking to his companion and the one who had served as clerk. Denton went right to Parmentier and, by talking louder than the nervous medical student already there, said, 'Could the throat have been slashed while the attacker was engaged in coitus with the victim?'

The great man eyed him. He paid Denton the compliment of immediately turning his attention away from the student as he began pulling off the rubber gloves. 'Do I know you, sir? Are you of the profession?'

'I'm a guest of Hector Hench-Rose's.' Making it a joke: 'Not a journalist.'

'I shall take it as given that your interest is not prurient. I don't know Hench-Rose, unless he's related to George Hench-Rose.'

'An older brother, I think.'

'Ah. I see him at old-boy dinners.' He tore at the left glove, which clung to him like skin, muttered, 'These damnable things—' and wrenched it off, dropping it on the floor with disgust. He took Denton's left arm and steered him towards the covered body. 'Yes, of course, if it was a man, it would be quite possible for him to support himself on his left elbow while grasping the hair with that hand and making that long, powerful cut across the throat with his right.' He removed the cloth; the body was still face-down. 'If you'll just lend a hand—' Denton took the cool, waxy ankles, and they rolled her over on her back; she seemed weightless. *Lighter than Emma.* 'Now, you see how it can be done – the elbow here – the knife in the hand—' Parmentier was bending over the girl as if he were the murderer still coupled with her, his eyes bright with enthusiasm.

'Was there ejaculate in the vagina?'

'Perhaps. It's going to be difficult to tell because of the state of the tissue; a good deal of blood and secretion in there. I'll have a look at it under a microscope. Are you in the police?'

'No.'

'I thought not. American? Canadian? American, yes.' He wiped his hands on the cloth.

Denton was examining the stab wounds in the breasts. 'You're satisfied she'd given birth,' he said.

'Oh, yes.'

'Thank you.' Denton searched for a compliment. He hadn't sat in on a post-mortem since he'd been a marshal and the local doctor had done an examination that lasted four minutes. 'An elegant performance, sir.' He had started to say 'doctor', but he couldn't remember which sorts of medical men liked to be called doctor and which thought the word an insult. Parmentier half-smiled, bowing his head.

Going out, Denton came face-to-face with Detective Sergeant Willey, who scowled but turned away as if his most cynical ideas of Denton had been confirmed.

CHAPTER FOUR

Emma.

Had he really said that to her – 'You're mine?' He didn't think so, but he remembered thinking it. Some atavism: the man owns the woman. It was what asinine juveniles said on the Criterion Theatre stage to pretty ingénues – 'You're mine at last!' And the ingénues agreed – 'I'm yours!' But that was metaphor. Wasn't it? Yet his reaction when Emma had thrown him over had been one of – redness. *Blood.*

Had that been Stella Minter's mistake, that she had left somebody who thought he owned her? He thought of the grey-green corpse on the table, Parmentier's scalpel; the feel of the girl's waxy, cool ankles; the watching, carefully controlled but greedy-eyed men. Yes, the savagery of the wounds might have come from that sort of passion. In the everyday world, the oldest of old stories, the lover jilted for somebody else. *She was mine.*

He had wanted to *kill* Emma; he saw that now, as if the postmortem had opened a window for him. He hadn't hit a woman, ever, even his wife when she was raging drunk and reviling him, although he had once shaken her when she was like that. Had he felt such shame then as he did now? What he remembered of the scenes with his wife was a deep loathing of both of them. Now, realizing his feeling towards Emma, he felt such shame as he had never known before, even in the worst of the war, when he had done some terrible things.

He tried to think about Mulcahy, but his mind kept straying to the post-mortem and the picture of the lot of them, sitting there in their overcoats, fascinated by the cutting-up of a woman. *Like a show.* Where had he seen those blank, rapt faces before? At a pioneer-country fair – open-mouthed farmers staring at a bored woman attempting the Dance of the Seven Veils in a booth.

Denton made his way to the British Museum. He had some hope of walking off the hangover, of course an illusion – outdoor air doesn't change the chemistry of alcohol. The rain had stopped, and now a wind was driving clouds against a hard blue sky. Even after years here, Denton lived mentally in Dickens's London, that place of twisting streets, poverty, gloom and idiosyncrasy; he always needed to adjust when he came out into such a day as this, when London was every bit its modern self – noisy, hard-driving, bursting at the seams and spilling out into new suburbs at the rate of thousands of houses a year. He was wearing some sort of tweed cape-cum-coat that blew around him in points and folds, its over-cape turning up over his head and half-blinding him when his back was to the wind. It had been a gift from Emma. Atkins had put it out for him that morning – an instance of Atkins's humour?

Emma. The insistent memory mixed with thoughts of the post-mortem, his mind unable to hold any image or idea for more than a fraction of a second. *Impossible that he'd lost her.* Stab wounds. Exvagination. *Impossible.* Had a baby, did that mean anything? Emma was *his.*

At the Museum, he went into the Reading Room and found the London directories and began looking for Mulcahy, R. The long rows of volumes didn't discourage him, but the lack of system did. One set was alphabetized, but it was a business directory, and unless Mulcahy, R. was a professional or a recognized businessman, he wouldn't be in there. Denton's memory of Mulcahy was that he wouldn't qualify, and indeed, he wasn't to be found. There were Mulcahys in business, but he saw none with a given name that started with R.

Kelly's directories were more inclusive. Entirely inclusive, if their foreword was to be believed, but the fact was that they missed many, maybe most people who rented rooms, especially in the slums. In theory, Kelly's post office directories included every male working-man in the vast metropolitan area; the frustration for Denton was that they were arranged by streets, not personal names. If you wanted to know who lived in every house on Praed Street, you could find out, but if you knew somebody's name and didn't know where he lived, you were lost. On an impulse, he looked for Stella Minter in the Minories, but of course he didn't find her. Stella Minter had been a transient, a grain of sand in a shifting ocean.

One thousand, one hundred and thirty-six pages in the 1899 Kelly's. And shelves of suburban volumes beyond. Denton sat, cold enough to have left the unfortunate coat on, turning pages, glancing at streets, as if the name Mulcahy might leap from the dense eight-point type.

It would take days. No, weeks.

And no hangover.

He sighed, put the directories back and carried his fragile head out to Museum Street. The Tavern beckoned, but he ignored it; he walked down to Holborn, then zigzagged west and south and headed again for the Metropolitan Police Annexe.

He announced himself to the porter and went up, put his head into Hench-Rose's room and was told that Hector was 'in a meeting of the Examinations Resolution Committee', whatever that was, and turned instead and went along the corridor to what he hoped was Detective Sergeant Munro's office. He got the wrong room, of course; an ascetic civil servant who seemed to be preparing for life in a Himalayan monastery – thin, bald, placid – put him right.

Munro was not delighted to see him. His expression was disapproving. 'We're being run ragged here just now.'

'I'll come back.'

'We're always run ragged.' They were standing in the outer room where the three clerks were bending over red-tied files. 'We don't really have time for gentleman detectives.'

'I'm not a detective, don't pretend to be.' He thought of Emma. 'And I'm not a gentleman.'

Munro's expression changed; was he amused? 'Five minutes.' He led the way, limping, to his inner office. 'You here about the murder again?' he said when they were seated.

'I went to the post-mortem. I told you, Mulcahy, the man who came to see me, had described a murder—'

'Yes, yes—'

'It was very similar.'

Munro shrugged. He was tying and untying the red tape on a file. 'Lots of murders are similar. No sign of your Mulcahy that I've heard of. City Police might have something – you did tell them, right? Have to ask them.'

Denton shifted his body, trying to find a position that didn't make his muscles ache. His head was pounding. 'I'd like to see her room. Where she was killed.'

'Why's that?'

'Mulcahy, Mulcahy.'

Munro fiddled with the tape, then joined his fingers and looked at Denton. 'This the western sheriff in you coming out?' Before Denton could answer, he said, 'Read a bit about you – a pal downstairs keeps a scrapbook, had a newspaper piece about you.' He was nodding. 'Funny, you were down in Nebraska the same time I was in Alberta. Mounties.'

Denton felt stupid, couldn't puzzle it out. A Brit in the Mounties?

'My dad emigrated from Scotland in 1847. I was born in Flodden, Quebec, tiny little place. I joined the Mounties in the second intake. Heard of the Sweet Grass Hills? Old Man River? Fort MacLeod?' He grinned. 'You weren't a whiskey trader, were you?'

'That's one thing I never tried.'

Munro grunted. 'Bunch of lowlifes selling flavored raw alcohol to the Indians on the Assiniboine. I put in twice my three years and came here – better job, better pay.'

'I went on west.'

'It was a rough place back then.' Munro leaned away from him. 'You really kill four men?'

He never talked about it. 'Two,' he said. He waited for Munro to see that it was a poor subject. Munro, however, had the look of a man who could wait him out. 'The other two died later.'

'Six-gun?' Said with a grin.

'Shotgun.' Said with a scowl.

Munro raised his eyebrows and shook his head. 'Always wonder how I'd have done, that kind of situation. But the Mounties were very big on not being like Americans.'

'Violent people.' Denton had thought about it. 'But we had slavery.' Slavery, as he had worked it out, made the slaver violent.

'Maybe the killer's an American.' Munro said it with another smile.

'My five minutes are up.'

Munro made a face as if to say it didn't matter. 'I might be able to get you into the scene of the crime and I might not. Bit difficult because it's City Police.'

'Plus Sergeant Willey more or less took against me.'

'Yeah, well— The truth is, Willey's probably so overworked he's forgotten you. No offence. But they've got a big thing going on bank fraud over there; a dead prostitute isn't going to distract them for long. Let me see what I can do through the Yard.'

'You've changed your mind about me.'

Munro was playing with the red tapes again. 'Apparently,' he said, and he grinned once more. 'You have the telephone?' Denton shook his head. 'Leave an address where I can get a message to you.' While Denton was extracting a card from his case with trembling fingers, Munro said, 'I'd give my right arm to be back in the CID.' He seemed to mean it as an explanation of why he was willing to help Denton now.

Denton's mouth tasted like burned metal.

He walked back like a man in a walking race. Always a fast walker, he seemed demented now. His balance was off; his back and head ached; still he plunged on. He had at first made for home, but he

45

detoured into Soho and threw himself into a Chinese noodle shop, where, surrounded by slurping Chinese labourers, he filled himself with noodles and broth and several small dumplings. He had discovered Chinese food in California, had been surprised that the cosmopolitan English looked on it as comical, possibly dangerous, meaning actually that it was lower-class and strange. ('We must never notice things that are unpleasant,' he had read in Dickens but not understood until he had lived in London a while.) The food made him feel suddenly better, and he was able to lurch his way up to Oxford Street and then east, turning up Museum Street again because he liked it and at last through rather awful byways to Lamb's Conduit. Always, the darkening blue was above him and the clouds were racing over as if leaping from the rooftops on one side to those on the other; below, looking up, trying to walk, he was made dizzy.

'Sergeant!' he shouted as he let himself in. He wanted to lie down but was damned if he would. He would make himself work, always a panacea, even though the work was no longer physical.

Atkins appeared in his little doorway at the foot of the stairs. 'You rang, sir?'

Denton tossed him the horrible tweed coat. 'Get rid of that.' He put his hat on the newel post. 'I don't want tea.'

'Good, else I'd have had to send to the Lamb. Nothing in the house.'

Denton started up the stairs; his head seemed to pull him backwards.

Atkins shifted the heavy coat to bring it more into view. 'When you say, "Get rid of it," you mean put it away or get it out of the house?'

'Throw it in the trash; give it to General Booth; wear it yourself.'

'Wouldn't be caught dead in it.'

He went up to his room. The unfinished novel made a pile of foolscap an inch high, written neatly enough but then scribbled over, crossed out, amended in trickles that fell off the end of the

46

line and ran down the page and sometimes looped around to the other side of the sheet. He sighed and sat down to it. The truth was, as he admitted as he read over the last ten pages, the woman he'd created was a piece of cardboard. A fiction, a convenience. She was another of his attempts to capture his wife – to capture what she had done to him, to his life – in fiction. The scene he was working on had been meant as preparation for the downward spiral that would leave her dead on a frozen pasture in winter, raving and wandering in the snow. (The real Lily had taken poison.) And destroying her husband in the process.

Stella Minter, dead and eviscerated by first her murderer and then the surgeon, was, he saw, more real, even in death, than the woman in his novel. He'd tried to recreate his wife, and he hadn't even created a corpse. He dropped the scene into the trash, then began to leaf back through the rest of the manuscript, pulling out pages, dropping them into oblivion. *Not the way a writer makes money.*

He heard Atkins breathing heavily as he came up the steep stairs.

'Copper looking for you down below.'

'I'm working.'

'Copper wants you.' Atkins produced a silver salver from behind his back. 'Message.'

'For God's sake—' Denton took the paper. 'The plate wasn't necessary, was it?'

'Might have touched it with my dirty hands otherwise.'

It was from Munro. *'Can you meet me at a public house called the Haymow near the Minories at six o'clock? We can have a look at the scene you were interested in. PC Catesby will tell you the way, as it is difficult. Please reply by the constable.'*

'I'll go down.'

PC Catesby had a foolish young face and blushed easily. He drew a map on the back of Munro's note as laboriously as if he were working out a problem in mathematics. In fact, Denton knew the streets he referred to as soon as he mentioned them, but there was no convincing the policeman. He went on pushing the thick pencil over the paper, printing names, making arrows, turning something easy into something tortuous.

'I understand; it's one street north and west of the Minories, right. The Haymow. Got it.'

'Yes, sir, if you tell the driver the Minories and *then* direct him to—' It was the third time he'd gone over it. Denton hadn't told the man he planned to walk, afraid that he'd get the entire route mapped for him on the same small sheet of paper. He kept saying yes, right, thank you, and finally PC Catesby took himself off, turning back in the doorway, then at the gate, to make some further point. Then he actually came back and said to Denton, 'The Haymow's rather low, sir.'

'Thank you.'

He wondered if he should have tipped PC Catesby, decided not. Giving policemen money had a bad reputation.

'I've put out the dark-brown lounge suit,' Atkins said when Denton came upstairs. 'You want another of them headache powders?'

'I'm all right.'

Atkins hesitated. 'Your coat come back from Mrs Gosden's. Also hat, gloves, stick. Also the derringer in the pocket.' He raised his eyebrows – music-hall astonishment.

'Somebody brought it?'

'Commissionaire. Coat et cetera in a box. Carried the stick.'

In a box. Everything ends in a box.

'Put the derringer in the hollow book.'

'Already have.'

Denton started to ask if there had been any message with the coat, any reply to the apology he had sent Emma, but Atkins would of course have told him if there had been. In fact, the coat and hat *were* the message. They were the full stop at the end of a sentence – the compound sentence that had been his affair with Emma and was never to become a paragraph.

CHAPTER FIVE

Denton walked to his meeting with Munro – down to Holborn, along to the Holborn Viaduct, to Newgate Street, Cheapside, Cornhill, Leadenhall Street, Aldgate High Street – almost the whole width of the City. It was nearly evening, but the streets were banging with mechanical life – steam diggers clawing up the earth, steam cranes lifting bundles of wood and stone into the sky. London was a mythical beast that was tearing out its own innards and regrowing them in a new form – new streets, new buildings, new tunnels and railways. It was destroying – or hiding – what was sick or poor or weak or decayed and putting up the new, the vigorous, the aggressive. No wonder the directories couldn't keep up with people like Mulcahy and Stella Minter: the city itself was flinging people from place to place.

He had spent his years in London walking as much as twenty miles a day, seldom less than eight or ten, Baedeker's in his pocket. He had walked from his house to Richmond on one side, to the Lea on the other; he had crossed the Thames and walked down to Greenwich and up to Kew, and he had found this mechanical pulse of renewal everywhere. London for Denton, when he pushed Dickens out of his head, was a clatter of modernizing machines surrounded by a sea of mud where new suburbs pushed relentlessly outward, chewing up whole streets, whole towns, each one succeeded by a newer that made the earlier one instantly mature.

He was not afraid of places or people, although if he walked at night he went armed – hence the derringer in the forgotten topcoat. Now, he knew London tolerably well – well enough, at least, that he found, when he got to the Haymow, that he had stopped in it once for a drink when he was walking down to the Tower. The woman at the bar, the few other patrons, hadn't been welcoming then – gentlemen didn't go into public houses, weren't welcome if they did, they had seemed to say. In fact, he'd learned a lesson from that visit to the Haymow. Gentlemen weren't welcome, but Bohemians were; if he had worn a wider-brimmed American hat (a 'cowboy hat', Hench-Rose had once called it, although it in fact had a fairly narrow brim compared with some he'd seen) and no necktie, like the Bohemians at the Café Royal, he'd have been tolerated.

The Haymow was one of the old pubs, small and simple, with a bar that ran almost the length of the far wall but no divisions into saloon bar or public bar or private rooms or any of the other embellishments of the great public houses that had bloomed over the last quarter-century. It was cream-coloured inside, or had been before a layer of smoke had been laid over the paint, then layers of what seemed to be amber shellac over that, so that the walls were shiny where the lights caught them and glazed as brown as a Dutch painting. PC Catesby had said it was low, but Denton saw nothing very low except a few working-men, hats on, smoke in a cloud around them. Munro was sitting on a faded brown banquette against the wall, far around to the right from the door.

'You found it,' he said when Denton sat down.

'PC Catesby gave meticulous directions.' Catesby, he figured, had been trying to do a good job; no need to speak ill of him.

'We're meeting somebody else.' Munro waved a hand, and a strong-looking woman nearing middle age – the same woman, so far as Denton could tell, who had served him before – came out from behind the bar and took Denton's order for a pint. They sat in silence until the ale appeared; then Munro leaned closer and lowered his voice. 'Pal of mine from Metropolitan CID's going to take us to the girl's room. The murder scene. He hasn't seen it yet, either, wants to have a look because the Ripper file is always open.

Mind, nobody believes for a moment it's the Ripper, but you dot every i. You're along as a favour to me.'

'My thanks.'

'Could be awkward if you're called one day to testify, I mean about Mulcahy, but we'll cross that bridge when we come to it. The tale we're telling is he wants to question you about evidence you gave Willey and will ask you to walk over the scene to see if any of it reminds you of something you might have forgotten. That's bollocks, but it's a tale.'

'Why's he doing it?'

'I told you, favour to me.'

'Why are you doing it?'

'Favour to myself.' They both sipped from the big glasses. 'A chance to think like a detective for a bit. Plus, I confess I'm curious what you'll do. You've a bee in your bonnet about your Mulcahy. Interests me.' He wiped his upper lip with a crooked forefinger. 'You think your Mulcahy killed that tart, don't you?'

'He could have. Likelier that he heard about it and got – excited.' *Remembering the rapt male faces ringing the post-mortem.* 'You believe men are evil?'

'I'd be a poor Christian if I didn't.' Munro drank.

'Men, I mean. Not women.'

'What, men worse than women?' Munro thought about it. 'Naw, give some women a knife, they're evil incarnate.'

Both were leaning on the pub table, their forearms only inches apart. Denton said, 'Killing prostitutes just seems such a male crime.'

'Well, yes. O' course. It's in the nature of the thing, isn't it?'

'What, killing's an extension of the – transaction?'

'Well, no, I didn't mean that, but—' Munro chewed his lip, made a face. 'Not many people here tonight. Scared of us. Place has been full of coppers – made this their sort of headquarters, Willey and his lot.' He sipped his ale and looked around at the other men, who seemed as weary and harmless as people could be. 'Inquest's tomorrow,' he said. 'Not here. Can hold an inquest in a pub, you know.'

'You telling me that because I'm an American?'

'Well, yeah, first time I ran into it here, I was surprised. As a Canadian.' He raised his eyebrows, looking over Denton's shoulders. 'Here's George.' Denton turned and watched a large man stroll to the bar. He was wearing a tweed overcoat that billowed around him and perhaps increased his bigness, but under it he was a large man, for sure. Forty, going to fat, but, Denton guessed, powerful and probably fast on his feet, as some heavy men were, maybe a clever dancer. His waistcoat was well filled, his shoulders enormous; Denton thought that his arms would look soft but be as big around as fence posts. Pushing his bowler back on his head, he was chatting up the barmaid and waiting for his pint; when it came, he turned and headed right for their table, although Denton hadn't seen him even glance their way.

'Georgie,' Munro said. As Denton half-rose, he said, 'Detective Sergeant Guillam of the CID, Mr Denton.'

Guillam sat. He looked at Denton over the rim of his glass. 'So you're the sheriff,' he said.

'I wasn't a sheriff – I was a town marshal. I get a little tired of people talking about it.'

'Yes, you would, wouldn't you.' Guillam had a pleasant baritone, pronunciations that for Denton added up to 'an accent', meaning only that it was 'London' or 'Cockney' or something other than the hieratic cooing of, say, Emma Gosden. 'So tell me about this man you've been going on about.'

Denton was irritated all over again, ascribed the irritation to the hangover, which had abated but had left behind, like trash on a beach, a general unease. There was also in Guillam's voice a little too much of the policeman, as if Denton were a suspect, not a witness. Or merely a looker-on. 'I've really nothing to add to what I told Sergeant Willey. He asked a lot of questions; the answers are all there.' When Guillam still simply looked at him, he said, 'My servant can bear it all out.' He sounded defensive and pretty silly to himself.

'Yeah, we're talking to him right about now. If he's home.' Guillam stared straight into his eyes. 'I got one interest, Mr Denton – that it's nothing to do with the Ripper. I just want to cross the t's and dot the i's and tie it in red ribbon for the great men who run Scotland Yard. So I'd like to hear your tale.'

Then Denton realized that he really was in some murky way suspect, if not *a* suspect. And then it struck him that of course Munro had been in cahoots with Guillam when he had asked Denton to meet him here. To see how he would react. Denton looked at Munro, saw that he was perhaps a touch embarrassed. 'Is this —' Denton gestured around the Haymow — 'just so you can quiz me?'

'No, no, no,' Munro said. 'Georgie's just being a good copper. He's got to follow up the loose ends, see?'

Denton glanced back at Guillam. 'Am I suspected of something?'

'Everybody's suspected of something — that's the copper's way. No, you're not suspected in this, unless it's spinning a tale about the Ripper for your own amusement. Which would *not* amuse me.' Guillam put down his empty glass. 'Willey's got his murderer—' Denton saw Munro's head come up, and his face must have shown his own surprise, because Guillam said, 'News to you? — a nigger he picked up with blood all over him, drunk out of his mind and unable to say where he'd been. So you're not a suspect, see? So please don't give me a hard time, Mr Denton. If you don't like talking to me here, I'll haul your arse down to the Yard and show you how we conduct an interrogation of an unwilling witness — because you say you *are* a witness. Now, get off your high horse, you.'

Denton felt a contradictory deflation at the news that Willey had the murderer, or at least a suspect; all at once, Mulcahy and his visit seemed irrelevant. He made the mistake of saying so to Guillam. Guillam bared his teeth the way angry dogs do and snarled, 'Just because you're a smart fella, don't try to do my thinking for me!'

Guillam would never have talked to Hench-Rose like that, Denton thought — he'd succeeded in convincing Guillam, at least, that he wasn't a gentleman. Oddly, the offensive tone made him like Guillam a little, and he laughed. 'What do you want to know?'

Guillam grunted. 'I read your statement to Willey and I think it's a bit peculiar that this fellow – Mulcahy? – just happened to come to your house.'

'I explained that.'

'Just came to your house, started to babble, he did.'

Denton tried not to sound defensive. 'It's the "sheriff" thing again. He was frightened out of his wits.'

'Tell me about that.'

'What?'

'How was he frightened? Tell me how you knew he was frightened.'

Denton looked to Munro but got no help. 'Are you two going to take me to see the girl's room or aren't you?' he said, annoyed again.

Guillam sat back, eyed him. 'Depends,' he said. He began working a thumbnail between his front teeth, moved the nail to the right into the next crevice, then the next, then turned the nail horizontally and chewed it. 'I'm thinking of doing you a service here. In return, I'd like some information. Then, if I'm satisfied, we'll stroll down to the crime scene because I want to see what you make of that – *if* you don't mind.'

'Munro said that was a tale, taking me along to see what I'd remember.'

'That's Donald's word, *tale*, not mine.'

'My God – you really do suspect me of something!'

Guillam hunched forward. 'Mr Denton, if we really suspected you, we'd have you at the Yard. Now tell me about Mulcahy being frightened out of his wits.'

He went through that, then through Mulcahy's flight, which Guillam said was 'convenient', then through Mulcahy's arrival and his choice of Denton for his 'babbling'. The more Denton talked, the weaker it sounded. The more questions Guillam asked, the more Denton thought that he was being looked at as one of those loonies who rush to the police after every sensational crime.

'City Police didn't find your tale about this Mulcahy very helpful.' Guillam gave a glimmer of a smile. 'I did send a couple of telegrams to check out what you say he told you, nonetheless.' He looked up at Denton, his huge face on his left fist.

'Where?'

'Yorkshire, Paris, Berlin.' He made a circle with his right thumb and forefinger. 'Nothing yet.' Guillam shifted, put both forearms in their heavy tweed sleeves on the little table. 'You write stories, Mr Denton, fanciful stuff full of ghosts and fairies. Tempting to think your brain's been too active, it is.' He held up his left hand again to shush Denton before he could speak. 'Don't get your dander up. I know that's insulting. But see it from my perspective – in walks this gent, feeds Willey a tale that doesn't help anything, gent turns out to be a professional storyteller, maybe one wanting his name in the papers. Willey's being run ragged, trying to fend off the press scum and satisfy his masters and solve a crime all at once; what he doesn't need is a fanciful invention from somebody who then wants to see the victim's body! Get it? You came across as a –' he shrugged – 'as eccentric.' He cocked an eyebrow. 'And maybe a bit more so when you turn up at the post-mortem.'

There is a stage in a hangover where the pain subsides and the nausea goes away and a curious serenity replaces them. Denton had suddenly reached that pleasant place, he found, perhaps helped by the ale. He let himself laugh again. He saw the figure he must make to men like these. 'Mulcahy isn't one of my inventions, Sergeant.'

Guillam glanced at Munro, then put his hands flat on the table. 'Let's go and look at the crime scene.'

'I passed the test?'

'There's been no test.' Guillam was standing over him now. 'But you didn't pass it, either.'

They came out of the cul-de-sac where the Haymow hid and turned left into Jewry Street, then right and almost immediately left again into a long, very narrow passage that his Baedeker's later told him was Vine Street. The sky, darkening now towards evening, was a mere slice overhead, the buildings on each side built almost to the kerbs, with paved walks only wide enough for one of them at a time. The street, macadam now but not so long ago cobbled, was itself used as a walkway, men and women moving aside for the barrows that came rolling up as if they would roll right over them. Guillam led them down past one narrow street that went off to their left and joined a thoroughfare that must be, Denton thought, the Minories; a hundred feet beyond, a constable was standing at another opening.

Guillam, walking in front, turned and looked at each of them. He muttered something to the constable, who pointed behind him. Denton expected again to be looking down a narrow street into the Minories, but what he saw instead was a gap between the buildings no more than a dozen feet wide, which opened into a court that was closed on the far end – Priory Close Alley. It was neither particularly clean nor particularly sordid; it was more or less quiet compared with the street; it had two skinny cats, several blown newspapers, weeds in the joints where the stone flags met the walls. All the buildings but one appeared to be commercial, and of no very successful kind.

A religious house had once covered the area of the Minories, its stones still incorporated into some of the buildings roundabout. Those in the court had nothing medieval about them, however, but were rather of some indeterminate style of the first half of the eighteenth century. Of different widths and heights, the four buildings, two on each side, all seemed to drop straight to the pavement from their eaves without setbacks or such luxuries as front steps; two were of blackened grey stone, two of brick so dark that only the pattern of the mortar made it possible to see what they were made of. The far end of the little court was closed by a wall seven or eight feet high, with beyond it an open space and then the upper storeys of a house that must face on the Minories.

Denton looked up and saw an even narrower slice of sky than over Jewry Street. The sun, he decided, would move more or less parallel to the court's long axis; if it actually shone here, it would light perhaps only the top two or three storeys on his left.

On his right were two buildings, one very narrow. The wider one stood a little advanced, as if shouldering the other aside. It had been, he thought, in one of its lives a warehouse, perhaps a combined warehouse and residence: high up under the eaves a beam thrust out from the façade, supported by a diagonal like a gallows; below it, a bricked-up rectangle suggested a former opening. Farther down were windows, several broken and pasted over with paper; farther down yet, a dead plant on a window ledge, a crockery dish on another, the window open a couple of inches. At ground level, the building had a central door reached by a single horizontal slab of blackened stone that was paler and concave in the middle from many feet. To the left of that door was another, smaller one where a window might have been expected, as if somebody had once decided to make a shop of the space behind it. This doorway was blocked by a sign on a wooden standard that said 'No Admittance POLICE'.

Guillam had an iron ring in his right hand with several keys hanging from it. He applied one to a new-looking padlock on the smaller door and turned back to them.

'Smell it out here,' he said. He moved the sign to his left and pushed the door open. 'We haven't let them clean up yet.'

CHAPTER SIX

'Judas Priest,' Munro muttered.

The smell burst out to meet them as if under pressure. Denton recognized blood and decay; memories of battlefields flitted down his mind, then an image of a short man he had shotgunned who had bled seemingly everywhere.

'You were at the post-mortem,' Guillam said. 'You know what to expect.'

Stella Minter had died in a room only big enough to hold her bed, a rickety chair, a stand that held a chamber pot, and a curtained area no wider than her shoulders, where her few clothes hung. High in the wall opposite the bed, in that part of the house that jutted forward beyond its neighbour, was an oval window, the long axis vertical, a piece of cloth pinned over it for a curtain. Guillam now tried to pull it aside and managed to pull it down.

'Touch nothing,' Guillam said.

'Anything been removed?' Munro muttered.

'Not supposed to've been.' Guillam pulled several folded sheets of paper from some inner pocket and handed it over without looking. Munro opened them and Denton, coming behind him, moved closer and waited for somebody to object. Nobody did. He saw at the top of the paper in a neat hand, *Inventory, No. 7-A, Priory Close Alley.*' He ran his eyes down the paper – '*1 dresses, 1 petticoat, 1 wrapper on floor, 1 nightgown on hook*', (indeed, there it was, next to the bed) '*undergarments, on chair; 1 pr. shoes; 1 reticule containing 2s 5d, 1 handkerchief, 1 Mason's toffee in paper …*'

Guillam was lighting the only gas lamp, in the wall above the bed, which had been fitted with a polished reflector that made the light briefly painful. When Guillam was finished, he closed the door, making a shooing gesture at somebody outside.

She had been killed on the bed, and most of her blood had soaked into the sheets and the mattress. Some blood, now dry, also lay on the wood floor like ink.

'She was laying this way, feet towards the door,' Guillam said. He sliced his right hand through the air, index finger up, palm to the left, parallel to the long axis of the bed. 'Legs were partly drawn up, arms—' He scrabbled for another paper. 'Got the City Police drawing somewhere—' He unfolded it – a stick figure on a rectangle. The arms were above the head. 'Could have arranged the body somewhat, our killer could. One foot off the end of the bed a little; maybe moved her, or maybe that's just the way she placed herself.' He glanced up at Denton. 'Notion is that he was a customer and all she was wearing was the wrapper; she opens the door, lets him in, lays herself down, and there you are.'

'He hit her in the face,' Denton said. 'Twice.' He met Guillam's stolid look. 'Post-mortem – two contusions on the right side.'

'Report didn't say that *he* did it and didn't say there was any damage to the brain or any of that. Whores get whacked all the time. Or, all right, she lets him in, he whacks her, she lays herself down.'

'Somebody she knew?' Denton said.

'Wouldn't have to be somebody she knew; she was a cheap toss, move them along and get them out, next chap in. Except this one killed her. What you driving at?'

'Nothing. Only if she knew him, it would have been easier for him. Where's the wrapper?'

All three looked at the inventory, then at the floor. Guillam muttered, 'Damn them,' and got on his knees and looked under the bed. He got up breathing hard, brushing his knees, muttering, 'Mistakes, mistakes—' He looked at the list again. 'Must've been taken as evidence.'

'Why that?'

'Blowed if I know.'

59

'Anything else taken as evidence?'

Guillam looked at him. 'You ask a lot of questions, you do.' Surprisingly, he grinned. 'Yeah, they took the washbowl, the soap dish and the pitcher because the killer might have handled them. Washing himself. Find maybe blood on them or his fingers' marks. Don't think much of the finger-mark business – not much to it.' He was going through the sheets. The last one was headed 'Seized for evidence at 7-A Priory Close Alley' and listed the toilet articles and the wrapper. 'Bit sloppy, putting the wrapper down twice. Damn them.'

Denton was trying to picture the jet of blood from the severed carotid artery. It would have sprayed the murderer, apparently had also sprayed the wall at the head of the bed. There was a line of blood down the wall beside the bed, as well, as if one spurt had struck it. Had he rolled her that way? Or had Stella Minter moved? He thought of the corpse he had seen at Bart's, the stab wounds in the breasts and the tearing incisions in the pelvis. Parmentier with one leg up on the table, miming intercourse and cutting her throat. 'He must have been drenched with blood,' he said. The two detectives looked at him. 'Even if he wore an overcoat – it would have been all over him.'

'He may have killed her from behind, then arranged her after.'

'What, while she was standing?'

'Yeah, a big man, easy to do – reach around, he's holding her with his other arm.'

'He's left-handed, then. Post-mortem made it pretty clear how the cut was made – right side of her throat to the left.' He hesitated. 'Mulcahy said he – the man he knew – murdered a woman while he was inside her.' Again, the two detectives looked at him, their faces unreadable. 'Killing from the front, his clothes'd have been covered with blood. Wouldn't have taken his clothes off, I suppose. Wash himself afterwards, or at least wipe himself down. Maybe with the wrapper?'

'"Mulcahy said."' Guillam folded up the inventory. 'Your Mulcahy was talking about something donkey's years ago, and anyway he made it up, if you ask me.'

'That's what he said, that it was long ago.'

'You got Mulcahy on the brain, excuse my rudeness, sir.' Guillam winked at Munro, who turned away. Guillam looked back at Denton, saw that he'd seen the wink, moved his whole torso inside the big tweed coat in what might have been a shrug. 'I'm about done here,' he said.

Munro was moving slowly around the outside of the room, apparently studying the bed and avoiding the stain on the floor. Denton, feeling that he didn't want the visit to be wasted, began to look at the walls. What had he missed? He looked at the ceiling – cracks, discoloration, a moulding that ended halfway along the wall nearest the bed and reappeared on the front wall as if there had once been an opening there, now closed in.

'No opening into the house?' he said. Guillam, staring at the dress, shook his head.

'Used to be.' That got no response. 'What's over there?'

'Number Seven – lodging house,' Munro said. 'Nobody heard anything. Nobody saw anything. Right, Georgie?'

'Nobody, nobody, nobody,' Guillam muttered.

Denton looked at the walls. Nothing – more cracks, more discoloration. Over the head of the bed, an engraving from a magazine of two young women, one praying and one ascending up what appeared to be a beam of light. Halfway down the bed, on the near wall parallel to it, a reverse painting on glass, much the worse for wear, of a castle in an exaggerated mountain setting. Denton stepped across the stain as Munro had done and worked his way down the narrow space between the bed and the wall to study the blood-splashed picture. 'Balmoral' was painted on a grey-green lawn that swept away from the castle, most of whose middle had flaked away, leaving a dark hole where the royal apartments might have been. Denton leaned closer.

'Mr Sherlock Holmes has found a clue,' he heard Guillam say.

If he hadn't said it, Denton might have spoken up. Instead, anger rising, he pushed his hands into his overcoat pockets and stared some seconds longer into the bowels of Balmoral and then turned back to the room, silent about what he'd seen. 'Not waiting for me, I hope,' he said.

Guillam was grinning. 'An admirer of Mr Sherlock Holmes, are you?'

Denton was still standing behind the bloodstained bed. 'I think it's claptrap.'

'You astonish me.'

'I liked the stupid doctor, what's-his-name. Reminds me of people I've known.'

'Coppers, probably.' Guillam's grin became tight. 'Coppers are stupid, that's the tale, isn't it? Stupid coppers can't solve a crime, call in the gentleman detective, all will be resolved with the application of one cigar ash, a baby's wail and eighteen generalizations. Brilliant!'

Denton worked his way down the bed, the space so narrow that he had to go sideways. 'I don't know any gentleman detectives.'

'Neither does anybody else – in real life!' Guillam guffawed, stopped abruptly and said to Munro, 'You done? I'm fair sick of this place, I am.'

Munro and Denton stood in the court while Guillam locked up. Munro said in a low voice, 'Don't mind him.'

'I don't.'

'Georgie's overworked. This is on top of everything else he has to do. He's a good copper.'

Guillam came to them. 'Talking about me?' he said. He gripped Denton's arm. 'Didn't mean to come down hard on you, Mr Denton. It's frustration. Always afraid I'll see something in these places that could be the Ripper. My nightmare.'

'Do you think it was the man Willey's holding that did it?'

Guillam held on to his arm, even massaging it slightly with his thumb. His eyes were fixed on nothing. 'I think it's a man. I think he's vicious. I think he owns a clasp knife with a five-inch blade. Or did own – may not any more, if he's got any brains.' He let go of Denton's arm. 'That's what I think. What I *think* isn't worth two tinker's dams in a pisspot until I *know* something different.'

He winked. 'But I can report that in my judgement it wasn't the Ripper, thank God.'

The constable saluted them as they went out, his eyes meeting those of each of them in turn as a mark, Denton supposed, of respect. They walked around to the Minories and Guillam got into a cab and, after thanking Denton in a slightly ironic voice, rattled away.

It was almost seven. Munro said he was expected at home. He was heading towards Aldgate station for the steam underground, why didn't Denton walk with him a bit? But he hesitated, looking down the Minories, hunched, and finally he said, 'I apologize for not supporting you better, Denton. Georgie can be hard sometimes.'

'I didn't expect you to support me.'

'You know what I mean. I didn't know he was going to come that rough. I really did think it was a tale, that about seeing how you'd react. He wasn't quite straight with me.' Munro looked at him. 'He's going to want to know where you were the night the girl was killed, you know. He didn't ask you yet, but I know him. He will.'

'My God, Munro, that's what the whole Mulcahy business was about! I was home!'

'He'll want to know about the whole night.'

'The girl was already dead by the time Mulcahy came to my house.'

Munro frowned as if he was worrying about Denton's situation, then took Denton's arm much as Guillam had, perhaps some sort of policeman's grip, and began to walk him north up the Minories. 'You could argue it was a good deal later. Office of Prosecutions can make that argument. Food in her stomach may not tell so much; as for rigor – all the blood run out, rigor's guesswork. Guillam's men will have talked to your servant by now, so they'll know about that night. You go out?'

He had gone to Emma's at eleven and she'd thrown him over. Then he'd gone to the Café Royal and got drunk.

'I'm not going to answer you, Munro. It's my business.' He didn't want to tell them about Emma. If he did, they'd question her. It occurred to him that she might even be angry enough to deny he had been there. No, surely not. *Frailty, thy name is—*

Munro made an unsatisfied grunt and muttered that the time would come when he might have to say something, want to or not. They turned into Aldgate High Street, and Munro, letting go of Denton's arm, said, 'This is where her pimp worked – here and up Whitechapel Road.' He nodded at the street ahead of them.

'I didn't know she had a pimp.'

'Kid himself, they say, name of Bobbie. No last name. City police can't find him. Not that they're trying what I'd call hard. Short on men, of course.' He fell silent for several steps and then said, 'Very modern pimp – used a photograph. It appears he had three, possibly four girls; he'd walk up and down, use that "Want my sister, sir? still a virgin but wanting a man, sir," and show 'em the picture. Customer says yes, he leads him around to Priory Close Alley and the thing is done.'

'Couldn't be that he's really her brother, could it?'

'Only if he's got several sisters, and I doubt they're all virgins, night after night. Damnable leech.'

'The girls are as much to blame.'

Munro glanced at him and looked away. Defensively, Denton said, 'You know what I mean. The girls aren't prisoners, after all. The oldest profession.'

'Might as well be, a lot of them.' He stopped. 'I'm over there.' He nodded across the street, where the underground station stood, next to it a chop house called the Three Nuns.

'What sort of photographs?'

'You know.'

'French?'

'Probably not that bad, they're actionable, but – suggestive, you know. Revealing. Kind of men who come birding here, it doesn't take a lot of female flesh to please them, all they get to see usually is the wife's shoulder when she's undressing in the closet.'

They shook hands. Before he turned away, Munro said, 'Georgie doesn't really suspect you of anything worse than muddying the waters. But don't annoy him, all right?' He touched a finger to his hat and moved away into a stream of pedestrians.

Denton watched him go, feeling that he was betraying Munro by keeping what he had seen in the girl's room from him – Munro a decent man, for all he'd allowed himself to be overawed by Guillam.

'Munro!'

Denton dived into the street, dodging a hansom and getting shouted at, then running past and around pedestrians like a footballer. He caught Munro at the door of the Three Nuns; somebody opened the door to go in and the warm smell of food was sucked out.

'Munro!'

Munro looked startled, then guilty, as if Denton had caught him at something.

'I've got something to tell you. Walk back there with me.'

Munro was clearly puzzled, thrown off by his sudden appearance. 'We could go inside.'

'No, I want to go back.' He set his face. 'I'm going back whether you do or not.'

'What the devil for?'

'I'll tell you as we go.'

Munro made a face – displeasure, disapproval – but turned back, and they crossed the High Street together, Denton for a moment thinking how crazy it was that this had actually once been a 'high street', the spine of a village. London like a monster child that ate its mother and never stopped growing. He checked his watch and wondered where he'd get dinner.

He led them back the same way they had come, Munro always a few inches behind him as if reluctant. 'I saw something in her room,' Denton said. 'I didn't say anything in front of Guillam; he'd got under my skin – as he meant to.'

'That's suppressing evidence.'

'Oh, come on! It isn't his case, anyway.'

Munro grunted. They were walking back down the Minories, fewer people out now, everybody seeming in a great hurry. Denton said, 'There's a picture on her wall. The frame is fastened to the plaster.' He waited for a response; none came. 'Not hanging out from the wall at the top, flat against it.' Again, nothing. Denton said, 'Never saw that done except in a sporting house, for looking through from the other side.' They had almost reached John Street. 'I want to see what's on the other side.' He didn't say how he knew the finer points of sporting houses.

Munro, interested now, came even with him, and they walked shoulder to shoulder, Munro actually in the gutter because of the narrow pavement. 'Let me handle this,' he said when they could see the constable at the opening of Priory Close Alley.

'Sir,' the constable said, touching his helmet.

'I wanted to check something.'

'Yes, sir.' Munro held something up and the constable shook his head and said, 'Remember you from before sir — sir,' this last to Denton. He suspected that what the policeman was really there to stop were journalists and souvenir-seekers, anyway.

Munro led the way into the court, the sky overhead now slate-blue-grey, several stars quite bright against it, as if seen up a stovepipe. The court itself was gloomy, lit only by the faded end of day and a single gas lamp on the wall at the back. The curtained windows in the former warehouse were unlit.

Munro crossed the court quickly and tried the larger door in the house where Stella Minter had died. It was locked. He knocked. The first knock brought no response, the second only more silence, but the third caused a rumble of footsteps, a clatter of locks and the appearance of a red face above a collarless shirt.

'It's unlocked, i'n't it?' the man bellowed. He turned the outer handle to demonstrate that the door was unlocked. 'Unlocked every night seven to half-eight, as everybody knows because you forget your bloody keys!'

'I have a few questions.' Munro held up his badge.

'Oh, crikey! We've had you lot for two days now, give it a rest!'

'See here, my man—'

'Come in, then, but give *me* a rest, I just got home; let me eat my dinner, good God, I ain't the fount of wisdom!' Then, knowing he'd given a policeman lip, he hurried off.

Inside, a long, dirty corridor ran away from the door; the man fled along it and disappeared where it made a jog to the right – another result, Denton thought, of some shift in the building's destiny.

Denton and the detective stopped just inside the door, Denton closing it firmly behind him and then leaning back on it. He studied the moulding at the top of the left-hand wall, on the other side of which was Stella Minter's room.

From the wall in which the front door stood to a place six feet along, no moulding existed; then, at a slight, not quite right-angle corner, the moulding began, turning again to run the length of the corridor. Denton pointed at it and said, 'There used to be an opening here into her room.' He was almost whispering, no rational cause.

In the wall below this gap was a door, narrower by a lot than the front door, narrower even than the two doors he could see along the corridor on the other side. It had a thumb-latch and a D-shaped handle, an apparently new Yale lock above it. With the front door open, this door would be partly hidden. Denton opened the front door to demonstrate.

Munro put his hand on the worn iron handle, his thumb on the latch above it. With a clank, the latch opened, and the door swung out, and Denton felt a stab of disappointment, because a door that hid anything important would have been locked. A smell, sour and disquieting, oozed out.

Over Munro's shoulder, he saw a narrow space whose floor was about the size of the inside of a coffin, its long rear wall made of open studs with strips of lath and clumps of horsehair plaster protruding between them – the back side of a plastered wall. Munro leaned in, began to rummage around in the darkness of the closet's farther end. So far as Denton could make out in the gloom, there were two long-empty night-soil buckets, apparently no longer used; a five-step ladder; a straight chair with a spindled back, missing three spindles; and a broom so worn that the bound-together straws had been reduced to a kind of club, the broom found only by touch while Munro was stumbling around. The smell proved to be recent vomit, now dry, from somebody who had eaten kidneys.

It made me puke, Mulcahy had said.

Munro backed out, forcing Denton out of the closet doorway, then standing aside to let the faint light from a fan over the outer door try to penetrate inside. 'What we need is a dark lantern. Can't see my own shoes in there.' Munro bent forward again and felt over the lath, down to the floor, then got on his knees and passed both hands over the old boards. 'Puke,' he muttered. 'Somebody lost his dinner. Kidneys, for sure – can't see enough.' He got up and wiped his fingers on a handkerchief. 'I hate to ask this lot for so much as a candle.'

Denton pushed past him and stood close to the lath-and-plaster wall. 'Close the door,' he said. 'Come in or not, Munro, but close the door. I want my eyes to adjust.'

Munro pushed in and closed the door, and the space was suddenly very tight, Denton able to smell both of them – wool overcoat, tobacco, sweat – and the slightly chemical odour of Munro's breath over the resident stench. He found himself holding his breath.

He waited.

'Bit far-fetched, this,' Munro said.

In fact, after several minutes, Denton could still see less than he had with the door open. What was he doing in here?

He felt over the walls with his fingertips, first low down, then standing to reach as high as he could, then standing on the chair and feeling over the upper part of the walls and the ceiling. It was a balancing act to stand on that uncertain chair in the dark; he started to sway, caught himself on Munro's head, pushing the policeman's hat down and hearing a grunt of complaint. He held himself that way until he located the light coming under the door, and when it snapped into focus his equilibrium came back and he was secure again. He raised his eyes, ready to work his way down the wall, and then he saw it – a thin line of lesser darkness in the dark where the laths ran.

'There.'

'There what?'

He slowly lowered himself and put one foot on the floor. From that level, the line of faint light was invisible. He worked his way up again, put his face against the clumps of plaster and the rough wood of the lath and looked down and so could see it. He put his hand on it, first hiding the light, then working the hand down until the light showed, then finding the exact lath and pushing on it and watching the light all but disappear.

He got down again, keeping his fingers on the lath. He tried pulling on it, catching it at top and bottom with his fingernails, and then he could see a little, dim line as the lath pulled away a fraction of an inch but wouldn't come free. He tried it several ways, and it was only when he pushed from the bottom that the lath moved upwards and could then be worked up over the roughness above it until it stopped, caught on something above. He felt the movable piece with his fingers in the dark and found that a piece of lath about two inches long had been scarfed on both ends so that they fitted under matching scarves on the strip in the wall – that, in fact, somebody rather skilled had cut the lath twice at an angle. Probing with a finger below this cut-out section, he found a hole.

He leaned forward. His hat brim hit the wall first; he removed the hat and put it behind him on the chair, leaned forward again, felt the tickle of a horschair. He put his eye to the dim light and found himself looking, as he expected, into the back of Balmoral Castle and, beyond it, Stella Minter's room.

The hole in the reverse painting was big enough that he could see all of the far wall and the oval window in it, through which the light from the outside gas lamp was shining. He could barely make out the shape of the bed, which was below him and close to the wall through which he was looking, most of it invisible because of the dark bloodstains. Yet, he thought, with the gas light on above the bed – now to his left and higher – especially with its silver reflector, somebody standing here could have seen a good deal. Everything that went on in the bed, certainly. He thought of the reflector on the gas lamp: that might have been the work of the person who had cut the lath, too.

'Have a look.' He pulled Munro into the place where he had been standing and put Munro's hand on the rough lath and plaster and led it to the hole.

'Voyeur,' Munro said after perhaps twenty seconds.

Odd, then, that the closet door was unlocked.

Munro pushed back, and Denton heard the door latch. 'This changes the price of fish,' Munro said. 'Willey will have to be told.'

Denton worked the cut piece of lath back into its niche and took up his hat and stepped out into the corridor.

The house was making sounds, as a house with a dozen or so people in it must. A medley of cooking smells reached him, too, not a bad odour at all, a blend like meat-and-vegetable stew, balm after the closet. Munro was straightening his hat, looking solemn; when the hat was right, he headed down the corridor towards the back of the house. Denton put his own hat on and walked behind him, passing doors on both sides, coming at the end to a kitchen on his left, the door open, and a water closet on his right, the door also open. The water closet was filthy, the kitchen fairly clean; both, he supposed, communal. Three people were eating at a table in the kitchen; two men, one of them the man who had opened the front door for them, were standing by a big coal range, staring into pots. When Munro stepped into the doorway, everybody looked at him and everything stopped. No need to say he was a policeman; the man in the collarless shirt had no doubt already told them what had happened at the front door.

'What's the name of the landlord?' Munro said.

Nobody spoke. After some seconds, a pretty, rather showy young woman said, 'Never see him. Wouldn't know him if he appeared in a car drawn by the royal family.'

'Don't make smart remarks, young woman! Who takes the rent?'

She looked at the others, blushing but apparently excited by her defiance. 'His collector slithers in on Mondays. A charmer, I *don't* think.'

'What's his name?'

'Clebbins,' the other man by the stove said.

'Just Clebbins?'

'All I ever heard.'

They didn't know where Clebbins lived or where he went or what other properties he gouged rents out of, although there was some sense that the owner might live in Chelsea, or possibly Hammersmith.

'Who uses that cupboard up at the front?'

Four of the five didn't seem to know that there was a cupboard up at the front. The fifth, an older, dour woman at the table, opined that nobody used it because it was always locked.

Denton pushed himself a little forward and gave them a quick description of Mulcahy. Had they ever seen him?

They had all seen him a thousand times, every day of their lives.

'That's all we'll get out of this lot tonight,' Munro said. He raised his voice to include them all. 'City of London Police will be back tomorrow. See you're ready to talk to them without a lot of lip.' The collarless man dropped his eyes to his pot; the young woman flounced or shrugged and looked sideways at a woman who had never spoken.

Out in the court again, Munro said, 'I wish you'd told Guillam.' He was looking up into the steely sky, apparently studying the stars – six or eight now – with his hands behind him under his overcoat tails. 'He'll be annoyed.'

'I can't help that.'

'You could have earlier.' It sounded petulant. Denton didn't respond. Munro straightened and put his hands into his overcoat pockets. 'It's possible to see it as a little too convenient – you finding it.'

'Wouldn't have been less convenient if I'd pointed it out an hour ago. What are you saying, that I'm a suspicious person because I found something the police missed?'

'*If* they missed it. Willey's people might have found it and not told anybody.' He breathed deeply, as if he was inhaling the night air for its odour. 'What d'you make of it?'

'You said "voyeur". That's about it.' He had been surprised that Munro had known the word, the sexual type. As this wasn't fair to Munro, he felt vaguely ashamed.

'Your man Mulcahy?'

'"My man," good God. Why don't you work it out and tell me.'

Munro bounced on his toes and said 'Mm' a couple of times. 'I'll do that. But you know, if you're so hot on your Mulcahy, you need to find him yourself. Nobody's going to do it for you – there just isn't enough *in* it. Enough likely information, I mean. We're not perfect, Denton, and there's not enough of us. We have to balance the likely gain against how many men and how much time.' He led Denton out of the alley and up Vine Street, saying nothing, and at the corner of John Street he stopped and gripped Denton's arm, this time while facing him. 'Come and see me in the morning. Georgie and Willey'll have it on paper by then. I'm on my way to the Yard now, file a report.'

'Feeling like a detective again?'

Munro grunted. 'Wife's waiting, dinner's waiting, kids're waiting. A policeman's lot is not a happy one.' Suddenly, he clapped Denton on the arm. 'Good work. You're all right, Mr Denton.' He limped away on John Street and disappeared around the corner.

It was growing dark. Denton found he was hungry. The evening loomed – no Emma, no dinner out. His interest in Mulcahy, however, had revived; it had sunk to almost nothing after Guillam implied that Willey had made an arrest, but the closet and the peephole had revived it. He thought about what Munro had said about finding Mulcahy himself. It would be a matter of time and people – both things that money could buy, although money was something he was not flush with just then. Still—

Denton walked another street and then hailed a cab and told the driver to head for Lloyd Baker Street; once there, he pulled one of the three bells that hung by the door of a run-down but still respectable house. This was the lodging of his typewriter, who translated his scribbled-over, crossed-out scrawls into legible pages. She lived on the first floor and he saw a light, but it was now night and he felt awkward about being there, a male figure in the dark when she opened the front door.

'Oh – Mr Denton.' Not particularly welcoming, nor particularly relieved. She was a very proper woman, he remembered too late.

'I know it's late, Mrs Johnson.'

'No, no – quite all right—' She looked anguished. Wondering if he would want to come in, perhaps.

'I won't come in,' he said. 'I only wondered if you could organize a, well – a job of work for me.'

'Oh, yes?' Dubious. She was a stout woman, still fairly young, widowed. She earned her living by typewriting, gave off no signals about having any other life.

'I need for somebody to go through the London directories to look for a man who came to visit me. He left no address, but it's important that I find him. It would take several people to do it.'

'I can't take time away from my typing machine, I'm afraid.' She had a shawl clutched tight at her throat with one hand, the other on the door as if she wanted to be sure she could close it on him.

'I thought you might know other people, other women, who could use the work. It would be several days' work. I'd pay them for a week – let's say three people – even if they finished before that.' He didn't confess that his bank account was running down towards zero; paying several women would probably get it there.

She looked out at the cab, which she seemed to see for the first time. The cabman was holding a water bag under the animal's mouth. 'I'm keeping you,' she said.

'No, I'm keeping you from your, um, meal.' Did you say 'supper' in this situation? Perhaps 'tea'. What the hell. 'I really need this to be done, Mrs Johnson.'

'Well – I know a few other typewriters from the agency— They don't get the work that I do.' Said with pride. She was good, and very fast.

Denton wrote 'R. Mulcahy' on a card and held it out. 'That's the name. And of course, I'd pay you for getting things organized.'

She stared at the card, which she'd taken with the hand that had been holding the shawl. 'I don't have any time open—' She clutched the shawl again, the card close to her chin. 'Still, because it's you— Can you pay them five shillings a day? They have to be assured it's worth passing up typewriting jobs for.'

He said that yes, of course, that would be fine, although he was thinking that twenty-five shillings for a week's work was more than working-men made. Still, he was in no position to bargain. 'And a bonus of a shilling for each R. Mulcahy they find.' He hesitated. 'There may be more than one.' If there were a lot of them, however, he'd done something stupid. But how many could there be?

She muttered a good night, and the door closed. Denton felt as he had with Guillam, suspected of something nasty and not exonerated.

Well, of course, he was male.

At home, Atkins had been grumpy because he was trying to recover from an uncomfortable hour with two detectives while Denton had been with Munro and Guillam. He had started complaining about it at the front door and had continued all the way through Denton's stepping into the hot bath he thought he'd earned. In turn, while he dressed again, Denton had told Atkins about the visit to the dead woman's room.

'What do you make of it?' Denton said now.

'Nothing.' Atkins jiggled the coat he was waiting for Denton to put on – the same brown suit he had worn earlier, now found déclassé by Atkins for evening wear but just right for Denton's Bohemian mood. 'They also serve who only stand and answer coppers' questions about their employer, leaving out the difficult bits like where you was going at eleven o'clock that night, the which I kept to myself.'

'And grateful I am to you for it. But I don't want to talk about that; I want to talk about the girl's death.' He sat on the bed and began to pull on a shoe. 'I'll tell you how I see it.' He looked up to see if Atkins was going to pout. 'Do you want to know how I see it?'

'Of course I do; it'll be better than Charlie O'Malley.' Charles Lever's *Charles O'Malley, the Irish Dragoon* was Atkins's favourite book, said by him to have been read twenty times. Apparently hearing his own tone, Atkins became apologetic. 'No, truly, Colonel, I don't have your gift for making a story out of a bunch of facts. Tell me how you see it.'

Denton paused with the other shoe in his hands. He moved the shoe up and down as if he were weighing it. 'All right—' He looked at nothing, the scene before his eyes like a play. 'Stella Minter opens the door. Maybe it's somebody she knows, although that's just a possibility. Anyway, he comes in – maybe pushes his way in, maybe doesn't. He hits her – twice, I don't know why. He undresses. Or maybe he doesn't. She either takes off her wrapper or he pulls it off her – interesting to know if there're any rips in it. I suppose the police won't tell me things like that. She lies down or he pushes her down. He has the clasp knife open in his hand but he's hiding it. He enters her.

'Mulcahy is watching through the peephole. I think that this is possible only if he has an arrangement with Stella Minter – he's put up the reverse-painted picture with the scraped-out place, also the reflector on the gas lamp. So he's watching. He doesn't see the knife until it's actually in her throat and the blood spurts. The killer stands up and starts to stab the woman in the bosom. Maybe she tries to roll out of the way, or maybe he moves her; anyway, blood actually spurts as high as the picture, so now Mulcahy sees it all through red.

'Mulcahy throws up. Maybe he makes noise doing it – people do, a coughing, strangling noise – or maybe he screams. And he opens the closet door and runs for his life.

'The killer hears the sound that Mulcahy made. He looks up, and he sees the light from the open closet door shining through the hole in the wall and the glass of the picture. He knows somebody has seen him.

'He panics. Or he doesn't panic. This is a clever man and a fast thinker, so maybe he doesn't panic. He wipes the blood off his naked body with the wrapper and drops it into the blood on the floor and puts his clothes back on.' Denton was seeing it as if it were a scene he was writing. 'He's still smeared with blood under his clothes, but there isn't enough of it to soak through. In the darkness outdoors, he'll be all right.

'He goes out. Now, he's almost certainly already mutilated her abdomen and cut out her female parts, because he's not going to go out and come back and do that – or is he? Is he that clever? That cold-blooded? Whenever he did it, he may have done it out of – what is it? rage? – or maybe that's where his cleverness comes in; maybe he's planned it that way to make it look like rage. Or insanity. Or maybe he thinks of it after he's dressed and has gone out, and he goes back in to do it. But, by the way, if he's planned all that out, then he's planned to kill her, and then I think he knew her and there's a personal reason for killing her – he's a rejected lover, maybe. Or, if it's just something he did, then he's a maniac. But a damned clever one.

'So he goes out, and he goes *in* the main door of the house, and he sees the closet door at once – open. Think of it, Sergeant – he was in that house, maybe somebody in the kitchen or the WC, and nobody saw him. He's clever and he's brave, or audacious, anyway. So he steps into the closet and he sees the hole and the lath, and this is where his cleverness comes in – he *pushes the lath back into place*, because he doesn't want the police to find it. He doesn't want them to have any clues to Mulcahy's existence, at least not before he's found Mulcahy first.

'Or that's the way I see it, because I think Mulcahy was so terri-fied that he wouldn't have stopped to push the piece of lath down. Nor to lock the closet door, by the way – the reason we found it unlocked. And the killer didn't lock it because he didn't have a key – it was in Mulcahy's pocket.

'So the killer's mind is racing. He knows he has to get out at once, but he knows he has to find whoever was in the closet. It's too late to try to follow him. What does he do?'

He looked up at Atkins. The sergeant let himself be looked at, shrugged, stood there. 'Runs like H, I suppose.'

'Well, yes. But suppose he finds something that Mulcahy has left in the closet in his terror – and that has his name on it.'

He was still looking at Atkins, who said, 'Well, it ain't his hat, because we had that, at least until the coppers took it away for evidence this afternoon. His coat? Unlikely to have his address in it, any more than his hat. All right, I'll bite – what did he take away that had Mulcahy's name on it?'

Denton shook his head. 'I don't know. Maybe nothing.' He saw Atkins's frown. 'I think that Mulcahy's a voyeur. He saw the crime. He was *there*, Sergeant – that's why he told us all those lies. He didn't want to confess what he was, but he wanted help.'

'No reason to want help unless he looked back and saw the murderer, covered with blood and gore, running at him with an axe, is there?' Atkins was being distinctly sarcastic. 'What I mean is – if he was so scared he come to you, he had a reason for thinking the murderer was on to him. Right?'

Denton was fastening his cuffs. He made an equivocal sound, like a small machine starting up.

'If you ask me, General, he's a damned lucky voyeur if he isn't dead by now. The man who butchered the Minter bitch wouldn't rest until he'd got Mulcahy, too, if he knew where to find him.'

Denton stood still to have his coat put on. 'That's what's got me worried. And there isn't a damned thing I can do about it. except – I put Mrs Johnson on getting some women to search the directories for him.' He saw Atkins frown – more money going out – but he ignored him and pulled his shirt cuffs down inside the coat sleeves. 'You going out?'

'It's one of my nights, isn't it?' Atkins had two nights a week off, part of the generous deal he had made for himself with Denton. There was much to be said, from his point of view, in serving a man who felt guilty about being served. 'Yes, I'm going out!'

Denton sighed. 'Enjoy yourself.' It was more than he expected, in his present mood, to do himself.

CHAPTER SEVEN

He walked again, enjoying the night but chewing moodily on the problem of Mulcahy. The streets were quieter, the city now a background roar, the hard sounds of digging and drilling ended for the day. He made his way to Glasshouse Street, looked in the bar of the Café Royal, then went around to the Piccadilly entrance and into the Domino Room. Unlike his visit of the night before, it was still early and the place was half empty.

There was an easy camaraderie to the Domino Room that belied its showy décor – high ceilings, mirrored walls, pillars like great trees in a fanciful forest, an overall colour scheme of peacock blue and gold. Bookies, artists, journalists, tarts, models, the would-bes and the has-beens, all mixed here with people from their own worlds and from that genteel one in which nobody worked but everybody was well off. Generosity, in the form of the casual invitation or the standing of drinks with somebody's last shilling, was the rule. Denton had learned to love the place. He loved to keep his hat on, to lounge against a banquette. You could do that in the Domino Room, and a good deal more – like last night.

Denton looked around and saw Frank Harris in his usual place; he moved to him and stood until the man looked up with hangover-reddened eyes. Harris groaned.

Denton collapsed beside him, ordered a milky coffee – a house speciality – and choucroute, part of the Royal's French past. When he said, by way of making conversation, how much he liked the Café, Harris growled, 'This place is the *boue* in *nostalgie de la boue*.

It appeals to the worst in all of us, and we all respond with a joy bordering on indecency.'

'Like last night.'

Harris groaned again. 'Did you drink as much as I did?'

'We stood on a table and bullied people into drinking to Wilde.'

Harris put a hand on his forehead. 'There's a stage after you've been drunk where you think you'll kill yourself, and then there's a stage of absolute euphoria. I think that I'd have been wiser to stop at euphoria and not drunk anything tonight.' He sighed. 'Not to mention what I had with lunch and the one or two before.' He sat back in his chair and clutched his head.

Denton said, 'I need a bit of advice.' Harris was supposed to have an encyclopedic knowledge of the darker side of London – indeed, of the darker side of a lot of things. 'Who can tell me about vice in the East End?'

Harris turned his red eyes on him, looked at him for long seconds as if he'd forgotten who he was. 'You're talking to an expert,' he said.

'There was a girl murdered there last night. I want to know who she was – where she came from, who her—'

'East End?'

'Well, the Minories.'

With his head back, Harris looked at Denton as if he were looking into a too bright light. 'What's the allure of a murdered tart? Idea for a book?'

Denton mentioned Mulcahy, said only that the man had told him a wild tale and been terrified – his now-familiar recitation.

Harris wrinkled his nose and stuck out his lips, then rubbed his eyes. 'You know Ruth Castle?'

'Mrs Castle?' She was a famous madam; of course he knew her. 'We all know Mrs Castle.'

Harris laughed. 'Could make a comic song of that. "Oh, we all know Mrs Castle here in London—"' He sang it a bit tunelessly. 'What the hell rhymes with London?'

'Done-done. Undone.' He looked at Harris's empty glass. 'Y'know, you'd do best to go home.'

'At this hour? My God, what would people say?'

'Why Mrs Castle?'

'Why not Mrs Castle? What are we talking about?'

'Vice in the East End.'

Harris waved a hand. 'She knows everything. Tell her I sent you. Better yet, *don't* tell her I sent you; I think she had me thrown out last time. But go and see her. Fount of knowledge.' Harris ordered himself another brandy and began to lecture about Bohemianism and the decline of art. Denton, finishing his choucroute as fast as he could eat, muttered a goodbye and got up.

He left Harris trying to start an argument about Fabianism with a man he didn't know and went out. He debated following Harris's advice to talk to Mrs Castle that night but thought his own advice to Harris was best: early to bed.

Home again, he dropped his hat and coat on a chair, added coal to his living-room fire, stood there looking into the orange heat that was still deep inside the black pile, thinking of the stupidities people, himself included, do.

He poked the fire and put the poker back in its iron stand and heard a sound that might have been the poker hitting another piece of metal but that might have been something else. He stood still, listening. He really believed the sound had come from somewhere else. Outside? Most likely not; it had been too muffled. And closer.

'Sergeant?'

They had had trouble with rats for a while. The sound was not unlike that of an animal dropping to the floor from a table. When they had had rats, a cat had got in once; it had made that sound, dropping in the dark on a rat to break its back.

Denton hated rats. He took up the poker again.

The gas light was on by the door nearest him, the only light in the long room other than the coal fire. If Atkins had been home, a lamp at the far end near his door would probably have been lit, too; instead, the room receded into darkness, past the dumb waiter, past the alcove on the left where the spirit stove and the makeshift pantry were, to the stairs and the window at their foot, now only a silvered reflection of the light.

Later, he would think he should have taken the derringer, but then he would think that it wouldn't have mattered. When the attack came, it came so fast that he was unable fully to react, and it came from his left side; the derringer would have been in his right. The poker – well, it saved his life, if not his arm.

He had started to pass the opening to the pantry alcove. He was listening, his head slightly cocked, and he was thinking that the light near Atkins's door should have been on, whether Atkins was there or not. He had reached the point of wondering why the light was out, and he was just beginning to appreciate an alien smell that was reaching his nose, when the attacker came in a blurred silver slash from the black alcove. Denton reacted away, turning, raising his left arm against that shining slice through the darkness, and his arm caught fire as something ripped through the coat sleeve and slashed him from elbow to wrist. He heard himself gasp in shock and something like indignation, then rage at himself for being so stupid, and then the blade, which had caught for an instant in the sleeve buttons, tore free and was being raked across his mid-section.

The attacker tried to move in closer; a hand grabbed at his coat, tried to pull him. Denton swung the poker against the man's side, then higher against the back of his head. He caught the knife arm with his left hand somewhere above the elbow. The knife was being held for a downward blow – not a knife fighter's grip, Denton would think later; a real fighter came in from below – and so, for the seconds that Denton could grip the upper arm before his own bleeding forearm weakened, the blade could only graze his ribs.

The attacker was a big man, and he stank. He stank of sweat and urine and of too long without washing. He had black hair, eyes that looked red in the thin light; his lower face was covered. The eyes were wide, frantic, as he tried to put the knife in and was held back. Then Denton dropped the poker and caught the face, his fingers trying to dig into the eyes, and pushed the head backwards as he brought his knee up.

The man roared. His weight came off Denton's arms as he surged back, trying to free the knife hand. Denton, his feet planted now, pushed; the attacker slammed back against the pantry arch; Denton turned his body into the knife, grabbed the arm with his right hand and slid the left down to the wrist. He was suddenly aware of the blood that was streaming down his arm, making the other man's wrist slippery.

Denton crashed the attacker's arm down against his right knee, trying to break it, and the man moaned. Denton's head was grabbed from behind and he was spun towards the wall, but he recovered and turned back, and, panting, the attacker fled down the long room towards the light, and then his steps thudded down the stairs and the front door slammed.

Denton was stunned. He leaned back against the wall, trying to clear his head. When he could think and move, he tottered down to the light, holding his left arm with a thumb in the crook of the elbow because he thought he could stop the bleeding. The light proved that idea foolish; the blood was coming from the outside of the arm; it had soaked the coat sleeve black and was running down his fingers and dripping in almost a stream on to the carpet. A trail of drops showed where he had come. He tried a crude tourniquet made from an embroidered runner from a table. It was a hideous thing; he felt a moment's illogical satisfaction in seeing it soaked with blood. Still, twisted around his upper arm, it slowed the flow only a little.

He would get light-headed and then weak, he thought. He needed a doctor.

He headed down the stairs and out to the street. The Lamb was closed, the street empty. Somebody described to him as 'a foreigner' had a surgery down opposite Coram's; would he be there at this hour? Denton began to walk in that direction, then broke into a trot. It was at that point that he saw a figure turn the corner and head his way.

It was Atkins.

Denton hurried towards him, his arm held out like an offering, blood behind him in round spatters right to his front door.

'Was it robbery, sir?' The constable was earnest and not tremendously bright. Dogged, at best.

'I've no idea.'

'You'd just got home. You heard a noise. You went to investigate.'

'Yes – as I've told you.'

Denton was lying in the 'foreigner's' surgery; the doctor proved to be a Polish Jew who spoke English with a music-hall accent but who was skilled at his art. He was swabbing Denton's arm with carbolic and then taking stitches while the constable made notes and another policeman stood at the door, as if either Denton or the doctor might try to run away. Atkins was slumped in an armchair, fanning himself with his bowler and looking desperate.

'I think it was attempted burglary, Tim,' the first constable said to the other one, who grunted.

'I am hurting?' the doctor said. He had given Denton morphine to take the edge off the pain, but the cut was deep and long, and he had to make many stitches.

'Not so bad.'

'You behafe well.'

Denton grunted.

'I am giffing you laudanum for after,' the doctor said. He had a rather long beard, a bald pate with a circle of black hair, like a monk. 'You don't sleep without.'

'Anything missing?' the constable said.

'I didn't look.'

'Didn't look, Tim.' The constable consulted his notebook. 'My advice, look first thing tomorrow.'

'I'll do that,' Atkins said. 'Crikey, don't you coppers realize the man's been stabbed?'

'Now, now!' The constable looked severe. 'Detectives will want a full inventory. They often close a case that way, knowing what's missing.'

'What, they see what's missing so they close it?' Atkins sneered. 'Regular Sherlock Bleeding Holmeses, they must be.'

'Now, now!' The constable moved to stand in front of Atkins. 'You mind your mouth, my lad.'

'Can't you see I'm in a nervous state?' Atkins looked up at him, gauged the constable's age, which was certainly less than his own. '"My lad." My hat!'

'He's in shock, Tim,' the constable said to the other one, who grunted. The constable returned to Denton. 'Black hair, smelled bad, tall. Correct?'

The doctor looked up from his work. 'When you are finishing? You vex my patient.'

'I wot?'

Atkins twirled his hat. '"Vex." It means to irritate, to bother, to be a royal pain in the bum. Couldn't apply to you, oh, no!'

The constable turned. 'Now, I'm telling you—' He pointed a large, blunt finger. 'I don't mind making an arrest for interfering with the work of a constable. Get me?'

Denton flinched as the needle went into tissue. 'Give it over, Sergeant. He's doing his job as best he can.' He moved a leg, which was going to sleep in the uncomfortable position required by the leather couch he was lying on. 'Yes, black hair, tall. Big man – heavier than I am. Strong. Maybe a little gone to fat; his arms felt big but not muscular. Foul breath. Hadn't washed – same thing with his teeth, I think. As if he'd been living rough.'

'A tramp? Lots of tramps turn their hand to burglary when they've a chance. Leave a window unlocked, did you?'

Atkins groaned. Denton said, more feebly than he'd intended, that a detective could look to all that in the morning. Then, perhaps only because the doctor wasn't finished and the constables were more comfortable in the surgery than on the street, they went through it all again. The doctor finished the arm and wrapped it tight in white bandage, which quickly discoloured with a line of oozing blood. He turned his attention to the ribs, which Denton had been surprised to find were cut, swabbing them with carbolic, which felt to Denton like live coals. His shirt was slashed, the suit jacket as well.

Denton found it hard to stand straight. Atkins paid the doctor out of Denton's wallet, made a face when he saw it was then almost empty. When Denton thanked him, the doctor – still in a nightshirt, a cardigan pulled over it – smiled and said they were neighbours. He saw Denton often, he said. 'My name is Bernat. For the next time.' He grinned. 'If you are cutting yourself at the shaving.' He gave Atkins a folded paper. 'Laudanum pills. I am old-fashion doctor – very believing of laudanum for pain and sleeping. Make him take them, please.'

Atkins helped Denton along the street. The two policemen followed them to the front door, where the one who grunted was to take up a post for the rest of the night. 'Just in case,' the constable said. Woozily, weakly, Denton thought, *In case of what?*

It was so hard for him to get up the stairs to the first floor that he asked Atkins to make him a bed in the easy chair. 'All I want to do is sleep.' Atkins picked up the hat and overcoat Denton had dropped there two hours earlier and came back with pillows, a blanket, his slippers and the derringer, which had been in the coat pocket. He put the little pistol on the table next to Denton's chair, then drew a pitcher of water in the pantry and poured a glass and gave him two of the laudanum pills. 'Medical officer says you're to take these. Orders.'

'I had morphine.'

'Do as you're told, Corporal.'

Denton took the pills, sipped the water.

'You think it was *him*, don't you,' Atkins said.

Denton stared at him, shook his head. He was too wobbly to think. He waved a finger at the decanter. 'Nightcap?'

'It's practically bloody morning, General!'

Denton stretched his feet out. 'I feel like hell. A little, Sergeant.'

Atkins set the glass where he could reach it. 'Medical officer didn't say nothing about mixing laudanum with brandy. Be it on your head.'

'It isn't my head, it's my arm. And my damned mid-section.' He sipped. The brandy, the taste of it, the strike of it, was far more satisfying than any pills. 'Go to bed, Sergeant.'

Atkins was looking at the carpets. 'Be a right treat, getting the bloodstains out of these. No bleeding rest for the weary!'

'Tomorrow, tomorrow.'

Atkins grunted and disappeared through his doorway, glad, apparently to get to his own spaces at last.

Denton might have slept a little, might even have slept and woken several times. Each time, his disengagement from his body and from the room seemed greater. A part of him knew it was the laudanum; part of him didn't care. The pain was gone, or reduced and changed, like a constant bass note that was not unpleasant. The brandy glass was empty. He stared at the blanket, which seemed to grow thick between his fingers, as thick as a snowdrift; his feet, mounded under it, were far away; he was like a vast field under snow, quiet, at peace.

And then, at the far end of the long room, Atkins's door was opening. A hand, turning out the gaslight. The man's smell reaching out ahead of him.

Denton watched him come down the room. Smelled him. Same smell, same man. Bottom part of his face covered again. He seemed to be coming a great distance, walking and walking and making no headway. Then suddenly he was there. With the knife.

Denton wanted to open his mouth and call out. He wanted to stand, to run to the door. A policeman was just outside.

He couldn't make enough sound to summon him.

He looked at the man's eyes, which looked at his. The man was sweating. Denton tried to force his hand to pick up the derringer and aim it, but he could command the hand only to move under the blanket to the arm of the chair and then, in a spasm, strike the edge of the table. Seeing the movement, the man with the knife moved faster. Their eyes remained locked. The man was trying to assess how best to do it, he thought, changing his grip on the knife and bringing it across his own body as if for a backhand stroke, as if he would perhaps grab Denton's hair with his left hand and sweep the blade across his throat. As he had murdered Stella Minter.

Denton's palm rested on the derringer.

The man with the knife moved.

Denton willed his arm to raise the gun, willed his eyes to aim, willed his finger to pull the trigger, but all that happened was that the gun, still on the table, went off, burning a crease across the tabletop, the bullet smashing through the thin, pie-crust edging and going into the wall.

The man with the knife cried out. He turned and raced back down the room, and Denton heard the sound of smashing glass. He was using something, maybe a foot, a boot, to break out the glass from the window at the foot of the stairs. The cooler air caressed Denton's face; there was silence; he smelled burning coal and the last of the man's stench. He tried again to call out, but nothing came.

Then a pounding on the front door. The policeman had heard the shot. Denton waited for Atkins to open the door. The pounding went on. Where was Atkins? But the man with the knife had come from Atkins's doorway, so where had Atkins been then?

He was waiting for us, Denton thought. *He never left the house. He slammed the front door but stayed inside, and he hid down in Atkins's rooms until he could deal with Atkins, and then he came up to deal with me.*

'Sergeant,' he managed to croak. His voice was expressionless. He was still covered in snow. Like being his own ghost.

Outside, the policeman was shouting, then blowing his whistle. Denton pushed with his right hand and the little table on which the derringer rested toppled over. Denton rolled himself off the chair. He lay on the floor, then pulled himself to his knees, up to a crouch to shamble towards the door. A huge effort to open it, then beyond it the stairs down; he held on to the banister with both hands but still fell halfway and wound up sitting at the bottom. He crawled to the door and opened it.

The policeman's face was terrified, then enraged. Another whistle was sounding somewhere. Denton tried to speak.

CHAPTER EIGHT

It was morning.

'How is Atkins?'

'He's had his head bashed in.' Detective Sergeant Guillam looked angry, apparently his normal expression. He glared at Denton with what seemed to be disgust. 'Didn't the constables even come into the house with you?'

Denton moved his head from side to side. He felt as if he'd ploughed a forty-acre field. 'I didn't ask them to.'

'It isn't your business to ask them! They're supposed to use their bloody heads!'

It was a little after eight in the morning. Atkins had been carried away to a hospital before daybreak; since then, the place had swarmed with police. Two of them were posted now, one in front and one in the back garden, through which, presumably, the man with the knife had escaped – classic closing of the door after the horse was gone. The window by the stairs, all its glass broken out except for sharp triangles along the frame, was hung with a blanket until the glazier arrived.

'You didn't see his whole face either time. He smelled. You say he looked frightened – what the hell does that mean?'

'He was sweating. His eyes were frightened.'

'Of what? You were there in your drug stupor; what'd he to be frightened of?' Guillam was a Puritan, Denton decided; 'drug stupor' was a deliberately outrageous moral statement. 'Why didn't he kill you if he had the chance?'

'The gun went off.'

Guillam glanced at the hole the bullet had made in the plaster. 'You're a brilliant marksman,' he muttered.

'I want my gun back.' The local detective had made off with it before Guillam had got there.

'You'll get it back, you'll get it back. You're going to get into trouble, having guns about.' Guillam was grumpy: it was early; he had been got out of bed to take the case. Without Atkins in the house, nobody was offering him even tea.

Denton used his good hand to point towards the pantry. 'There's an alcohol stove in there. Water. You could make us tea.' His throat was sore, his mouth dry. 'All of us.'

'That where he attacked you the first time, is it?' Guillam lumbered down the room and looked. He still had his bowler and his overcoat on. It was raining again; the smell of wet wool had come in with him. A certain amount of banging from the pantry indicated he was trying to make tea. He cursed. While the kettle heated, he pulled the now wet blanket aside and looked out of the broken window. 'Probably cut himself,' he said. 'Not enough to matter, I suppose.' He came towards Denton, looking at this and that in the room, sizing it up. 'You sure it was the same man both times?'

'Yes.'

'No burglar stays inside once he's been seen. He skedaddles, he does.'

'Not a burglar.'

'I know he's not a burglar! Judas Priest.' He had his hands deep in his coat pockets, dragging his shoulders down. 'You think it's *him*, don't you.'

'Him?'

'You know who I mean! Don't get cute.' He went past Denton, looked at the books beyond the fireplace, took one down and riffled its pages. 'Because of your Mulcahy.'

'*My* Mulcahy.'

'Well, nobody else's claiming him. You think it's the man killed the Minter girl, you do. Hooked up somehow through your

Mulcahy. Well, I won't have it. Anyway, Willey's got his Cape Coloured in custody; they'll move to a charge as soon as he gets a confession. You look disappointed, Mr Denton. Myself, I'm happy with a nigger sailor.'

'Don't use the word "nigger" in my house.'

'This is a police investigation! I'll use any bloody word I want! What're you, the society for the improvement of bloody Africa?'

'I heard enough of that talk during the war. Cork it, Guillam – I mean it.' Denton stared him down; Guillam shrugged and looked away. Denton said, 'Find Mulcahy. He can tell you at least whether the murderer was a black man or not.'

Guillam put the book back and turned on Denton. 'Very cute of you to spy out that peephole in the girl's room. Terrifically cute of you not to tell me about it yesterday.' He loomed above Denton. 'Why didn't you tell me about the peephole yesterday?'

'You would have made some joke about Sherlock Holmes.' Denton pulled his blanket closer; he was in the green armchair again. 'If Mulcahy was behind that peephole when the girl was killed, you've got a witness, you know.'

'I have to be told about the peephole by Munro, who's got a bee up his arse because he fell off his own roof and isn't in CID any more, and he's just delighted to know something that I don't! Well, it was well done, and my congratulations to you, Mr Denton!' Guillam took his hat off and made a deep bow. 'Brilliant, brilliant! The coppers look like idiots again, and the amateur sleuth finds the clue!'

'Go suck eggs.'

'Don't you talk to me like that! I'll put your arse on the floor as soon as look at you!'

'Well, do it while I have one arm in a sling; it's your best chance.'

Guillam stared at him and burst out laughing. He went back up the room shaking his head, and two minutes later he came out with a pot of tea and two cups without saucers. 'Sugar's coming.' He went to the window and called something down, and a minute later one of the policemen came up. By then, Guillam was laying out more cups and the sugar bowl and some vaguely suspicious-looking milk.

'Yesterday's milk,' Denton said.

'Smells all right. Oh, hell!' Guillam had poured some into his tea, and apparently it had separated. 'Forget the bloody milk.' He muttered to the constable to take a cup down to his pal and get a move on, and then he brought his own cup and lowered himself to the hassock near Denton's feet.

'I don't like it,' he said. 'I don't like it that the bastard was so determined to kill you that he came back, and I don't like it that it's you, with your interfering and your nose into everything. Nothing personal, Denton, but you're not a helpful part of the landscape.'

'I didn't invite him to come and try to kill me.'

'Put an advert in the newspapers, did you, trying to reach your Mulcahy?'

'I did not.'

'"If R. Mulcahy will reply to this address, he will hear something to his advantage"? None of that? It would explain how the bastard found you.'

'Sorry I can't make it easy for you.'

Guillam sipped. Slurped. 'Damned hot tea.' He pushed his hat back on his head. 'Could be he followed your Mulcahy.'

'Then waited a night and a day?'

'You don't know what else he was doing. Maybe things didn't come together for him until yesterday. You don't know what else was going on in his mind. You don't know but what he's certifiably lunatic. Normal rules don't apply.'

'You agree, at least, that it has something to do with Mulcahy.'

'I do not. I'm only playing your little game to see where it leads me. I can give you a dozen reasons for somebody coming after you. He read one of your books and thinks he's the demon of the plains.' Denton's first book had been titled *The Demon of the Plains* – astonishing that Guillam knew it. 'Or he's part of a secret conspiracy that originated in Salt Lake City, Utah. Or he's trying to avenge a crime you committed in India. The theft of a fabulously valuable jewel.'

'I've never been in India.'

'But the valet chap who got knocked on the head has. Told my boys that yesterday.'

'I'm not in a humour for jokes, Guillam.'

'Glad to hear it. We'll stop the games then, shall we? I'm only trying to show you how stupid the idea of your Mulcahy is. Think of it from my point of view – I have to consider all the reasons for somebody knifing you that I've come across over the years. Such as, he saw you with a woman he fancies. Or he's got an old grudge against you that you haven't told us about yet. Or he owes you money. Or you owe him money. You rogered his wife. He blames you for something you don't even know you did. Crikey, there's more reasons for people to go slashing each other than Mudie has books.'

'Or, he saw me at Stella Minter's yesterday with you.'

'There you are. Which wouldn't mean he murdered Stella Minter, but only that he didn't like your face or your hat.'

'I've given you a reasonable motive for his coming after me.'

'Motives be damned. I like facts I can send to court to hang the bastards.' He finished his tea and hitched the hassock closer. 'Now, see here. He came in your skylight, must have been while you and your man were both out. Between nine and eleven p.m., was it? He waits in the pantry, tries to knife you, does half a job but you fight him off. Then he pretends to run but hides again, whacks your man with an iron doorstop, and comes up here and tries it on again. Which you end with a gunshot. I see two things that don't hang together: one, he's a determined chap; and two, he scares off easy. You tell me.'

Denton had been trying to think about it through the fog of the laudanum. 'He isn't a natural killer.'

'What the devil's that mean?'

'He didn't use the knife on Atkins, didn't kill him. He didn't try to kill me with— There was none of the frenzy he used in killing Stella Minter.'

'There you go again!'

'None of the frenzy *somebody* used in killing Stella Minter.'

'So what? He didn't really want to kill one of his fellow men?'

'Oh, wanted to, yes. But *had* to – I don't know.'

'You've lost me.'

'Whoever killed Stella Minter would have done it no matter what. If it was the same man here, he had less – passion.'

Guillam looked disgusted. 'We'll put out a call for men six feet and above, twenty stone, don't kill with passion.'

'Don't kill *men* with passion.'

'Oh, no you don't! Now you're saying it's the Ripper. I won't have it. The Ripper's ancient history, he is!'

'Isn't that why they gave this to you? Because it might be connected to the Ripper, and you're their Ripper man?'

'They gave it to me because I'm in CID and you were already part of a matter I investigated.' Two detectives from E Division had been there before him, had turned it over to him and left. They hadn't wanted to hear about Mulcahy and Stella Minter; they had looked for evidence of burglary – footprints in the back garden. Glad to leave it to somebody else.

Guillam heaved himself up and collected the cups. 'Anything else you want to tell me before I leave to write this up? You been making trouble for me anywhere else?'

Denton told him about hiring Mrs Johnson to look for Mulcahy in the city directories. 'He's a potential witness, Guillam.'

'Yeah, we thought of that, but it would take detectives off other cases and it isn't worth it because frankly we think you're spinning us a tale. Nevertheless, when you get the results, you'll give them to me – understood?'

'You going to reimburse me what it cost?'

'I am not! But you'll give it to me, otherwise you're withholding evidence.' He lumbered to the pantry, returned. 'Anything else?'

'I thought of trying to find the kid who's supposed to have photos of Stella Minter. Her pimp.'

'So are we, so give it up.' He flexed his arms, a motion oddly like a rooster preparing to crow. 'I don't want interference. We clear on that point? If you don't give up all this amateur-detective crap and I find out about it, I'll come down on you like a hod of bricks.' He pulled his hat forward and shrugged himself deeper into his coat. 'I want to have a look at your attic for form's sake, and then I'm off. Might be as well for you to get away for a rest somewhere, wouldn't it?'

'I live here.'

'Yeah, but you've got no man, your window's broken, and between laudanum and loss of blood, you're a sorry spectacle. Find yourself a nice spot in the country for a week or two. *Let us do our work.* You get my meaning, Denton?'

'Mind my own business.'

'Couldn't have put it better myself.' He laughed, turned away. 'Gentleman detective!'

Guillam went off up the stairs. He was down again so quickly that Denton wondered if he'd even walked the length of the attic. Still, he'd certainly been up there, because he said, 'Intruder smashed a pane of the skylight. If you hadn't been out, you'd have heard him. Floor's wet now. He didn't see the guns you've got up there, else he might have used one. No light, I suspect. Daring chap. Dark house he's never been in before, and so on.' Looking at a notebook. 'You've a lot of guns about, I must say.'

'Mind your own business. Some wise advice I had recently.'

'My business if you shoot somebody.'

'I won't tell you if I do. Anyway, I'm not likely to do it with a parlour pistol.'

'Wouldn't be the worst thing in the world if you loaded that Colt and kept it by you.' He'd hardly been up there for three minutes, but he knew the Colt wasn't loaded, meaning he'd opened the case. *Impressive.* Guillam began to button his coat. 'I don't believe he'll come back, but you never know for sure. You really might think seriously about going elsewhere for a bit.'

'Worried about me, Guillam?'

'Yeah, you've touched my heart-strings.' He pulled at his hat brim in a gesture that might have been a salute or might simply have been a clothing adjustment, and he went out.

Denton had fallen into an exhausted sleep, to be woken by the constable from the front door, who wanted to know if he should let in a Dr Bernat, a Jew, sir. Denton said of course, and Bernat examined him, put on fresh dressings and asked after Atkins – word of the second crime had travelled through the neighbourhood.

'He's at University College Hospital in Gower Street. I can't find out a damned thing from here.' He touched the doctor's shoulder as the man was bending over him. 'Can I hire you as his physician?' He flinched at 'hire', knew he should have said 'retain'.

'I am not being of the faculty,' Bernat said. 'I have no hospital.' He gave a smile, more resigned than amused, no need to say to what. 'Except the Jewish in the East End.' He meant the hospital for indigent Jews.

'I can write you a letter. They can't object to that.' Bernat had to fetch paper and pen from Denton's bedroom. Denton wrote the note, trying to make it florid and stuffy – 'my personal physician,' 'to advise on the condition of my man Harold Atkins,' 'yours most very sincerely.' Bernat took it without reading it and then shook a pudgy finger at Denton and said he was to go to bed; he was not to think of going out; he was to drink beef tea, apparently by the gallon. 'Replacing the blood,' Bernat said, shaking his finger. 'We are replacing the blood, Mr Denton!'

When Bernat went off, the policeman came up with a nervous-looking, very young man and said apologetically that he wasn't put there to answer the door, he was sorry, sir, it was job enough to keep the press away, as they was flocking like pigeons around an old lady with a bag of breadcrumbs.

'Name is Maude, sir,' the nervous young man said the moment the constable stopped talking. He was wearing a new suit, new round hat, new overcoat, none of the best but not the worst, either. 'Sent by the Imperial Domestic Employment Agency, sir. Recommendation of –' he peeked at a card – 'Mr Harris.'

Denton's head was still muzzy, his vision filmed. He was quitting the world of laudanum and entering one of something like influenza. 'What for?'

'I'm filling in currently. Until something permanent transpires. Sir.'

The policeman was still in the room, waiting in fact for Denton to tell him to go. 'He's a valet, sir,' he said, making it 'val-it' but clear enough. 'Can I go, sir?'

Denton was putting it together in the fog. Harris, valet, employment agency: Frank Harris had sent him a servant to replace Atkins; therefore, Harris knew what had happened. Harris was famous for knowing all sorts of things; he was also famous for doing all sorts of things, many of them scandalous, scurrilous, or actionable, but sometimes – like now – inexplicably generous. Denton waved the policeman away and said to the young man, 'I've got no room for you. His – the permanent man's – rooms are a crime scene.'

'Only coming in by the day as a temporary, sir. Accustomed to making do.' Seeing, probably, that Denton was unconvinced of the need for him, he said, 'Somebody to answer the door in this trying time quite important, sir. Not proper for the cop – policeman. Not well yourself, if I may say so, sir, helpful to have somebody about. There's also the matter of clothing, your morning newspaper, letters and calling cards—' He held out the morning mail and the newspaper, which he had been holding all the time he had been there.

'Can you cook?'

'Oh, no, sir! But I can serve a proper dinner.'

Atkins could cook. After a fashion. What he called 'curries', mostly meaning that he threw some things together and used spice from a tin he bought at the Army and Navy Stores. Plus eggs, gammon, toast, coffee and various sandwiches, always served with chutney and pickle. The Indian background.

'But you can make a pot of tea.'

'Why, yes.'

'Good. Do it. Your hat and coat go in that closet. When the tea's made, take a cup to each of the coppers outside – one's at the back. Then I want you to go up to the attic and get some things for me, and then we'll talk about drawing me a bath. You'll get lunch for both of us from the Lamb, plus anything the officers want. Can you do that?'

With the air of a man of parts, the boy – for he was only a boy, perhaps sixteen – said, 'Of course, sir.' Leaving Denton to wonder why Frank Harris, who was only an acquaintance, had gone out of his way to help him. And what he would want in return.

Denton found the confirmation of what Guillam had told him buried on an inner page of the newspaper:

CAPE COLOURED SEAMAN
ARRESTED IN MUTILATION MURDER
Confession Imminent, City Police Say

Joseph Abrahams, a Cape Town seaman, has been detained for the violent murder of a woman in the Minories two nights ago. Abrahams was found in an inebriated state and covered in blood, City police say. Detective Sergeant Steven Willey said he expects to lay charges tomorrow. Abrahams's ship, the *Ladysmith Castle*, will sail from the Port of London today.

'Mr Atkins is comatose,' Dr Bernat said several hours later. 'Very bandaged, so I could not examine the wounding, but the resident was helpful.' He tut-tutted. 'A bad blow to the back of the head.' He touched his own large dome behind his bald spot. 'Concussion for certain. But not to despair yet. I am seeing many woundings of the head in Poland.' The resigned smile again; no need, it said, to tell him who had been wounded and who had done the wounding.

'I'd like you to see him again this evening. If you have time.'

Bernat bowed, a curiously courtly and old-fashioned gesture. He raised one of Denton's eyelids, then the other, then looked inside Denton's mouth. 'Laudanum was new to you. It is very forceful that way sometimes. The brandy was not wise.'

'I know that now.'

'The doctor cannot predict is coming in a burglar to kill you. Sleeping is what I wanted for you, not knifing. But the brandy was foolish.' He waved a finger at Denton. 'Now you know better.'

'I'm learning.'

Bernat gave him the smile, then rattled through advice – sleep, lots of liquids, red meat if he could eat it; rest, rest, rest. And *no* spirits. 'You have no wife? No woman?' A look of disapproval. 'The man without a woman is prey to mental vexations. Woman is soothing and also is love, as well the conjugal activity of pleasure. Every life needs softness!' Then he laughed, and Denton laughed, and he went away.

By then, Maude had handed the tea around, answered the door four times (three newspapermen, one Christian Scientist), brought Denton the late newspapers (*Famous Author Wounded in Dastardly Attack*, which made Denton ask himself why, if he was so famous, he wasn't rich), and made himself a tiny space at the top of the stairs that ran down to Atkins's rooms and the kitchen – inside Atkins's space, as it were, but not inside the crime scene.

'Bath, sir?'

'Attic first.' Denton explained exactly what he wanted and made the boy repeat what he had said. 'Now help me up to my bedroom and bring me the stuff there. Then the bath.' A few minutes later, he was lying against three pillows on his own bed, loading the Colt. Then he had the bath. And his third cup of beef tea.

Frank Harris turned up in the early afternoon. He looked pretty much as bad as he had the night before, but cleaner. Denton received him in his bedroom. 'Informal but understandable, I hope,' he said.

'Ah, the author's lair!' Harris's eyebrows went up and down. He had a lot of self-mockery, for surely he included himself in the idea of 'author'. 'How's the temporary valet working out?'

'Well enough that I want to thank you for him. I'm pretty much marooned here; it wasn't working, having a copper for a doorman.'

'I thought something like that. Plus it gave me an excuse for paying you a visit.' The eyebrows went into their act again. 'You ought to get away.'

Denton made it clear that he was sick of hearing about getting away.

'Yes, yes, that's all very well, but you need to get away. You've been stabbed; a madman is after you. Your house is practically uninhabitable. Paris is the place for you!' He grinned as if they shared a joke.

'You've something in mind.'

'Well. Yes. It's this way, Denton—' Harris hitched his chair closer, leaned in as if to share a secret. 'Somebody from the Café Royal crowd, somebody *literary*, has to show the flag at Oscar's funeral. We have to be seen to send somebody of some *gravitas*, don't you agree? It's the day after tomorrow.' His eyebrows went up and stayed there. 'All sentimental crap aside, Oscar Wilde can't go into the ground with the world thinking nobody in literary London cared!'

It was typical Harris. Two days ago, he might not have been ready to subscribe two-and-six to a fund for Oscar Wilde, but a combination of contrariness and old friendship now made him Wilde's champion. Plus he had once set up a famous meeting with Wilde and Shaw at the Café Royal, trying to persuade Wilde to skip his trial. Plus his bravura performance at the Café, in which Denton had supported him, probably appealed to his sense of self-dramatization.

And now Denton knew what he was supposed to do to repay him for the valet.

'I'd go myself,' Harris said, 'but I've got a magazine going to hell under me, and anyway, the Paris authorities are not, mm, quite happy with me yet.' He reached out and tapped Denton's calf. 'It's about *art*, man. About art and this ridiculous, stuffy, suffocating, hypocritical society we live in! Everything's regulated; everything's marked out ahead of time – whole lives! – except for art. An artist can go anywhere – until he goes too far. Then the bastards turn their backs on him and sneer. We can't let Oscar go like that, Denton. We owe it to *ourselves* as artists.' Then he guffawed – a sound loud and abrupt enough to make Denton flinch – and said, 'Heard the one about the tart who gave service *à la bouche* while playing "The Lost Chord" on the pianoforte with her toes?'

Denton said he hadn't. Perhaps he had, but he could never remember jokes, and he had a puritanical distaste for off-colour ones, a leftover from his New England boyhood.

'Well,' Harris said, settling into it with a grin. 'Fellow goes to this tart, et cetera, et cetera, and she has the speciality as noted, so she begins, and he's delirious with pleasure, and she's swinking away, playing Sullivan with her toes, and he's just a jot short of a climax when she stops dead and says, "I can't remember how this part of the music goes." Well, the man is beside himself! He shouts, "Play anything – anything – make something up!"' Harris roared with laughter, and Denton, thinking this was the end, smiled; Harris, however, wiping his eyes, said, 'So – so the tart rears back, and she says – she says –' he couldn't keep from laughing – 'she says, "Make something up! Sir – I'm an *artist*!"' And he became help-less, laughing.

Denton at least chuckled at that, but when Harris had recovered, Denton made the mistake of asking what *à la bouche* meant, and Harris became glum and said the joke was ruined. 'I don't know which is worse, Denton, your utter lack of humour or your sexual prudery.'

'I don't think that not knowing French makes me a prude.'

'Ever hear of a man named Havelock Ellis?'

'*The Psychology of Sex*. Downstairs on my shelves. Volume one, anyways.'

'You astonish me. Well, how can you read that book and still be a prude?' Harris leaned forward. 'I suppose German and Latin would be too much for you, or I'd put you on to Krafft-Ebing. *Psychopathia Sexualis*. Set you straight.'

'Ever occurred to you, Harris, that sex isn't all that important?'

Harris looked poleaxed.

'I mean,' Denton said, 'it's fine in its place. Pleasure is nice. But it's not worth writing whole books about. Maybe you have sex a bit too much on the brain.'

'You're the one who's mad about murdered tarts and voyeurism and sexual mutilation!'

'But not because of the sex.'

Harris stared at him, shook his head, and sighed, like an actor trying to make a point to a particularly stupid audience. He looked at his watch; then he pushed his hands down into his trouser pockets and sank even farther down in his chair, his legs out. Then he shook his head. 'Thesis, antithesis, synthesis,' he muttered.

To cheer him, Denton said that he supposed he could go to Paris, but— 'Why me?' he said, although he knew why. *Because there was nobody else.* 'Are they all so afraid?' he said.

Harris sighed. 'Since Oscar was jailed, everybody with a lingam behind his flies has been terrified to so much as own a copy of *Dorian Gray*. Actually, you're the perfect one – you are, if I may say so, the epitome of the hairy masculine. Not a hint of English neurasthenia about you. Come on, Denton – if not for Oscar, then for me.' He grinned – much show of teeth – and said, 'After all I've done for you!' It was both a joke and a solipsistic plea.

All Denton could say was that he'd think about it. He didn't say that he wasn't going anywhere until Atkins was out of danger. Otherwise, the idea of a flying visit to Paris was not unattractive. Except that, of course, it was doing exactly what Guillam had advised him to do. And he shouldn't spend the money just now. 'I'll think about it,' he said again – grumpily, as he realized when he heard himself. 'I can't leave Atkins unconscious in a hospital.'

'Better in a hospital than somewhere else.'

'I'll let you know tomorrow. There'll still be time to take the night mail and get there.' Harris looked at him with the terrific frown that had made him feared – sheer uncivilized ferocity, as if he planned to club you to death and eat the remains. Denton wasn't impressed, but he wondered how sane Harris was. He reminded himself that he didn't know Harris at all well; they were Café Royal acquaintances, and not very frequent ones, at that. In fact, his only contact with Harris outside the Café had been when the man had asked him to provide 'anything on American fiction' more than a year before, and Denton had written something on Stephen Crane. So far as Denton could remember, he'd never been paid. Which wouldn't have been much to begin with, its being Harris. To forestall more talk about Paris, Denton now said, 'Did I ever get my money for that piece on Crane?'

He should have said 'Where's my money for the piece on Crane?'

because Harris, given the possibility of its already having been paid, said, 'Of course you did!'

'I don't remember it.'

'Shock. Loss of blood.'

'I think you gave me the loose notes from your pocket when I asked for it. I think it was about ten pounds short.'

Harris became magisterial. 'I don't think we should bicker over money when Oscar is barely cold.'

'I'm not bickering – I'm asking—'

'Crane just died, of course. How about doing a piece on that? We could split the difference.' Not getting encouragement for that idea, he rushed on to say, 'Oh, another thought I had.' Harris smiled, then touched his forehead and frowned. 'Would it be possible to get a drink, do you think? Something is always welcome at this time of the day.' It was not yet one o'clock.

There was no bell, and Denton had forgotten the boy's name. 'Bellow down the stairs. Tell him what you want.' What Denton wanted was for Harris to go; he was feeling disoriented, floaty, weak. Not up to the Harris personality. 'Or you could just go next door to the Lamb.'

'A public house? Good God! Only an American would suggest it.' Harris went out and, instead of bellowing, said something in a low voice and then went on down the stairs. He was back in two or three minutes with brandy; Denton was almost asleep, and the smell woke and nauseated him. Harris drank, sighed, massaged his temples. 'You really need to get away for a day or two, Denton. The boy isn't to be here at night, he tells me; you'll be alone.'

'I'll think about it, I said.'

'Of course, I'll cover your expenses – take up a collection.'

'Take up one for the Crane piece, while you're at it.'

Harris finished his brandy with great briskness and banged the glass down. 'You disappoint me.' He paused at the doorway like an actor with an exit line. 'The Café Royal is counting on you.'

Later, Maude – by then, Denton had remembered the boy's name – brought up a lunch from the Lamb and more beef tea, of which Denton was getting noticeably weary. Denton asked him if Harris had paid his wages.

'Oh, no, sir, that's for you to do.'

Of course it was.

Towards six, Dr Bernat puffed up the stairs, a glass bottle in his hands full of what looked like blood. Denton was ready to shout that by God, he'd gone too far; he'd put up with beef tea, but not blood! But Bernat explained that it was Russian beet soup made especially for Denton by Mrs Bernat. 'The beet is being full of mineral, which is also the blood. Drink.'

'Now?'

'When better?'

Denton had had enough beets in his childhood to last a lifetime, but he didn't want to offend Bernat. Mentally holding his nose, he drank – and liked it. Borscht, he found, when made by the right cook, was very different from boiled beets. He smiled. Bernat smiled. They both laughed. Bernat said Denton was 'very game', an Englishism of which he seemed proud. He had been to see Atkins again. There had been a period of consciousness, he had been told, some indications that Atkins could see, move his limbs and ask questions, or at least say, 'What the bloody hell?'

'Now, he will improve, but he is having a nasty wound. Some days yet he must be in hospital.'

'Can I visit?'

'Tomorrow, maybe yes, maybe no. But you need rest yourself. Today, absolutely no.'

Denton looked grim. 'Somebody wants me to go to Paris. A trip to University College Hospital won't compare.'

'Paris!' Bernat frowned. 'Paris is not a restful place. I trained in Paris. During the—'

Maude was standing in the doorway. 'Now there's a gentleman named Munro to see you.' He looked aggrieved. His work day had ended two minutes earlier, and here he was, announcing yet somebody else. Denton said to show him up, and the boy said that *then* he was leaving the house, sir, and he clattered downstairs.

'I am going,' Bernat said.

'No, no, stay.' Bernat had a half-finished glass of sherry. He looked uncertain, probably embarrassed. Munro, however, seemed unfazed by either patient or doctor. He was carrying his hat and coat and grinning. 'Your man flew out of the house before I could give him my things.'

'My man's a kid, hardly out of short pants. Sling them on the bed.' He introduced the two men, said that Bernat was a doctor and Munro a policeman. 'Two professional visits in one,' he said. 'Munro, if you want a drink, you have to get your own. Atkins got his head broken.'

'So I heard. Nothing for me, anyway.' He looked at Bernat. 'Well, how is he?'

'Our host? Generally in excellent health, his wounds stable, still weak and I think a little shocked. But promising.'

Munro looked at Denton. 'I'd like to hear your tale of what happened. Guillam's keeping his own counsel – his prerogative; he's being a good cop. Tell me what happened.'

Bernat said he shouldn't listen to private police business; no matter how much both men insisted, he drank off his sherry and left. He had seemed at ease with Denton, clearly was not with Munro, or perhaps only with two other people instead of one. 'Shy,' Denton said. 'Been through the pogroms; maybe it's because you're a policeman.'

'Coppers have that effect. Part of the job.'

Then Denton told him the story of the two attacks, ending with Guillam's visit and Guillam's disdain for the Mulcahy story. 'Guillam hates my guts,' he finished.

'That's just Georgie. He wants to be a superintendent, at least; always on the make. To him, you're a rival. I know, it's stupid, but he's like that. He doesn't want anybody else to have an idea. Down on me because I had your observation about the peephole before he did.'

'He wants me to "get away".'

'Yeah, that would suit him. Plus you must admit, he has a job to do.'

'Which I don't prevent him doing.'

'Yeah, you do, if you get in the newspapers and spout ideas that the coppers then have to deal with – which he's afraid you will if a reporter ever gets hold of you. It's really hard enough being a London copper without civilians saying it should be this way or that way. As if you had to listen to Guillam tell you how to write books.'

Denton grunted. 'Somebody else wants me to go to Paris.'

'Happy to go in your place. You'll buy the ticket?'

Denton laughed. His visitors had made him feel better. 'How about you go next door to the Lamb and get yourself some beer and a couple of plates of beef? The boy servant seems to have forgotten that I eat in the evening.'

Munro stood. 'I'll get beer for me and beef for you. Mrs Munro expects me at home, and she expects me to eat what's put before me. If you're eating to help that arm, you should have liver.'

'Beef. The redder the better.'

Munro was whistling when he came back. The whistling got breathy as he struggled up the last flight of stairs with the tray, but he made it – a little red-faced, a little winded – and laid out the beer pitcher and a glass, roast beef (not very red), mash with sprouts, a bottle of some sort of sauce. 'Barman at the Lamb sends his best. Shocking you're hurt. Crime is a scandal, and the police should all be sacked.'

'You didn't tell him you're a copper.'

'Didn't seem friendly to disabuse him.' Munro took a long pull at the beer and sighed happily and began to cut up Denton's meat for him. 'So – you think it was *him*?'

'The attack? Yes, I think it was him.'

'Well, you've seen his face now. He'll either come again or go to ground.'

'I saw half his face.'

Munro glanced at the Colt. 'You expect him back, I see.' He put the plate on Denton's legs. 'Constables going to be kept at your door?'

'A few days.' He ate some of the roast beef. 'I might as well go to Paris.'

'And give up on Mulcahy?'

'Mulcahy's dead by now.'

'You surprise me. Why?'

'There's no point in attacking me unless he's already got rid of Mulcahy. I think he was afraid that Mulcahy had told me something.'

'What?'

'I wish I knew.'

Munro drank his beer and frowned at the wall and said, 'Willey's got a solid case on the Cape Coloured he grabbed. They kept a lot of it out of the papers, but the long and the short of it is that the poor bastard was covered with blood and drunk as a lord when they found him, plus he gave them a confession. Willey laid charges a couple of hours ago.'

'What's that to me?'

'Willey's got the girl's killer. Whatever your Mulcahy and the man who attacked you do or don't have to do with the great scheme of things, they didn't murder the Minter girl.'

'Because Willey has a South African sailor who's too frightened to know what's happened to him? Munro, you know either of us could get a confession from a man in his situation even if we knew for a fact he was innocent – black man in a white country, found drunk and bloody, probably can't remember what the hell he did that night, afraid they'll hang him and so willing to say anything. And who made the peephole – the black man?'

'The peephole's neither here nor there. Denton, there's no evidence that it had any connection with the murder at all! Or with your Mulcahy, for the matter of that. Fact, Willey's people tracked down the landlord of the house in Priory Close Alley – lives out in Staines, never goes near his property, has an agent to do all the dirty work. The agent rented the closet to a man who gave the name Smithers, can't remember anything of what he looked like. Paid six months in advance. Smithers may have been Mulcahy, but it's wasted time to Willey.'

'It means he probably has a witness.'

'It means there's an *outside chance* of a witness, but Willey has a confession, and if the coloured boy's lawyer wants to go hunting for Smithers-Mulcahy, he's welcome to do so, but Willey can't spare the resources!'

Denton swigged borscht and chewed beef and shifted his position in the bed. 'The girl,' he said. 'We have to learn more about the girl.'

Munro grinned and shook his head and, finishing his beer, clumped down the stairs and let himself out.

CHAPTER NINE

After night fell, he lit the gas in his room and on the stairs, and then, the loaded Colt in his hand, he went down and lit a lamp in the long room. He felt only a little dizzy, still weak but clearer in his mind. After sitting for a few minutes in his chair, he went down to the ground floor and lit the gas there and opened the front door. A different constable was standing out by the street but came hurrying when he saw Denton.

'Something wrong, sir?'

'Only putting my head out for air.' The evening was cold, hazy with vapour that was condensing on the stones and starting to drip from the eave. 'Still somebody in the back?'

'Yes, sir. Bit dark back there, I expect.'

Denton went through the corridor that ran along Atkins's part of the house, lighting the gas, speaking a few words with the constable out there before going upstairs again. He tried sitting to read, found his eyes not focusing on the page, got himself water, then thought about a drink of some sort and rejected it. The arm hurt, but not unbearably; Bernat had brought him a black silk bandanna for a sling, and it eased the pain.

He got a lantern from the old kitchen, climbed back to the bedroom, legs a little rubbery, got the Colt and then went on up to the next floor and then the attic. 'Getting back on the horse,' he muttered to himself. The attic was deeply shadowed. He shone the feeble light around, feeling unsteady, hating his own nerves. The skylight had been re-glazed and nailed shut. The Flobert pistols were put away. The dumb-bell and the rowing machine looked like grotesque animals, casting huge shadows. He shivered.

Back on the floor below, he locked the attic door and went down to his bedroom and undressed and got into his bed and tried to go to sleep. Fifteen minutes of racing brain later – worry about Atkins, a new awareness of his arm, visions of the attacker's mad eyes, his smell – he was dressing to go out. The after-effect of the laudanum, he supposed, was an insomniac tenseness and sense of hurry. And, perhaps, dreams. The idea of repeating the nightmare about his wife decided him that he wouldn't sleep yet.

Doing buttons one-handed was difficult, and he was tempted not to put his left arm through his coat sleeve, but he made himself do it, hearing his grandmother's voice, 'If it hurts bad, it must be good for you.' He put the arm through Bernat's black sling. A necktie gave him far more trouble and he finally abandoned it, pulling the tie through itself and letting it bulge above his waistcoat like a stiff ascot.

'The glass of fashion,' he muttered, aware for once of where the quotation had come from. He put his right arm into the sleeve of an overcoat, drew the left side over his sling and buttoned a button to hold it, then pushed the Colt revolver into the right-hand pocket. It made a mighty bulge, but he wasn't going without it. He might be getting back on the horse, but he was nonetheless afraid that his attacker would come back.

'Going out, sir?' the constable said again, exactly like the first time. He was an older man than the first, heavily jowled and pretty well girthed. He sounded parental, as if Denton was to account to him for his movements.

'Tired of being cooped up.'

'Wet, sir.' The damp air had by then produced a fine drizzle. He moved past the constable, waiting to be stopped – the idea was absurd, but Denton felt as if he were doing something underhanded – and moved away as quickly as his still-wobbly legs would allow. Walking lasted only as far as the corner; he knew he couldn't make it much farther.

He went by cab to Mrs Castle's famous house, commended to

him by Harris, the house otherwise known simply as Westerley Street. Other houses stood in Westerley Street, but only the one was known by the street's name; more than one of her clients, drunk or sober, had said that it must be awkward actually to *live* in that street. But all the cabs knew the way, and they all knew what a man meant if he said 'Westerley Street'. Denton had no idea what they thought if a woman said it.

As higher-class houses went, it was a little shabby, but that seemed to be a sign of its authenticity. Mrs Castle herself was always soberly and tastefully dressed, if not in fact sober and tasteful; she always had champagne at hand and loved to talk politics or racing or what she called 'so-sigh-tih'. A certain shabbiness of speech, as well – the odd dropped H, the even odder dropped final G – went with the patchily worn carpet or faded chair. It was said that she had been the mistress of a personage, had chosen to be a madam rather than a milliner afterwards, knew that the best houses were sometimes the worst kept and kept hers accordingly.

'Well, sir, it's you,' a big man said as he opened the door to Denton.

'Hello, Bull.' Fred Oldaston had fought bare-knuckled as the Lancashire Bulldog for fourteen years and had been the first Englishman to take Denton into a public house. He had also – same evening – taught Denton how to put a thumb into a man's eye while punching him. Now fifty and two stone heavier than when he had fought, he was Mrs Castle's conscience: 'I keep them honest,' he had said, meaning the clients. Now, he murmured, 'Hurt your arm?' as he closed the door behind Denton.

'Somebody stabbed me, in fact.'

'Fighting with knives, bad business, best stay out of it.'

'I didn't have much choice.'

Oldaston took his coat and pointed through a fringed and swagged doorway. 'You know the route. Something to drink?'

'I'd pass out.' He went through the drapes and into a large parlour that was a couple of decades out of date, too much furniture and too much darkness, and that smelled of cigars and good perfume and coal fires. A man in evening dress was sitting in a corner with two women, one of whom looked expectantly at Denton; he passed on to a room beyond where a large table lamp with a globe painted with cherubs cast a glow the colour of a sunset. Mrs Castle was sitting where she always sat, in a large armchair surrounded with cushions, so that it was not possible to stand right next to her; the walls, surprisingly after the décor in the other rooms, were covered with a William Morris paper, but the rest was like the parlour – velvet and lace, a bulbous piano with paisley hanging from it like melting icicles, a sideboard big enough to have served as a back bar.

'Well, here you are, then,' she said. She held out a hand. 'I 'eard you'd been 'urt. They say 'e tried to kill you, that true? The black silk thing is ever so elegant.'

Denton squeezed her hand and sat down. She was probably in her forties but looked both older and younger, her face well preserved but weary, her abundant hair her own, her voice firm, her figure overstated but good. He thought her attractive but had never got any encouragement from her. 'A bad cut is all,' he said.

'But in your own house, my dear.' She had firmer control of the H that time.

'You seem to know all about it.'

'Well, friends of friends in the press, you know.' She sipped champagne. She was one of those drinkers who are always one or two drinks gone but who never seem drunk; one day, he supposed, it would all crash down on her. 'Can I call somebody for you?' she said.

'It's you I came to see.'

'Oh, I'm flattered. Poor old me.'

She started to tell him some long story about HRH, whom she actually did know, although not absolutely recently. A lot of it was about horses, and Denton's mind wandered. He watched, through the doorway, two or three more men in evening dress come in, then several women from another direction. The sound of male voices rose, then a woman's, singing. Denton realized that one of the men was Hector Hench-Rose. When he sensed that Mrs Castle's voice had changed tone, he knew that her story was over, and he smiled and nodded. When she stopped to pour herself more champagne, he said, 'Maybe you can help me.'

'My dear, I'd be delighted. Anything.'

'I'd like to talk to somebody who knows the girls who work the street around the Minories.'

'You're 'urtin' my feelin's, my dear. Not going to be loyal to Westerley Street?'

'Business. Writer's business.'

'What then, somethin' about that killing? Is this about your arm?'

'I'd like to find somebody who might help me talk to some of the girls.'

Mrs Castle smoothed her gown. '*I* don't know anybody in that end of town, *I'm* sure. Bit of a ragtag and bobtail there, little of everythin'. I never hire from there, you know, they don't 'ave the style.' She looked hurt. 'Cow-girls and goose-girls.'

'I didn't mean it that way.'

'Surprised you'd think it of me.'

'I didn't. I only thought you might know somebody who did. Know that area, I mean.'

He had to apologize again, then wheedle her out of her mood, if it was genuine. She became roguish, then suddenly confiding. She really did know, or know of, all sorts of people, all sorts of stories. She seemed to be coming to some point, perhaps even a name, when Hector Hench-Rose came in with a very young woman, laughing and red-faced and rather tipsy for that early in the night.

'Denton!' he shouted, in case anybody in that part of London had missed his name. 'Saw you when I came in! How's that arm? I thought you had one foot in the grave, the way the papers went on. This is Yvonne, who's a charmer, ain't you? Ah, Mrs C, handsomer every time I see you.' He kissed Mrs Castle's hand and accepted a glass of champagne and proceeded to tell her all about a lot of police business that was almost certainly confidential. Yvonne stared into space, laughing when she thought she was supposed to, pulling at her clothes as if she had dressed too fast. Other people wandered in and out; an organ started to play a waltz a couple of rooms away. When Hench-Rose had finished his gossip, Mrs Castle looked at an ormolu clock and said, 'Supper room's open.'

'Aha!' Hench-Rose stood. He winked at Denton. 'Join us? Little sustenance? I've a mind to visit the last act at the Palace of Varieties in Greenwich – care to join me?' He didn't wait for an answer, but in the doorway he called back over his shoulder with another shout of laughter, 'Making rather a night of it!' He was married, with several children; his wife was said to be shy.

'Janet Striker,' Mrs Castle said. '*Mrs* Janet Striker.'

Denton let his expression ask the question.

'The person you want, my dear. 'Ench-Rose can be an exhausting soul, can't he. Thought he'd never come to the point. Gave me a chance to think, though. Mrs Janet Striker. The Society for the Improvement of Wayward Women.'

'Sounds awful.'

'It *is* awful. But she ain't. Tough as tripe, but a lady, and not your mealy-mouthed do-gooder. She understands the lives the girls live. She tries to find other work for them, get them off the street, which is like tryin' to bail the Serpentine with a fish fork, but she *means* well. I wouldn't send you to most of the hypocrites in that line, but Janet Striker's a woman who—' She smiled, cat-like, disingenuous. 'You'll have to meet her to see what she is.' She rested her chin on the fingers of one hand and stared at him. 'I'm not sure she'll take to you, Denton.'

'That's flattering.'

'She doesn't think much of men.'

'And she's a Mrs?'

'All the more reason.'

'What's her husband like?'

'He isn't like anything – he's dead.' She raised the champagne bottle out of the bucket and found it empty. 'Tell them to send in another as you go out, will you, my dear?' she said. She was tired of him.

This time, when he got home to bed he stayed there. A pleasant languor had overcome him in the cab. He took one of Dr Bernat's powders and crawled between the sheets and fell off the edge of the world.

The Society for the Improvement of Wayward Women had an address in Aldersgate. The street was commercial but not prepossessing; the building was grim but not impressive; the office was as squalid as a land company in the Dakotas in mud season. Generations of heads had left hair oil in a smear above the chair rail; thousands of hands had left dirt on the doorjambs; God knows what had chipped the grey-green paint that covered the walls. It was not a setting where he expected to find women, but everybody there was female – a rather sullen, plain woman who guarded the outer office; a younger, morose woman behind a typing machine inside; and, in the far corner between two windows, Janet Striker.

Her look of weariness reminded him of Mrs Castle's, although it had been earned in another school, he thought. She had a face that had once been unmarked perhaps, was now frankly guarded, any stock of pity or sentimentality expended. Her hair, very dark, was pulled tight back over the top of her head and wound in flat circles that hid her ears like some peculiar helmet. She wore greys and browns, both dark, not so much nun-like, however, as business-like, the dress years out of fashion and mended down near the hem. If a man, she'd have been a manufacturer, he thought, of something entirely practical, shovels or water closets. Or perhaps a policeman; there was, in her steady, appraising look, something of Guillam.

She had his card between her fingers. Denton was watching her eyes but taking in the fact that she had a telephone on the wall, wondering whatever for and then thinking it might be for calling the police. He didn't know why he thought that – something fortress-like about the office, he thought. Warrior women.

'What is it you want, Mr Denton?' Her voice was soft, surprisingly low, genteel.

He was still standing. There was no offer of a chair. There were no chairs, in fact, except in the outer room, where they were lined up around the walls like those in a clinic for the poor. He said, 'I'm hoping you could help me.'

'We're not here to help men, I'm afraid.' She put his card down towards him as if giving it back.

'It's about your, uh, particular area.'

'This is an office that tries to help women find their way out of prostitution. As men are the reason they get into it, I doubt I can help you.'

'I'd have said women get into prostitution for the money.'

'Yes – and men have the money. When you're starving, you sell what you can.'

It wasn't an argument he wanted to get into. The view that marriage itself was a kind of prostitution had once shocked him, now seemed fairly sensible – dramatized by Shaw but hardly original. 'I'm sorry. I'm not here to argue.'

'We're busy here, Mr – Denton; please don't take up our time.'

He felt himself flush. 'It's about a girl who was murdered,' he said too quickly.

'That's a police matter. Are you with the police?'

'I—' He fought his irritation. 'May I sit down and explain this to you?'

'Do you mean will somebody fetch you a chair? No. There's nobody to do that here. We don't have *time*, sir.'

So, standing like a schoolboy at the teacher's desk, he ran through the high points of the story of Mulcahy and Stella Minter. He wasn't going to go into the attack in his house because she didn't need to know that to understand, but she said, pointing at his sling with a pencil, 'What happened to your arm?'

He sighed. 'Somebody attacked me in my house. The man who killed her, I think.'

'What's this to do with us?'

'I was told you might be able to put me into contact with some of the girls who knew Stella Minter. The other young ones on the street. *Somebody* must know her story.'

'Surely that's a police matter.'

'The police are slow.'

'You're very foolish to take matters into your own hands. Is this some male idea of revenge for the arm? You'd do better to go to bed.' She started to look at something on her desk and then looked up again. 'Who told you I might be able to put you into contact with street girls?'

'Do you know Mrs Castle?'

It was the first time she had smiled. 'Mrs Castle of Westerley Street? Of course, you must be one of her clients, then. How I do loathe your sort.' She said it quite casually.

'Stella Minter was murdered in a horrible, ugly—'

'I know how she was murdered.'

'Aren't your – clients – frightened?'

'Of course they are.'

'Then why don't you want to help get her murderer off the street?'

'The morning newspapers say that the police have her murderer and he's confessed.'

'Do you know how easy it is to get a confession from somebody who's alone and terrified and probably brutalized, Mrs Striker?'

She raised her eyebrows, pursed her lips, not looking at him, and he had the sense of her looking inward, for the first time affected by something he'd said. He leaned a few inches towards her over the desk. 'The police don't believe me about Mulcahy. The City Police aren't exactly bowled over by Stella Minter's death. It isn't that they don't care; they've got other fish to fry. I'm willing to take the time to pursue it. I'm paying a number of women to look for Mulcahy in the directories. I'd like to look for Stella Minter, too – who she was, why her killer chose her. I'm not trying to pick up young prostitutes, if that's what you think, Mrs Striker!'

She toyed with the pencil, then looked up at him. 'What is it you want from us?'

'Ask the – your clients – if they knew Stella Minter. If they did, ask if they'll meet with me – and you or somebody else or a policeman, if you like – and tell me what they remember about her. That's all. I swear, that's all.'

She retrieved his card, looked at it, and put it down in front of him with the pencil. 'Put her name and the other man's name on it. You'll hear from me if I learn anything.'

That was that. When he was done writing, he found himself looking at the straight parting in her dark hair, her attention entirely on something she was reading. There were no goodbyes.

He visited Atkins in the hospital on his way to the Paris boat train. The sergeant's head was wrapped in cotton, most of it on the top and back but one wrap coming around the forehead as if to hold things together. His face looked small, rat-like, rather old.

'Still, you're alive,' Denton said.

'Take more than that to kill me.' The voice was small. He had had concussion and his eyes looked strange. 'Bastard hit me from behind.'

'Dr Bernat says you're on the mend.'

'Old biddy wants to keep me in here a week.'

'It's necessary, Atkins. You've been wounded.'

'Most soldiers die in hospital, not the battlefield – ever hear that?'

'This isn't a soldier's hospital. It's where you need to be.'

'Feels like a soldier's hospital to me.' It was a ward, with a long range of beds down both sides and an aisle up the middle. Coughs, sighs, the sounds of other visitors swept up and down the big room.

'The soldier's hospitals I saw,' Denton said, 'they laid them on the ground. In the rain.'

'Yes, well, that was a war.' Atkins sighed. The short visit was tiring him out. 'And he almost killed you. What a bastard.'

'I'd better go.'

'Paris, eh?' Denton had already told him about Wilde's funeral. 'Funny how things turn out. Five years ago he was king of the hill; now he's got you going to his funeral.'

'That's a come-down, I admit.' Denton was smiling. 'Do what the doctor tells you.'

'Yes, yes – 'course—' Atkins was drifting into sleep. Denton asked a nurse if that was a sign of anything, and she said it was a sign he'd stayed too long.

Paris at the beginning of that December was wet with a cold downpour. During the night, a wind had come up, and Denton's ship had rolled and tossed, and between the rolling and his arm he got little sleep. He went to the Hôtel des Anglais, where he had stayed before with Emma Gosden; it was her hotel when she was in Paris. Had he chosen it because of her, or had it been simple laziness? Or had he really come to Paris hoping to see her? To make it up? He had a delicious, partly sexual moment of dreaming of meeting her, finding her glad to see him, and their going off somewhere together – the south, maybe Italy, and the hell with Mulcahy and Stella Minter and—

He slept for an hour and then had the French idea of a breakfast and read a London newspaper and looked at the rain. The funeral was across Paris, the interment miles out in the suburbs some-where; he would have to make an early start. Still there were hours to fill. He was not one for museums or shops. He wondered what he was one for. Work, probably. Except his work had come to a halt, something deeply wrong with the book he was writing – the woman, he had to admit it was the woman; she was all wrong. He was all wrong, that meant.

He sat in an armchair with the newspaper over his lap and watched the Parisian rain and thought off and on about Emma Gosden. Hell of a day for a funeral. His mind kept swinging back to Mulcahy and Stella Minter. He was sure that the man who had attacked him and the man who had killed Stella Minter were the same; why wouldn't the police see it, too? Guillam did see it, he thought, but wouldn't admit it out of orneriness – no, out of prag-matism, a black sailor on remand being better than an unknown on the loose. Anyway, Guillam wasn't really part of the Minter investigation.

He thought about Emma Gosden and getting together – would she do that—?

He'd have to see Sergeant Willey when he got back, try to make the City Police get going on finding Mulcahy or Mulcahy's corpse. He'd have to—

He'd have to start minding his own business, he thought. Drop it. Rewrite your novel and make some money. He'd have Bernat's bill to pay now, Atkins's hospital bill, plus the household bills he hadn't yet paid—

He went up to dress and found that Maude hadn't packed black gloves, and the hat was the wrong one but would do. The concierge supplied gloves, although they were too small, but there was no time to buy others because with one thing and another, Denton was late by then and had to hurry out and ask for a cab. To his surprise, the rain had stopped. The streets were still wet and shining, very noisy, nervous. Out on the boulevard, the number of motor cars astonished him; he had never seen so many, never a third so many, in London. When the boy came back with a horse-drawn cab for him, he was sorry he hadn't told him to get a motorized one; it would have been a spot of interest in a gloomy day.

He had paid the boy and was standing there, reaching up with his good hand to grasp the rail beside the cab door, when another drew up behind his and a female foot appeared, then the edge of a skirt, then an elegant woman in, he thought, the latest Parisian fashion. It was only when she was on the pavement that he realized she was Emma Gosden.

His hand froze on the handrail. It was the unexpectedness of it, of actually seeing her in Paris, the fantasy of a few hours before made flesh. She looked wonderful, probably in a new gown, something of the real – that is, the expensive – Paris, where funerals and knife wounds didn't enter. It was he who didn't belong, not she; she was of the place. As he looked at her, his heart announcing itself with great thumps, she turned her head and saw him. Her entire body gave something like a quiver, a start; he thought she might have been ready to take a step away from him or even a step towards him. Her right hand, her free hand, the hand not holding her purse, moved upwards; if it had continued, the gesture would have been a greeting.

Even a welcome.

Then the hand stopped, then dropped the few inches to where it had been. Inches. But the gesture told him everything: more than anything she had said that last evening, more than her anger or his, more than the return of his hat and coat, more than her silence since, the few inches of movement told him that it was definitively over. *Like something written by that silly old woman Henry James – so much subtlety you think you've died.* The end of a love affair in a motion.

Then a man came out of the hotel and she turned to him with a smile. They walked away, she on the man's arm. Denton thought he might be younger than she, impressively good-looking. *I've found somebody else. Be a man.*

The church service for Wilde was grotesque. Denton counted fourteen people, including himself. He wouldn't have recognized Wilde's old lover, Alfred Douglas, except that he was apparently the head mourner and so greeted the others, who slipped into St-Germain-des-Prés like fugitives. The fourteen, all men, seemed to Denton to be a collection of odds and ends from anywhere, dressed for a funeral but gathered there apparently by coincidence. Nothing connected them to the Wilde of legend – no green carnations, no hint of aestheticism, no witty remarks. The church itself was cold and damp, puddles collecting on the floor from their coats and umbrellas; in another chapel, a better-attended funeral mass was punctuated by tears and a female voice that moaned like a hurt dog. The sounds of their grief threw the silence of Wilde's mass into relief, only the voice of the young Irish priest audible. Denton, depressed by what he was taking part in, tried to think about Emma Gosden and found only a sense of emptiness.

The flowers he had ordered through the Hôtel des Anglais looked showy and vulgar, and the card, which should have said they were from the Café Royal writers and artists, said, 'Form the writters and artistes du Café Royale.'

After the service, the others got into four carriages that were nominally the official vehicles and followed the hearse; Denton, wanting to be by himself, came after in a cab, clopping miles into the wet suburbs. If the mass had been grotesque, the graveside service was ludicrous: the rain pelted down, its noise blurring the spoken words; umbrellas hid every face; the priest's hands shook from the cold. Finally, it was over; what was left of a great and sometimes awful man went into the ground, Denton thinking at the last, as he dropped wet clods on the coffin, that Wilde had been the emblematic man of the century's last years – brilliant, duplicitous, too arrogant to survive.

He would say later that, although it had had a month to run, the nineteenth century had ended on the day of Wilde's funeral. Privately, he would think that it had ended for him with Emma Gosden's gesture.

CHAPTER TEN

Back in London, he climbed his stairs like an old man. The funeral had been hellish. It had all been a kind of comedy, but he found it sordid and humiliating for the dead man. *We all end up in a box, but it doesn't have to be a Jack-in-the-box.*

At the top of his stairs, he opened the door to his sitting room. He had expected nobody – Maude hadn't come to the door, so Denton figured he'd decamped – but at the far end of the long room, just in front of the window through which his attacker had vanished three nights before, a mysterious figure could be made out, crouched, indecipherable, as if caught in some dubious act. The hair on the back of Denton's head prickled, and he reached for his pistol, slow as he was to recognize the figure's necromantic gown as Atkins's tattered Indian robe, then to recognize Atkins's face above the collar, and finally to understand that the seemingly disembodied helmet above the face was a black bowler resting on a swathing of bandage.

'You gave me a start,' Denton said.

'Nothing to what you gave me, Colonel. I might of shot you.' Atkins was coming forward, now holding up a hand with the derringer in it. 'Copper brought this by.'

'You're supposed to be in hospital.'

'Couldn't lump it another day.' Atkins took off the hat, revealed a kind of turban. 'Shaved my head. I look like a bleeding fakir. So I had to wrap it in something, didn't I? Old scarf of yours, hope you don't mind.' He put the hat on again. It sat about two inches above his forehead. 'Reckon if I'd been wearing this hat when the bastard hit me, I'd never have had to go to the hospital in the first place.'

'You're a sight for sore eyes, Atkins.' Denton found himself smiling. He touched Atkins's shoulder. 'Glad you're back. Where's the boy servant – what's his name? – Maude?'

'Sent him packing. Wet behind the ears. Did you know the only experience he'd had was as a footman in some jumped-up manufacturer's manse? Family hopped off to the Continent for a year, gave him his marching orders. Too young to be out alone. All right if I sit?'

'Well, of course—'

'Bit wobbly still.' Atkins fell into the armchair and put the derringer on the table, which still showed the damage from the bullet Denton had fired, the flash mark a burn like a black teardrop. 'I'll stagger back downstairs presently.'

'Like hell. You'll take it easy until you're fit. In the meantime—' Denton, still standing, reacted away from more movement down the room. Atkins's door had swung open and an indeterminate shape had appeared. Denton snatched at the Colt pistol. 'What the hell's that?'

'Oh—' Atkins turned, looked down the room. 'I was getting to that.'

Denton stared into the gloom. Something that might have been a recently sheared sheep seemed to be standing there. 'What the hell?' he said.

'Yes, well – he's a comfort to me. Frankly, General, I'm jumpy. No point in denying it. Old soldiers know better than to fake the courageous. I still jump at shadows. Can't stand for anybody to be behind me; I think that chap's going to brain me again with the doorstop. So, see, I was glad to have Rupert's company.'

'Rupert.'

'Prince Rupert. Loan of a friend who's in the dog trade. Racing, and so on.'

Rupert didn't look as if he did much racing. He was in fact, one of the fattest dogs Denton had ever seen. He was also big, ugly and enthusiastic. He had almost no tail, but the rump around the stump vibrated with what might have been joy. He was mostly black but with a white face, and mostly rounded, except for a head and muzzle that were oddly angular. His eyes were more like those of a pig than a dog, slightly slanted, rather smaller than you'd want if you were designing a dog, and pale blue. He went straight to Atkins and tried to hoist his bulk into Atkins's lap. Atkins managed to push him down; he sat, staring at Atkins, his stump whisking the carpet. 'Bull terrier in that head,' Atkins said. 'Intelligent breed.'

'I see some Rottweiler in the rear end, myself. The middle looks like whale. But, if he's a comfort—' Atkins's confession of fear had reminded him of his own nerves when alone in the house, the loading of the revolver. He shoved the revolver back into the overcoat pocket.

'Pardon me saying it, Colonel, but it looks like you're carrying an anvil in that overcoat.'

'My revolver.'

'So I saw. Your tailor would have a fit.'

'It isn't really a pocket pistol. But I'd as soon not get stabbed again.'

'Hand over that coat and I'll do something to fix it. Open the bottom of the pocket, is my notion – run the barrel down there, maybe sew something like a holster into the pocket to hold it upright. You'll look like you're carrying the blacksmith's hammer instead of his anvil.'

'The real way to carry it is on its own belt around your waist.'

'Yes, well, that ain't the fashion in London these days. Take what you can get, I say – hand over that coat.'

Denton, grateful, put the overcoat in Atkins's lap and said, wanting to make some gesture, 'You'd like the dog to keep you company for a while?'

'Well – to stand watch, as it were, Colonel. Only until—' He pointed at the layers above his scalp.

'Dogs have to be fed, watered, walked, cleaned up after—'

'I've done latrine duty before, General. He eases my mind, if you know what I mean.'

'I think I'll have the Infant Phenomenon back until you're well.

No, no – I'm not going to have you busting a seam somewhere by going back to work too early – no—'

Atkins made pro forma objections – no recent footman going to mess in his household, couldn't cook, left a shocking amount of litter, no taste – but gave in easily enough. The man was exhausted, aching and nervous; even a boy on his first job would be a help.

'But the dog,' Atkins said with spirit, '*I* feed the dog! Because dogs cleave to them that feeds them.'

'Well, don't let him cleave too closely. He's a loan, correct? Temporary? Until—?' He, too, pointed at Atkins's turban and hat.

Rupert grinned from one to the other and, with a satisfied sigh, collapsed at Atkins's feet.

Denton had settled to read his mail with that feeling of the just-returned traveller that he has been away for weeks, is therefore surprised that so little has accumulated. In fact he had been gone barely thirty-eight hours, and he had only a few pieces of mail – a note from his editor, asking about the progress of the novel he was supposed to deliver in three months; an invitation he wouldn't accept; and a short, brisk letter from one of his sons in America.

And, hidden by the others, a long envelope from his typewriter, Mrs Johnson. He slit it with a pocket-knife and pulled out several sheets, all but one covered with typed names and addresses.

Mr Denton, I enclose herewith the list of R. Mulcahy's found in the postal directories, with addresses. There are one hundred and thirty-seven in all. I enclose also a bill for the services of the three employees. One woman is continuing, at my instruction, to look at the advertisements in Kelly's and also in Grove's, in case the name appears in any of those; she will finish tomorrow and will submit a separate bill. I hope this is all right.
  Yours, L. Johnson.

A hundred and thirty-seven names. At a shilling a name.

Denton looked at the lists – looked and despaired. The addresses were all over Greater London and there was no way to tell one from another – which might be promising, which not. He had promised Guillam he would hand the list over; now that he saw it, he was quite willing. The job of sifting through it would be enormous, too much for one man. Guillam was welcome to it. But he was disappointed, he realized. Let down.

'I'm going out,' he called towards the stairs.

'I'm staying in.' Atkins's swathed and bowlered head appeared. 'Unless you've got other plans for me.'

'You're convalescent. You want the derringer?'

'I've got Rupert.'

Denton carried his bag up to his bedroom and bathed and changed and, after sending a note off to the employment agency to send Maude back, made his way down to New Scotland Yard, the revolver riding uneasily in a mackintosh while Atkins doctored the overcoat.

Guillam was there but wasn't available; then he was available, but he was somewhere else in the building. Denton, not sure whether he was being toyed with or was simply suffering the inevitable effects of bureaucracy, made himself calm and chatted with the almost elderly constable who served as porter. Made sympathetic, the man sent off a much younger constable to make 'a special effort for this gentleman', with the result that Denton was eventually led through the ants' nest that was New Scotland Yard to an office door, behind which sat four detectives, one of them Guillam.

Guillam saw him, jerked, bobbed his head in a kind of greeting. When Denton was standing by his desk, Guillam, head down now over paperwork, grunted. After thirty seconds, Denton said, 'Could I sit down?'

Guillam looked up, bobbed his head towards a chair against the wall – the only spare one in the room, testament to the rarity of visitors – and Denton got it, lifted it one-handed and carried it back and set it down. He sat, crossed his legs, watched the top of Guillam's head. Five minutes later, Guillam said, 'Well, now.' He stared at Denton. 'To what do I owe the honour of the visit?'

Fighting irritation, Denton took out the sheets Mrs Johnson had sent him. 'You wanted the addresses of the R. Mulcahys in the London directories.'

'I did?'

'You said you did.' Denton hadn't quite succeeded in hiding his annoyance. 'I told you I was having it done, and you said it was evidence and you wanted it.'

'I might have said something like that. All right, chuck it in the basket.' He bobbed his head towards a wire basket on the far corner of his desk. 'That's it?'

'You're not even going to look at it?'

'Willey's manor, not mine. I'll send it to him.'

'Today?'

Guillam's head had already gone down twice, as if he was going back to his paperwork; now, it stayed up as he eyed Denton. 'When I get to it.'

'Isn't it more important than that?'

'That's for me to decide.' Guillam's head went down. 'G'day.'

'I'd think Sergeant Willey would want it as soon as he can get it.'

Guillam's look was ugly. 'Willey's got other things to think about!' he roared. The other detectives looked at each other, grinned. 'It isn't going to run itself over to the City just because you paid for it!' He touched his pen to his fingers as he counted. 'A day to get logged here. A day to send it with the messenger's lot to City Police. A day for them to log it. A day for it to get to Willey, who'll take one look and chuck it into a basket identical to mine and hope it gets buried until he's got nothing better to do! Now mind your own business, Denton!'

Denton had one of those instantaneous internal debates – hit the man? No, don't hit a copper in his own office. Erupt in curses and threats? No, they'd laugh at him. Complain to his superiors? – and stood, his overcoat over his good arm. 'That does it, Guillam. If I had my hand around Mulcahy's neck, I wouldn't deliver him to you.' He started out, turned back. 'You're one rotten cop.'

'Go to hell.'

Denton strode out. He heard laughter before the door closed behind him. He knew his face was flushed and set; he was barely able to be polite to the old constable in the lobby. He wanted to kill somebody. Barring that, complaining was all that was on offer. He headed for the Annexe and Hector Hench-Rose.

A florid-faced civil servant with the manner of a church usher bowed his head and said, 'Sir Hector will see you now, sir.'

Before Denton had digested the *Sir Hector*, he was in the office and looking at the man himself. Surprisingly, Hench-Rose was wearing deep mourning. Denton, despite seething over Guillam, took in the black and wondered what had happened, a mystery best taken care of at once. 'I take it you've had a bereavement,' he said. 'I'm so sorry.'

'Only my brother,' Hench-Rose said in a chipper voice, 'and I couldn't stand him. Rather a swine, in fact. However, he was nice enough to make me rich and pass on the title to me. You may now address me as *Sir* Hector.' He guffawed.

'I thought the Queen did the knighting with a sword.'

'Baronetcy, not a knighthood. Hereditary.' Well, that explained the flunky.

'I'll never understand England.'

'That's what you get for rebelling against us. You're a sight for sore eyes, I must say – how's that arm?'

'I've had worse.'

'The black hanky is quite romantic. Also the pallor – is that loss of blood? You've come to ask me to lunch, I hope.'

'I've come to complain about an ass at the Yard.'

'What, only one?' Hench-Rose roared. 'I may be leaving the police, actually. The Yard is losing its fascination for me, now I'm wealthy.'

Denton said something about Guillam and stupidity in general and then added, a little desultorily, that he hoped the London police weren't too much for Hench-Rose.

'Not that at all; police are all right as far they go, not too bad when you've got a sinecure. Trouble is, I've got a grouse moor and my own mountain now.' He smiled, waggled his eyebrows. 'What I'm trying to work out with the powers that be is something that would allow me to drop in one or two days a week, keep my hand in. Advisory or consultative, that sort of thing. Not during the shooting season, of course.'

Denton had seen one or two men like that in the publishing business, partners who came and went like ghosts making visitations. They, however, had money invested in the firm. 'Maybe,' he said, 'you should buy into Scotland Yard.'

'What? Oh, not possible. Can't buy a government entity.'

'I was joking.'

'Oh? Really? Oh, I see!' Hench-Rose laughed. Perhaps in retaliation, he said, 'Do you know you've dog hairs all over your clothes? Your man is not doing his job.'

'It's his dog – long story.' To change the subject, he said, 'You were having a good time at Westerley Street the other night. Did you get to the variety at Greenwich?'

'What? Oh, I did see you, didn't I! One forgets. Yes, yes, that charming girl. No, I didn't, as a matter of fact. Got dragged to the Adelphi to look at the tarts – some real smashers there, quite remarkable, but no good to me after Yvonne. My word, that girl'd exhaust a monkey! No, oddly, I was asleep in my own bed by one o'clock.'

'So much for your night on the tiles.'

'Well, it started rather handsomely. You didn't stay at Westerley Street, did you?'

Denton told him about the hugger-mugger trip to Paris. Hench-Rose seemed scandalized by the idea of going to Oscar Wilde's funeral, muttered something about public morals. Denton said, again to change the subject, 'Does the name Janet Striker mean anything to you?'

'Striker.' Hench-Rose had a vast family and was probably sorting through third cousins and in-laws by marriage, his eyes cast up. 'Mmmm-no – wait—' He swung around to look out of the window, one finger on the end of his nose. 'Striker. Yes, by God!' He swung back. 'There was a Striker – let's see; it was a long time ago – I was billeted at Salisbury, I think, not so bad as it sounds because of the trains, possible to be in London at the weekend – and there was a tale. Mmm. Woman who killed her husband, as I remember. Must have, because she went to prison. Yes, that was it. Newspapers very circumspect; you had to read between the lines, understand that a lot of very racy stuff was involved. Yes, Striker. Interest you as a novel or something?'

Denton dodged the question. He told himself it couldn't be the same woman. Hench-Rose asked again if Denton was taking him to lunch; Denton answered that he thought that, as Hench-Rose was now rich, it was his turn. That seemed to delight Hench-Rose, who grabbed a black hat and led the way out, heading for his club. As they were going out, Hench-Rose said, 'Ah!' and turned around to stop Denton with a finger to his chest. 'I've made up a quip. It's rather good.' He grinned.

'Let's hear it.'

Hench-Rose cleared his throat, the rigours of creativity making him flush. 'All gals are divided into three parts: mothers, tarts and the ones we're allowed to marry. Eh? Eh? Rather good, isn't it? "All gals are divided"?'

Denton didn't get it. It had to be, he knew, one of those references that Hench-Rose had learned in school, therefore must have something to do with Latin. He said, 'I've told you, I left school when I was twelve. I don't get it.'

'"All gals" – get it? "Gallia est omnis divisa—" Eh?' Hench-Rose could never accept the idea that Denton hadn't been to an English public school. '"All Gaul is divided into three parts"! All gals!' He chortled, but, seeing Denton's incomprehension, stopped, became deeply gloomy. Halfway through lunch, he explained his joke again, a process that he said was like taking out one's own gall bladder, and he added – unwisely – that Denton lacked a sense of humour. Denton made the mistake of saying that he didn't think that Hench-Rose's joke displayed much sense of humour, either. Hench-Rose, now annoyed, said that Denton didn't know any more about humour than he did about women, as shown by the fact that Denton 'was wasting his time on some stupid bint who had got herself murdered.'

Denton's jaw set and he was about to say something ugly when Hench-Rose, his face red, almost shouted, 'And another thing! That Striker woman! She *murdered* a man, and you're asking me about her as if you're *interested* in her!' His voice rose; heads turned towards them. 'Everybody said the husband was as nice a chap as you'd ever want to meet, and she *murdered* him. Or as good as – she might as well have put the pistol to his head and pulled the trigger herself! She's obviously an awful woman! Awful!'

Then Hench-Rose realized that he had been shouting and had committed that worst of crimes, calling attention to himself. He seemed to shrink in his chair and, with his face almost in his plate, he mumbled, 'Fellow feels strongly about certain things. Things have to be said.'

And Denton, who liked Hench-Rose no matter what, felt his own anger evaporate, and he said in a gentle voice, 'You said it for my own good, Hector. You're a good fellow. Should I try the spotted dick?'

CHAPTER ELEVEN

'I wash my hands of the whole damned business!' Denton raged as
he went up his own stairs. He meant Stella Minter and Mulcahy,
but Guillam most of all, and Hector Hench-Rose into the bargain.
He was angry about Guillam's handling of the lists of names – days
of work, money, tossed into a basket to moulder – and Hench-
Rose's lack of sympathy had made it worse. *I wash my hands of
it.* His mood, if anything, was blacker than when he had left
Guillam's office; Hench-Rose's easy brutality hadn't helped, nor
had the stodgy lunch and Hench-Rose's going on about that joke.
'Another joke about women, my God,' Denton said out loud.

'What's that?' Atkins was leaning out of the alcove to look at
him as he came in the doorway; another head appeared, this one
Maude's; then, at knee level, the angular muzzle of the dog.

'I wash my hands of the whole damned lot!' Denton shouted.

'Good enough for Pontius Pilate, should be good enough for
you, Major.'

Atkins's voice changed to a martial bellow as he began to order
Maude about. Apparently the cleanliness of the alcove hadn't
been to his liking. After explaining that he didn't give two hatpins
whether Maude thought that cleaning was part of his job or not,
Atkins said something disparaging about servants who thought
they were too genteel to get their hands dirty; then he leaned into
the sitting room again and said, 'There's mail for you.' His voice
took on a hectoring tone. 'More bills, I'm sure.'

'I wash my hands of them, too.'

'Oh, no you don't!' Atkins came down towards him; Rupert padded behind, panting like a blacksmith's bellows. 'You neglect the bills, I'm on my way to the agent's for a new position.' He stood beside Denton's chair, quite unembarrassed now by the hat's sitting on the bandage, the Indian robe. 'You wash your hands of Mulcahy and the dead tart, all well and good; best get to work on that book, then.'

'You're as good as a mother-in-law.' Denton was opening bills and putting them with others he hadn't paid. Soon, he'd have to write apologetic letters and ask for time. Bad. He opened a plain one that looked like a begging letter – he got those now and then; people thought writers were rich – and took out a note of a different size, scrawled in an almost illegible hand. It was from the woman he'd visited, Mrs Striker: he could talk with three young women if he would come to her office at five o'clock on the second.

Today was the second. It was barely two.

Telling himself *No, I'm done with it, done with all of them*, he slit another envelope with a finger without looking at its origin and realized only when he held the contents in his hand that it was from his typewriter and that the women she'd hired must have found more Mulcahys in the directories. *More expense.* With it was a mere phrase scribbled on a blank sheet – '*As promised, the names from the adverts*' – and her bill. He crumpled that before Atkins could see it but couldn't keep his own eyes from going to the total, which was startling.

'Oh, no,' Atkins said, reading over his shoulder. 'Not more Mulcahy! Send it off to that copper, Guillam.'

'Never again.'

'You just said you've washed your hands of Mulcahy – didn't you? You did; I heard it with my own ears. You're done with Mulcahy!'

'I'm more done with Guillam. I wouldn't send him my old drawers.' He was looking at the new list Mrs Johnson had sent. Only seven addresses, all businesses; four were far from the metropolitan centre, all suburban shops that seemed to offer him nothing. Of three closer in, one was a Regina Mulcahy, Fine Linens – not likely; one was a Richard Mulcahy, Processed Beverages, the

Famous So-Do-Pep, Health Drinks for the Health Conscious –
possible, but nothing leapt out at him; and one was a Regis Mulcahy,
Now Proprietor of the Photographic Inventorium, Under New
Management, the Famous Periscopic Lens, Patent Applied For.
'Photography!' he said.

'Wash your hands of it, General!'

'A camera, Atkins! That's what he could have left behind in the
closet – a camera! And that's why the murderer went after him –
he thought Mulcahy had taken a photo of him and had run out
with the plate. *And maybe he had!* My God, no wonder Mulcahy
was terrified!'

'You're making it up, General!'

'It fits.'

'You're writing fiction. Go make money off of it.'

'It all fits, damn it!'

'I'll have fits if we don't pay some of those bills!'

Denton turned on him and was ready to say something ugly, but
he was stopped by Atkins's ridiculous costume and his ridiculous
dog. He grunted, shook his head, said, 'I'm going out.'

'Oh, no – no, don't, Captain! Bloody hell, you'll be in it up to
your elbows again!'

'Just this once.'

Atkins groaned, but Denton was already grabbing up his mackintosh and hat. He grinned. 'Don't wait up.'

Atkins met him at the downstairs door with the overcoat he'd
been working on. 'You can't wear a mac on a day like this – what
would people say? Take it off.' He took the Colt from Denton and
demonstrated his handiwork: the revolver's barrel slipped through
a hole into the overcoat's lining; a kind of envelope of canvas-lined
tweed held it upright, the grip ready to the hand.

'Ingenious,' Denton said. He put the coat on. The pistol's weight
dragged it down on the right side, but he could draw the weapon
easily without having to fumble for it as he had before. 'And it's
practically invisible,' he said.

'It's invisible the way Nellie's mistake's invisible in about the
sixth month, General, but it's better than it was and you're not

an embarrassment to me going out in it. Though I say again, you ought to be filling the coffers and not chasing will-o'-the-wisps.'

Denton put a fingertip on Atkins's shoulder. 'Was it a will-o'-the-wisp that put that turban on your head?' He withdrew the finger. 'Expect me when you see me.'

The Photographic Inventorium was in a tall building behind Camden Passage in Islington, a former house that may once have stood alone. Denton's eye told him it was eighteenth century, maybe a bit earlier; it looked asymmetrical because one rank of windows had been bricked up, but in fact it had a centre entrance with two bays on each side, small pediments over the windows like plucked eyebrows, and a shallow hip roof that hung over the top storey. Only from the side could he see two tall dormers in the steep part of the roof, the window open wide in one of them.

If the neighbourhood had ever been up, it had come down; lower houses on each side had weeds where there might once have been grass, broken windows stuffed with rag or filled with paper. From somewhere behind the street, the sound of a machine thudded, and there was a faintly chemical smell. Denton went close to the building on one side, trying to look along it, but a tall wooden gate closed off the narrow space between it and the next house. Looking in through a crack, he could see only weeds, in a space the sun never touched.

He went up the three steps to the central door. On one side, the remains of a stone urn, in which torches had long ago been extinguished, remained; the other had been tipped down into the lower entry, where it lay in pieces among smashed bottles and weeds. The door was open; through it, the thudding noise was louder, rather menacing, and the chemical smell was strong. Denton stepped inside. Straight ahead was a stairway, and beyond it another door, also open; through it, he could see part of a yard and a wooden building. To his right, a door was closed; that was the side where the windows had been bricked up. To his left, a large opening showed where a wall had been pulled out; three men, stripped to the waist, were working over vats of poisonously coloured liquid in there.

Denton walked to the back. The yard was littered with metal castings and wooden boxes; at one side, a workman was hammering sand into one of the boxes. Denton knew enough of manufacturing to see that the box was a mould; the workman was preparing a sand casting. The foundry, he guessed, was still farther back.

He went in again and looked into the big room with the vats. Two of the men were lowering a casting into a vat with a chain hoist. *Plating*, he thought. *Or cleaning.* He tried to get the attention of the third man but was ignored; maybe it was the noise of the thudding, ponderous machine, probably a drop forge but sounding like the footsteps of a monster.

Finding no sign to tell him where the Photographic Inventorium might be, he went up another storey. Here, a single door on the left opened on a space the length of the house, undoubtedly made from two or even three old rooms – the cornice changed halfway down; a ragged scar ran across the floor where a wall had been removed. Far down the room, a dark man in a skullcap stood on a small dais, a kind of counter around him. The rest of the room was bins, both along the walls and down the middle. While Denton watched, a young man rummaged in a bin, pulling out bits of lace, studying them, picking out one or two and dropping them into a sack. When Denton moved deeper into the room, he saw a sign behind the dais: *A. Gold: Findings, Trimmings and Best Remnants.*

'Mr Gold?'

The man on the dais folded his arms over his chest, cocked an eyebrow. Standing up there gave him an advantage, and he was aware of it. 'So?' he said.

'I'm looking for something called the Photographic Inventorium.'

Gold pointed skyward.

'You know the man who operates it?'

Gold shook his head.

'Have you seen him in the last few days?'

Gold shook his head.

'Thanks.'

Denton went up to the next floor. There, a young man who was planing panels for a door said he didn't know Mulcahy and wouldn't recognize him if he fell over him, and he'd seen only one person on the stairs in the last week, and he didn't know him, either.

'What'd he look like?'

'Who wants to know?'

Denton offered a couple of shillings, glad Atkins wasn't there to see him, and the young man said what did he think he was, a flunkey? 'I'm a self-employed craftsman; I don't take charity and I don't take bribes. You see this here door I'm making? It takes skill. It's hard work, and not many can do it. And nor can I if you won't let me be!' He turned his back and began to run a steel-bodied, rosewood-filled plane across the wood. Denton wanted to linger, the odour of the wood enticing, the artisan's concentration impressive, but the young man gave him an angry look and he left.

The Photographic Inventorium, Under New Management – no mention of Mulcahy – was on the top floor. Two doors stood up there, silent and closed; the other, if it had an owner, bore no sign. The door to the Inventorium had two hasps, both locked with big Brahma padlocks. Denton knocked and waited and knocked again, but nobody came.

The Inventorium was closed.

The drop forge thudded. The cabinetmaker sawed a plank. Denton tried the other door and called out Mulcahy's name, but the building, if it knew something, was dumb.

He was up in the part of the building, he thought, where the dormers projected from the steeply pitched hip roof. Yet the stairs, which had moved from the centre to the far side of the house on their way up, here broke off and, like a snake cut in two, continued in a different place. He found them only by prowling the corridor and seeing, right at the back, the walled-in stairway going up. If he was right about how high he had come, these stairs led to the roof.

He went up.

The stairs turned once and ended under a trapdoor that must, he thought, open in the almost flat part of the roof that covered the centre of the house. Denton could come within only four steps of it; even then, he had to duck his head. The trapdoor had been locked with a chain heavy enough to haul logs, and a padlock as big as his fist.

Which had been broken.

Denton felt his heart lurch. He looked at the lock, which hung from the chain as if still locked, perhaps arranged so that the casual eye would think it was. He put his eye close to it, his hands on the dirty stairs, his hat off. A gouged scar marked the inside of the lock's curve, but he saw nothing to tell him when it had been made. The metal was dark with time, the gouged line hardly brighter. It could have been made months before. Or yesterday. He reached to take the lock out of the loops of chain, stopped himself, thinking of Guillam. *Tampering with evidence.* Would he even tell Guillam about any of it? *Well, just in case—* He took out the white handkerchief that Atkins insisted he carry and removed the lock with the care of a man stealing an egg from under a hen. Then he used the handkerchief between his fingers and the trapdoor to push it open.

The trap must have weighed thirty pounds. He let it rest on his head and neck while he peered under it over the roof. Here, the roof was made of four triangles like pieces of a square pie that met in the centre; at their outer edges, the roof plunged into the steep decline he had seen from the street. Orienting himself, he turned his head towards the side where the Inventorium sat behind its locked door.

He made himself breathe slowly. He knew he was going to have to go out on the roof, and he was afraid of heights. But he would go out only to look. Only to look.

He lowered his head, letting the trap down; gloom closed in on the stairs. He laid his folded overcoat on the top stair, then put his hat – grey, American, soft and somewhat wide-brimmed – on top of it. He hesitated. It was early December, cold outside; the grey sky threatened wet snow. He decided against taking off his jacket. He breathed.

Unable to postpone things any longer, he raised the trap again and got ready to step out. Then, thinking that somebody (but who?) might put the broken padlock through the chains while he was on the roof, he used his handkerchief to slip the padlock into his pocket. Only later did it occur to him that anyone who wanted to lock him out need only loop the chains – no padlock needed. But it would be too late to go back by the time he had the thought.

He went up a step; his head rose above the roof, and he was able to look along the slight incline and beyond to the grey sky. Up another step, he could see housetops and chimney pots, and if he'd dared look that way, he could have seen the edge along the Inventorium where the roof plunged down its final dozen feet to the eave. He went up another step.

Edgar Allen Poe had written a story about the pull of an abyss on the onlooker, 'The Imp of the Perverse'. That imp had tempted Denton all his life – on barn roofs, on cliffs, on the rail of a steamship. Now, it beckoned to him from the edge of the roof: *Down here – come down – look over the edge, it's lovely – take a step out into the void—* His fear was not so much of heights as of the imp, and what he might make Denton do.

The central peak was to his left, the slope down towards the Inventorium's edge to his right. Ahead – he didn't dare turn his head yet – was the peak and then the panorama of London. Even dimmed by autumn mist, it seemed inhumanly large, the sky as huge a bowl as over Montana. Far off to his left was St Paul's; nearer to his right, the sand-coloured bulk of St Pancras station, Euston beyond it; move the eyes a bit to the left, there was the British Museum. The Thames was there somewhere in the middle distance, hidden by buildings, but he could make out London Bridge and the clock tower at Westminster. Looking from a height at this distance, the depth of the house separating him from the void, he didn't hear the imp.

He took a breath and went out. Not daring to stand out there, he sat down. He looked all the way around, the entire compass of London. The thudding of the machine was clear, but under it, around it, was a steady roar made of iron wheels on pavement, the scuffing of shoes, voices, music, hooves, the clatter of machinery – the city.

He would have to look at the Inventorium's side of the building, which was the side, he was sure, where he had seen an open window. Only look.

He removed the black silk that served as a sling. He took off his shoes. His stockings were instantly wet from the slates, which were shiny from the mist and which had moss growing in their chinks.

He swung around with his feet pointing down the gentle slope and his heels trying to dig into the moss. The roof was slippery with condensation, but at intervals of a dozen feet or so iron prongs curled up like monkeys' paws to support roofers' or repairmen's ladders. A few were broken off; all were rusty. Still, as he started to work his way down on his rump, he clutched one for as long as he could. It felt solid enough, as did another, and then one crumbled away in his hand, and his heart rate accelerated and he had to lie back with his head on the slates.

Come on, the Imp said, *down here – just slide down and look over—*

He started down again. His injured arm ached. He thought he must look like an inchworm, sliding his rump down until his knees pointed up, then straightening his legs and sliding again. His suit was being ruined. He didn't look where he was going but used the lines of the slates as a guide, his face turned to the sky, until he felt a change under the backs of his calves and knew he'd reached the end of the easy part, and his feet were now sticking out over empty space. The imp was shouting with glee.

He told himself he couldn't go any farther. He told himself he was too frightened to go farther.

He wished he'd taken his coat off, because he was running with sweat. He could feel it in his hair and trickling into his eyes. He breathed once and forced himself to look towards his feet.

He saw his own legs and shoeless feet, then empty air, London rooftops a distant background. His heart lurched. The next building was a storey shorter, but he could see its peak and part of its roof. It seemed far down. Down there, four storeys below, he thought, was the weedy gap he'd peeked at through the gate. Dizzied, he looked to his left: there was the roof he was lying on and, jutting from it, the triangular bulk of a dormer – if he was right, a dormer of the Photographic Inventorium.

Well, he had looked. He didn't dare do more.

He brought his feet back and reversed the inchworm motion of coming down, pushing himself up several slates, palms slipping, then crab-crawled sideways until he could by reaching – heels braced, legs flat against the roof, back arched to keep his balance back – touch the beginning of the dormer.

Now.

He wouldn't try to go down, but if he did, the worst part would come right at the beginning of the last descent, when he would have to put his feet on the sharp pitch downwards but couldn't yet get a grip on the dormer eave. A glance told him that there was no gutter there, only a rotten soffit and eave and the slates, one of which was hanging out into space from a single nail.

Heart pounding, Denton inchwormed down. His buttocks reached the beginning of the sharp downslope. His palms, braced on the tiles, were just at the point of sliding. He told himself that he hadn't committed himself yet; he wasn't really going down there; the imp wasn't tempting him—

He rolled on his belly. He put his feet down until toes felt slate, his torso and arms extended up the central, gentle slope, his right hand with a death grip on an iron monkey's paw. He groped left and right with his toes, then up and down, looking for one of the iron supports, trying not to think of what he was doing – lowering himself to a seventy-degree pitch with no support. Sweat was running stingingly into his eyes; he tried to wipe it off on the moss that was pressed against his face. He swore.

His left foot found an iron paw. He pushed on it; it felt solid. He put more of his weight on it. Still solid. He looked to his right, twisting his neck, to locate the dormer. Three feet away. Could he put his weight on the iron support and still reach out for the dormer eave and—?

The iron support broke. Not slowly, not crumblingly like the other one, but like a snapped twig, and he slid off the central part of the roof. He was still twisted towards the dormer and he made a grab at it, actually touched the broken slate, but the slide was accelerating, and he tried to get on his back, not knowing why – what good would it do? – but down he went, fingers scrabbling at the slates, nails breaking, like a nightmare, the worst of nightmares realized: he was going over the edge and into the abyss.

The iron paws had been put up in lines at right angles to the eaves, so that one jutted up eight feet below the broken one. His foot caught it, slid over, and would have gone on except for his turn-up, which snagged and held – good British woollens. The paw sagged, bent, but held. He felt it, felt his direction change from a downward plunge to a swing as the turn-up became the centre of a circle on which his weight spun, throwing him down and to his right, closer to the dormer. He dug with his hands, his arms; he tried to force his chest into the slates; his injured arm felt a jolt like electricity as it took all his weight. His hands, swinging around, struck the side of the dormer and he slowed and stopped, his hands spread against the wood as if he were a suction-toed frog, held for as long as his trousers and his arms could hold out; and then there was nothing for it but to look down, terrified, down the steep slope to the vertical drop-off. Just short of the edge, another iron support jutted up, closer to the line of the dormer than his right foot, which had got within inches of the edge. He thought he could have hung there longer except for the pain that was burning up his injured arm and into his shoulder, now spreading over the top of his left arm towards his clavicle.

He moved the foot over and caught the iron paw. And then hung there. Listening to the imp.

He could see the dormer's corner now; it rose in line with the building's external wall, about eighteen inches from the edge of the roof. He was still two feet above the corner, his right foot six inches below it. He had either to move his left foot so as to put all his weight on the one support, or move his hands down the dormer wall until he could grasp something, perhaps a window ledge, to pull himself up.

The fingers of his right hand inched down the wall, palm flat against it. At the bottom, an irregular brick gave a kind of finger-hold. Then he inched his left foot off its support and moved his left leg over towards his right, finding it impossible to put both feet on the paw because he couldn't get his left leg under his right, and then he was lying partly on his left side. Bending his legs, he let himself down the dormer and felt around the corner, up, then a few inches across the face, and at last to the sill of the open window.

He found a handhold in the windowsill, a blessed, blissful hand-hold, and he pulled his weight to the corner and then up, and then he could pull his right foot up and put the left foot briefly on the paw, and then he was sitting in the open window with his feet on the slates, his toes six inches from the edge of the roof.

Then he was going to be sick, and the imp was tempting him to be sick over the edge, and he scrambled through the window, his knees on the floor inside and his belly on the windowsill, and he bent forward, ready to vomit, his chin where his toes had been, almost at the edge. And he looked down, straight down into the void, and saw the black walls of the buildings like the sides of a funnel, and the strip of weeds at the bottom, and among them an unrecognizable dark shape like a twisted dark star.

He had found R. Mulcahy.

CHAPTER TWELVE

He stood up and turned towards the room inside the window. The corpse below, he had decided when his eyes had made sense of it, had to be Mulcahy's if this room was the Photographic Inventorium, as of course it was – a huge wooden camera stood on a wheeled tripod; a smaller device, a black cloth, and the corner of a dais on which, perhaps, photographic subjects posed were just visible before the inner corner of the dormer cut them off.

Straight ahead of him across the thirty-foot-wide space was a heavy door – the door with the two padlocks on it, he thought, the door to the corridor and the stairway. The camera and the dais were to his left as he faced the door; to his right, a counter or work table ran towards him and disappeared behind the dormer wall.

He walked on still-trembling knees out of the dormer's enclosure into the room proper and found it large, almost airy, the feeling of space increased by the enormous paned window that took up most of the wall to his left, the rear of the building. This was the source of the photographer's light, which poured through even on this gloomy day. The dais he had glimpsed was set at an angle to this window, undoubtedly movable, because the wooden floor was scarred with long marks. As he moved farther into the room, he found that the dais was backed with some sort of framed canvas, over which, on the photographer's side, a piece of black velour like a theatrical curtain was hung; in front of it, a carved armchair crouched. The camera, as big as a small trunk, looked like some resting animal.

The work table on his right ran from the wall in which the locked door stood to within five or six feet of the facing wall, its far side tight against a wall that ran almost the width of the room, leaving only a narrow corridor between it and the outer wall. It was neither the corridor nor the work table itself that caught Denton's attention, however, but a shrine-like arrangement of dying flowers on the table's far end. He went close and examined it – two pink roses in a cracked vase, dropped petals on the tabletop; a water glass of once-green weeds, drooping now; a brown bottle, perhaps originally meant for chemicals, with a nosegay of the sort girls sold at the theatres stuck into its mouth. These were in a triangle, the roses at the apex. In front of them and resting against the vase was a cabinet photograph of Stella Minter, the face recognizable as that of the waxen, bruised girl of the post-mortem.

She was sitting in the ornate chair that now stood on the dais, her body turned away from the camera but her face in profile. Her back was almost bare, as was her near shoulder; one lacy strip rose from the froth of clothing at her shoulder blade and crossed her upper arm almost at the elbow; the arm, pulled back, revealed one breast just to the top of the nipple. Her lips were open, as if she were speaking – as if, still a child, she were asking, 'Am I doing it right?'

In front of the photograph and flat on the table was a sheet of business letterhead, with 'The Photographic Inventorium' and the address at the top, and 'Under New Management'. On the white sheet was written in a large scrawl, '*I love her but I cant have her so I killed her. I got nothing to live for.*' It was signed '*Regis F. Mulcahy*'.

Denton bent close to the paper, as if smelling out its secrets. He was in fact looking at the writing, which was very slightly shaky, the result perhaps of excitement or even a fit of weeping. The paper had no blots or bulges from tears, however, and no smudges or stains.

He went to the chair and made sure that it was the chair in the photograph. There was no mistaking its hideous griffin's heads on the arms, the overdone curlicues on the upper back that would have made sitting in it torture. Denton looked it all over, back and front, bringing his eyes as close to it as he had to the paper. The upholstered seat had a faint smell – urine? Excrement? Using his handkerchief, he tipped the chair back – it was as heavy as a library table – and then forward. He took particular interest in the joints where the back legs met the seat, where, by looking very close, he could see a few red threads caught. Seen from one angle, several of the threads glinted – silk or satin, he thought. He looked then at the arms but found nothing, then at the back and, in one of the many piercings that made the thing notably ugly, two more of the red threads.

Denton stood back by the camera and looked at the dais. Black curtain, chair. Light from the photographer's right.

He walked to the work table and looked again at Stella Minter. The light had come from the photographer's right, yes, but not at all harshly. There were the chair and the velour curtain. But on the left side of the photo, the velour curtain curved down and towards the right, caught back by a rope, revealing what seemed to be a pastoral scene with a waterfall and some sort of tree.

He went to the left side of the curtain and raised it with the back of his right hand. There were the waterfall and the tree and, in fact, a painted landscape that must fill the entire space. This was the explanation for the canvas-covered frame – a sort of theatrical flat; and indeed the scene might once have been some sort of drop curtain.

Denton looked for the rope by which the curtain had been caught back in Stella Minter's photograph. He didn't find it, but he did find the hook to which it had been tied, and, in the thin gap between the hook's backplate and the wooden frame, several red threads. So, a red rope with a decorative knot and a fringe, to judge from the photograph. Of which some threads had also been caught in the hideous armchair.

He spent an hour in the Inventorium, walking up and down, looking into things, trying to understand Mulcahy's life. And his death. Along the corridor behind the work table were a door to the photographic darkroom, where Mulcahy also kept a grubby cot and an extra shirt. The cot, its single sheet wrinkled in long lines, had a smell, and, his nose almost down among the soiled folds, he recognized the smell as that of the man who had tried to kill him with the knife. It brought that night back; unconsciously, he grabbed his left arm where he had been cut. *He was here. He slept here and waited for Mulcahy.* Beyond the darkroom was a newer, narrower door with a patent Excelsior water closet behind it, filthy but fairly new. It was a long walk down to the privy in the foundry yard.

On the far end of the work table from Stella Minter's shrine were rolled-up papers that proved to be mechanical drawings, all apparently by Mulcahy and all competently done. Several showed stages in the development of the Mulcahy Moving Picture Machine, parts of which (in wood) lay on the work table with the drawings. The machine, Denton guessed, had never worked, certainly had never reached manufacture. Edison's patent was safe.

Drawers in the work table held glass negatives and prints, one drawer devoted to girls like Stella Minter. A few had been photographed against the background of the curtain and the pastoral scene, but most were against a cheaper-looking background of two-dimensional pillars and a balustrade – Mulcahy's lesser resources before he moved to the Inventorium, Denton supposed. The photos themselves were much the same, neither quite art nor quite French postcards, the girls always young, partly undressed, seemingly passive.

The poor sonofabitch, Denton thought.

He looked everywhere for the red cord. When he was satisfied that it was not in the Inventorium, he leaned out of the dormer window again and looked down at the body. He ignored the imp. Denton didn't think that what was left of Mulcahy had a red rope around his neck – and who would hang himself by jumping out of a window? And if he had done such a daft thing, why was there no sign of the cord's having been tied off up here? No, Mulcahy hadn't hanged himself.

Where, then, was the red cord?

Denton stood in the window for some minutes trying to work it out. Then he stood there for several more, thinking about how he would go back up the roof to the trapdoor.

When he was ready to go, he was shaking.

CHAPTER THIRTEEN

'You're late,' Mrs Striker said. She was rushing towards him from her scarred door, thrusting a hatpin through a flat black hat that did nothing to flatter her. In the outer room, Denton was waiting with half a dozen women who, if they were prostitutes, gave him none of the smiles he might have expected.

'I was working late,' he said. In fact, he'd been to a cheap tailor on Whitechapel Road whose sign he had remembered – 'We Press, You Wait.' An ascetic-looking Eastern European had shaken his head over Denton's suit and tut-tutted while he brushed off moss and sewed up tears; Denton had waited, trouserless and jacketless, in a sort of booth with a swinging door, until the tailor appeared and, helping him on with the jacket, had said, 'A shame – a shame – such good cloth—' But Denton had walked out looking more or less respectable again, the damage of the roof muted. 'I'm sorry,' he said now.

'I've another appointment at eight.' She made it sound as if he had already made her late, although it wasn't quite five.

'Which are the ones I'm supposed to meet?' He looked around at the unsmiling women.

'Oh, they wouldn't meet you *here!*' She gave him a little push towards the door. 'We're going up Aldgate High Street.' When they were out on the pavement, she said, 'We'll walk,' and strode away. Denton caught up, did a sort of dance to get on her left, and found her laughing at him.

'*Quite* gentlemanly,' she said.

'Do you mind?'

'It's nothing to me either way.' They walked a few strides and she said more soberly, 'These girls won't go near my office. They think I'll send for the police – as if I'd do such a thing! We're meeting them in a public house, not a very nice one – they feel safe there.' Another stride, and she had changed the subject – a habit he would eventually get used to. 'I asked some of my nicer acquaintance about you. They said you were "entirely respectable". Otherwise, I'd not have let you meet these girls.' She smiled. 'Did you ask about me?'

Denton thought of lying, didn't. 'One friend,' he muttered.

'A man? What did he tell you? That I'd killed my husband?'

Startled, Denton jerked his head and made a sort of grunt.

'It's what they usually say,' she murmured. Pointing ahead, she again shifted ground. 'There's the place where we're meeting them. Let me speak for you, please. They're like wild kittens.' She walked faster and led him to the saloon door of a large pub with an electric-lighted front and several entrances. With her hand ready to push the door open, she said, a rather sly smile turning up her lips, 'I didn't kill my husband, in fact, no matter what your friend said.' The smile turned wry. 'Did he say I'd spent four and a half years in an institution for the criminally insane? Well, I did.' And she pushed her way in.

The pub was huge, pounding with human noise, most of it coming from the other side of a wall to their right. The interior managed to be both muted and garish, dark green walls punctuated with the white, glaring electric globes. Part of a mahogany bar that must have served the whole house in a shape like a racetrack jutted from the wall in front of them, disappeared in a wall at their left; in that same wall, a door with frosted glass and 'Private Rooms' stood just beyond the bar's curving end. Above the bar, coloured glass panes made a screen. The overall air was of activity and seediness, false elegance blurred by a fug of pipe smoke and coal.

'In there,' Mrs Striker said, again shoving him, this time towards the private rooms. 'I'll find the girls.'

Denton stopped. 'I don't really like to be pushed,' he said.

'Oh.' She frowned. 'I didn't know I'd done it. Oh, I'm sorry.' She muttered something about bad habits and, flustered, disappeared through a door marked 'Ladies' Bar'.

Denton waited. His suit smelled of the pressing – hot cloth, his own sweat. The memory of the roof made him sweat again. He was still rattled by it, not really able to focus well. He wished he could go home, have a hot bath, sit in the green armchair with a drink.

'One, anyway,' Mrs Striker said, coming through the door. She was pushing a thin girl in front of her with jabs between the shoulder blades. 'Move along, Sticks.'

The girl whined something about a shilling; Mrs Striker explained that the only way she'd been able to get the girl to come was to promise her a shilling. 'After,' she said to her and gave her another jab.

'Leave off!'

Mrs Striker rolled her eyes and indicated the private rooms, and Denton hurried to open the door. Inside was a row of half a dozen swinging doors, theirs the third one along. Denton pushed through, found a space a little bigger than a coffin with a narrow banquette on each side covered in greasy, almost napless brown velour. At the far end was the same coloured glass that stood above the long bar, and a hatch that he guessed was for service.

The child – eleven, Denton thought, emaciated, not pretty – fell into one of the banquettes and stuck her feet out. Mrs Striker said she was off to find the others; she turned back before she went out and said to the girl, 'Mind your manners, Sticks. *You know what I mean.*'

When she was gone, the child said in the door's direction, 'Cow.' She looked at Denton and said, as if on a dare, 'Stupid old cow.'

'Don't say that.'

'Hate her.' It was like trying to understand another language; he had got 'cow' all right, but she ran her words together, and she had an accent he couldn't follow. He sat down next to the door, finding himself embarrassed, not sure why.

'JerwantaFrenchwye?' the girl said.

'What?'

'Frenchwye, *French wye*! Yer deaf? French, I does't betternor'ny. Ask any gemmun. Quick, I am. Bring yer off in lessnor minute.'

Denton stared at her. What struck him most was how entirely sexless she seemed. Yet he supposed that 'French way' meant the same as Harris's *à la bouche.* 'How old are you?' he said.

'Fourteen, wot bus'ness't to you? Yeserno, you wannit 'fore the cow comes back? Shilling.'

Denton said no, and she flounced back against the greasy velvet and folded her thin arms. She had no breasts at all that he could see, nor any hips; if she was fourteen, nature hadn't brought her any maturity yet.

'Wantersee my place?' she said. He felt himself flush. She smiled. 'No hair on it. Tenpence.' She reached down to grasp the hem of her skirt; the door pushed open, and Janet Striker came in.

'What are you doing?' she said.

'E made a nindecent purposition ter me.'

Mrs Striker glanced at Denton and then at the girl. 'You're a terrible little liar, Sticks.' She looked back at Denton. 'I found the others outside the public bar; they'll be right along.' She sat on the same side as Denton, facing the girl, two adults apparently allied against her. 'I know you better, Sticks. Drop it.'

The girl crossed her arms over her chest again and pouted her lips. 'Where's my shilling?'

'After, I told you.'

'Five shillings, you said!'

'That's if you had anything to tell us about Stella Minter. Well?'

'Yerfinkiblab everyfink I know?' She wiggled herself deeper into the banquette. 'Fer five bloody shillin'? Make me larf.'

Janet Striker's voice was tired. 'She doesn't know anything. I knew it was a mistake to spend time on her, but— Give her a shilling and I'll send her on her way.'

'I know wot I knows!'

'Yes, nothing.'

Denton was trying to find a coin in his pocket, wondering if the tailor had taken his money. No, there it was—

'I do know somethink, so there! Stella Minter tole me all her secrets!'

Mrs Striker took the coin and held it out. 'Oh, Sticks – get out.'

The girl grabbed the coin and jumped up. 'Stella Minter got the clap!' she shouted and, giggling, ran out. She collided with two other girls, who shouted at her and she at them, and they came in red-faced. Both wore demure blouses and dark skirts and little round hats with brims. They looked at Denton and then at Mrs Striker and everybody seemed deeply embarrassed.

'Sit down, do,' Mrs Striker said. 'That's Lillian, and that's Mary Kate.' Lillian was plump, rather sleepy-looking, perhaps sixteen; Mary Kate was thinner, freckled. 'This gentleman wants to know about Stella Minter, the girl who was murdered in the Minories. He'll give you a shilling for being here and five shillings if you know something useful.'

The two girls looked at each other. They seemed still more embarrassed. Denton realized it was because of him – something about its being all right to sell themselves to a man like him but not all right to discuss their profession in front of him and another woman. Mary Kate put her feet flat on the wood floor and looked at her shoes; Lillian stared around as if she had never been in such a place before and then fanned herself with a hand and looked over Denton's head. All at once, Mary Kate said, 'Had a baby.' Three words, and he knew she was Irish.

Mrs Striker looked at Denton and then back at them and said, 'Stella Minter? When?'

They looked at each other again. Lillian said, her voice so soft he could hardly hear it, 'Wile ago.' She glanced aside at Mary Kate and then murmured, 'Waren't married or nothin, she waren't.'

'What happened to the baby?' Denton said. All three women turned towards him – they had been talking to each other – and frowned. Mrs Striker gave him a look and said that it was a good question, and did the girls know?

''Dopted,' Lillian said.

'She gave it up?'

Mary Kate studied her shoes but said, 'She went to the Humphrey, an' they kep' it and all.'

Mrs Striker said aside to Denton, 'The Humphrey is a home for unwed mothers.' Then, to the other two, she said, 'You're sure? This is important information – you must be sure.'

'Sure 'n' I'm sure as sure,' Mary Kate said, and Lillian giggled and got red.

'Did she tell you?'

'Sure, wasn't she Lillian's special pal, then? She was allus tellin' you everthing, wasn't she, Lil?'

'Well, not *everythin'*.' Lillian blushed deeper. 'Oney oncet she tole me that when she were feelin' low. She were a sad girl, she was. A'ways.' Her face, which didn't seem to know how to show sadness, got blank. 'Never had no fun.'

'Was she afraid of something?' Denton said, and they all looked at him again.

'Maybe. But I dunno. I do know she tole me oncet about the 'Umphrey and the awfu' time they give 'er. Workin' girls to death.' She looked up at Janet Striker.

'Yes, I know, dear.' She glanced at Denton. 'It's like an old-fashioned workhouse.' Then, turning back to the others, she said, 'Is that all? There's nothing else you remember?'

They looked at each other once more, then around the little space as if for escape, and Lillian murmured, 'Ever so eddicated.'

'What's that?'

'Stella was eddicated. Nuffin' she din't know. G'ography. Reading.'

'She owned a book,' Mary Kate said.

Denton didn't remember a book among Stella Minter's belongings. Was that significant?

'Name weren't Stella, neither,' Lillian said so low he wasn't sure he had heard right.

'What?'

'Her name weren't Stella. We was standin' down Aldgate, nobody comin' along, nuffing! And we was both sad and tellin' things and she says, "My real name's not Stella." Well, lots o' the girls change their names, don't they? So I said, "Wot is it, then?" and she says, "Ruth, like the Bible."'

'Ruth what?'

'She wooden tell that, would she? Oney Ruth.' Lillian's eyes were almost closed; she might have been a medium, hauling up these titbits from a trance. 'Her sister's name was Becca. Becky, but she says Becca. *Re*-becca. She's ever so worried 'bout Becca.'

Denton leaned in. 'Worried about what?'

'So much younger, wasn't she? Go the same way she done, I s'pose. She said something like, "Wind up like me." And crying.' Lillian looked at Mrs Striker. 'We had such a good time at the hop-picking last summer, the three of us. Now she's gone.' Tears shone in her eyes. 'That's all I know.'

Mrs Striker raced along the pavement, Denton striding to keep up with her. 'You're a fast walker,' he said, meaning it as a compliment.

'I shouldn't have brought Sticks. She's a vicious little brute. Did she offer herself to you?'

'More or less.'

'I'm trying to reach girls like her. I apologize for using your shilling to do it. Anyway, it didn't work.' She strode on as if late for her appointment, although there was more than an hour yet. 'You needn't accompany me.'

'I want to talk to you. About what they said and – other things.'

Perhaps she misunderstood; perhaps her own life was on her mind. Whatever the reason, she was silent, seemingly angry, and then she burst out, 'I told you I spent four and a half years in an institution. Now I shall tell you why.' She raised a finger to point to a turning to the right as they were entering the City. 'My mother sold me to Frank Striker. It was called a marriage, but it was a sale. I was cheap goods – no dowry, no beauty. I was my mother's only capital. She raised me to be marriageable, tried to teach me to please men, gave me all the useless capabilities – I could pour tea but I couldn't boil water. When I was seventeen, she put me on the market.'

'Edith Dombey,' he said.

'What? Oh, I suppose. Anyway, she found Frank Striker. He got me, and she got a yearly stipend and a flat in Harrogate.' She fell silent again; he glanced aside at her and saw her face spottily reddened, her jaw set. Then she started talking again in a hard, half-strangled voice. 'My husband liked two women at a time. That was my wedding night – a prostitute and me. I stood it for a year and then rebelled. He came for me one night with a belt and gave me three welts on my bare back, and then I tried to push him downstairs. He had me committed. Well, it's perfectly logical, isn't it? Any woman who'd raise her hand to her husband must be insane.' She slowed, looked at her watch and strode on. 'Four and a half years later, by whining and wheedling and saying I was a good girl now, I managed to get my release. He sent a servant for me. I jumped out of the cab and went straight to a woman lawyer I'd heard about in prison, and I started suit for divorce the same day. Two of his prostitutes testified for me – they were sorry for me. The prison doctor testified about my scars. We were going to win the case, and the night before the jury returned the verdict, he took his revenge – shot himself and left every penny to his Cambridge college.' She laughed rather horribly. 'My mother lost her stipend and her flat and tumbled on me to care for her. I sued to break his will, but I hadn't a penny. Have you ever tried suing one of the colleges of our great universities? The nurseries of our great men, the treasuries of our best thought, the preserver of our highest traditions?' She hooted.

'What did you do?'

She laughed more quietly. 'I did what women always do. I went on the street.'

He felt her look at him; he met her eyes and saw the challenge. '"Hard times will make a bulldog eat red pepper,"' he said lamely.

She laughed, this time a real laugh, almost a masculine one. 'Wherever did that come from?'

'My grandmother.'

'Irish?'

'Scotch.'

'Scottish. Scotch is whisky.'

'We say Scotch.'

She looked at him again, smiled, shrugged. More cheerfully then, as if it were all a kind of shared joke, she said, 'I didn't know a thing about going on the street. I knew only the words. So I went out on Regent Street. I didn't know it was the French girls' pitch. Two of them pushed me into a doorway and slapped me about and told me if I ever came on their territory again they'd cut my nose off. But it was rather pro forma; when they were done, one of them told me to try Westerley Street, where they might have a taste for a woman like me. I thought she meant prison-worn, but now I know she meant English and conventional. Anyway, that's how I met Mrs Castle. I wasn't much good to her as a prostitute, except for a few men who wanted to be able to say that they'd had the woman who killed Frank Striker, but she sent me on a bookkeeping course and I became her accountant and played the piano in the parlour for the gentlemen, and so I had a home and an income and a skill.'

Ahead, he saw one of the Aerated Bread Company's tea shops. 'May I buy you a cup of tea?' he said.

'You mayn't buy me anything, Mr Denton. But I'll buy my own cup of tea and drink it with you, if you'll be quick.' It surprised him. He realized that she wanted to talk.

'You're going on to dinner?'

She hooted again. 'I'm going to speak at a temperance meeting at a Methodist chapel.' She looked at the watch again. 'I'm due in Euston Road at eight.'

'I'll put you in a cab after we've had some tea.'

They were at the shop door. She looked at him with a kind of weariness. 'You won't put me into anything. If I take a cab, I shall take a cab.'

Inside, flanked by a teapot and cups and a plate of aerated bread and butter, they were awkward. The silence between her tirade on the street and their seating themselves had made them both diffident – strangers again. He felt intimidated, yet knew she had told her story to have this effect – and to force him to know, from a curious egoism, who she was – and yet he felt a kind of diffidence towards her because of it. What she had said, the brutality of her saying it, seemed to invite – to challenge? – a response of the same kind. His voice tentative, he said in almost a whisper into the silence between them, 'I was married when I was young.'

She was pouring tea for herself. Sharp eyes touched his. 'And?'

'She killed herself.' He could have stopped there, had meant to, but it seemed self-pitying, and suddenly he was rushing to tell her. 'She drank lye. She took the lye bottle out into a field and drank as much as she could stand and then began to scream. I was in the barn. I heard her, but I thought she was just— I was used to hearing her scream. She lived for three days. We were thirty miles from a doctor. I took her in the wagon; it was all we had.' She wasn't going to pour him tea, he had seen; he had one hand on the teapot, but his eyes were staring off into the far side of the vast room 'She'd had four babies in six years. Two stillborn. She was carrying another when she did it. She hadn't told me.' He was silent. 'That one died, of course.'

Janet Striker said nothing. Her eyes were on his face.

'It was too much for her. *I* was too much for her. We had— We'd done it together. As if we'd conspired to make something that would destroy her. And we called it *love*.' As he said it, he saw all of a piece what was wrong with the book he had been writing, and he saw the book he should write; he saw the image of a man and a woman making a beautiful and then hideous thing together as they laughed and endured cold silences and made love and hated each other, and he saw the title: *The Machine*.

'Do you blame her?'

'She took to drink. I've always blamed her for that, but I guess I shouldn't. We did it *together*.' He felt his hand hot and looked at it and saw that it was still embracing the Britannia-metal teapot. 'The saddest words of voice or pen – we meant well.' He grasped the teapot's handle and poured himself tea, his hand shaking. He gulped the tea, then said, 'I've had a damnable day.' He told her about Mulcahy then, and the roof, and what he'd found in the Inventorium. 'Getting back up that roof was the hardest thing I've ever done in my life.'

'I wondered about your clothes.'

'I sent a note around to a policeman I know. They'll be all over that place by now, and the body. I suppose they'll make trouble for me over it. But I know now that Mulcahy didn't kill Stella Minter.'

'Why do you care?'

He opened his mouth to speak and then hesitated. 'Because – because Mulcahy was a pathetic little man who came to me for help. And I didn't help him. And because—' He chewed on his moustache with his lower teeth. His left hand was clenched at the edge of the table. 'I went to the post-mortem. It was all men. All of us – like a theatre, like— No better than Mulcahy. *Watching*, you know.' He stammered a few syllables that made no sense. 'I saw – Mulcahy made me see— It's something about men and women.' He shook his head.

'Men hate women,' she said, as if she were saying that tea was made with tea leaves and hot water.

'That's damned nonsense!'

After half a minute's pained silence, she said, 'You weren't surprised to hear from Mary Kate that the Minter girl had had a baby.'

'The surgeon at the post-mortem found something about – milk—'

'She was still lactating? Oh, the stupid girl! If she'd come to me, I could have found her a place as a wet nurse. The money isn't much, but she'd have had a roof over her head and a leg up on a servant's place.'

'Maybe she didn't want to be a wet nurse.'

'"Hard times will make a bulldog eat red pepper."' She grinned. It was a peace offering. 'Did the girls tell you anything worthwhile? Were your twelve shillings well spent?'

'Thirteen,' he said, meaning Sticks. Atkins would have been

furious. 'Yes, her name. And her sister's name. And that about being educated – I think that's significant.'

'Lillian wouldn't know what education is. "Eddicated" may simply mean that Stella – Ruth – spoke better than the others. Or she knew where Norway is.'

'Still – maybe she did have more education. How would she have got it?'

'Oh – perhaps nothing more than doing her lessons. That would make her "eddicated" to Lillian, I suppose.'

He stirred his tea, although there was nothing in it to stir. 'It's grasping at straws, isn't it.'

She poured herself more tea, then, after hesitating, poured some into his cup, as well.

'I'm sorry.'

'It isn't your fault.'

She chewed a piece of the bread and butter, saying it was all she'd get to eat until she got home. Thinking of what her 'home' might be, he said, 'What's become of your mother?'

'She's become a drunkard. She lives with me.' She finished the bread and wiped her fingers. 'You can't keep them away from it. You do everything. Finally, you give up and let them drink.'

He remembered all that. Seen through the gears of the machine they'd built, he realized now that Lily's drinking had been an effect, not the cause. 'Your life isn't easy,' he said.

'No life is easy. I curse those mindless women who swan about in carriages and dress for dinner and have everything done for them – the women who live the way my mother meant me to – but in fact I know that even their lives aren't easy. Theirs are lives of ease, but not *easy*.'

He frowned, chewed his moustache, bit something back and at last, having thought of Emma Gosden and Stella Minter and Sticks and Janet Striker and his dead wife, he settled for mumbling, 'Yes.'

Out on the street, she strode off without waiting for him. 'The Humphrey,' he said, catching up.

'The Humphrey Institution for the Betterment of Unwanted Children. Yes.'

'I want to talk to them.'

'Grasping at more straws?' She hesitated. 'I suppose I could help you – I know them from my work, not that they think much of what I do. They're not such very nice people.' She grunted. 'People who do good often aren't.'

'Would you go with me?'

She seemed to be totting up a column of figures in some moral account book. 'I suppose. If I have the time.' She was walking as if trying to outpace him, and she said, 'I shan't want company beyond this point, thank you.' She stopped and put out her hand. He took it, saw there was no going farther with her. He said, 'You don't really believe that men hate women, do you?'

'Of course I do,' she said and walked away.

CHAPTER FOURTEEN

A constable was waiting at his front door to tell him that Munro would be by to see him soon, and the police would greatly prefer him not to leave his house until they had spoken.

'And if I do?'

'Just giving you what I was told, sir. Please to tell me where you can be found.'

Denton changed his clothes, realizing that he felt guilty and that the suit was incriminating. In law, he assured himself, he had done nothing by going to Mulcahy's Inventorium – a bit of breaking and entering, perhaps, but hardly at a level to interest Munro – and in fact he had done the Metropolitan Police a favour. Unless he'd gone down the roof and seen the body, there'd have been no justification for their going into the Inventorium, as he was sure they'd done by now.

A public benefactor, he thought. The truth was, he'd set himself against doing anything that could help Guillam, and he was damned if he would tell Guillam first about what he thought he'd found in the Inventorium. As a result, he'd sent a note about it to Munro. On the other hand, what he'd learned from Janet Striker's girls, although it hadn't been much, was *his*, and he'd keep that to himself. And as for his having told Atkins that he'd washed his hands of it, well – that had been before he'd crossed the roof.

He ate something sent in from the Lamb and sat staring at a book, saying nothing to Atkins about where he'd been or what he'd done, not wanting to involve him. Atkins had forgone the hard hat that had crowned his bandages. Dressed now in a sober suit, he looked almost normal except for his tight white turban. Looking at the suit that Denton had worn to cross Mulcahy's roof, he made noises and raised his eyebrows and muttered 'Bloody hell'. Getting nothing from Denton, he had snatched up the suit and said, 'Can't weave a new seat into these trousers, you know.'

'What's wrong with the old seat?'

'Ha-ha. You got a new pal with rawhide chair seats, or where were you today?'

'Mind your own business, Sergeant.'

Munro came at last after nine. Denton heard him limping up from the front door, his breathing heavy. His face, appearing in the doorway, was exhausted and angry.

'Well,' Denton said. Munro waved a hand, as if the idea of Denton wore him out. He wouldn't sit. Denton, nervous and trying to seem calm – nervous because he liked this man and wanted to be liked by him – sat, offered drink, food, finally silence.

After the silence had got long and ugly and then threatening, Munro said, 'You were in that damned place today.' His voice expressed controlled outrage.

'What place?'

'Don't try that on with me! You put me in the middle of this business instead of going to any copper on the street as you should have! Well, by God, I'm not going to make it easy for you! What the hell were you trying to do, Denton? Did you think I'd lie for you?'

'I thought you'd do exactly what I believe you did – turn it over to the right people.'

'Oh, is that what you thought! You mean, anybody but Guillam, isn't that what you thought? Well, you guessed right; I didn't take it to Guillam. You got me bang on with that, Denton. I didn't see it right off; then it was too late. You knew I'd keep it away from Guillam so I wouldn't stir him up – and that's exactly what I did.' Munro looked at him bitterly. 'You didn't even tell me it was Mulcahy.'

'I couldn't know it was Mulcahy.'

'Straight below his window and you didn't know it was Mulcahy! What do you take me for, an idiot?'

'What makes you think I was inside that room?'

Munro pushed his hands so deep into his trouser pockets he seemed hunched. 'You're too good an old copper not to have been.'

'Two padlocks on the door. No keys.'

'You went over the roof, don't guy me.'

'I'm afraid of heights, Munro.'

'Yeah? Show me the physician who's treated you for it.'

'Heights *terrify* me.'

'You went over the roof! Look me in the face and deny it – go on! Will you lie in my face, man?'

Denton looked at the exhausted, angry eyes and couldn't hold them. He glanced away; Munro gave a sigh of disgust. Lamely, Denton said, 'Guillam doesn't care rat's piss about Mulcahy.' He turned back, almost pleading. 'Guillam tossed aside a list I paid people to drag out of the directories of all the R. Mulcahys like it was, was – trash!'

'This isn't Guillam, Denton. This is me.'

'Guillam's the police.'

'*I'm* the police.' He pointed a thick finger. 'You had no business going in that room!'

Again, Denton couldn't face him. After several seconds, he got out of his chair and paced up the room to get away, then went on and fetched himself a brandy from the alcove and a bottled ale for Munro. He felt bone-weary now, hardly able to haul himself back up the room.

Munro opened the big bottle with a tool from his pocket and watched a mushroom of foam rise to the lip and subside. He sat down, poured ale into a glass. 'You should have gone to a police station.'

'I went to you.'

'You sent a bloody note!' Munro's voice had risen and he knew it. 'You look like death. Where's your sling for that arm?' Before Denton could answer, he growled, 'It must have been hell going down the last pitch of that roof. No wonder you look bad.' He sipped the beer, repressed a sigh of satisfaction, but he was over the worst of his anger now. In a voice more weary than enraged, he said, 'You could be up on a charge, Denton.'

'For what?'

'Trespassing. Destroying evidence, if somebody like Guillam got hold of it. And if you come up on a charge, you can kiss living in England goodbye! If Guillam doesn't see to it, I bloody well will!'

'Hasn't Guillam got it by now?'

'I went direct to N Division and got a not very bright detective named Evans up to Mulcahy's place with a couple of constables, and so far it's an N Division matter. I told Evans we had an informer who said there was a body – now, that won't last past Evans's first report, and it won't make it to the coroner, because N Division aren't simpletons – but it'll do for tonight and maybe tomorrow morning. By that time, if you're lucky, Evans will have his jaws tight around the case and he won't give it up to Guillam or the devil himself. Guillam'll hear about it like everybody else in a day or two, and that'll be that.'

'Thanks.'

'There'll be nothing to thank me for unless you tell the truth. Tell me and then tell Evans.'

'What's the truth?'

'Goddammit, Denton, don't try that! Your buttock's in the crack in the privy seat, and I'm not entirely out of it myself, thanks to you. Look – I didn't tell Evans that a gentleman author sent me a note about this body he found, but if I had, you'd be at N Division right now explaining all the hows and whys and wherefores.' Munro took a gulp of beer. 'I'm giving you a chance to tell them to me first.'

'Concoct a tale?'

'I'd punch another man for saying that to me. I don't concoct tales and I don't help other people concoct them. No, I want the truth. And the truth is what'll go into the case file.' He heaved his bulk up and stood facing Denton. 'You and I've been square with each other, haven't we? We seemed to hit it off.' He was embarrassed by this revelation. 'Don't make things worse – get it?'

'I looked through a crack in a wooden fence that runs alongside that tall brick building. I saw a body.'

'You can't see the body through the fence. I tried.'

'I'm taller than you are.'

'Don't do this, Denton!'

Denton sipped the brandy and, finding it too much, set it down. 'What is it you think I did?'

'You broke the lock on a trapdoor to the roof and climbed down to Mulcahy's window and saw him and then went into his room.'

'I broke no lock.'

'Denton, two people will testify they saw you in the building. I can put you there, man.'

'I was in the building – of course I was. And, yes, I found the stairs to the roof. But the padlock on the trap was already broken. I didn't break it.' He crossed the few feet to the window.

'And you went out on the roof!'

Denton, his back still to the policeman, was fingering a green cord that held back the velvet curtain. The cord was twisted like a rope, the surface shiny, but as his fingernail ran over it, individual fibres separated: the green silk was a kind of sheath that surrounded a stronger, more prosaic fibre. 'Did your Evans go over the roof?' he said to Munro.

'He broke the locks. He'd sent a constable over that gate – it didn't take a bloody genius to see he'd come out of that open window.'

'Then you don't need anything from me.' Denton was holding a shiny green fibre up to the gaslight and studying it. 'I didn't push the dead man out the window, and I didn't destroy any evidence anywhere, so I don't see what you're on about.' He turned to face Munro. 'Was it Mulcahy?'

'Of course it was.'

'And was it suicide?'

Munro gave him a shrewd look, then shook his head, perhaps in disgust, perhaps in disbelief. 'Evans likes the suicide idea. So does

Willey; Evans called him in as soon as I told him about the dead woman in the Minories. If there's no other evidence, Evans will go for a coroner's verdict of suicide while temporarily insane.' He stared up at Denton. 'Is there any other evidence I should know about?'

Denton dropped the green cord. 'Munro, I swear – *if* I was even in that room, I touched nothing and removed nothing. *I have no evidence.*'

'The coroner will sit on this on Saturday. You'll be called, and you'll by God testify. Under oath!'

'Fair enough.' It was Tuesday. 'You'll get your truth. Under oath.'

Munro shook his head again. 'You've got something; I know you've got something; and you won't tell me because you think it'll get to Georgie. Well, I'll admit he's behaved like a right ass, but that doesn't justify you withholding *anything*, Denton – all right, you don't have evidence! – any idea, any suspicion!'

'Do you believe Mulcahy killed himself?'

'Do you?'

Denton took two steps to the bookcase and back. 'Will Guillam?'

'Georgie'll be pleased as peaches and cream. Another crime that isn't the Ripper.'

'Mulcahy confessed in a suicide note?' He knew perfectly well what the note in the Inventorium said, but he wanted to see what Munro would say. Munro screwed his mouth up, looked up at Denton through shaggy brows and shook his head.

'You're damned devious,' Munro said. He drank some of the beer. In other words, just in case Denton actually hadn't been inside the Inventorium and seen the note, he wasn't saying anything, either.

Denton pulled the hassock closer to the green armchair in which Munro was sitting and lowered himself to it, putting himself in an apparently subservient, almost pleading position at Munro's knees. 'If Mulcahy murdered the girl and killed himself, who broke in here and tried to kill me?'

'Georgie will say it was a burglar and that's that.'

'What do you say?'

Munro eyed him, held up his glass to the light as if to look for lees, and said, 'I think that's a damned violent burglar. Even for London.'

'So you don't believe Mulcahy killed her.'

'I don't say that. Mulcahy's mind was unhinged – you said as much the night he came here.'

'With terror, not murder.'

'Your impression. Look, Denton—' Munro bent forward with the glass between his hands; the two men's heads were almost together and his voice fell very low. 'I know what you're thinking – it serves Willey's and Guillam's and even Evans's purposes to have Mulcahy the murderer. But that's not my way. I'm in this because you pulled me in. Now, look here – I'll keep your counsel until the inquest if you'll tell me what you have. Because by God, man, I know you have something.'

It was a kind of declaration of friendship, as real as if they had touched. Denton felt a lurch of memory, thought of his response to Janet Striker's story of her life: a desire to answer like with like. To accept what had been offered. When he spoke, his voice was even lower than Munro's, a conspiratorial rumble. 'I've nothing but an idea, and you already know that. That Mulcahy didn't kill her, and somebody else did,' he said. 'But no evidence.'

Munro was staring into his eyes. They were close enough to have kissed. His voice fell to match Denton's, almost a whisper. 'Why do you want to hold off until Saturday, then?'

'I was with a couple of young tarts who knew Stella Minter today. They told me a few things.' The man's eyes stared into his. Denton murmured, 'She'd been at a place called the Humphrey – unwed mothers. I'm trying to get in there to ask about her. Her real name was Ruth. She had a sister, younger. She seemed "educated". That's it – that's all of it.' He looked down at his own glass, swirled it, met Munro's eyes again. 'Give me until Saturday. And don't tell me to give the information to Willey or Guillam. They'll pitch it in a wire basket.' He put a finger on Munro's coat sleeve. 'You want to do something, look for evidence that Mulcahy was tortured.'

'*What?* You're daft. What, tortured to sign a suicide note? Not a chance.'

'Had he pissed himself? Was there shit in his trousers?'

'After falling four storeys, what do you think?'

'I think a man who was tortured would have soiled himself.'

'You're weaving stories, Denton.'

'You asked me what I think.' He waited. 'There going to be a post-mortem?'

'Evans won't ask for anything fancy. The man fell four storeys and he'd been down there a couple of days, at least.' Munro looked shrewd, one eybrow raised. 'What kind of torture?'

'Something that wouldn't show up easily after a four-storey fall.'

Their heads remained together, their breath mingling, the mixed smell of brandy and beer thick between them. After several seconds, Munro grunted, leaned back, drained his glass and put it down with a knock against the table. He threw himself back in the armchair. 'Torture! That would put the cat among the pigeons.' He sniffed, pressed on his eyes with thumb and fingers. 'I'm not even sure there'll be a post-mortem. Some local doc, if there is. Evans won't want to stir things up.' He stuck a fist under his chin. 'Your "burglar" breaks into Mulcahy's place, waits for him, then tortures him. Just to sign a suicide note?'

'To find out where he's been and who he's talked to.'

'Which is how he gets to you. Then – what? He tortures Mulcahy until he signs the suicide note and then throws him out of the window? Is that your tale?'

'Something like that.'

'What does he think Mulcahy told you?'

'I wish I knew. Not that wild tale about them being kids together.'

'Where is he now, your torturer?'

'Gone to ground.'

Munro tapped his fist against his chin and stared at the ceiling and abruptly burst into laughter. 'They'll say it's one of your novels, Denton!'

Denton shrugged. 'It's what I think, anyway.'

Munro struggled out of his chair and put a hand on Denton's shoulder. 'I'll try to put a bee in Evans's bonnet about a careful PM. I can't float an idea of torture past him; he'd see that as interfering and he'd go into his shell. Evans is a plodder, workmanlike but sensitive as Bunthorne's bride. That's the best I can do. Maybe drop a hint if he's in a good mood. As for where the girl had her baby and her name and all—' He shook his head. 'Willey's got access to the same tarts you have; let him find out for himself. How'd you connect up with them, anyway?'

'A woman I know.'

Munro stared at him, tossed his head, pulled down his waistcoat as if straightening himself before leaving. Denton, still seated on the hassock, said, 'What do you think "educated" means to the girls who knew Stella Minter?'

'Not at the Varsity, I expect.' He was looking around. 'What the hell has your man done with my things?'

'Look in the alcove – up at the other end—' As Munro stamped off, Denton raised his voice to say, 'More schooling? Could she have got more schooling? Some sort of public school for girls?'

Munro's voice was muffled, and he came back down the room with his hat crooked on his head and a huge, hairy overcoat balled in his arm. 'Public school and she got herself in a fix and went to a home for unwed mamas? I doubt it. More likely—' He was struggling into the coat; Denton got up and tried to sort out the collar and a sleeve while Munro seemed to be trying to take them away from him. 'More likely – what the hell – more likely, she— You know, I might better do this myself. Just – there – well—' Munro shrugged himself into the huge coat. 'More likely she might have stayed on at school for a term or two. Mandatory they stay to age eleven – I know; I've got kids. But they can stay on as long as fourteen, depending on the school and how they do. That'd be "educated", I suppose, to one of the eleven-leavers. Especially if she came from a decent home, learned to speak more or less properly. This is England, Denton; you are how you sound.' He was buttoning the coat. 'Up to a point.'

170

'Who would know about girls who stay on at school?'

'You don't give up, do you? Metropolitan Schools Board, I suppose. But it'd be a needle in a haystack.'

'Like R. Mulcahy in the London directories. Metropolitan Schools Board another monument to red tape?'

'One of our finest.'

'How about helping me with a letter to cut through it?'

Munro thought about that, then tapped Denton's shoulder with his bowler. 'Your friend Hench-Rose is the man for that. He doesn't have to worry about a pension.' He started for the door, said, 'You heard he's come into money?'

'He told me.'

'Lucky sod. Except it isn't luck, is it? They leave it to each other – keep it in their hands and out of ours.' He jammed his hat on his big head and opened the door. 'You didn't hear me say that. Good night, Denton.'

Thirty seconds after the front door had closed, Atkins came up from seeing Munro out. Rupert, drooling and grinning, swayed along behind.

'Heard everything, did you?' Denton said.

'Enough.'

'You know what's going on, then.'

'I know you're in it up to your oxters again, is what I know! "I wash my hands of it," my hat!' Atkins picked up the beer bottle and glass. 'If you're keeping on with the late Mulcahy, I'm off to the agencies in the morning to list myself for a new place.'

'Oh, now—'

'I don't mind the odd rough-up as a condition of working for you, General, but I can't have my employer's bills going unpaid. I know it's fashionable, but I ain't the glass of fashion.'

'You've always been paid.'

'And mean to continue to be. It's me for the agents.'

Denton knew that if he had been an English gentleman he'd have given Atkins a tongue-lashing and sent him packing, but he felt a probably North American, certainly democratic, guilt towards Atkins. Or maybe it was simply the guilt of a man born to a dirt-poor Maine farmer. At any rate, to scold Atkins would be failure, as if he had abandoned some ideal of equality.

'Sergeant, not so fast! I'm meeting with my editor tomorrow. I mean to ask him for the money in my current account – the publishers always have money they're holding back. You know my business well enough for that; they pay up every six months, and it accumulates between times. They'll give it to me.'

'Enough?'

'There should be an American payment, royalties on the last book – there's others on the backlist—'

Atkins made a mock curtsey. 'I leap at the opportunity to remain with you, then. I'll wait to visit the agents until – Friday, how's that?'

'The day before Mulcahy's inquest.'

'Mulcahy! I wish I'd thrown him down the front steps and slammed the bleeding door!'

'Well, you didn't. As you say, I'm in Mulcahy up to the – what was the word—?'

'Oxters. What you'd call armpits.'

'All right, that deep, so, so are you. You might help, not snipe.'

'You was actually in his room, was you?'

'Of course I was.'

'But wouldn't tell that copper that.'

'I'll tell him before Saturday.' He caught Atkins's eye, was irritated to see it wink. 'He'll get the truth!'

'What'd I say? I didn't say nothing. So did Mulcahy leave a note saying he was going to kill himself and – what? He done the girl? – and then he threw himself out of the window. Very neat. Which you think is all night soil because the madman that crowned me did the nasty to him and made him write? And then threw him out of the window. God!'

Denton thought of what that fall must have been like for the frightened little man – if he'd still been alive – and winced. His own memory of the roof and the imp was still too sharp.

'Well, then,' Atkins said, 'what did you find that you wouldn't tell the copper about?'

'Nothing.' He saw Atkins's disgust. 'All I can do is work back from the girl – her real name, her sister. If we find who she was, maybe we'll find her lover, boyfriend, whatever he was.'

'Another needle, another haystack.'

'She'd given birth within the year – say last December. That would make her pregnant the previous March at the earliest. Say she ran away from home in her fourth or fifth month – August or September, perhaps. Or, if the condition didn't show, maybe as late as October. It might show up in the school records.'

'You're hopeless, you are.' Atkins shook his head. 'I suppose you mean to spend more money on it? 'Course you do. Well, it's yours to throw away. Until Friday.' He went up the room, grumbling to the dog. 'Best officer I ever worked for, throws me away like the Orient pearl! A fool and his money, Rupert – lucky you're a dog. Bloody hell.' He turned at the door that opened on his stairway, light spilling up from below and casting a huge shadow. 'Mind you see that editor tomorrow, Colonel! Time is short.'

In the morning, Denton sprawled among the newspapers in his armchair, sipping tea and looking for articles about Mulcahy. They were disappointingly small, except in one sensational rag ('Man's Corpse Found Fifty Feet from Busy Street – Lay There for Four Days – Jumped to Ghastly Death'), suggesting third-string reporters cadging details from police desks, not from anybody who had actually been on the scene. *The Times* buried the story deep inside and barely raised its voice above a hieratic murmur:

MAN'S BODY FOUND IN ISLINGTON

The dead body of a man identified as Regis Mulcahy, instrument maker, was discovered yesterday behind a hoarding in Islington. Metropolitan police refused to give details, but an open window four storeys above appears to have indicated the spot from which the victim may have precipitated. A coroner's jury will sit on the matter on Saturday.

'They make it sound like he slipped on a patch of mud,' Atkins said. 'Nothing about suicide, is there?'

'They're keeping the note to themselves. God knows why.'

'Nail it down at the inquest before they give it to the papers – "death by his own hand while temporarily insane", then give a juicy account of him killing the girl. What'd the note say?'

'He loved her.' Denton cocked an eye at Atkins. 'Not a word to your pals at the Lamb, mind.'

'What d'you take me for?' Atkins gathered up the dishes. 'Time you was dressed to go and see your publisher, isn't it? Money don't wait, you know, Colonel.'

Denton had sent his editor a note asking to see him at eleven. It wasn't a meeting he wanted to have: he hated asking for anything, especially money; he hated having to admit that his book was in the trash. Still—

'He must needs go whom the devil driveth,' he said. He clambered out of the chair.

CHAPTER FIFTEEN

'Horrors! Horrors, Denton! I want horrors.'

Diapason Lang had been his English editor since Denton's second book. Lang was older than Denton, almost emaciated, his skin taut over his cheekbones but ruddy with good health. His father had been a noted organist, hence the first name. Denton liked him well enough but found Lang's seemingly wilful mislabelling of his books as 'horror' irritating. More than irritating, in fact.

He had come to his publishers by way of Mrs Johnson's, charging her again to mobilize her women for an assault on the Metropolitan Schools Board. She had, with a toughness she usually masked, pointed out that the women hadn't been paid in full as yet. Embarrassed, Denton had stood at her door and counted out notes, then coins, not finding it easy to make up the total. 'The bonus – for finding each Mulcahy – ah, I'll bring that by another time—' He had walked away very quickly.

And so he had come to his publishers. The firm was in a narrow building off Fleet Street, only two houses from the one once occupied by Izaak Walton; it had a look of untidiness that correctly embodied the business it housed: door jambs tilted, floors sagged, cracks in the plaster had become so institutionalized that baseboards had been cut to accommodate them. Yet the firm itself was a good one with a notable backlist in fiction and botany, the combination pure accident, the reasons no longer remembered. Diapason Lang had been with them for more than thirty years and was in good part responsible for the fiction list. A type not unknown among editors, he often misunderstood the books he selected but selected well, nonetheless. Like his saying now, 'Horrors, Denton! I want horrors!' Then he leaned forward and said, as if they were friends with a common passion, '*You* know!'

In fact, Denton didn't know. He would never have told Lang that he was there because if he didn't get some money, his manservant was going to leave him; and he hadn't yet had the gumption to tell Lang that he had decided to abandon the book that he was due to deliver in three months. Or – the worst – that he nonetheless wanted another advance. 'I'm never quite sure what you mean by "horror",' he muttered. Playing for time.

Denton hadn't started out to be a horror writer – if that's what he was, and he didn't see it – or in fact to be a writer at all. All he'd managed to become after the war was a failing young farmer who didn't know he was failing, able to keep going by not adding up his debts. Then, after he failed completely and everything was gone, his wife dead and his sons sent off to his sister because he had failed as a father, too, he had gone farther west and rattled about, done his marshalling, gone on to California. Then he'd begun writing because his head was so stuffed with sorrow he thought it would burst, and he had had to get it out. He had written half of a novel called *William Read* before he realized it was self-pitying claptrap – more failure. Then, disciplining the self-pity by realizing that it was not the same thing as sorrow, he had begun to set down experiences as if he were writing instructions on how to harness a team to a plough, and the result was *The Demon of the Plains*. That first novel ended with the farmer-hero hanging himself in the barn he had built with his own hands, and his body being wrapped in a horse blanket, already frozen, and stacked with the cordwood until the ground might thaw enough to bury him. Denton had found his method: a plain, unfeeling style that embodied appalling events.

The Demon of the Plains had given him a reputation beyond America. The French had made comparisons to Poe (whom he despised), the English to Le Fanu (whom he didn't know). In fact, he saw no horror in *The Demon of the Plains* except the horror of solitude and unending labour and failure, and the hero's sense that a force, a demon or perhaps a ghost of the Indians who had lived there, persecuted him. Denton thought he had made it clear that the demon was only in the character's mind, a way of making the untractable and the appalling comprehensible, but the word 'demon' set people going. When his second book, *At Battle's End*, proved to have ghosts in it (who were not ghosts to him but fantasies of the war-maddened hero's collapse), the word 'horror' was everywhere in the reviews. At Lang's urging (at that time not yet met in the attenuated flesh, expressed as a letter to his American publisher), his third book was titled *Jonas Sniden's Horrors*, and it was compared favourably to the Stevenson of *Dr Jekyll and Mr Hyde*. Diapason Lang, when they finally met in the late nineties, had told him he was the best horror writer in the English language.

It had made Denton squirm.

Now Lang bent forward over his desk. 'We English *love* horrors. It comes from hiding everything from us as children; we have dreadful nightmares. Unaskable questions answered out of our imaginations. Do you know my picture of the nightmare?'

Lang had spoken of it before, so of course he knew it; Lang in fact had a print on the wall, was pointing at it with a bony finger without turning his eyes towards it. Elihu Vedder. Denton nodded. 'I suppose it refers to something sexual,' Denton said. It showed a hideous figure – demonic but certainly male – crouching over a nude woman in a bed. He thought of Janet Striker's idea of men and women.

Lang looked pained. 'Americans are so much more outspoken than we are.' Now he glanced at the painting. 'Perhaps – perhaps. You think she's having a nightmare about the sex act itself?' His voice was high, a bit cracked. 'Fearing it? All women do, you know.'

'Not knowing what it is, more likely. But possessed by it.'

'It isn't titled "Desire", my boy. I've never asked a woman what she thought the painting meant. Nor would I, of course.' He tittered. Lang's sexual preferences were matters of speculation but no evidence.

Denton smiled. 'I don't think it's just children you English keep things from.'

'There are some things one doesn't mention. To women, I mean.'

Denton thought that Lang travelled in the wrong circles. Among Emma Gosden's friends, anything could be said; the same was true among the artists who clustered at the Café Royal. Denton looked again at the painting. And, he suspected, anything could be said to Janet Striker. 'I had a man tell me recently that he'd been watching another man cut a woman's throat while coupled with her. Maybe that's what the nightmare is.'

Lang blinked. 'Ah. Mmm.' He grew cheerful. 'Might be a book in that.'

'The sex act itself a kind of murder,' Denton said, still looking at the picture. Like his wedding night. The blood, of course. He shook the idea off. 'I wanted to see you, Lang.'

'Yes, yes, yes, and I wanted to see you! I have an idea – a *horrible* idea!' He cackled. 'But routine business first – how's the new book coming?'

There it was. Denton looked into his eyes, pursed his lips, said, 'I've thrown it into the trash.'

Lang tried blankness, then a titter – it must be an American joke, he seemed to imply – then severity. 'You're not serious.'

'I'm afraid I am.' He tried to explain the revelation he'd had while he'd talked with Janet Striker – the woman not a real woman, the marriage all wrong, the book sick at its very heart.

'I've always thought your women quite good,' Lang moaned. Denton didn't say that this might say more about Lang than about Denton's women, or that perhaps Hench-Rose had been right when he'd said Denton knew nothing about women. He brushed residual drops of rain from his hat, which was on his lap; the warren of publishing offices had no place for visitors' clothes – hardly room for visitors, in fact. 'But you *can't* have thrown it out,' Lang said. 'You can't!'

'I did.'

'It's what *first* novelists do. It's what *young* men do.'

'I have a better idea. A new book.'

'Pull it out of the trash, Denton, we can salvage it. *I* can salvage it.'

Denton waved a hand. 'I've got a better idea, I told you.' Lang looked sick, then profoundly annoyed, then, with an effort, attentive – that smiling, wide-eyed look that women learn to put on when men talk. 'It's called *The Machine*,' Denton said.

'*The Machine*. A little too H. G. Wells?'

Denton sketched it for him: a young husband and wife who build together the machine that destroys them, their marriage.

'But a machine? I'd think something organic would be more likely, something that they nurture—'

'I see it as a machine.'

'Well – of course, it's your idea—' Lang sounded dubious. 'Rather fashionable, perhaps – machines, I mean. Fear of the clang and bang of modern life, the dark Satanic mills, all that. *Motor cars.*' He raised his eyebrows and waved a hand. 'But a machine as the embodiment of horror, Denton—'

'Oh, forget your damned horror!'

'Oh, dear, oh, no—'

'Lang, the horror is something you've all read into the books. I write about people, about suffering, about—'

Lang waved his fingers again. 'Writers don't know what they write about. It's horror, take my word for it. But a machine, oh dear—' He tittered. 'Perhaps a runaway motor car with an evil engine? Something that goes about murdering people at crossings? You're not amused, I see.'

Denton put his hands on the desk and spoke slowly and with great emphasis. 'Lang, I need money!'

'Ah. Oh, it's that way.'

'It's exactly that way.'

Lang looked about as if for a secret exit he'd forgotten the exact location of. 'I suppose we could do something—'

'My royalty account.'

'Statements aren't due yet, you know.'

'But there's money you owe me. There always is!'

'Well, I suppose— Oh, well, of course – as you're such a pillar of the backlist—' He rang a little bell. Heavy footsteps sounded in the corridor, and a young man materialized in the doorway. Lang cleared his throat. 'Ask Mr Frewn to step around, please, Meer.'

The heavy footsteps went away, went up some stairs, faded. Lang tapped on his desk. He said, 'Frewn doesn't get around as well as he used to.' Denton put his coat and hat on the floor and crossed his legs. When slow, light footsteps sounded overhead, Lang smiled and murmured, 'There we are,' but it was another long silence, marked by increasingly loud footsteps, before a white-haired, bent man looked in. His black suit hung on him, giving him the look of a wet raven. In a surprisingly deep voice, he said, 'You wanted something?'

'Mr Denton – you know Mr Denton, one of our best authors, one of our *most successful* authors, Frewn – would like a cheque for the balance current in his account.'

The old man stared at Lang, then at Denton, as if he couldn't believe his own rather large ears. 'A *cheque?*'

'Yes. Now, we've done this before, Mr Frewn – you remember, I'm sure, it can't have been more than half a dozen years ago—'

Frewn shook his head. 'Never heard of such a thing.'

Lang smirked at Denton and muttered, 'We've done it again and again; it's just—' He smiled at Frewn. 'Of course there's a balance in Mr Denton's account, Mr Frewn.'

'No idea.'

'There is, of course there is. So please, have Mr French write a cheque for the full amount for Mr Denton to take with him when he goes.'

The old man sucked in his breath. '*Today?*'

'Now, Mr Frewn, this is too bad of you – of course, today – look here, I'm writing it out so you'll have something on paper, eh? An authorization, all right? "Balance of account to this date, to be paid by cheque—" That's quite clear, eh?'

He came around the desk and put the sheet of paper into the old man's hand; he brought it close to his eyes, and his breath hissed in again. He muttered something, in which Denton caught only 'ruin', and patted off up the corridor, his voice mumbling on. Denton saw, as he left the doorway, that he was wearing carpet slippers that were almost hidden by remarkably long trousers, possibly somebody else's, possibly his own from some earlier, longer-legged self.

'Mr Frewn is rather a character,' Lang said. 'Quite the stuff of legend in the firm. I don't know what we'd do without him.'

'He's the accountant?'

'Ah, no, not— He's actually a, mm, the— Mmm. Hard to explain – rather a vestige of an older way of—' He smiled wanly. 'He's a kind of bottleneck for anything one wants to get done.' Almost to himself, he added, 'But things do get done. They really do. You'll see—' He tapped some more on his desk, looked at *The Nightmare*, and, apparently taking inspiration from it, said, 'Well, this gets no books written. Not to pry, Denton, but – do you want to pay us back the advance on the book you've so rashly thrown away?'

'Of course I don't. I can't.'

'Then—'

'Then I want to substitute *The Machine* for it.'

Lang made a face. 'On the same schedule?'

'Can't be done. There isn't time, Lang.'

'No-o-o, there isn't. Well, I suppose an extension of six months—'

'During which I have to live.'

'One would assume so, yes. Yes, quite.' Lang squeezed the bridge of his nose between long, thin fingers. 'You're going to ask for more money, aren't you?'

'It won't hurt you to raise the advance on the book I trashed to something like what my books actually command.'

Lang rapped on the desk with a knuckle. Denton fell silent; it was as if the editor had called a meeting to order. Lang gave another, more decisive rap, and sat up very straight. 'I told you I have an idea,' he said.

Denton looked at him, thinking, *My God, not a book idea—*

'Transylvania,' Lang announced. He sat back. 'There!'

'Transylvania.' Denton had the vaguest idea what Transylvania was. He lacked the British elite's passion for travel, usually for sport – Norway for salmon, Switzerland and beyond for game – and lacked as well the Latin that might have led him to make a translation of the word. But he was honest. 'What is Transylvania?'

'Oh, my dear!' Lang tittered. 'It's the far end of the Alps, the place everyone was thinking of when they used to write about haunted castles and ghastly vales and mountain peaks. A place of legend and lore – and peasants who speak unintelligible languages.' He leaned forward. 'Werewolves! *Vampires!*'

'Fairy tales.'

'My dear Denton, I've made a *study* of vampires. Hardly fairy tales, unless very grown-up ones. Did you know there was a play called *The Vampire* way back before our dear Queen was crowned? Now Stoker's gone and written *Dracula*, and why, oh, why didn't you get in ahead of him with the idea?'

Denton shook his head. 'Sucking blood? Doesn't interest me.' Although the mind, he thought, of somebody who *believed* he was a vampire would interest him.

'The vampire in the old play had to marry a virgin before sunrise or *die*. Doesn't that touch a chord in you, man?' It didn't, and Denton let his stoic face say so, although he had a brief and bad moment thinking again about his wedding night. Lang put a pleading note into his voice. 'They *rise from the dead!*'

'So do my debts. I need money, Lang.' He stuck out his lips under his drooping moustache. 'I can try to finish *The Machine* in four months, how's that?' Lang made a face and Denton said without conviction, 'I suppose I could write about this man who told me he'd seen a tart murdered – it was in the newspapers—'

'You cannot! I won't let you.' Lang sounded like a petulant child. 'Real crime's been quite taken over by the lowest kind of journalist; you'd ruin your reputation by associating with it. *Prostitutes*. Oh! Unspeakable mutilations, I suppose.' He shuddered. 'No, no – I want *literary* material, Denton, *artistic* material. Like the vampire. You may say it's sensational, and that of course is part of the point, but I believe that there is something in vampirism that *touches* us. Deeply. Blood – insatiability – the application of great force in pursuit of a perverse sort of desire—' He sighed and leaned back. 'You don't see it, I can tell. Oh, dear.' He groaned, then threw himself forward to try again. 'Vampirism could do for you what She-who-must-be-obeyed did for Rider Haggard!'

'Haggard is claptrap.'

'But claptrap that touches our souls, Denton! There's something *in* his fantastic stuff – something – repellent but irresistible— Something – forbidden— A profoundly desirable horror, how's that?'

'Like *The Nightmare*?' Denton said.

'Oh-h-h—' Lang twisted in his chair in disappointment. 'Look here, I'll talk to Gwen –' Gwen was Wilfred Gweneth, the publisher – 'about your, ah, financial *crise*, and I think I can get his approval to offer you expenses plus your usual for a *travel* book about Transylvania. *The Land of Horrors*. We'd make up an itinerary to take you to the sites of legends and great tales – Mary Shelley's *Frankenstein*, for example; now you'll say that's Switzerland, I know, but—'

In fact Denton didn't know; he'd never read *Frankenstein*.

'– you could start there, poetic licence, and move through Bavaria – isn't that Monk Lewis territory? – and so on, and then concentrate on Transylvania. You apply your great powers of description, that relentless honesty that makes your work so—'

'Lang, I don't give a hoot about legends and lore.'

'You're so very *vexing* sometimes. You *Realist*! Have you had lunch? We could walk to my club and have a late lunch and talk this over—'

'I have to meet with some women about a girl who may have left school to get herself murdered. One of the desirable horrors of everyday life in London.' He boosted his hat and coat back to his lap. 'A travel book – me?'

Lang gave him a suddenly shrewd look. 'Money, my dear – you need money.'

'You told me once never to write for money.'

'I am an idealist. But you are a Realist. And your creditors are literalists – they want twenty shillings in the pound. Come now,

Denton – I'm sure I can get you the money for the right sort of book. A nice journey down the Rhine, some pleasant miles by train – Continental railways are perfectly acceptable, I believe – then, to be sure, a somewhat less luxurious mode of travel in Transylvania itself – colourful local carts, an ancient post-chaise, even a sledge—'

Denton was both angry and amused. He got up slowly and then went behind his chair and leaned his forearms on the back. Grinning none too pleasantly, he said, 'A *motor car* to Whatylsvania.'

'That's an appalling idea.'

'I'll do it that way – but that's the only way I'll do it!' Denton didn't really mean it; it was simply something to say to vent his sense of outrage. '*By Motor Car to the Land of Vampires.*'

'A motor car! That would ruin everything! It's so – so disgustingly *modern.*'

'All the more reason. Combine the new with the old, progress with legend and lore.' He was improvising, atypically manic. 'Start from Paris – I could pick up a car there; they've got thousands of them – and head east. Outrunning the werewolves in a Panhard Twelve! Flying over the steppe on a fuel of garlic and potato spirits!'

Lang was shaking his head and saying that Denton was being *too bad*, simply *too bad*. 'You're ragging me; I see what you're doing. This is your little joke. Well, laugh. Surely you don't think we'd buy you a motor car. Gwen doesn't mind taking a flyer, but he's not an outright idiot. *Motor Car to the Land of Vampires*, indeed!'

'Buy the machine, keep ownership while I do the trip, sell it after. Famous motor car, used in Mr Denton's best-selling new book. You'd make a fortune, Lang.'

Lang sniffed. 'I despise commerce and everything it stands for.'

'But you want me to write a book about horrors because it will sell.'

Lang waved a hand. He put the left side of his jaw on the thumb and three fingers of his left hand, the index finger resting on his leathery cheek, and he said in a dry voice, 'What I had envisioned was some colourful narrative of native carts toiling up the Alps.'

'It might come to that. Motor cars aren't much in mountains – you did say there were mountains?'

'The Transylvanian Alps, which are always represented as the teeth of a saw.'

'Motor-car enthusiasts would love it – conquering the mountains. Breakdowns while the werewolves howl. Tyre punctures in the dead of night. We run out of petrol and are pulled across the snow by a team of vampires!'

'Yes, make a joke of it. You're the one who needs money, not I.'

Denton hunched farther towards him over the chair back. 'So I am.' He'd forgotten. He shrugged. 'Actually, it doesn't seem such a bad idea, Lang.'

'My dear Denton, *motor cars*—! They're simply – *vulgar*.'

Denton heaved himself up, laughing. He saw Lang's confusion and guffawed again. 'So am I! So am I!'

Then Mr Frewn padded in with Denton's cheque, which was for seven pounds, five and ninepence. Denton, having expected ten times as much, swore and rushed out.

The women whom Mrs Johnson had assembled in her meagre parlour were both sceptical and respectful – he had paid up, after all – and in their way not so different from the young whores he had met with Janet Striker. A similar embarrassment and distrust were plain. Denton tried to outline what he wanted, tried to guess what the Schools Board's bureaucracy would be, but one of the women had worked there and could tell the others all about it, ignoring him.

'The lists are handwritten, a lot of them in an appalling fist, and not at all up to date. The school heads aren't held to the fire; they've too much else to do.'

When it was clear that he wanted them to search the lists for all of Greater London for the previous school year, one of them laughed outright. When he had difficulty explaining what he wanted, another muttered, 'A local habitation and a name,' and told the rest that what he meant was that they were to search for a girl named Ruth, who'd left school and who had a sister named Rebecca, who hadn't.

'And if we find them?'

'Then you'll find their last name.'

'And then? We'll have only their school. Only their town or village or ward.'

'Then you'll look for the family in the post office directories.'

He suggested the census, but they pointed out that the last census had been taken in 1891. He went home and told Atkins not to talk to him. Using pantomime, Atkins pointed him to the mail, then took himself downstairs with his nose in the air, like a music-hall comedian playing a duke.

Among the bills was a note from Janet Striker. They could visit the Humphrey the next afternoon; she suggested that he bring a letter attesting to his character.

Tomorrow would be Thursday. It would leave him only one day to find the man who had now killed both the girl named Ruth and the man named Mulcahy. On Saturday, if he found nothing, they would rule that Mulcahy had killed himself while insane, and they would close the case. He could go on looking after that, but he sensed that he would not. He was about out of threads to wind on his spool.

And why did it matter? Mulcahy was nothing to him, nor the girl, either. Yet he thought of that thin body laid out on the table at Bart's, the murderer's crude gashes and the surgeon's neat cuts, the men in rows around her watching, watching – and he cared.

Lang wanted horrors. This would be horror, indeed – meaningless, dehumanizing death, and his own failure to do anything about it.

He went out again to Hector Hench-Rose to ask for a character letter. Hench-Rose surprised him by being abject, ashamed of his behaviour of the other day and pathetically ready to do anything Denton wanted. Denton thought it odd – Hench-Rose was now wealthy, presumably powerful or about to be, with a parliamentary seat at his bidding, an estate, tenants, forelock-tugging ghillies, as Denton imagined them – but Hench-Rose seemed desperate for Denton's approval. Odd, very odd – a need to have the world without exception approve of him? Or something special about Denton? Or was he, as Denton was with Atkins, caught in some snare of pride? Denton, at any rate, liked him better for his discomfort; the truth was, he had felt more comfortable with Hench-Rose the modestly poor ex-officer than Hench-Rose the wealthy baronet.

'My distinct pleasure, old man,' Hench-Rose said as he scrawled a note under the letterhead of the Metropolitan Police. 'Want me to order the populace to cooperate or ask them? Asking's probably better – flies and vinegar, and so on. Hmm?' Hench-Rose proposed supper, promised no jokes, but Denton said he couldn't, had too much to do. A drink at the club? Would Denton consider an expedition for salmon in February? Denton's thought had been that the one thing he needed, money, and the one thing Hench-Rose had, money, was the one thing he couldn't ask Hench-Rose for, although he suspected that Hector would have started flinging notes on the desk if he had asked for them. But Denton couldn't ask.

CHAPTER SIXTEEN

The Humphrey Institution for the Betterment of Unwanted Children was in Hackney Wick, the Lea running almost at its back, although Denton wasn't to realize that the river was there until almost the end of his visit. It was a wet, raw day, a fine drizzle boring down like somebody's bad intentions, drenching and chill. It smudged distance as if a fog, and as Denton and Mrs Striker jogged through unfamiliar streets in a mouldy cab, he thought that this might be one idea of hell, going on endlessly towards a dimly glimpsed nowhere in the damp discomfort of the grave.

'I'd like a hot drink,' he said, when neither of them had spoken for several minutes.

'A lap robe would do.'

He grunted. They were crawling through mean streets where nothing else seemed to move. It was as if the entire city had died. He shrugged himself deeper into his overcoat. 'Poor people around here,' he said. 'Not enough money to buy a louse a wrestling jacket.'

'Your grandmother? Definitely Irish.'

'Scotch and proud of it. Worshipped John Knox, believed a blow was healthy for a child, saw the world as good or bad, white or black, all choices made on principle.'

'Hard to live with?'

He hesitated. He had been talking for the sake of talking; now he had to think about what to say next. 'It sounds peculiar, but she wasn't. Sure, she whacked us now and then, but she was protective.'

'Against the world?'

'Against my father.' It came out slowly, an intimate admission, painful. 'She used her hands; he used a piece of firewood.'

'On you?'

'Until I was as big as he was. Then he tried it and—' He shrugged himself into the coat again, shivered. 'We fought.' His shoulders were trembling with cold, perhaps with memory. He wondered what she would do if he moved closer to her for warmth. 'I joined the army when I was fifteen.'

'I wouldn't think they'd take you so young.'

'I lied. I was big for my age. My grandmother signed the paper.' He smiled. 'She could read and write. That's Scotch, not Irish.'

'Was that her way of protecting you?'

He looked out at the wet house fronts, an ironmonger's shop, a scene of water and soot and lifelessness. He had never told anybody this story. 'It was for my sister.' He felt the fine drizzle on his cheek, realized his trousers were getting damp. 'She was fourteen. She didn't have a dowry. I got a hundred dollars for enlisting.'

'For her?'

'There was somebody would marry her if she could bring some money. My grandmother told me to do it.'

Janet Striker was silent, staring, too, at the bleak, blackened bricks. Then she said, 'Because of your father?'

The question surprised him, an insight straight to his secret self. He had his hands in his overcoat pockets, his long legs stretched out; he moved, a kind of squirming, acutely uncomfortable. 'My mother died,' he said uncertainly, almost stammering, 'when we were kids. Fever. Josie never had a proper mother. My grandmother—' The memory was acutely painful.

'Did you understand what was going on?'

'I don't think anything was really—' He trailed off. He couldn't picture his sister as she was at that time; had he erased her? But he had 'understood' something about her – and about his father. He mumbled, so low he was never sure she heard him, 'My father said things to Josie – he started touching her—' He trailed off. 'My grandmother said it was best for Josie to get married.'

She looked at him. 'You could have been killed in the war.' As if she distrusted the effect of her eyes, she turned her head towards the street and leaned back. 'Did it work out for her?'

'She had four kids of her own and raised my two, after— When I couldn't. She seems content enough.'

'And you? The army suited you?'

It made him laugh, part of it relief at the changed subject. 'The army doesn't give you a chance to say if it *suits* you. It was war. I went in a private and came out a temporary lieutenant, got shot at and paraded and marched and starved and rained on and thrown into battles like a piece of meat to a hungry dog. No, it didn't suit me. But I did it, and it took me off the farm. The army showed me another way to survive than trying to grow potatoes out of rocks. The army's a hard mother and a hard teacher, but there's worse. Far worse.'

'Were you ever wounded?'

'Twice. A musket ball and a bayonet. Neither fatal. Obviously.'

They rode along. The horse's hooves rang on the wet street, now wider, opening out into the newer, less impoverished neighbour-hoods beyond Victoria Park. A few living beings appeared – a dog, a shopkeeper in a doorway, two women with a child. Janet Striker said, 'And your father?'

'He married again. He left the farm to his widow.' Ahead, he saw a grey building, stone, neoclassical by suggestion but essentially ugly; he guessed it was the Humphrey Institution. 'I never went back,' he said.

'And your grandmother?'

'I hated my father. But after I'd knocked around a while—' He stared at the ugly buildings along the cab's slow progress. 'Poverty drove him mad. He worked and worked—' He made a gesture of futility. 'My grandmother died while I was away. There was nothing for me to go back to.' But there had been his sister – why hadn't he gone back to her?

The cab pulled up opposite the building's entrance, a set of double doors up two stone steps from the street. The doors looked as if they had been closed and locked when the building had gone up, closing in a prison for lifers. They got out and he paid the driver, a hopeless-looking man who neither smiled nor thanked him but wiped his wet nose on his sleeve and passed his whip over the horse's back as if too tired to lift it higher, and the cab passed away into the drizzle like a phantom. Denton and Mrs Striker were left standing on the narrow pavement, the only living things to be seen in a square of which the Humphrey took up an entire side; inside an iron fence, five leafless trees reached up like blackened hands. There was a smell, familiar but unpleasant, that Denton couldn't place.

'Hell,' he said.

'Its entrance, anyway.' She went up the steps and yanked a bell-pull. After several seconds, she said, 'Somebody's coming.' She looked down at him, seeming to gauge him, to estimate just what he might be. 'I think you're a far better man than I first took you for,' she said. The door opened.

The smell was laundry. Wet laundry, soap, steam. The Humphrey Institution for the Betterment of Unwanted Children operated a sizeable commercial laundry that took up the entire rear of the stone building and two sheds behind, as well; it was in the laundry that the wayward ones earned their keep.

'Work is their salvation,' the woman who met them said. 'They scrub clean their souls.' The words seemed to be quotations that she had by rote. Mrs Opdyke was a big woman in a black dress a few years out of fashion, the cut emphasizing her bigness, her chest and abdomen, as if she were some male figure of power whose belly was called a 'corporation', but within this was a less certain woman. She was tall, made taller by grey hair piled on her head in lustreless clumps like dirty wool, and she stooped as if her tallness was a burden. Keys jingled at her waist, suggested a saintly emblem – the keeper of the keys – that was belied by her wary eyes. Denton wondered if she was afraid for her job. 'We would do them a disservice to indulge them.' She meant the women.

'How many live here?' Mrs Striker said.

'We have close to a hundred at any particular time.' She bent her head to look at Mrs Striker; there was a sense of expecting contradiction. 'But they don't *live* here. They are permitted to await the birth of their babies here.'

'And then—?'

'And then they must make their peace with the world, as we hope they have made their peace with Him who sees all transgression.'

'Do they understand transgression, do you think?'

'We always say, show me a young woman who is weeping in her bed, and we will show you a soul yearning for its maker.' Again, she seemed to be quoting somebody else.

'And the infants?' Denton said.

Mrs Opdyke glanced at him. She flinched, as if he had surprised her, perhaps the rarity of his maleness. 'Forgive me, sir,' she said. She had a big voice, big like the rest of her, but raspy, as if she had used it too much. 'I caught your name but not your purpose.'

'I'm looking for a young woman who gave birth here.'

'Are you a relative? Her father?' She seemed ready to disbelieve him. 'An uncle?'

'The young woman is dead. I'm trying to find what happened to her.'

'It seems to me you already know what happened to her, if, as you say, she's dead.' She dropped her chin and looked at him over the top of silver-rimmed glasses. 'Are you a policeman?'

'Mr Denton is a famous author,' Janet Striker said. 'He is acting philanthropically.'

They were standing in a lobby that lay immediately behind the front doors, a long, bleak room almost without furniture but overseen by the life-size portraits of two elderly men in the fashions of the seventies. Denton had been wondering which of them was the founding Humphrey, had decided that the more severe and lifeless of the two probably was he, the other being altogether too ruddy and too plump. Now, he smiled at Mrs Opdyke, trying to look philanthropical.

'We encourage good works,' the woman said, but the idea of philanthropy seemed to worry her, and she frowned. 'Many gentlemen are able to practise good works through us. Many.' She turned to stare at the portrait that Denton had *not* chosen as that of the onlie begetter. 'We were founded by a man. Men serve on our board and our inspection committee.' She turned back to stare at Denton. 'Good works are one route to bliss.'

Denton was confounded by this – not the idea, but *bliss*, which seemed to him dated and poetic and, anyway, unattainable – and he said weakly, trying to smile, '"Inasmuch as ye have done it unto one of the least of these my brethren, ye have done it unto me."'

Mrs Opdyke's frown deepened. 'I don't see the aptness of that,' she said. For the first time, she seemed stirred to something other than quotation, and her cheeks reddened. 'Forgive me if I miss something, but the aptness of that escapes me, escapes me altogether. Is this intellectualism?' Before he could answer, she rushed on. 'There is too much intellectualism. We don't allow our girls to engage in it.' She turned to Mrs Striker as if for support, common understanding. 'Our charity is based on the founder's ideas and is straightforward and simple – work and prayer. "Work to weariness, pray to tears." We always say that to new intakes, and I say it to each as she leaves. Work and pray, work and pray, I tell them – your lives are over, you are ruined, pray for release, nothing more can be expected.' She raised a hand towards the portrait. 'Our founding philosophy.'

'I was quoting scripture,' Denton said.

'Were you ironic? We detest irony. It is part of intellectualism.'

'The girl's real name was Ruth,' Mrs Striker said in the voice of somebody bringing a meeting to order. 'But after she left here, she called herself Stella Minter.'

Some of the colour left the woman's face and she seemed to slump back to her normal posture. Denton had the sense that she saw him as an enemy, even *the* enemy – because of the men who had got her women pregnant? Or, more likely, because of the founder and the all-male inspection committee? At any rate, she was far more at ease with Janet Striker, to whom she now said in a lower, almost confiding voice, 'I don't understand this gentleman's interest. I have a duty to protect the, mm, the premises.'

Mrs Striker produced the two letters they had prepared, the one from Hench-Rose about Denton's sterling character, one from her own organization. 'He is above reproach,' she said.

Mrs Opdyke removed her glasses to read the letters. Her eyes looked undefended, timid. 'Well—' she said. 'Well.' She read both letters twice, then folded them and handed them back. 'Well – very well.'

'What can you tell us?' Janet Striker said.

'I can't say anything, standing here in public.' Only the three of them were in the draughty hall; nobody else had passed through it; nothing suggested that anybody else even had access to it. 'We must go to my office. I'm sure you will want to see the work rooms and other, other – facilities.' She had replaced her glasses, now looked at the portrait of the founder as if hoping the subject might step down and order them to leave.

'Who's the other fellow?' Denton said. He jerked his head towards the other, more severe figure that he had thought the founder.

Mrs Opdyke stared at it. She drew a breath. 'My predecessor,' she said. She turned away and moved towards a door at the far end of the long room, seeming to move on rollers, her skirts giving no hint of legs moving beneath them. Denton, wanting to get away as fast as possible, still cold and miserable, looked at Janet Striker. He was astonished to see her wink.

The visit became a kind of tour of inspection. Denton thought that they missed nothing except the water closets and perhaps some secret room where the staff sipped gin and smoked cigars. They were shown the kitchens, the dormitories, the chapel (stark), the classroom (girls under twelve were given two hours of lessons a day), the refectory (scrubbed wood tables, grey-green walls, a lectern for 'improving lectures' while the women ate), the lying-in rooms, the nursery, the infirmary, the morgue. 'Yes, we have our deaths,' Mrs Opdyke sighed. 'Little deaths, mostly.' She waved a hand at a pile of fresh wooden boxes that might have held papers but were infant coffins.

Ten women, all young, had been nursing babies in the nursery. They had thirty minutes off from their work, four times a day, Mrs

Opdyke said. None of the young women looked at them. Their faces were healthy but tired, perhaps sullen. The kitchens told him in part why: great piles of cabbages lay on central tables; more young women with the same healthy, unhappy look were splitting the cabbage heads with cleavers, then chopping them and flinging the pieces into huge pots.

'Boiled salt beef once a week,' Mrs Opdyke said. 'Fish on Fridays. Milk, four glasses a day, the last before bed with patent malt extract. Porridge found to be excellent for their general health. We do not approve of sauces.'

The lying-in rooms were closed to Denton, but he was allowed into a huge space where babies, new-born to four months, lay in rows like bullets in a belt. Surprisingly few of them were crying. Two women in striped caps and dark aprons moved among them but never picked one up.

'They get no coddling?' Janet Striker asked.

'They are fed, changed, kept warm. Mothers don't feed their own babies; they don't know which are theirs, in fact. No, we don't believe in coddling. These children face a harsh world.'

'Where?' Denton said. 'Adoption?'

Mrs Opdyke turned eyes as weary as those of any of the women on him. 'One in twenty is adopted. The rest go to institutions.'

Coming out of the babies' room, they met a spry, angular man who was introduced as Mr Orkwright of the Eugenical Sterilization Society. He shook hands and passed on, grinning at the staff women, who all seemed to know him. Janet Striker stared after him and murmured to Denton, 'Trolling for victims.' If Mrs Opdyke heard her, she said nothing.

The work rooms were last. These were, in fact, the two wooden buildings that stood behind the stone structure and were the source of the smell that hung over the place and spilled into the square.

'Our clients are some of the finest firms in London,' Mrs Opdyke said.

Women, mostly visibly pregnant and with their sleeves pushed up and their damp hair falling down, stood over vats full of clothes; others turned the handles of big wringers; still others, using sticks like oversized broom handles, lifted wet cloth from the vats and turned it, stirring the water and the thick mass within. The air was wet; condensation clouded every window and lay as big drops on every cool surface; the floor was slippery. The women, like the others inside, had the ruddy, almost chubby look of the founder, like well-fed animals readying for slaughter.

'Work and weep,' Janet Striker said. 'Dear God.'

In a separate room, six women sat at mangles and foot-pumped the dry cloth over big, heated rollers. Against the far wall, ten more, their bellies prominent, stood over ten ironing boards, running ten sad irons over shirts and collars. In the middle of the room, an oversized stove held a coal fire; irons and mangle cores stood all over its surface. The temperature, Denton guessed, was close to ninety.

'Are they paid?' he asked.

'Of course not.'

'I'd have thought there was a law.'

'We are a charitable institution.'

Going back out through one of the wash houses, his eye was caught by a white bit of cloth hanging from a rolling basket between the wringers. It was damp but not soaked; he picked it up, smoothed it, recognized the Napoleonic emblem and the regal R – it was a napkin from the Café Royal. Perhaps he had wiped his mouth on it a couple of evenings ago. He dropped it back into the basket.

'I think that now you have seen everything,' Mrs Opdyke said.

'Enough, at least,' Janet Striker said. She smiled. 'Enough, I mean, to appreciate what you do here. May we talk about Stella Minter now?'

Mrs Opdyke had perhaps hoped that they would somehow not get to the moment – perhaps they would change their minds, or die – but she tried to straighten her slumped shoulders and led them back into the stone building and along a wood-floored, scarred corridor to the front, again into the lobby with the portraits, and through a door in the far side. Beyond it was a dark-panelled office that might have suited a particularly hard-hearted banker: everything was dark, nothing was comfortable, not even Mrs Opdyke's chair. Boxes with faded orange ties and labels rose up the walls on shelves perhaps meant once for books; only two black-and-white engravings relieved what wall space was left, one of them, Denton guessed, having something to do with Rome and rapine, the other too dark to see. A single window, barred, heavily draped in old brown velour, looked out on the square, where it was still raining.

Denton was assigned a chair too low for him, so that he sat with his knees up and his hat beside him; Mrs Striker got something a little better, although hard and straight. Mrs Opdyke, seating herself behind a black oak desk that seemed to have the mass and weight of a safe, sighed, as if to say *So we've come to this ugly business at last*, and said, 'What was it you wanted, again?'

'A young woman named Ruth, also known as Stella Minter,' Janet Striker said.

'Ruth. We've had several Ruths. Many, in fact. We don't use last names here. Ruth or Stella, then.'

She bent and unlocked a drawer with one of her keys, removed a large ledger, opened it and, forehead propped on her left hand, began to turn pages. Janet Striker told her when they thought Stella Minter's baby had been born, about when they thought she had left the institution. Mrs Opdyke made ambiguous sounds and turned a number of pages at once. Denton described the girl as he had seen her in the operating theatre and as she had appeared in Mulcahy's photograph, and Mrs Opdyke seemed to recognize her, for she sniffed mightily. She seemed then to be looking for something specific, not browsing names, and she seemed to have found it when she said, her voice almost angry, 'Oh, *yes*.'

Denton tried to sit forward, almost fell off his inadequate chair. 'You have her?'

'A bad child. An *evil* child.'

'Ruth?'

'I could hardly forget her – rebellious, ungrateful, vicious. What happened to her, then? Did she take to the streets? I predicted that she would – dirt seeking dirt. Did she?' She glowered at Denton.

'If it is through *that* connection that you know her, you will leave at once, sir.'

'She was murdered, ma'am. I learned of her only after she was dead.'

Mrs Opdyke nodded. 'Murdered. Of course.' She shook her head, spoke to Mrs Striker. 'It was foreordained. We could see it in her from the first week she was with us. Twice, I considered ordering her out. A bad child.'

'Do you have her name?'

'Ruth – what I have is Ruth. I told you, we don't deal in last names. They come to us with their histories behind them; they leave us, we hope, with no history whatsoever. If they return to families, that is their business; if they go elsewhere—' she waved several fingers – 'so be it. We are here to accept the innocents they have carried. Did she go on the streets?'

'She did.'

'She was far too knowing for a girl of her age. A sly girl, her language sometimes highly offensive. I would say she had already been on the streets, but she insisted not. But they lie, of course – they lie.'

'Who was the father of her child?'

Mrs Opdyke held up both hands. 'We dare not ask; if we learn such a thing, it is locked up in our hearts and never committed to paper!' She looked in her book again, rubbing her eyes. She read off the dates when Ruth had arrived and left; Denton wrote them down on a cuff. 'Demerits, demerits, punishment, *severe* punishment, more demerits – a thoroughly bad young woman.' She raised her head. 'She disappeared two weeks after she gave birth. We make every effort to keep track of our women, but this isn't a prison. She went out through the laundry gate, we think – chatted up one of the draymen, I should imagine. She could be charming when she chose. Without a backward glance or a thought of her child, I'm sure.'

They asked more questions – Ruth's age, anything she'd said about parents or family, any idea of where she'd come from, anything – but Mrs Opdyke's ledger was unyielding.

'Was the birth registered?' Mrs Striker said.

'Our legal adviser keeps a record by date and sex, but without names. No other formality is required by law.' She drew her lips in. 'He makes an annual report to the registry office.'

'And her baby?'

'I am not at liberty to tell you. The child is long gone from here, at any rate. And from its mother, to its eternal benefit.' She put her glasses back on. 'Murdered, you say.'

'Quite savagely.'

'I shall not be so unkind as to say that she put herself beyond God's mercy with her wilfulness.'

Denton smiled. '"And one of them shall not fall on the ground without your Father."'

She glanced quickly at him; her cheeks reddened again. 'Sparrow me no sparrows, sir – she was an evil girl and I was glad to see the last of her. Rather than concern yourself with an object of God's justice, you might turn your attention to good works.'

Denton struggled to his feet. 'Finding the girl's murderer is a good work, ma'am. Maybe I'm an agent of God's interest in sparrows, too – in my way.'

She stared at him, then said, 'Hmmp,' and stood. Janet Striker tried to ask another question, but Mrs Opdyke said, 'You know everything I am able to tell you,' and moved towards the door.

Out on the front steps with the door closed behind them, they stood close together and stared into the rain. Janet Striker took his arm and held it as if glad for its warmth. 'What a God-awful place,' she said. 'Do you suppose it was a day like this when she ran off? Oh, God, if she'd only come to me!'

He wondered how they were going to get a cab. He didn't want to think of what it would be like to be out on such a day with no money, no warm clothes, nothing. 'I wonder how she found this place,' he said.

'Maybe she lived nearby.'

'Or the opposite – she wanted to be as far as she could from – from whatever it was.'

They stared into the rain. 'We didn't learn much,' she said.

Abruptly, as if she'd just realized what she'd done, she jerked her hand out of the crook of his arm.

Nothing moved. The smell of laundry was thick, troubling. She said, 'I wish one of us had brought an umbrella.'

CHAPTER SEVENTEEN

His house felt icy. The door closed with a slam like thunder, echoed by the real thing from somewhere south of the river, a great rolling crescendo like kettledrums. Water dripped from his soaked hat, and he whipped it off. Mrs Striker had been right; they should have had an umbrella. It had been difficult to find a cab, and they had both been wet and grumpy when at last he had dropped her at her office.

Atkins was standing near the alcove with his arms folded, watching the young would-be valet, Maude, who seemed to be operating a boat pump. For an instant, Denton thought there must be water in the sitting room; he even looked up at the ceiling. The idea was rejected almost as soon as he had it – the absurdity of using a pump in a room, the lack of damp on the ceiling – and he tossed his hat at the green armchair and tried to struggle out of his coat. Atkins, who knew where he had been going that afternoon, came forward and said, 'Looks like the baby factory wasn't no help, am I right?'

'You're always right, aren't you?' Free of the wet coat, Denton looked through his mail, found an envelope marked '*Deliver by hand*' from Mrs Johnson, inside a note that said only, '*Nothing yet.*'

Yet seemed unjustifiably hopeful.

He tossed the envelopes aside and leaned forward to stare at Maude and the contraption he was working. 'What the hell?' he said.

'Patent vacuum sweeper,' Atkins said with what sounded like pride. 'Very latest thing.'

Relieved of the coat, Denton took a couple of steps towards Maude, whose face was running with sweat and whose breath was rasping as he pumped the wooden handle of a long metal tube that did, in fact, look like a boat pump. Maude looked up, misery on his childish face.

'Labour-saving miracle,' Atkins said.

'Doesn't seem to be saving Maude any labour.'

'He's not used to it. That device is going to put the housemaid out of business. It's going to liberate a generation from the drudgery of beating rugs. It's going to—'

'You've got money in it, is that it?'

Atkins bristled. 'How could any intelligent person not see the advantages of it?'

'Another of your investments? Sergeant, Sergeant—!'

Atkins draped his coat over the fire screen and scampered to the device. Pushing Maude aside, he bent down and twisted a latch in the metal tube and a door popped open. Behind it was a grey mass of fibres that looked like something a mouse had put together against the winter. 'Look!' Atkins cried. 'Look!'

Denton bent to look. 'Rats or squirrels?' he said.

Atkins grabbed the mass with his fingers and pulled it out. 'Dirt!' he shouted. Dust and fibres floated out into the room. 'From your floor, General! Your carpets! You think you can get that kind of filth out of a carpet with a broom? Have another think, then – only the Patent Pneumatic Vacuum Sweeper can pull fibres, dust, dirt, lint, microbes, insect bodies, effluvia—'

Denton put his face close to the mass. 'Dog hairs,' he said. 'Looks like there's a lot of Rupert in there, too.' He straightened. 'You mean to say this contraption actually got this stuff from our floors?'

'Every bit.' Atkins dropped the mass into a wastebasket and then began spreading newspapers, on which he dumped more from the tube as he talked. 'This thing *works*, Colonel. It sells itself. Trust me. Every young matron behind every front door in every new terrace in London wants one of these the moment I open that door and show her the results. Magic!'

'You're already peddling it?'

'I've made a few experimental visits in Maida Vale and associated areas.' He held up a hand. 'On my evenings off!'

'Well don't use "effluvia" when you sell it, or they'll think you're saying something naughty.' Denton picked the device up, saw that it had a sucker-like mouth that rested on the floor. At the other end was an oar-shaped wooden handle attached to a shaft that ran down into the metal tube. It was in fact a simple pump – push the handle down, a plunger descended, forcing air out through two valves; pull it back up and the valves closed and a weak vacuum was created at the mouth. Denton pumped it a couple of times, saw why Maude was sweating. 'The new matrons are going to get damned tired,' he said. He pumped again. 'The handle's wrong – who wants a handle in line with the shaft when you have to pull? You want something at right angles, like a shovel handle.'

Atkins shrugged. 'We got a price on some oars. Of course, we intend to refine the product as the company grows.'

'How much have you got in it?'

'Ten pounds – fifty per cent share.'

Denton put the mouth down on the carpet, pumped twice, felt a suction that drew the end of the carpet off the floor. He handed it to Maude, who had collapsed in a chair. 'Makes more sense to put an electric motor in it.'

'We thought of that already,' Atkins said with a hint of getting one over. 'Won't work – to pull the handle up, you need a great thing like a derrick working at the back.'

'You don't need to pull the handle up. There are rotary pumps, aren't there?'

Atkins stared at him, then took out a notebook and a pencil and scribbled. 'Good idea, Captain. Mind –' he held up the pencil – 'it was given freely in conversation! Maude here's a witness – no royalty or percentage due for it.'

Denton grunted and turned back to the morning's mail. More bills. A quick survey of them told him that he owed more money than he had. 'Damn,' he muttered. His real concern was paying the women who were working for Mrs Johnson. If he hadn't bought this house, he'd be all right. Or if he'd been able to finish the book that was due, he'd be all right. Or if somebody owed him money—

He grabbed the wet overcoat from the fire screen. 'I'm going out!' he shouted down the room.

'You're soaking wet!'

'It suits my mood.' He clapped the wet hat back on his head and was off.

Money, money, money. He went into the Domino Room for the first time since Wilde's funeral and nodded to a few people he knew but headed straight towards the Glasshouse Street side. It was Frank Harris he wanted – he intended to get his reimbursement for the Paris trip.

'Been looking for you,' Denton said, sinking into a chair. Harris was sitting alone at a small table, staring at an empty brandy glass.

Harris looked up. It seemed to take him a couple of seconds to realize who Denton was; then his usual look of malevolence vanished and the corners of his eyes crinkled. Denton's face must have told him everything, because Harris frowned, then shrugged and grinned. 'I have some money for you,' he said.

This was so surprising that Denton thought Harris must think he was somebody else. His prepared speech of appeal and outrage stuck in his throat.

Harris began to pull money from various pockets and drop it on the table. 'Took up a collection. To cover your expenses in the Paris expedition. People surprisingly generous. You sent flowers, did you? Damned good of you to go at all – can't have you out of pocket—' He grinned. 'Actually, I think you'll do rather well out of it—'

'The flowers were as ugly as anything I've ever seen, but at least they were flowers. The card said, "Form the writters and artistes du Café Royale" – with an e.'

'Was the funeral dreadful? Was it all terribly Catholic and *French*?'

Denton told him about the almost empty church, the miles-long ride to the cemetery.

'Well, I'm grateful. Oscar liked to get his Johnson into funny places, but he was an *artist!*' Harris pushed the crumpled notes and a pile of coins across the table. 'Genius forgives everything.'

'That's what people say about Wagner.'

'You're not a Wagnerite?'

'Lot of people screaming at each other in German. Pretentious horseballs.'

'Don't let Shaw hear you say that. You get along with Shaw?'

Denton was stacking the notes, mentally counting as he started to sort the coins, thinking he could pay off the shilling-apiece R. Mulcahys. 'He's delighted to meet me every time we're introduced.'

'Doesn't remember you?' Harris laughed. 'Bit of a snob, actually. Typical Fabian – help the working-man, bring culture to the middle class, but Oh, please, don't introduce me to one of them!'

Denton ordered a coffee and told Harris he was in a foul mood because he'd about run out of direction in his murdered-tart business, and he'd spent a dismal afternoon in a home for unwed mothers; meanwhile, he was counting money and checking off in his head the bills he could now pay.

'Go back to writing.'

Denton made a face. 'Actually, I've got an idea that might pay, thought you might like to buy it. Spent the afternoon at this God-awful place where the murdered girl had her baby. No wonder she preferred the streets – I've seen better prisons. I've *worked* in better prisons!'

Harris got his hungry look. 'Anything in it for me? An exposé, something of that sort? I'm between magazines right now but I'm starting a new one, a society mag, in the spring. This suitable?'

'Would take some digging.'

'Getting down in the night soil and raking out diamonds? Like the man in *Pilgrim's Progress*? Upper class love that, so long as they're not expected to do anything.'

'Pregnant women being worked like slaves, would that entertain them?'

Harris shook his head. 'Social reform, not a good idea for my audience. They want something that they can tut-tut over before they have their after-dinner belch.' Harris played with the foot of his wine glass. 'Sex in it?'

'Well, the women got pregnant, didn't they? But there's exploitation, injustice, ill-treatment—'

Harris shook his head. 'Maybe if we got somebody inside. Maybe a woman journalist, posing as in the family way. Nice angle, that, actually.' He signalled to a waiter. 'Have another?'

'The Café gets its linen done there. You could buttonhole Oddenino, get him to tell you what he pays. They're making money, and the women aren't getting it.'

But Harris wasn't listening. 'Actually, I could write it myself under a female pseudonym. I wrote as Mrs F. B. Strether a couple of times; I could resurrect her. I always saw her as a middle-aged woman with glasses and a huge *embonpoint*. Somebody younger for this, though – "How I Was Enslaved by My Unborn Babe," by Elsie Dampknickers. "Your Clean Linen is My Dirty Secret – Chained to a Mangle by a Moment's Indiscretion!"' He banged on his glass for a waiter. 'Sounds rather fun. You'd supply the eyewitness account of the deplorable conditions in this workhouse, and I could fabricate a couple of pathetic tales from recent inmates, with some titillation about how they got – do you say "knocked up"? In my days in Chicago people did. Wouldn't need to put somebody inside, in that case. Might even pick up one or two of the post-partum graduates with a well-placed advert, in fact. But maybe not worth it. Get into trouble, advertising for women. Slant it towards the solid middle class – much moral indignation about child labour and the rights of women, "even women and girls who, though fallen, deserve better of England." Eh? Catches the tone, you think? Maybe *Pearson's* would take it. I'll give you, let's say, ten per cent for the idea and the information.'

'I could write it myself.'

'Not your manor, Denton; you haven't got the properly low touch. Fifteen per cent?'

'Half,' Denton said, pocketing more than twenty pounds and

admitting to himself that Harris could write such a piece better than he could.

'That's an unkind cut.' Harris hunched over his empty glass. 'A quarter.' He glared at Denton. 'Not in advance, you understand. What's this about, then? You on your uppers, Denton?'

Denton shrugged.

'Then let's talk about something more your line: the new mag might lay out a few pounds for something about this murder that fascinates you so. Or what about this attack you suffered? Fellow stabbed you, didn't he? Have to treat it in a genteel fashion – gentleman astonished by lower-class lack of civility. Invasion of your premises, working-class brute, collapse of civilization. Eh?'

'Actually, he tried to *kill* me. Twice in one night.'

'"Famous Author's Night With a Monster", something like that?'

'You make it sound as if we went to bed.'

Harris waved a hand. 'Scare the knickers off the well-to-do – if it could happen to you, it could happen to them.' He smiled at the fresh glass that finally appeared in front of him. 'Actually, if you're hard up, there's a market for a, shall I say, more *specific* account of your girl's murder. Something, shall we say, *graphic*. Not for a, mmm, press you'd recognize – rather special, by subscription, your own name wouldn't go on it – but spiced up with a few scenes of the right sort – first-person account of her early experiences, properly moist descriptions of what your man saw through his peephole on several occasions, then the gory murder – "What Mulcahy Saw." Mmm. Nice. I'd take only ten per cent.'

'Pornography, in short.'

'Well, what's in a name, Denton? We mustn't think ourselves too grand for other forms of art when we're hard up. It is art, you know – what is it if it isn't art? It has its laws, its forms, its necessities.'

'Old men in bedrooms with their tongues hanging out.'

'And not just their tongues. Old *and* young, Denton, middle-aged and juvenile. What a sheltered life you've led! *All* men, my friend, *all* men. Pornography is simply what we all think but few dare to put on paper.'

'I know a woman who says that all men hate women.'

'We do! Yet we can't live without them! They have that magical thing, that locus of fantasy, the monosyllable that begins with C, and *we want it!* We must have it! And they hide it, protect it, make us scrape and plead and marry them to get at it – and we hate them for it! The only workable relationship between men and women is prostitution; the only revealing literary form is pornography. The woman who told you that we hate them is very wise – do I know her?'

Denton hesitated; there was the usual proscription against discussing women, plus some personal distaste in this case. 'A woman named Janet Striker.'

'Oh, I know of her! Formidable woman. Remarkable. Rather like the Hindoo whatsit – the thing that rolls over you—'

'Juggernaut.'

'That's the one. Janet Striker, my God. A virago with a halo. However did you meet her?'

'She took me to the Humphrey this afternoon.'

'Yes, her line – saving women from men. Unwed mothers our speciality. Hopeless, but no more so than Fabianism.' Harris drank, his eyes now rather red, his voice rising as he warmed up for the argumentative stage of his evening. 'It's *all* hopeless. It's all going to crash, Denton! All this do-gooding, all this genteel putting of plasters on suppurating sores. Crash! Down it's all going to come – you, me, magazines, pornography – out with us, I say, good riddance. Down come all the old ways of doing things, all the hypocrisy, all the good intentions, all the pretence that gentility is anything but greed tinted golden – there's a fall coming, a plunge into an abyss – inevitable! Some cataclysm, some disaster – pestilence, famine, *war*! It'll all be over in a quarter of a century!'

'That's pessimistic.'

'On the contrary, I'm an optimist. It can't go on. *We* can't go on. Look at the hellhole you just visited – and that's supposed to be for some greater good! Look around you – look at England's *artists*. Dear God, Jesus laughs – artists! Art should be the hope of creation, and what do we have? The RA! Alma-Tadema! Composers who've never heard a minor key in their lives – little nightingale farts about their *feelings* while contemplating bloody nature! Poets with their lips pressed to the warm buttocks of privilege! Henley – dear God – "I am the master of my fate; I am the captain of my soul"!' He held up his fists like a strong man, braced his head and back like a hero on a horse. 'Dum-de-de-dum-dum dum de-dum! All the rhythm of a drunkard tupping a slattern in an alley.' He shook his angry head. 'Let it end! New art – we must have new art that's jangled, mysterious, incantatory, wondrous – paintings that don't have subjects, poems that don't scan, novels about life as it's never been—!' He glared at Denton. 'You don't believe a word I say.'

'I have an editor who wants me to write a book about vampires.'

'Editors will be the first to be swept away!' Harris laughed; Denton joined in. 'How would twenty-five pounds do for the rights to the baby-factory idea plus an article for the new mag on your night of horror?'

'In advance?'

Harris laughed again.

Denton got to his feet then, muttering about having to go; he could take only so much of Harris when he started to rant. After several long seconds, Harris said, looking away from him, 'It's all coming to an end. It has to. All going to crash.' He looked up. 'Indignation's no good, Denton. The Fabians, the do-gooders, the reformers – not a hope! We need a revolution.' He lifted his almost empty glass. 'Or another drink.' He waved at a waiter.

Atkins was asleep in the armchair when Denton came into the sitting room; the sergeant's swathed head glowed in the gaslight. As Denton closed the door, Atkins jerked awake and said, 'Been thinking.'

'Congratulations.'

'Stella Minter. Why'd she call herself that?'

'I thought you were fed up with all that.'

Atkins was helping him with his overcoat. 'You gave me a bit of an idea about the vacuum broom; thought I'd return the compliment. Why'd she call herself Stella Minter if her name was Ruth?'

'She had to call herself something.'

'Yes, but why that? Plucked it out of the air? Saw it on a hoarding? Name of somebody she knew?'

'Spill it, Sergeant.'

Atkins shook out the coat. 'What do blokes do when they want to be somebody else? Had a pal, had something going with a woman he'd met – never told her his real name so's she wouldn't come after him when it was over. What name'd he use? Mother's maiden! What name does everybody what had a ma and pa have in the back of his head? Mother's maiden. Bet you can tell me right now what your mother's maiden name was, Captain.'

'Burrell.'

'See? Mine's was Orping. Just for a test, I asked the Infant Phenomenon. His's was Smithers. So.'

'So?'

'So when you haven't got a certainty, you go for a likelihood. The likelihood is your tart's mother's name was Minter. Forget the Stella; that could of come from anywhere – sort of trashy-classy name a young girl might wish to give herself airs with. But Minter – that could be her mother.'

'So all we have to do is locate all the women whose maiden name is Minter, and ask them if they had a daughter named Ruth. Shall we start a house-to-house canvass? Perhaps you could ask the new matrons as you peddle the boat pump.'

'The registry, General, the registry! You know how old the girl was – about sixteen, correct? She was the oldest kid, right?'

'So far as I know.'

'So what's the likelihood? That ma and pa were married seventeen, eighteen years ago. You could try to locate the marriage, but lots of marriages don't get into the registry; they're in the parish records or they're nowhere at all. So what's the likelihood? That the birth *was* registered, and I know for a great, bleeding fact that the mother's maiden name *and* the child's name go on the registry, *as does* pa's name. So there you got them!'

'All I have to do is search the thousands of babies born over two or three years.'

'Work of a day for a smart chap.'

'And then what? Go through the directories again with the father's name? You know how many R. Mulcahys they found? Suppose it's a name like Smith or Jones or Wright or, or—'

Atkins stared at him. 'You're giving up, aren't you?'

'It's what you've been asking me to do, isn't it?'

'I've been asking you to make some money, *which* I thought Mulcahy was in the way of, but if you just give up Mulcahy altogether without a fight, you'll sigh and moan and hang about here making life miserable for me, and what's the good of that? Have a little backbone, Major! It's only one more day's work!'

'You going to do it for me?'

Atkins apparently had already thought it through. 'The Infant Phenomenon's capable of handling the house for one day. I'll read him the manual of arms and the courts-martial act before I go. All right? Does that nod mean yes? Yes?'

Denton sighed, grunted.

'Good! Wonderful! Your enthusiasm is like cool drink to a dying man.' Atkins turned away, then swung back, dropped his voice as if there might be somebody else in the house who could overhear. 'By the way, young Maude's wages are due, if you've got some loose coins about you—'

CHAPTER EIGHTEEN

Friday morning.

He was awake before Atkins and went downstairs to make his own tea in the alcove, the spirit stove giving off a blue light, the space otherwise dark with the sun not yet up. The window had been replaced at the bottom of the stairs, but the curtains hadn't yet been put up; now he wanted sunlight to spill through, to tell him that the world was alive, life was good. Instead, he stared at the blue flame, smelled the burning alcohol, thought of the man who had lunged out of this place to attack him. He rubbed his arm. Where was Stella Minter's murderer now? Awake, walking the streets in fear? Sleeping the sleep of the just? More likely the latter, Denton thought, a man without conscience, reckless, clever. He'd have seen the newspaper stories about Mulcahy's body, have been watching for them, sure that when the body and the note were found, he'd be safe.

Denton took the tea back up the stairs, sipping as he went, feeling it scald his upper lip; he went on past the bedroom floor and up to the attic, stumbling in the darkness. Was the murderer up here, waiting? No, he'd finished with Denton; he'd realized days ago that if Denton had learned anything from Mulcahy, something would have happened. Now, he thought he was safe. Or all but safe. One day, one fact, one sliver of investigative hope lay between him and complete escape. And it depended not on Denton but on five women making lists and, perhaps, a soldier-servant with an idea.

Not much.

He began to row on the contraption. The attic was cold and silent; the rowlocks groaned. He hadn't slept well – dreams, long waking periods, tormenting himself with old failures, old humiliations, back to childhood: failure begat failure. His mind turned, twisted, raced, as it had done all night, reviewing everything about the killings, about Mulcahy, the attack, the girl. On and on, over and over. Nothing new, nothing helpful.

He lifted the hundredweight dumb-bell, then lighter weights for each hand. Nothing, nothing, nothing. He fired the parlour pistols, then stood with the old percussion Colt held at arm's length. Two minutes, three minutes, four, the sights never wavering from the target. He would have liked to shoot the killer right then. Wonderful if he had loomed out of the shadows – a bullet in the eye.

But the killer, he thought, was laughing at him, sitting at his breakfast by now, devouring sausage and potatoes and laughing around the half-chewed food.

Nothing, nothing, nothing.

Atkins was full of himself and his mission, so was particularly hard on Maude that morning, bustling and hectoring, outfitting himself with pads of paper and pencils from Denton's desk, appropriating a never-used leather dispatch case given him by Emma Gosden ('You're never going to use this, right? Shame to waste it'), then swaggering off like a diplomatic courier in mufti. He left behind him an already exhausted Maude who was, as well, terrified of Rupert and who armed himself with biscuits to be produced whenever the dog looked his way.

'I think I'd like to give notice, sir,' Maude said as he was taking away Denton's breakfast dishes.

Mindful that he hadn't paid him, Denton produced a half-crown he'd got from Harris and said, 'Could it wait until Monday? It's rather a bad time.'

'Oh – yes, sir – it's only Mr Atkins is so— He's very particular.'

'One of his finest qualities.'

'And then there's the dog, sir.'

'Just keep feeding him biscuits, Maude; he'll follow you around like a, mmm, dog.'

Maude picked up the coin. 'Is this in addition to my wages, sir?'

Denton sighed, muttered that it must be.

Maude went down the room with the tray; behind him, Rupert kept pace, anticipating a feed before they reached the bottom of the stairs.

Denton could do nothing until other people brought him information. It was no good to say that he should have done the work himself; in fact, he had neither the knowledge nor the patience to do what Mrs Johnson's five women were doing. Nor could he cause them to work faster, although he now tried to do just that: he walked over to Mrs Johnson's and asked how the work was coming, then muttered that today was their last day.

'They're entirely aware of the day, Mr Denton!' Mrs Johnson, although she depended on him for work, was not going to suffer him gladly. 'It does no good to try to hurry them along.'

'I wasn't trying to, mmm, hurry... Only thinking, maybe something had, you know, uh—' He held out a ten-pound note. 'This is for the earlier, um, bonus.' She seemed relieved to get it but didn't encourage him. He said, 'If you hear anything—'

'Mr Denton, I will send you a message by hand the *instant* I know something! Until then—' She stood in her doorway like a guard, her chin out.

'Yes, mmm, of course – you're right, yes— But the instant, the moment – as soon as you know something— Time really is of the—'

She thanked him for the money and closed the door.

So Denton walked. He thought he walked aimlessly but found himself outside the building that housed Mulcahy's Inventorium. No policeman was visible, so he crossed the street, at first merely pacing along the building's front, then going in and retracing his steps of days before. The massive locks were gone from Mulcahy's door, replaced by two smaller ones and a sign that said 'Metropolitan

Police Premises – Keep Away'. The broken lock to the roof had been replaced, as well, the new one sealed with a police tag. Nobody was about, however, and nobody approached him either coming in or going out: the press had lost any little interest it might once have had in R. Mulcahy.

He walked some more, now down City Road to the warren of old streets around Finsbury, then found himself standing in the Minories and going on to look again at the door behind which Stella Minter had been killed. The constable and the police sign were gone; the room, he was sure, was as yet untenanted by anybody else. Might never be, in fact, its legend now too grim.

He turned away and walked through the new terraces south of Victoria Park, the great bustle of the city nowhere more visible than in these places where building was going on – carts moving in and out, carpenters on scaffolding, a monstrous machine driving piles somewhere with a sound like that from the forge behind Mulcahy's building – a sense of impending event, of something coming for which great hurry and noise were necessary. The event being, he supposed, the building of the next London terrace, and the next, and the next.

Then he walked back to Mrs Johnson's ('I haven't been home; I thought you might have— No? I'm so sorry—') then west, then north on York Road along the cattle market and into Kentish Town and another plain where new houses would soon stand. At the moment, it was a field of rubble, devastation as if after a war, with, near the centre, a raw, new building rising alone – a pub. This one was faced with green tile that shone in the white winter light. As he watched, two wagons, looking like centipedes, crawled in from the farthest corner, and men the size of ants began to unload iron pipe, the rattle and clink of the pipes reaching him long after he had seen them dropped. Then he headed south again, paralleling the Great Northern and Midland lines, the trains pounding along the tracks towards the depots in Camden and Somers Towns, their whistles like screams. He wondered how anybody in the new houses that would rise could tolerate the noise, then realized that they could and would: this was *London*, where there must be always more noise, more houses, more workers – cram them in, stuff them in, subject them to noise and dirt – they will accept it and then love it. He thought of Harris's *We need a revolution* and thought, *No, he's wrong; this is what we want, this world, this noise, this bustle.* This *is the revolution.*

In the midst of which a murderer, eating his morning sausage, laughs.

I could do with a revolution that took him with it, Denton thought, heading homeward. But perhaps, then, the murderer was the revolution Harris wanted, an eruption of violence from within. It would be a grim revolution, then. Harris, he thought, had something more dramatic and final in mind.

He stopped again at his own house to ask Maude if any messages had come, learned none had, went off to Privatelli's to eat Italian food he didn't taste; then he walked on, down into the City, across the river (looking north, trying to see where Mulcahy's roof must be), crossing back over Waterloo Bridge, his legs tiring now, grateful for clocks that told him that the day was looking towards its end: grateful because it would be over soon, failure looked in the face, something else waiting up ahead.

And so he came back to his own house about four. He let himself in, took off his coat and hung it, walked up and down the long room, put water on for tea. Only then was there a sound from below – slow footsteps on the stairs (he whirled around, startled despite himself), then the door opening. It was Atkins, much chastened.

'My very own Isandhlwana,' he said. 'Disaster.'

Denton watched his last hope die but smiled to reassure him. 'Well – you tried.'

'Oh, yes, the saddest words of voice or pen, "I tried."' Atkins looked under Denton's arm. 'You making tea? Maude's got tea downstairs. Want some?'

'No, the water's hot; I'll make fresh.'

'Well, then. Pour me a half cup, if you will. My confidence in myself is shaken.'

They sat by the cold fireplace, Denton in his armchair. Atkins had dragged the hassock to the hearth and sat with his chin on his fists, staring into the cold grate. 'Bloody hell,' he said.

'No Stella Minter, then?'

'If you wanted grown women, maiden name of Minter, Stella, I could provide you with two! But neither had a girl child between 1883 and 1886, did they? I could provide you with several dozen ladies, maiden name Minter, who had girl children between 1883 and 1886, but none of them by name Ruth! And none of them match to any woman, maiden name of Minter, what had a baby girl she named Rebecca between 1885 and 1888. Now, I can give you two Rebeccas born to women whose maiden names were Minter, born in the right years, but they don't have older sisters, do they? Oh, brothers, oh, *yes*! They got brothers enough to relieve the siege of Ladysmith, but they don't have sisters! You follow me, General? My idea about the maiden names was bleeding stupid!'

'Now, now—' Denton made comforting noises that he didn't feel. He let Atkins sputter and run down, and, as sop to Atkins's vanity, he said, 'She lied. Not your fault.'

'Who lied?'

'Stella Minter. I suppose her real name wasn't Ruth any more than it was Stella – she lied when she used it at the Humphrey, and she lied when she told the other tart it was her name. She was a really frightened girl – not trusting anybody. It isn't your doing, Sergeant.'

'What, I spent the day looking for Ruth and there ain't no Ruth?'

'Ain't no Ruth and ain't no Rebecca, I suspect, and ain't no Stella Minter, either.'

Atkins pushed his chin harder against his fists and growled. 'Yes, *that* one there is! A Stella Minter there is.'

'Two, you said. Wrong age – they're mothers?'

'One yes, one no. A girl, born – I've got it written down some-place – it's in me dispatch case – born in the right years. Named Stella Minter – there she was, plain as currants in a cake. You do all those names, column after column, you forget what you're looking for. I'd already done the Minter maidens; I was doing baby Ruths, but I got confused or sleepy, God knows, and there's a Stella baby, father's name Minter, and I wrote it down. Stupid, I'm just stupid. It's a wonder you put up with me, Major.'

Denton stared at the angry servant's profile. The room was cold; he'd been feeling it for a quarter of an hour, only now realized it. 'Light the fire,' he said. He stood. 'I'm going out.'

'You just came in.'

'I want the information you took down about the infant Stella Minter. Chop-chop.'

Atkins looked up at him. 'What for?'

'Maybe we've been working on a wrong assumption. Maybe her name really *was* Stella Minter.'

Atkins got up slowly. He fetched matches from the mantel, bent over the grate, in which Maude had laid a fire that morning, then straightened. 'Bloody hell,' he said again. 'Now who's been stupid?'

'I want you to be there,' Denton said to Janet Striker, 'in case it really is the one. At best, it'll be telling somebody their daughter is dead.'

'Surely they've seen it in the paper.'

'You'd think. But people are funny – they could be recluses; they could just be people who don't want to know things. It was a very small notice.'

Mrs Striker raised her chin. 'They never reported her missing, if her name really was Stella Minter.'

'We don't know that.'

'*I* know that, Mr Denton. I get a list of missing women every month. I looked, the first time you visited me.' They were in her office, the workday coming to an end. She gestured at a scruffy stack of papers behind her. 'If it was her real name, you're dealing with people who never declared their daughter as missing.'

'Anyway, I'd like you to be there.'

She stared up at him, her face weary, the skin shiny as if she had a fever. 'You're going now?' He nodded. She looked at a watch pinned on her breast, looked around the office as if to see what was left to do. 'How far is it?' she said.

'Kilburn – off Kilburn High Road. Twenty-seven Balaclava Gardens. That's the address on the birth record, at any rate.'

'And they're still there?'

Her questions irritated him; he wanted to go, to get it done, even while he knew her doubts were good ones. 'I'll find out when I get there,' he growled.

She opened a drawer and burrowed under papers and took out a small, fat book. 'We shall see.' She turned pages, asked him to read off the address again, ran a finger down a page and up the next one, and said, 'Balaclava Gardens, number twenty-seven – Alfred Minter, licensed accountant.' She closed the book with a snap. 'Still there last year, at any rate.' She stood, tall and thin and weary-looking, then raised her voice to almost a shout. 'Sylvie, I shall be out on business. Answer the telephone, please.'

A heavy voice came from a surprisingly small woman on the far side of the office. 'Yes, Mrs Striker.'

'You think they'll just let us waltz in,' she said to Denton.

'I brought my police letter. You can tell them what a noble sort I am.'

'And who's going to tell them how wonderful *I* am?'

Balaclava Gardens was a terrace on the west side of Kilburn High Road beyond Shoot Up Hill. Denton recognized it as recent but not new, part of an estate developed long enough ago that the trees were nearing maturity and the front gardens looked obsessively trim and spiritless – the real gardens would be at the back. The cab had come along the edge of a more recent building site to reach the street: the area had been built up in stages, was now, he thought, almost complete.

Number 27 looked like all the others, was perhaps a touch nattier, its garden a notch more obsessive, but what set it well apart was the Headland Electric Dogcart parked in front, its rear axle attached by a chain to a ring in a concrete block.

'Bloke thinks it's a blooming horse!' the cabbie guffawed.

'Or he thinks his neighbours are thieves,' Denton said. He paid the man but asked him to come back in fifteen minutes 'just in case', as he murmured to Janet Striker. 'We don't want to get marooned in the wilds of Kilburn.'

'I can't make a living hanging about,' the cabbie said.

Denton gave him one of the coins he'd got from Harris. 'Find the pub, have one on me, come back.'

Mrs Striker was looking at the electric motor car. 'It's quite unusual,' she said.

'Small.'

'Look – there's not another on the street.'

'Maybe accountancy pays.'

'And likes to declare itself. I wonder, does he ever drive it, or does he leave it here to remind the neighbours of how successful he is?'

They turned to the house, a yellow brick in a terrace of identically built houses, now rather hysterically individualized by touches of paint, the occasional bit of sawn fancy-work under an eave, names like 'The Cedars' (next door, though there were no cedars). Denton had already seen the lace curtain in the front window of number 27 twitch; in that house at least – perhaps all up and down the street – an arrival by cab had been noticed.

'You do the talking,' Denton said.

'In heaven's name, why?'

'You do it better than me. Anyway, people trust a woman.'

They went up the short walk between two rows of bricks half-buried on the diagonal, two rows of rigorously trimmed box beyond them, English ivy and a monkey puzzle tree in each ten-by-twelve-foot plot. 'You expect too much of me,' she said.

'You can do anything, is what I think.'

She gave him a look – amused? annoyed? – and rang the bell. The door opened too quickly; the middle-aged woman behind it had been waiting. She was wearing a nondescript dress, but Mrs Striker seemed to know she was the maid (and would be the only maid in this house, and would live out somewhere) and wasn't the mistress. Denton wanted to say that this was a perfect example of her abilities, because he'd have got it wrong and thought her the mistress.

'We should like to call on Mr and Mrs Minter, if you please. Will you show us in?' She held out a calling card.

The maid frowned. Her face said that she was neither bright nor well paid, so why should she be forced to make a decision in such a matter? Then her face more or less collapsed, as if to say, *It's beyond me, it really is.* She said in a whisper, 'Wait, please.' And closed the door.

Janet Striker rolled her eyes. 'Not done,' she said softly. 'Poor frightened soul—!' A murmur of voices came from inside the house; Janet Striker smiled unpleasantly and said, 'Now she's being scolded. Mrs Minter will be saying, "What will the neighbours think? Everybody's seen them come by cab; we can't leave them on the doorstep, Alfred! It will cause the most awful gossip! They'll think, oh, what *will* they think—!"' She displayed a talent for mimicry he hadn't expected, then remembered her contempt for 'nice' women. 'And he'll be saying, "Can it be the religious canvassers, do you think? At *this* hour?"'

With that, the door opened again and the maid, now red-faced, whispered, 'Come in, please, miss,' and stood aside. They passed through into a tiny vestibule with a tiled floor, beyond it a narrow hall with oppressively dark but very shiny woodwork and a staircase. At the far end of the hall a man was standing, pulling at the bottom of his waistcoat and looking severe. *In the middle of his tea,* Denton thought.

'Show our guests into the front parlour, Mrs Wick,' the man said in the voice of a clergyman welcoming somebody to a funeral.

The room was small – twelve feet on a side – with a coal grate, unlit, and the same dark and brutally shiny woodwork, and dark furniture, vaguely Eastlake, that could be dated to the beginning of the Minters' marriage. Antimacassars everywhere; on the walls calligraphic certificates in which the name Stella Minter could be made out, and on the dark mantel a tinted photograph (not one of Regis Mulcahy's – wrong pose) of a plump young woman holding a book.

'I'm afraid I am not cognizant of the reason for your visit,' the man said. He was short, bald, plump and entirely sure of himself.

'I am Alfred Minter,' as if to say, *I* am the reason for all this magnificence.

Janet Striker smiled as brightly as the woodwork and held out her hand. 'I am Janet Striker of the Society for the Improvement of Women. And *this*,' indicating Denton as the prize item in the menagerie, 'is Mr Denton, the famous author.'

Minter touched her hand and inclined his head, moving it in a quarter-circle to take in both of them. 'And the reason for—?' he said.

'The matter is rather delicate.'

He looked at her, then Denton.

'Your daughter—' she said. Minter's head snapped up. 'We'd like to ask you about your daughter.'

'This is most unusual.' He tugged again at his waistcoat. 'Most surprising. I fail to see why you – why anyone – would ask me about my—' He made a gesture, as if the word 'daughter' was too sacred to pronounce.

'Do you have a daughter named Stella?'

He pulled himself up to his full five feet six inches. He raised a hand and moved it slowly past the row of calligraphies on the wall. 'An accomplished young woman. *Thoroughly* accomplished. The apple of our eye! I don't understand your interest, madam.'

'Might we see her?'

'Certainly not. She is a girl, a sensitive and good girl. I see no reason to, mm, expose her to the—' He frowned. 'To strangers. Who, I must say, give me no reason to entertain, mm, to have confidence in, mm, to know who or what they are! I don't *know* you, madam. Or you, sir.'

Janet Striker gave Denton a look; he got out a calling card, then searched his pockets for Hench-Rose's letter, now somewhat battered. He handed both over. Minter took them, held the card low and well away, tipping his head back, then went to the front window and studied them there. After that, he held the letter at arm's length and read it. He looked back at Denton, perhaps to determine if he could really be the Sir Galahad described by Hench-Rose, then returned to the letter and apparently read it again. At last, he came back to them and stood in the same spot in front of his fireplace, defender of the hearth. 'What is all this about?' he said a little hoarsely.

Janet Striker sat, the chair dark and overwrought, both hideous and uncomfortable-looking; she took up only the forward two or three inches of it. 'A young woman using the name Stella Minter has met her death. We are looking for her parents.'

His left hand went unconsciously to his chest; the idea of his daughter's death caused a spasm of pain on his face. 'But she is alive and well!' he gasped. 'In this house. At this moment!'

'May we see her?'

Minter's lips moved; he hesitated, decided, went to the door and called into the darkness of the hall, 'Mother! Please to bring our Stella to the front parlour. At once – please.' He turned back to them. 'You will see—' He touched his forehead. 'You gave me a turn. To suggest that our Stella—'

'I'm so sorry, Mr Minter. I didn't mean to suggest that your daughter was the victim. Only that we are looking for her parents.'

He went back to his place by the hearth and stared at the floor. 'That was cruel,' he murmured.

A middle-aged woman paused in the doorway, then came into the room; behind her, holding the woman's hand, a young but very large girl followed, clearly the girl in the photograph. Both were taller than Minter, neither 'good-looking' by most standards, the girl's face broad and long, her colour good, her hair lank. Both, Denton thought, were overdressed: did they put on their best to welcome Papa home to tea? Or were the clothes a declaration of status, like the little motor car?

'My wife, *Mrs* Minter,' Minter said, drawing her still farther in, 'and our beloved daughter, Stella.'

The family stood together. They looked expectant. Minter stared at Janet Striker as if for help. Yet she looked at Denton, who saw it was his turn. 'I'm happy to see,' he said, 'that Miss Minter isn't the young lady we're looking for.'

'Looking for!' the woman cried. 'Why should you be looking for her?'

Minter turned his head to say something to her, but Denton said loudly, 'It's a case of mistaken identity, ma'am. Another young woman of the same name.' He didn't say how disappointed he was.

'I should think so!' she said. 'Very mistaken, indeed, I should think! You really ought to determine your facts in a better fashion, I think!'

'Now, Mother—' Minter managed to say.

'Anyone who knows her knows that there can't be any confusion about who she is! I can't hardly understand how her identity could be confused! I think you must be very ignorant people!'

'Oh, Mama—!' the girl moaned.

'Hush, dear.'

'My wife is overwrought,' Minter said. 'Stella is the apple of our eye.'

'Apple, indeed!' Mrs Minter shouted. 'A girl of such accomplishments—!'

'That's enough, Mother!' Minter said. He had reverted to the clergyman's voice; the effect was instantaneous, Mrs Minter's mouth remaining open but no sound coming out. The girl blushed and looked at Janet Striker in appeal, perhaps apology; she looked at Denton and gave him a tentative, awkward smile. She was sixteen, the birth record had told him that; she had the adolescent's embarrassment at her parents, however they loved her and she them. Her smile to Denton seemed to ask for an understanding of that, and on an impulse, he said to her, 'Is that your picture on the mantel, Miss Minter?'

Her mother started to answer for her, but Minter said, 'Now!' in a warning voice; the girl, after a second or two, blushing some more, said, 'I was just finished at the common school. I was only fourteen then.'

'And look,' Minter said, 'at all she's accomplished since! She's won a scholarship to the Roedean School!'

'And will go on to university – her teachers say so!' the mother burst out.

'That's wonderful,' Denton said. 'Wonderful. You went to the local school, then? And stayed after age eleven, and went on as long as you could.'

'I love studying.'

'What's your favourite?'

'Science. I'm going to be a scientist.'

'Or a teacher,' her mother said; unresolved conflict hovered over the words.

'Yours is an unusual name,' Denton said. The girl nodded, blushed, as if to suggest that the name was not her doing. 'I wonder,' Denton started, looking aside at Janet Striker, the idea forming in his head as he asked the question, 'if any other girls have ever used your name. Pretended to be you.'

'What, as a kind of cheat? To get money or something?'

'No, dear,' Mrs Striker said, picking up Denton's notion, 'no, more from, perhaps, admiration. Or envy. "The sincerest form of flattery," do you know that saying?'

'Yes, but that's imitation.'

'Well, yes, dear, that's I think what Mr Denton means. Imitating you. Has there ever been anybody like that?'

Mrs Minter laughed, a dismissive, contemptuous laugh. 'They *all* envy her.'

'Oh, Mama—'

'Well, some are quite nasty, you've said so yourself! The green-eyed monster, that's what afflicts people.'

Denton crossed his arms over his chest, his words trying to pull the talk back to his question. 'But has there ever been anybody – some special friend, some girl who admired you, maybe talked like you, even said she wanted to be like you—?'

Stella Minter looked at her mother, made nervous movements with her shoulders, said, 'Alice, I suppose.'

Her mother sniffed.

'Well, she did admire me, Mama! She said so!' She looked at Denton. 'She was ever so unhappy, she said, and she wanted to make something of herself, to become somebody. She hadn't my advantages, you see. We were such good friends, and she came here and she asked questions about everything, about—'

'When they were very *little* girls; I think that when they are still in the age of innocence, *little* girls can be accepted where, later, they cannot,' her mother said.

'She wanted to know what a maid did, and what all the books I owned were, and how to play the piano, and – just everything! She was so sweet and she was my best friend, but—' She glanced at her mother. 'As Mama says, it was all right when we were little girls. She used to come here every day. I couldn't go to her house, you see—'

'A public house,' Mrs Minter said. 'We didn't know, in the beginning. Then – it would have been most improper.'

'Alice,' Janet Striker said. 'Alice what?'

'Satterlee,' Mrs Minter said. 'The Satterlees, we found out too late, were low and common.'

'Oh, Mama—'

'You don't understand these things yet, Stella. I couldn't know her mother – to think of such a thing makes me ill; was it right that her child should know you? We decided not, finally. The girl was appealing when she was little, but at twelve, you can understand our position. It wasn't proper.'

Minter smiled. 'But it was a spectacle to see them together! Little Alice was another Stella! She *did* talk like our Stella; you could hear her using the big words, hear her trying to talk proper. She'd borrow books and try to read them, I suppose.'

'Steal them, you mean.'

'She didn't!'

'One of your books simply disappeared!'

'She wanted to learn things, Mama.'

'Giving herself airs,' the mother said.

'Mama, she was trying to better herself. She was trying to *be* proper.'

Janet Striker said, 'Did she ever play at *being* you?'

The girl blushed again. 'I suppose. Maybe.' She looked at her mother. 'We had a game. When we played me giving a tea party with my tea set. I'd be somebody – oh, it's awfully silly, but we were children – I'd be one of the royal princesses or a maid of honour, and she'd be me. It was just a game.'

'And she called herself Stella?' Mrs Striker said.

'That was the game. She was Stella.'

'But you said,' Minter interrupted, 'that a girl using the name had passed away.' Mrs Minter said 'Oh' in a tiny voice and turned her daughter aside as if to protect her, but the girl shrugged her off. 'Do I hear now that you think this other girl might have known our Stella?'

Denton and Janet Striker exchanged a look; she said, 'It seems possible.'

'You mean Alice Satterlee?' Stella said. 'She's – passed away?'

'We don't know,' Denton said. 'We're trying to find out.'

Tears stood in the girl's eyes, and Denton realized what a nice girl she probably was – truly touched, probably lonely, sentimental, treasuring the memory of somebody who had worshipped her. Her mother saw the tears, however, as danger and, after a glare at Denton, pushed the girl from the room.

'Mrs Minter is very protective of our Stella,' Minter said. 'She doesn't allow emotional scenes.'

'How well did you know the Satterlees?' Denton said.

'As Mrs Minter said, they weren't our sort of people. We never crossed paths, as the saying is.'

'They lived in a pub?'

'That's a bit of an exaggeration. I believe they lived *next* to the public house.'

'Satterlee was a publican?'

'Satterlee was something for the building estate – over there on the other side of Crimea Way. He did something while the site was prepared, before the houses were put up – I remember walking Stella over there once and seeing the great expanse of it, levelled and nothing on it but the pub. Stella makes it sound as if they were friends for years, but it can't have been awfully long; I think at most a year. Then they were gone.'

'What's the name of the pub?'

'Oh—! I've never been in it.' He frowned to indicate disapproval of the public house. 'I think something about a rose. I really wouldn't know.'

A silence fell; Denton knew it was over. Janet Striker stood, and then they were out in the front garden again, and the cab was waiting at the kerb.

'You know a pub beyond Crimea Way called the rose, or some such?' Denton said to the driver.

'Just been there, many thanks.'

'Take us there.' He winked. 'You can have another and then take us to the station.'

In the cab he leaned back against the stiff cushions, aware of how tired he was and how disappointed. That morning, he had despaired; now, they had come close, he thought, perhaps very close – yet not close enough.

'I liked that girl,' he said.

'She has a hard row to hoe. As your grandmother might say.'

The Rose and Rooster was less than half a dozen years old but looked as if it came from the seventies or eighties, a public house purpose-built to the designs of a man who specialized in pubs for a large syndicate. Its dark wood, stained glass and gleaming brass were meant to evoke those earlier houses in which such details had been innovative, were now 'pub style', to be expected by the patrons. The tiled front, the name in gold letters, were stand-ins for a national nostalgia – the roast beef of old England.

Denton steered Janet Striker around to the saloon bar, now comfortably full, the usual fug of pipe smoke hanging at chest level, women mostly sitting quietly while men in bowlers laughed or wrangled.

'What'll it be, then, love?' the barmaid said to him as soon as they sat down at a small table. She was thirtyish, cheerful, professionally flirtatious.

Janet Striker said, 'A half of your best bitter.'

'Two,' Denton said, 'and I'll have a word with the publican, if I can.'

'He's that busy, I wouldn't put money on it, dearie. What's it about, then?'

'Tell him it's personal-historical.'

228

She laughed, showing big, cream-coloured teeth. 'You're not a debt collector, I hope.' When she was gone, Denton said, 'Well?'

Janet Striker shook her head. After several seconds, she said, 'I was thinking of that poor girl – Satterlee. Wanting so much to get out of what she was and not knowing how to do it.'

'And ending up dead. If it was her.'

'The mother was a piece of work.' She meant the real Stella Minter's mother, he knew.

He said, 'Defending her chick.'

Janet Striker snorted. 'Defending the proper and the prudish, you mean. Ambitious for the girl, probably driving her husband as hard as she drives her daughter, wanting she doesn't quite know what – more of something: more propriety, more money, more *things*, more signs around her of how proper and accomplished she is – through her husband and her daughter. You can build empires with women like that pushing people.'

'You think the motor car is his idea or hers?'

'His, of course. He handles the money and makes the decisions; she pushes and mostly sets the terms. I'm sure she wants a better house – wouldn't surprise me if she has one picked out for the moment when Stella is launched from university and a success. Suburban, detached, *stylish*. What a weight that child has to carry!'

'But carries it pretty well,' he murmured as the barmaid came back, placed the two wet glasses neatly in front of them and said, 'Landlord's drawing pints for a party of nine and then he'll pop in, but he says to tell you – his words, not mine, don't take it out on me, love – "If it isn't important, I'll be back drawing pints faster'n Jack Sprat."' She bent down so that her hair brushed Denton's face. 'His bark's worse'n his bite.' She giggled again, straightened, winked at Janet Striker and whirled away.

They toyed with the glasses, sipped – neither wanted the ale – tried to make the time pass. Janet Striker said, 'Don't jump at its being the Satterlees.'

'I know, I know. We have to be dead certain. I *want* to be certain, that's the trouble – it's tempting to jump ahead.'

'Don't jump.'

He studied her face, saw its intelligence, its hardness, wondered if he could ever get past that. She looked at him, looked away, then back; their eyes joined and held. It was disturbing: long, shared looks were supposed to be examples of intimacy, thus with her were embarrassing. He knew he was getting red, face warm; she looked cool and detached. He wanted to say something, to do something like touch her hand, but he didn't dare.

'Now then,' a big voice bellowed next to him, 'who wants to see me?' He was a wide, solid man, shorter than Denton, confident and even brassy. Ex-military, Denton thought; he put on more assurance than he felt and said, 'My name's Denton.' Taking the chance, he added, 'Ex-sergeant, infantry. Sit down, will you?'

He was holding out his hand; the other man took it, gripped it hard. 'Penrose, gunner. Like calls to like, eh?' He let go. 'Can't sit down, no time.' Then, to Mrs Striker, 'Evening to you, ma'am.'

'Janet Striker,' she said, holding her own hand out. He touched it but turned back to Denton; men were for business, he seemed to say. 'What's up, then?'

'We're trying to locate a family named Satterlee.'

Penrose tipped his head back as if to have a better look at Denton. 'This the personal or the historical?'

'Little of both, I expect. We were told they used to live here.'

'In aid of what?'

'An enquiry.'

'You got do better than that, ex-sergeant. American, are you? What army?'

'Union. Our Civil War.'

'Oh, that one. Saw a lot of it, did you? Yes, I think you did. I was lucky – thirteen years in South Africa, I never got so much as a stone thrown at me. All right, ex-sergeant, tell it to me straight what you want – I've a lot of thirsty people waiting.'

Denton looked at Janet Striker, saw her nod, said, 'A girl is dead. We think she might be a Satterlee.'

'The little one or the big one?'

Janet Striker jumped in. 'There were two? Only two, or more?'

Penrose drew a chair from another table and sat, opening his attention to include her. 'You're not the police,' he said. 'Not that it'd matter if you were; we're clean here. There were two girls, Alice, the bigger one, and a younger one named – now let me think – Eadie – that's what they called her, but it wasn't Edith – Edna. Edna! Alice and Edna.' He leaned a forearm on the table. 'They didn't live in the pub itself; I and the missus live upstairs and always have. The Satterlees lived in the extension next door – other people in there now. When they put these buildings up, they build on the extension for the company's business – works manager, engineer, whatever it is – and then it becomes the sales office when the houses are ready to sell. When all the houses are sold, they rent it out.'

'Satterlee was the works manager?'

'Nothing quite so fancy. More like the work gangs' foreman.'

There was a silence. Denton, fearing the man would run off, said quickly, 'What were they like?'

'Weren't like nothing, because you never saw them. I saw the girls now and then in the back, playing out there, but him only when he wanted me to. And her, never. See, they kept to themselves and shut the rest of us out – curtains always closed, never going about or chatting like normal folk, wouldn't hardly open the door to the postman's knock. My missus said we ought to extend the hand of neighbourliness; I said they could go to the hot place, pardon me, miss. I mean, here we was, two families marooned in the only building in the middle of a bleeding metropolitan desert, and they wouldn't offer to share a cup of cold tea!'

Janet Striker leaned forward. 'What were the girls like?'

'Pathetic. Not out of want, I don't mean pathetic that way, but off to themselves all the time and lonely. You could tell. Like they was dying for company, for conversation. Nice enough girls, mind.'

'Did you ever hear them talk about Stella Minter?'

Penrose stared at her. '*That's* an odd one. That's right odd, I mean it.'

'Why?'

'How could you know about that?' He looked at them with sudden suspicion, as if they had revealed some incriminating secret –

a tail, or an odour of brimstone. Then he thought better of it. 'It was a game they played, the two sisters. It was sort of a tea party or something – all in dumb show, mind, except for the odd old cup or a rock they'd picked up. But I'd look down from our window – I'd have put my feet up for a bit – and, there they'd be out in the garden, except there wasn't no garden then, jabbering to each other and playing at pouring tea – I got that much – and other stuff I couldn't tell, like talking to people that wasn't there, and so on. I went down one day, I had something to fix on our back door, and the little one sees me and she says – they was always eager to talk – she says, "We're playing cellar-minto." Or that's what I thought she said. Made no sense , but I thought it was some word they'd made up; *I* don't know kids' games. Then later, another day, she said it again and I got it as stellar-minto. Stellar-minto, all right, makes no sense to me either, but so what? Now here you come along and say it again, I haven't heard it in, what? – four years. And it all comes right back. What's it mean, then?'

'It's a girl's name – Stella Minter.'

He looked at her, frowned. 'What's that mean, then – we're playing Stella Minter? Playing at somebody else? Making fun?'

'More like being somebody else.'

Penrose went on frowning, then shook his head; he put his hands on the table as if to push himself up, and Denton hurried to say, 'What sort of man was Satterlee?'

Penrose grunted, a single scornful sound. 'Harold Satterlee was the sort you don't want hanging about. Full of himself. Drove his workmen like billy-o; that's why the company hired him, I suppose. I had one run-in with him, that was all I needed to see of him.'

'What happened?'

'Look, mate, I've really got to go. I'll make this quick.' But it was clear that Penrose liked the chance to tell the story. 'Satterlee comes to me and says he wants me to refuse to sell beer to his men in the middle of the day – says it slows them down in the p.m. I said that was bleeding nonsense and I wouldn't do it. He says if I don't do it, he'll go to the company and close me down. Well, I laughed in his face! I said to him, see here, my man, they didn't build this pub first because they liked the look of it, you know; they built it so the workmen can grab a pint! You go and tell the company to shut it down, and they'll shut *you* down. *You'll* be out on the street, not me. Well, he knew I was right, but he got mad as a wet hen. Swore terrible, put his face in mine, said he was going to pound me. So I showed him my friend in need –' Penrose pulled only the handle of a leather-covered truncheon from his trouser pocket – 'and said I'd have him level on the ground before he could swing a fist. Well, he knew I'd do it, so he stomps off bellowing and never spoke to me again. Nor could his kids after that – they'd look away if they saw me. I felt that sorry for them. The bigger one, Alice, she could have been pretty, but she had a hard time of it. And a hard time since, I'd wager.'

'It's she who's dead, we think,' Janet Striker said.

'Ah, poor tyke. How?'

'Murdered.' She glanced at Denton. 'If it's the same girl. Look here, Mr Penrose, it's important that we find the Satterlees. I take it they're not here any more. Where have they gone?'

Penrose, on his feet now, shook his head. 'No idea, and good riddance. The company might know – he might've gone some-place else to do the same job for them.' He shook his head again. 'Murdered! You never know what tomorrow will bring, do you?'

'What's the company?'

He looked perplexed, as if everybody knew what the company was. 'Britannic Improvement. Their name's all over London.' He said the name again, as if they might be slow. Then he shook hands with both of them, muttered 'murdered', and was gone.

Neither of them had done more than sip the ale, so they left it on the table. Both were silent in the cab, heading back through evening streets towards the Marlborough Road station. It was colder and a few flakes of snow were falling, melting as they touched the pavement. At last he said, 'I've got to find him.'

'Them,' she said. 'It's the whole family, Denton – and they may be the wrong ones.'

They rode along. He said, 'How do we find them?'

'The company, I suppose. If they'll tell us. Tomorrow's Saturday;

the company offices will be open, but if the important people aren't there, it might be hard to get them to tell us. "Oh, you must wait for Mr Smith to return on Monday." Does it really matter, Denton, whether it's tomorrow or Monday?'

'It matters to me.'

They waited on the cold platform, then sat silently side by side like a long-established couple who'd been having an argument. At Baker Street, they changed to the Metropolitan Line and went on, silent, swaying, until he said abruptly, 'We'll get out at King's Cross and walk.'

'I don't want you to walk me home.'

'We're going to my typewriter's on Lloyd Baker Street. I think I know how to find the Satterlees.'

'But it's impossible, Mr Denton!' Mrs Johnson was less scandalized than usual because Denton had a woman with him; she had even let them both inside the front door. 'It's after seven o'clock, Mr Denton – they've worked all day and they're not going to work all night!'

'I'll pay double! Triple! They won't have to work all night – it's one name, one name!'

'Mr Denton, they've been three days, looking for Ruths and Rebeccas; now you want them to look for Alices and Ednas. I'm sure they'll be happy to try again on Monday.'

Janet Striker said in her most severe voice, 'The Metropolitan Schools Board building is open until nine o'clock. I know, because I've had to go to meetings there. We have two hours – more, Denton, if you're not averse to bribing people.'

Mrs Johnson sucked in her breath, as harsh a rebuke as she ever allowed herself.

'It will also cost something to prise the records out at this hour. Mrs Johnson, do you know what records they were looking at and in what office?'

Mrs Johnson wilted under Janet Striker's tone. She didn't know, she murmured; she hadn't been doing the work, only organizing it; Frederica Tilley had been the one actually there and running things.

'Where is she now?' Janet Striker demanded.

'Home, I suppose, slaving all day as she's been doing. Several streets away. No, of course I don't have a telephone – nor she – it's ten minutes' walk—'

They made it in six, to find Frederica Tilley relaxing with sherry and sausages in a room above an upholsterer's. Once she'd got over the surprise of the visit, she told them quite lucidly where the records were in the Schools Board building, and precisely which volumes would hold the most recent reports. 'But it's way down Blackfriars Road and a frightful walk from the tube station! You'll never—'

Then they were in a motorized cab speeding through freezing streets to the south bank. The city was dark but peopled, everybody hugging himself, shoulders hunched, hands at throats to hold collars closed against a wind that seemed to be blowing from the Arctic. Overhead, clouds scudded in the reflected light of London, low and fast and spitting a snowflake now and then. Paying the cab fare, Denton counted his money and wondered if it would last.

Janet Striker, he found to his surprise, knew all about bribing people. When she saw his hesitation, she held her hand out for money and said crisply, 'I'll do it.' She got them into the building – a shilling for the night porter – and into the records room – half a crown for the clerk, half a crown for the watchman – and down at a table near the records themselves. It cost them another crown when the building closed at nine, and then they sat in a big, cold room, the brass Aladdin lamp on the table the only light, bound books of handwritten school reports piled around them.

'Have you any more money?' Mrs Striker said at ten-thirty.

He blushed. 'Coins.'

'We never had supper.' She disappeared and came back after ten minutes. 'The night porter's gone for food. And drink. I'm afraid we're entertaining two watchmen, the porter and somebody he calls "Old Geoff".' She smiled into the island of light. 'If any of "the upper staff" find we're here, it'll cost a good deal more.' She sat down. 'Your money ran out. We're on my shilling now.'

'I can't let you.'

'You can't stop me.' She opened a book with a bang. 'What bad fists people have! My eyes are crossing from the handwriting.'

At half past midnight, she suddenly slapped her worn hand down on the ledger. 'I have them!' She raised her voice. 'Satterlee, Edna, aged 12, East Ham Progressive Central School.' She looked up at him, her face weary, ironic, smiling. 'Don't,' she said, 'don't do it, Denton,' because apparently she knew he wanted to kiss her.

CHAPTER NINETEEN

A hard frost had laid a sheen of palest grey over grasses and had left a gloss of black ice on the streets. East Ham beyond the train station was a bleak expanse of seemingly identical streets of identical houses, all joined into two-storeyed rows under shallow-peaked roofs. At intervals, ancient wetland persevered as dun-coloured grass, now almost white, matted into clumps and hummocks and marked here and there by pools of open water whose edges had frozen overnight. Always, beyond any view that opened – inevitably over the marshes – there was a jagged skyline of factories and the rising plumes of smoke and, this bitter morning, steam.

Denton and Mrs Striker, their cab jogging slowly between the rows of houses, were silent. It was only a little after seven; workingmen were moving on the street, dinner buckets hanging from one hand; an odour of pipe smoke, coal and food hung on the chilly air. Denton shivered in his overcoat; the revolver, snug in its pocket, was icy to the touch.

East Ham had been a village for centuries, an inhabited place before the Romans, probably; it had seen farms and orchards in the middle ages and later. Now, London had engorged it as a place for the working people needed to stoke the great British engine. *Mean streets*, he thought as they clopped along, but that expression had been used for a place far worse than this, the streets here in fact not mean but simply spiritless, grim, repetitive. The farmer in him disliked the erasure of the farms.

'There are far worse places,' Mrs Striker said as if they had been discussing it. He grunted. She said, 'People don't leave places like East Ham to go back to the farms, Denton.'

'That's because there's no work on the farms.' He sighed. 'They'd pave the whole country, if they could.'

'And if people needed houses to live in, I'd say it was a good thing.'

He glanced aside at her, thought how unsentimental she was – not always an attractive trait. This morning, she looked ugly to him, pinched, her face closed as if by the cold. He wished he'd come on this part of the journey alone. They jogged on for another several minutes, and he said nothing, and she, probably understanding him, didn't try to talk.

'Almost there,' the driver called down to them.

Denton put his head out to look. Off to their left, a different kind of prospect was opening – no low houses and streets, for a change, but a levelled field of the kind he'd come to recognize. It was big, perhaps ten acres, stretching away as flatly as a bed; on three sides, the streets lined it like walls; on the fourth, he could see open space, a line of trees and, distantly, a steeple: this, for now, was the end of the gobbling-up of East Ham.

'You sure you want the pub?' the driver said. He was pointing with his whip. The building was far over towards the outer edge of the field; between them and it was a frosted expanse with sewer pipes and water connections sticking up where macadamized streets would run.

'Is there another?' Denton said.

'This's the only one where they're still building. I can't get you closer than the edge here – can't do it! Wouldn't risk the horse on them fillings.' After another hundred yards, he pulled the horse up. 'Can't get no closer.'

They got down. Their breath steamed in the windless air. The driver was pointing again, showing them how they could pick their way among piles of building stone and lumber. Denton had already seen the route, noted how it had been pioneered by other feet.

'Good enough for the workmen, I guess it's good enough for us,' he said to her. 'You needn't come, if the walking's too hard.'

She gave him a look. 'You can't get rid of me now, Denton; it's too late.'

They walked into the field. It was made of fill; nobody had been too choosy about what the fill was or where it came from. Denton saw broken crockery, a rusted gear poking up like a jawbone. There was a thin smell of sewage: it was said that some of the new London was built on the cleanings of the old London's privies.

'We can ask there for Satterlee,' she said, pointing at a cluster of men by a stack of cut stone.

'We can see the pub,' he said.

'If the Satterlees are still there. Let's ask.'

She irritated him, but he did as she wanted. They turned off the track that others had beaten and crossed the rough ground towards the men. He stumbled once over something hard, almost entirely buried and now frozen in, swore, caught himself, the pistol swinging heavily in the overcoat. When they came to them, none of the men paid any notice but stood as they were, gathered in a semicircle around a well-dressed man who had laid out a piece of paper as big as a tablecloth on the building stone. He was saying something about the water table and hydraulic pressure and cellar walls, but when Denton moved around the men to have a look at him, the man glanced up and said, 'Yes?' It was less a greeting than a challenge.

'I'm looking for the site manager.'

'I'm the site manager.'

'Satterlee?'

'You want Satterlee? Should have said so sooner.' The man gestured over his shoulder with a thumb. 'Try the public house – might still be there, might not. Removal van was there at six.' He looked down at the paper plans, looked up again and said, 'Satterlee's part of the job is over; he's moving on.'

'Where's he gone?'

'I told you, I don't know if he's gone yet. If he's gone, I don't know where. Ask at the company office. In the City.' He looked down at the plans again and began to trace a line with a finger, talking about four-inch pipe and 'domestic connections'.

Denton looked towards the pub. Janet Striker was doing the same thing. He could see now that what had been from the road a white dot at one side was now a closed wagon; a horse had separated itself, too, from the dark brick of the building.

'Removal van,' Denton said.

'Too late,' she said.

'We don't know that.' He started to stride across the rubble; she almost ran to catch up. She told him to slow down, but he paid no attention. Closer by then, he could see two men carrying some big, dark piece of furniture up a ramp to the van's innards, and he strode faster. When they were a hundred feet away – the men clear now, faces, one taller than the other, a red scarf at a neck – she caught his arm and almost pulled him off balance. 'Denton!'

He swung around on her.

'Don't!' she said. 'Don't go in there like this!'

His instinct was to pull away and charge on. She was panting, more colour in her face now, and he remembered the other days, his liking for her. She became somebody else, not the woman he had resented in the cab. She said, 'We don't *know*.'

He chewed his lower lip. He breathed out – he, too, was a little out of breath. 'All right.' He put his hand into the pocket where the Colt rode. 'You lead.'

Her hand was still on his arm. She passed in front of him very close, and she said, 'He isn't your father.'

She led them more slowly over the hard earth, her skirts lifted a little in her hands. Behind her, shortening his stride, he held the bulge of the heavy pistol against his hip with a forearm. When they reached the back of the removal van, they found a kerb and a pavement; the smell of horse surrounded them, straw-filled dung on the ground.

'The Satterlees?' she said to one of the removal men, who was coming out of the house with a small armchair held against his chest. He jerked his head back. 'Inside!' He was sweating.

She stood aside for the other man, also coming out; she was right at the front doorway then, turned back to Denton, giving him a look as if to say, *Now, mind your manners.* When she turned back to go in, a young girl was standing in the doorway.

Denton knew it was the right Satterlee because of her. Later, he would be able to anatomize her and explain why he knew, but at that moment he knew only that he could see the dead young woman in her face and his sister in the entirety of her – pose, smile, clothes – which told him all he needed to know about her and about her relationship with her father. A terrible realization struck him: *This was how Josie looked. I didn't remember, but I do – it was this, this look of – of not being a child.*

'We're looking for Mr and Mrs Satterlee,' Janet Striker said.

'Looking's free,' the girl said. She laughed.

Mrs Striker glanced at Denton and said, 'May we come in?'

The girl looked not at her but at Denton. She gave him a smile, cocked her head, gave another smile. *Flirting.* Denton said, 'You're Edna, aren't you.'

'I might be.' She made a movement with her whole body, swaying forward and dropping her right shoulder and then straightening, never taking her eyes from him, the finish of the movement leaving her partly in profile so that if she'd had breasts they'd have been shown well. 'What'll you give me if I am?'

'Is your mother here?' Janet Striker said.

The girl laughed. 'She is for as long as the gin lasts.' She laughed again and looked at Denton. 'She's here, but she's not all there, if you know what I mean!'

The removal men pushed past them then; the girl flattened herself against the open door, but as the younger of the two went past she moved forward so that he brushed against her and she looked up into his face, smiling. The man looked at Denton and Janet Striker and muttered something and went on inside, down a narrow hall to stairs at the back, and up.

'We'll come in,' Janet Striker said.

The girl shrugged. 'Suit yourself.' She gave Denton her smile again.

The hall ran right through the house to another door at the back, now standing partway open. Two doors on the left led to a parlour and, at the back, he supposed, to a kitchen. The hall was small, barely big enough for two people, he thought; the walls, papered in a small pattern in shades of grey-green, were nondescript, probably depressing after a little time; the woodwork was dark but dull.

Janet Striker looked back from the first door, nodded at him, and he followed her, feeling the girl close behind him.

The parlour had been emptied of furniture except for one arm-chair, in which a woman in a dark coat and a small black hat was sitting. She looked at them with dull eyes, said nothing.

'Mrs Satterlee?' Denton said.

'Oh, she won't say nothing; she never does.' The girl giggled.

Denton went closer to the woman, bent down to see her face. Under a layer of powder, it was lined and blotchy. The eyelids quivered.

'Mrs Satterlee, we're looking for your daughter – Alice.'

'I told you, she won't say nothing! She don't know nothing!' The girl danced into his line of vision. 'Ask me; I know lots of things.'

He felt real physical revulsion, wanted to slap her. In a hard voice, he said, 'Where's your sister Alice?'

'She went away.'

'Where?'

'How should I know? She went away and she didn't come back, now my story is all told.' She gave him the smile, then bent her torso forward and put her right hand into the small of her back as if to deepen the curve of her spine. The posture was that from a cheap postcard – a woman offering herself, the pose designed to reveal the breasts, cleavage if she had had such a thing. Denton felt his attention lurch, saw his sister at thirteen, and in an angry, pained voice, he cried, 'Don't! You stupid little—' He'd have said *bitch*, but a louder voice from the stairs stopped him, stopped them all, and their eyes, even the seated woman's, went to the door, hers open with fright.

'You bloody stupid bastards, I told you to be careful! Now look what you've done to the plaster, you stupid bastards! God, man, lift it—!' Something heavy bumped against the wall; there was a thump, a different voice swore, and a third male voice said, 'You talk to us like that any more, guv, I'll drop this bloody thing on your toes.'

More sound – bumps, a dragging along the floor, men's heavy breathing – and the first voice shouting, 'Have a care – you shouldn't be allowed to move stones, you bloody imbeciles—' and a man backed down the hall past the doorway, one side of a chest of drawers in his arms, then another man at the other end.

And then the third man came, his eyes on the two who were carrying the dresser.

Satterlee was tall, very solid but with a heavy gut; his hair was dark, almost black, his face red from shouting, sun- and wind-burned. He looked into the parlour as he was passing; his eyes took in the four of them, and he recognized Denton just as Denton recognized him. Neither had any doubt. Denton didn't need to see more than the eyes and the forehead.

Satterlee reached into the right rear pocket of his trouser; Denton was putting his hand into the overcoat, then closing it on the Colt and feeling the pistol catch in the fabric as he tried to draw it out. Satterlee by then had his hand out, a dark shape in it that, with a flick, became a heavy-bladed knife.

The girl screamed. She ran towards her father. She shouted. 'Papa, don't!'

Denton, wrestling with the pistol, trying to tear it loose from the pocket, still had part of his brain respond to the words: *Of course, that's what Mulcahy heard the other girl say – Don't, Papa – Oh, Christ—*

Whatever Satterlee had intended – to kill Denton, probably, to eliminate the only one who could connect him with the attack – he was momentarily frustrated by his daughter. She reached with both hands for the hand that held the knife (knowing? having reason to fear it?), managing to catch his arm; she was saying, almost crooning, 'Please, Papa, no—' over and over, as if with this voice she was able to quiet him.

Satterlee shoved her with his forearm, then wrenched himself free of her and tried to turn; she tried again to grab him. Denton, trying to tear the pistol out of his coat, missed what happened next but saw only the result, a spurt of red that spattered the floor and the wall as the girl spun away; then he heard her scream and, behind him, the screams, all alike and repeated as if by a machine, from the woman in the chair.

Satterlee looked at him. His eyes were manic, enraged. He might have come at Denton then, but the Colt was at last coming free, the curve of the handle visible above the pocket, Denton's thumb cocking the single-action hammer. Satterlee in one grab pulled Janet Striker to him; the shoulder of her coat and dress ripped with the violence of the movement, and then he was dragging her out of the room and she was screaming at Denton. Satterlee shouted at somebody in the corridor; there was a crash and a male scream.

Denton had the pistol out and crossed the parlour in two strides, saw down the hall the two workmen, one on the floor, blood on the wall, Janet Striker being pushed out of the back door. He tried to run down the hall, jumped over the fallen man, cannoned off the narrow doorframe at the back and fell to one knee as he failed to see the step down from the house to the rubble outside. When he was up again, Satterlee was forty feet away, dragging Janet Striker, who was struggling with him, trying to punch and kick him and failing.

'Satterlee!'

Denton put himself into a sprint. There was no way Satterlee could outrun him if he held on to the woman. Denton ran wide of their path, meaning to swing around him and come in at an angle where he could have a shot, but Satterlee looked back and in one move – the man was powerful and fast – swung Mrs Striker against him and held her there as a shield. He had the fingers of his left hand wound in her hair and her head pulled cruelly back; the knife was against her throat, and already a thin ribbon of blood was trickling down.

'Get off!' Satterlee shouted at him. 'Back off or I'll kill her!'

Denton stopped. He raised the pistol.

Satterlee ducked his head behind Mrs Striker's. His voice came, heavy and dangerous, 'Throw down that pistol, or I'll kill her now!'

'Kill her, and I'll kill you.'

Satterlee pulled her head back still farther. Mrs Striker had hooked her left hand inside the arm of the hand that held the knife, but there wasn't a hope that she could keep the knife from slashing her throat. Denton's mind raced through possibilities – shoot one of Satterlee's feet, his shoulder – but none would stop him from killing her.

'Throw the gun down or I'll do it!'

The cleared field stretched behind Satterlee to the line of trees, still white with frost despite the low morning sun. Not another figure was in sight.

He had been holding the gun at arm's length since Satterlee had swung around to face him. The front sight was steady on the point where some part of his head might appear. Denton thought that he needed only a fraction of a second, two inches of skull. He waited. His own breathing quieted. If somebody could go around Satterlee from behind—

But nobody would. Denton knew what Satterlee would do next, and he wouldn't wait much longer. He'd slash her throat and run, risking the bullet. And she'd be dead.

'Janet—' he called.

Her head was pulled back again. Satterlee shouted, 'I'm going to bloody kill her!'

Denton thought about risking a shot close enough to graze her and hit Satterlee, but he couldn't. And Satterlee would react automatically; the knife would do its work no matter what. He kept the pistol level, aimed, ready.

The sound that Janet Striker made was like an animal growl that rose to a scream, like some big cat that went from menace to hysteria in a single cry. The scream was purely the triumph of the body over pain: she had moved her left hand from Satterlee's arm to the razor-sharp blade of the knife, which she grasped as if it were a lifeline, at the same time twisting her head down and away into the blade against Satterlee's hold so that Denton heard hair rip from her scalp.

Blood covered her fingers. Satterlee roared and pulled the knife, through her fingers and down, and then blood flowed from her face and her throat, but she had given Denton his fraction of a second and his two inches of skull.

He pulled the trigger.

CHAPTER TWENTY

'They've put off the inquest on Mulcahy.'

'I'd have kept my promise to be there, Munro. If this hadn't happened.'

It was past one in the afternoon. They were sitting in a room in the East Ham police station, overcoats on against the dead, damp chill of the place. Munro was sitting by a scarred wood table, from time to time rapping his knuckles on it in either frustration or impatience.

'You might have told us,' he said.

'There wasn't time.'

'You ought to have told us.' Munro rapped with his knuckles. 'More tea?' When Denton shook his head, Munro looked at the third man in the room, an aristocratic face above an impeccable suit and a fur-collared overcoat. 'Sir?'

'Thank you, no.' He was, as Denton had to keep reminding himself, Denton's lawyer – sent out by his publisher as soon as they could gear themselves up to action.

'I don't like being treated like the criminal in the thing,' Denton said.

'You are the criminal in the thing. Until we prove otherwise.'

The solicitor cleared his throat. Munro looked at him, shrugged. The man of law said, 'I think you would be wise, Sergeant, not to slander Mr Denton.'

'I'm here as a friend, Sir Francis, not as a copper.'

The long, lawyerly face – similarities to some horses in the nose and upper lip – smiled, and he said, 'Once a copper, always a copper. You must be careful what you say.'

Munro shrugged again. He hugged himself, poured some now cold tea from the brown earthenware pot that sat on the unpainted table. He sipped and made a face, then rapped on the wood. 'Guillam had a fit when he heard.'

'Good.'

'He's raving about prosecution, or was when I saw him at the Yard. Georgie wants to make super, I told you.'

The lawyer shifted his long, elegantly trousered legs. 'Any policeman who prosecutes the man who shot a brute who had just stabbed his own daughter and a workman and was holding an innocent woman at knife-point is likelier to find himself a constable on a beat than a superintendent. There isn't a jury in England who would convict. And not a judge who'd be patient with the prosecutor who brought such a case.'

Munro frowned. 'You may know that, Sir Francis, and let's say for the sake of argument that *I* may know that, but George Guillam has decided that he despises Denton, and he's a man who can let his rages run away with him.'

'Happily, then, the decision to lay charges is not your Sergeant Guillam's. It's East Ham's.'

Munro made a sound, doubtful, equivocal. 'CID're in it now.'

'They at least believe in prudence.'

Munro had surprised Denton by turning up an hour before, explaining not too helpfully that he had 'picked up a ride with the deputy super' of CID. Only as the hour wore on did Denton gather that Scotland Yard was in a subdued uproar over the coming together of the Mulcahy and Stella Minter cases, resulting in the postponement of the coroner's inquest on Mulcahy. Denton himself, held now in the death of Harold Satterlee, had been treated like both a criminal and a hero – two hours of questioning, but no jail cell, and an immediate response to his request to send a message off to his publisher. (He'd thought first of Hench-Rose, but had decided he didn't want that indebtedness.) He'd thought that Lang would send the legal nonentity who advised the publishing firm on contracts, but, to his astonishment, Lang had sent Sir Francis Brudenell, of whom even Denton had heard; he had introduced himself as 'your solicitor, not the one who'd represent you in court – that's a barrister – but we'll never go to court.' Now here they were, waiting for Denton didn't know what – news of the girl or Mrs Striker, perhaps, or the evidence that Sir Francis insisted was all that was needed to send him out a free man.

'Well,' Denton said, 'I did shoot a man.'

Sir Francis made a face. 'Sergeant Munro will forget he heard that, I hope. Mr Denton, you must stop offering information.'

'But I—'

'Hush, sir! At once!'

Munro was embarrassed; he jumped up and said, 'More tea,' to nobody and everybody and rushed out with the teapot. While he was gone, Sir Francis gave Denton a lecture on saying nothing; in fact, he had already given it, in short form, earlier. When Munro came back with the teapot newly filled and obviously hot – he was carrying it in a not very clean towel – Denton and the lawyer were sitting as they had been, both quiet. Munro tried to bustle, offered tea, poured, produced from a pocket two scones wrapped in baker's paper, apologized for the lack of a plate, and said, 'The woman's going to be all right.'

'Mrs Striker?'

'She'll have a bad scar.' Munro shook his head. 'Pretty much all the way down one side of her face, I'm afraid. Terrible for a woman.'

'Not for that woman,' Denton said. 'What about her hand?'

'They're trying to save her fingers.' Munro offered the scones and, refused, took one for himself and perched with one buttock on the table. 'Local men didn't want to deal with it, so they took her off to Bart's. Word just came back.'

'And the girl?'

'Pierced the intestine, opened her abdomen, but she'll survive. Or so they say. Lot of problems when you cut into the gut – sepsis, all that.' He chewed his scone. 'The workman got it in the shoulder and arm, won't be doing any lifting for a couple of months, poor devil. They're trying to get a statement from the mother, but the medico says she's catatonic, and anyway she's still drunk and they want to dry her out. We'll get something from her eventually, I'd say, but — not right away.' He rubbed his fingers together and brushed crumbs from his partial lap. 'Bit tricky, what we'll get from those two.'

Denton glanced at Sir Francis, then said, 'You won't get much from the girl. Not until she admits — what happened to her. And she won't tell that to a man.'

'You think he molested her, too.'

'Of course he did.'

'You don't know that.'

Denton looked at him, hard-eyed. 'You only had to see her move. To listen to her.' He put his head in his hands. 'She's only a kid. She knows he did something terrible to her, but she also knows she gets a lot of butter with it. She's the queen of the household. Woman of the house. She may even think she loves him and loves — it.'

'But you can't *know* that.'

Denton looked at him between his fingers. He said nothing. Munro sat at the table again, rapped, shifted position. 'You're in a foul mood, I must say,' he muttered to Denton.

Denton looked up at him again. 'Ever kill anybody?' Munro grunted. Denton put his face in his hands. Munro was embarrassed and made desultory talk with the solicitor. Denton, taking a turn around the room, stopped in front of Munro and said, 'When can I see Mrs Striker?'

'You can't go anywhere.'

Sir Francis said something about patience. Denton had a cup of tea, fidgeted, waited. After a few more minutes, a constable put his head in and said to Munro, 'You're wanted, please.' Munro gave Denton a half-comical look and went out. Sir Francis said, 'The plot thickens.'

However, it was another half an hour before things were thick enough to produce a result. The door opened and a constable held it for Munro and the East Ham detective who had questioned

Denton, and then for a burly man, whom Sir Francis seemed to know. The burly man was introduced as the deputy superintendent of CID, and he said, 'No touching.' He indicated a wooden box, which the East Ham man had put down on the table. 'We want an untainted evidence trail. Everyone clear on that?'

Sir Francis said that he must take them for fools; both he and the deputy superintendent chuckled. The deputy super said, 'Munro, this is your party, I think. Your stroke of genius, isn't it?'

'I happened to get there first.' Munro looked at the others. 'This is stuff from the remains of a fire out behind Satterlee's. Ashes were still warm.' He took the top off the box, which was far too big for the things inside. Using a pencil as a pointer, Munro indicated one of them – a blackened, at first shapeless mass the size of a doll's head. 'Know what that is?' he said to Denton.

Denton bent down, studied it, saw bulges that seemed to suggest pattern but couldn't make it out. He looked up at Munro.

'Decorative knot from the end of a rope. A red rope.' He grinned at Denton. 'You were right; we hadn't done our best when we went into Mulcahy's. You seemed so sure of torture when I talked to you that night, I thought, "Maybe he's got something; maybe I missed it and he got it." So I went back next day. It took me two hours to catch on to the missing red rope, but once I got that, I looked at the chair. I did see the fibres without a hint, thanks very much. Now we'll see if our experts can match them to what's left in that burned mess.'

'He told me about somebody's maybe torturing Mulcahy yesterday,' the deputy superintendent said. 'Strictly sub rosa, as they say. A good copper isn't supposed to go outside the lines of command, but a really good copper does, now and then.' He winked at Sir Francis Brudenell. 'If we can match the fibres, we can put Satterlee at Mulcahy's, and the thing's as good as done.'

Munro pointed his pencil at several bent wires, what appeared to be a blackened metal plate. 'Remains of a photographic camera. The lens is cracked but it's still there, and we think there're letters around the rim. If we can identify it as definitely one of Mulcahy's, with his "Inventorium" on it – I've got a man up there now, looking at his other cameras – then we'll go to court with your theory, Denton, that Mulcahy left a camera behind in that closet where he had the peephole, and Satterlee found it.'

He pointed at a blackened key. 'Might be the key to Mulcahy's closet. Mr Denton believed that Mulcahy carried it off with him that night – maybe Satterlee found it in Mulcahy's clothes. Would have taken it to keep anybody from connecting him with the peephole and the girl.'

'Another nail in the coffin,' the solicitor said.

Munro indicated a shallow brick of burned paper and scorched cardboard. 'What's left of a book. Denton told Sergeant Cobb here –' he indicated the East Ham detective – 'that the real Stella Minter may have had a book that the Satterlee girl took – borrowed or stole, doesn't matter. This is certainly a kid's book – the other side has some titles you can read, all for kids – and we're hoping the Minters can identify this one. If we're fantastically lucky, there'll be a legible name written in it. We haven't opened it – that's for the experts.'

Denton said, 'Satterlee didn't do a very good job of burning.'

The deputy super shook himself, said, 'Books are hard to burn, actually. He managed to destroy the camera and most of the rope well enough. But this type of man may like souvenirs. May have been reluctant to get rid of them.' He looked at Sir Francis. 'Seen it twice before.'

'Plus he's reckless,' Denton said. 'Very reckless.'

Sir Francis put his long nose down towards the box as if to smell it. After some seconds, he said, 'So you believe that you have evidence that links the man Satterlee to the man Mulcahy and to the murdered girl, is that right?'

'We think so, yes.'

Sir Francis put a hand through the deputy superintendent's arm. 'May we talk?' he said, and they went out. A moment later, the East Ham man had closed the box and taken it to the door, cradled in his arms like a baby. Munro said, 'Mind that doesn't leave your sight! We'll want an affidavit—!'

The detective turned in the doorway, the door hooked into his right foot so he could pull it closed. He gave Munro a look that meant *What do you take me for?* With the slow delivery that mocks patience and suggests the speaker is talking to a fool, he said, 'It's going back with you and the super in the CID van.'

'We'll still want your affidavit!'

'Yeah, yeah, yeah—' He went out and pulled the door to with his toe.

Munro smiled at Denton. 'Hurry up and wait some more, eh?'

'I want to see Mrs Striker.'

'She, uh— Is she a, umm, your—?'

Denton was grim. 'She risked her life so that bastard wouldn't get away.'

Munro nodded his head. 'Right. Right.'

Five minutes later, Sir Francis came back in. He put his hand on Denton's shoulder. 'No charges will be laid. You're free to go on my recognizance until they're certain of the evidence.' He gave Munro a small smile, turned back to Denton. 'I have my motor car; may I give you a ride to town?'

'I'm going to Bart's.'

'I can drop you, then.' He nodded at Munro. 'I'm sure I'll be seeing you again, Sergeant.' He turned back to Denton. 'I'll just have a word with my chauffeur.'

When he was gone, Denton said, '"Seeing you again"?'

Munro looked sheepish. 'They want to talk about me going back to CID.' He leaned back against the table. 'Metropolitan Police were about to do something that would have been wrong and stupid – close the Mulcahy case. They were doing it because it was easy and because, let's face it, people had persuaded themselves they were right. Powers that be were, so they say, beside themselves when this broke this morning. Even though I was in too little and too late, they think I fell down the privy seat and came up with a diamond, so maybe I can go back to CID despite the leg.' He grinned. 'I owe you one.'

'Not at all.' He put out his hand. 'All's well that ends well.'

'I do have a question, though.'

Denton waited.

'What would you have done if your shot had hit the woman instead of Satterlee?'

He had Denton's hand; Denton returned his pressure, withdrew his hand. His voice was gruff. 'I'd have got him with the second shot.'

Denton had to wait in the upstairs corridor until the solicitor's motor car came. He was told to stay away from the windows 'because of the vultures from the press'. He peered out with his face against a window frame and was astonished to see more than twenty men clustered where he supposed the station's entrance was. He saw mostly the tops of bowler hats, the occasional soft hat on somebody more daring; voices reached him, words unclear but the tone sometimes sharp, sometimes mocking.

'They're all there for you,' a voice said behind him.

'Harris!' It was as if the man had materialized out of the stale air in the corridor. 'What the hell?'

Frank Harris, less red-eyed than usual, smiling his shark's smile, rubbed a thumb and three fingertips together. 'Lucre changed hands, copper showed me up the back stairs. Corruption in the bastion of law.' He grinned. 'Always think the worst of your fellow man – you'll get farther.'

'What are you *doing* here?'

'Little bird told me a notorious murderer had been shot by a well-known author. I bustled. Rather early in the day for me to bustle – I do my best work in the dark – but I made an exception, and here I am with an offer that's going to make your heart twitter with delight! You may want to kiss me, in fact.'

'What've you done?'

Harris craned to peek out the window. 'Not a word to that crowd of poltroons. We're dedicated to one rag and one rag only, the *News of the World*, because they're paying us a hundred pounds for your story!' He grinned again, preened. '*How I Tracked and Shot the East Ham Monster with my Colt .45!*' He waited. Clearly, he expected more than Denton was giving. 'Well? *Well?*'

'It wasn't a .45; it was a .36. And what's this "we"?'

'Ah, well, y'see, I thought that as I negotiated, in fact *invented* and negotiated this arrangement, fifteen per cent seemed justified. For me. Of *a hundred pounds*, Denton! That's eighty-five for you, man – any money troubles you had are over! Eh? Eh?'

Denton stared at him. Anger had hit him first, now was giving way to some sort of humour, perhaps hysterical, a reaction to the shooting. He found that he was laughing. The more he laughed, the more perplexed Harris looked, making Denton laugh that much more. Denton leaned against the wall, feeling himself light-headed and knowing it was nervous reaction; soon he would feel emptied, then despairing. Pulling a trigger is easy; the labour comes after. 'I'm sorry,' he said to Harris.

'Sorry for what?'

'Can't do it, Harris. No deal.'

'I can't get you more than a hundred. I tried – I said, "A hundred guineas!" but they wouldn't budge. It's no good—'

'*No deal.* I won't do it. No. N-O.'

Harris's voice was hoarse. 'Why in the name of God not?'

Denton thought how best to explain it, saw that there was no way to explain it that would pierce Harris's cynicism. He said, 'I can't make money from killing somebody.'

'Why the hell not?'

'I just can't.' Denton shrugged. 'I just can't.'

Outraged, Harris put his swollen eyes close to Denton's face and shouted, 'Don't you try to give me any crap about honour!'

Below, an elegant motor car was slowly herding the newsmen out of the way as it pulled up close to the station entrance. He smiled at Harris. 'I wouldn't have the guts to try.' He raised a hand.

Janet Striker had been put in the women's ward. Denton had arrived out of visiting hours and had been made to wait for more than an hour; leaning back against a wall in a bent-wood chair, he had felt himself slide into that state that is like exhaustion but that doesn't come from labour. It is the emotional collapse after a single instant of action, the body raised to a pitch, then everything released, the result an inanition that could last, he knew, for days.

He had tried to explain a few times why anybody who could kill without affect was a monster, but he supposed you had to live it to understand it. In the dime novels, on the stage of people like Cody, killing was easy and there were no awkward emotions afterwards. Life was a bit different.

'You may come along now,' a sister said. She was young, sweet-faced, but severe in her manner. 'We're making an exception for you.' He supposed this to mean that it still wasn't visiting hour.

She led him along a tiled corridor and through a pair of double doors, seemingly into a different building – older, darker, a lingering smell of ether and carbolic. Ahead, a door was open and a trim, small man with a moustache was standing outside it. No introduction was made; he simply grasped Denton's arm and turned him away from the open doorway, through which Denton had seen a small room, not much more than a closet, with a railed bed and a lot of white sheet.

'We've brought her out here rather than have you on the ward. All-female, and so on.' He was a lot younger than Denton but clearly in charge, certainly patronizing. 'The police wish us to accede to your wishes as much as possible. You're the husband?'

Denton had to swim up from his exhaustion to say, 'A friend. I was there when she was hurt.'

'It was my understanding you were the husband. This is irregular. Well, as you're here— I'll have to ask sister to stay in the room with you.'

A hard remark occurred to Denton, but he suppressed it.

'She will have a scar.'

'I know that.'

'Her left hand is another matter. There is damage to nerves and tendons; I don't know how much use of it she'll have. We had to transfuse her twice – great loss of blood.'

'You were there for the, whatever it is. Operation?'

'I performed the surgery. I am a specialist.'

Denton couldn't think of anything to say to that. Something seemed required – hosannas, perhaps. He said, 'Can I see her now?'

The surgeon arched his eyebrows once and said a little stiffly that of course, if that's what he wished. He steered Denton back into the tiny room.

The room was almost too small for the two men and the metal bed. The insistence on propriety – he couldn't go on the ward out of hours – seemed stupid to him, wasteful. She was walled off from him by metal bars that were painted pale yellow and chipped along the upper edges, as were the head and foot of the bed. Her right hand, even against the white sheet, was pale. The left side of her face was covered with white gauze, secured under her chin with plaster; her left hand was entirely swathed. Behind him, the nursing sister muttered, 'They gave her morphine. She'll be going to sleep any time.'

She looked asleep now. Denton said, 'Can I talk to her?'

'You can try.'

He leaned over the bed. Before he could speak, her eyes opened. They were unfocused, in fact not looking at him but at the ceiling. They swung towards him and she frowned.

'I came as soon as they'd let me,' he said.

She seemed to concentrate, to recognize him. 'Did you kill him?' she said in a hoarse voice.

'Yes.'

'Good.'

'Well—'

'It weighs on you?'

'Yes.'

She drifted away, came back. 'That's good, too.' Her eyes closed, and he thought she had fallen asleep, but after several seconds she stirred and even moved her right arm, as if to turn towards him. 'They say I shall have a scar,' she said.

'It doesn't matter!'

'It does to me. Astonishingly. "Vanity, vanity…"' Her eyes closed and her voice sank away.

He glanced at the sister, who looked annoyed. Mrs Striker's breathing became slow and regular, then caught, and her eyes opened. 'You're still here.'

'It hasn't been long.'

'You saved my life.'

'No, *you* saved your life. You were – magnificent.'

She didn't say anything for several seconds, her eyes narrowed as if she was perhaps seeing it all again, evaluating it. 'Better a scar and no fingers than having my throat slashed.'

Denton laughed. He knew he shouldn't have, because he heard the sister's sharp intake of breath, but he laughed for the relief and the release of it. 'You're a tough bird,' he said.

She smiled, winced as the smile pulled on her slit cheek and jaw. 'A tough – sparrow—' she said, and again her eyes closed and her breathing fell.

Denton waited. This time, he didn't think she would come out of it. The sister said, 'She's fallen asleep, sir. She'll sleep for twelve hours now. The morphine.'

'Well—' he began. Then Janet Striker's eyes opened and searched for him; when they found him, she smiled again and winced again. 'Come back,' she murmured, and fell asleep for the night.

Denton rattled home in a cab for which he had barely enough money. He could, he thought, sleep for days. At the same time, a restlessness filled his brain with disconnected thoughts, now of money, now of the man he'd shot, now of Janet Striker. He should get to work. He needed money. He was a fool to have turned down Harris's offer. Was there possibility in Janet Striker's *Come back*? Perhaps he should sell his house. Perhaps he should go back to America. Could he have taken Satterlee alive – or had he wanted an excuse to kill him? And whom was he killing – was Satterlee only a stand-in for his own demons? He made a sound like a groan wound around a sigh. He needed something – wanted something—

His own house looked strange to him. The evening was dark now and cold; the morning's frost had never melted where the shadows lay. A wind had risen, nosing around chimneys and skittering leaves and pieces of paper. He shivered.

He went up the stairs and let himself in and was astonished

to see Diapason Lang sitting in his own green armchair. Denton stared at him stupidly.

Lang bounced out of the chair and rushed towards him. 'Oh, my dear boy! Oh, you're all right – are you all right? Oh, sit down, do sit down – brandy? Have brandy. Where's that man of yours? Hoy! Was it horrible? Yes, of course it was. How horrible for you! Horrible, horrible!' Denton was trying to get out of his overcoat; Lang was dancing around him, getting in his way; surprisingly, the man had tears in his eyes. 'Brandy – servants quite useless when you want them—' Lang had rushed to the table behind the armchair; something fell over with a crash. 'There!' Lang poured from the decanter, his hands shaking so that the neck rattled against the glass. When he handed it to Denton, the brandy slopped over their hands. 'Oh, look what I've done! Oh, I'm such a useless old fool. Did the lawyer come? Are you a free man?'

'Free, yes – he came—' It seemed long ago.

'I went right to Gwen as soon as I had your message. Gwen was a brick! "The best, we must have the best!" he said. I had no idea of such things, so I asked Frewn, you remember Frewn, crime is his hobby – he said Brudenell. Was Brudenell good? Frewn said that up to the moment you go into court, Brudenell's the best man in England. Was he good? Did we do well by you?' He had fetched a chair from farther up the room and carried it behind Denton and was pushing it against Denton's knees, almost forcing him to sit. 'Is that comfortable? Are you sure?'

Despite his fatigue and his racing brain, Denton was touched. This was an utterly different Lang from the dry androgyne of the publishing office: now emotional, now unsure, now concerned, he was like a very nervous hen with too many chicks. Denton assured him and assured him again, and finally Lang fell back into the green armchair and took a sip of sherry and calmed himself. Then, abruptly, he sat up again.

'Oh, you must think me insane! I haven't told you what I'm here for. I've been here since four. Your man gave me sherry and biscuits. I may have drunk too much of the sherry. At any rate, I have a purpose that I've never told you!' He nodded his head several times. 'Good news!' He banged his hand on the arm of his chair. 'I've good news! I think. I hope you'll think it's good news. Oh, dear! I think it's good news.' He leaned towards Denton. 'Gwen *loves* your idea!'

Denton wondered if he was drunk already. 'What idea – the new book? *The Machine?*'

'*By Motor Car to the Land of Vampires!* He absolutely loved it. I told you he's a motor-car enthusiast, quite mad, he's the money, of course, but noisy contraptions, smelly, too, but he *adored* the idea. "Lang," he said, "row fifty for the minute on this one. Go all out! This is a twentieth-century idea!"' Lang sat there and enjoyed his own good news. 'Here is the arrangement: eight hundred pounds in advance against your usual royalty plus expenses plus the firm will provide the motor car. Between you and me and the gatepost, Gwen means to pick out the motor car himself but he was going on about making a trip to Paris with you to find absolutely the right one, because he believes the French make the best motor cars in the world, which is *not* very loyal, if you ask me.' He sipped his sherry again. 'Where was I? Expenses, the car – yes, subsidiary rights, ah, yes. We want to serialize – sixty per cent for you, the rights already sold in England – oh, yes, my dear, I moved quickly – to *Every Other Week* for three hundred pounds, including Ireland. I have a cable from Chapman at *Century* in New York – where is it, where is it—? Doesn't matter, he's offering ten thousand dollars for North America. I haven't heard from *L'Affiche d'Aujourd'hui* or *Kunst*, but I will. You're assured, in short, of at least three thousand pounds.' He looked up with the guilelessness of a child. 'Is that all right?'

'All right?' As Lang had talked, Denton had felt the black mood slipping away. *Everything's going to be all right*, he thought. *Everything*. He jumped up and pulled Lang from the armchair and threw his good arm around him. The editor gasped; Denton tightened his grip into half of a bear hug. 'Oh—' Lang cried, 'oh, this is too— Oh, *dear*— You Americans are *so* emotional— Really, you needn't—'

And then Atkins was coming from the stairs, Rupert lumbering behind him. Atkins was shouting, 'Congratulations, General! Well done, sir! No need now to go to the agent's, nor did I want to—!' Any pretence of not having eavesdropped was out of the window. 'Three thousand pounds! Out of funds, my hat!'

Everything would be all right; he would be rich – and then he thought of Janet Striker, the injured face, the moment when he pulled the trigger, and he understood that if he accepted Lang's offer he would be gone for months. What would she think of him? Or – what was worse – would she even care?

Denton let go of Lang, who fell back into the armchair. Atkins poured him another sherry without taking his eyes from Denton.

'You heard?' Denton temporized, his mind still on Mrs Striker.

'I couldn't help, the gentlemen having a rather carrying voice and clear enunciation.'

'Transylvania,' Denton said. 'It's a long way.'

'In Europe, in't it?'

'By motor car. We'd be gone a long time.' Thinking, we can write to each other; maybe it will be even better – get to know each other a different way— But he wanted them to get to know each other in the usual way – dinners, walks, then—

Atkins grinned. 'Three thousand pounds!'

'You'd have to learn to drive, Sergeant.'

'How difficult can it be? Look at the fools what smashes them up all over London.'

'To Transylvania, Sergeant. You're willing to travel with me all the way to Transylvania?' Wanting Atkins to say no, to cause him not to go. Knowing he had to go, had to have the money, and at the same time wanting that damned woman who lay in a hospital bed with her face slashed.

Atkins raised his head, pushed out his lips, then hesitated. 'If there's room for Rupert.' He looked down at the enormous dog. 'You'd like to see Transylvania, wouldn't you, old fellow?'

The stump of tail thumped on the floor. Denton stared at it. He sighed. He would write her *lots* of letters.

ABOUT THE AUTHOR

Kenneth Cameron is a former US Navy intelligence officer. He lives most of the year in the woods of New York State's Adirondacks, where he writes regular contributions to the fishing magazine *Waterlog*.